El Diablo

USA TODAY BESTSELLING AUTHOR
M. ROBINSON

1

Copyright © 2016 M. Robinson
All rights Reserved.

No part of this book may be used or reproduced in any manner
whatsoever without written permission of the author.

This book is a work of fiction. References to real people, events,
establishments, organizations, or locations are intended only to
provide a sense of authenticity, and are used fictitiously. All other
characters, dead or alive are a figment of my imagination and all
incidents and dialogue, are drawn from the author's mind's eye and
are not to be interpreted as real.

Connect with

WEBSITE

FACEBOOK

INSTAGRAM

TWITTER

AMAZON PAGE

VIP READER GROUP

NEWSLETTER

EMAIL ADDRESS

MORE BOOKS BY M

All FREE WITH KINDLE UNLIMITED

EROTIC ROMANCE

VIP (The VIP Trilogy Book One)

THE MADAM (The VIP Trilogy Book Two)

MVP (The VIP Trilogy Book Three)

TEMPTING BAD (The VIP Spin-Off)

TWO SIDES GIANNA (Standalone)

CONTEMPORARY/NEW ADULT

THE GOOD OL' BOYS STANDALONE SERIES

COMPLICATE ME

FORBID ME

UNDO ME

CRAVE ME

EL DIABLO (THE DEVIL)

ROAD TO NOWHERE

ENDS HERE

KEEPING HER WET

Acknowledgments

To ALL my readers and my VIPS!
Thank you for allowing me to do what I love every day of my life.
I couldn't do this without you!

I LOVE YOU!!!

Boss man: Words cannot describe how much I love you. Thank you for ALWAYS being my best friend. I couldn't do this without you.

Dad: Thank you for always showing me what hard work is and what it can accomplish. For always telling me that I can do anything I put my mind to.

Mom: Thank you for ALWAYS being there for me no matter what. You are my best friend.

Julissa Rios: I love you and I am proud of you. Thank you for being a pain in my ass and for being my sister. I know you are always there for me when I need you.

Ysabelle & Gianna: Love you my babies.

Rebecca Marie: THANK YOU for an AMAZING cover. I wouldn't know what to do without you and your fabulous creativity.

Heather Moss: Thank you for everything that you do!! I wouldn't know what to do without you! You're. The. Best. PA. Ever!! You're NEVER leaving me!! XO

Silla Webb: Thank you so much for your edits and formatting! I love it and you!

Michelle Tan: Best beta ever! **Argie Sokoli:** I couldn't do this without you. You're my chosen person. **Tammy McGowan:** Thank you for all your support, feedback, and boo boo's you find! I'm happy I made you cry. **Michele Henderson McMullen:** LOVE LOVE LOVE you!! **Dee Montoya:** I value our friendship more than anything. Thanks for always being honest. **Clarissa Federico:** Thank you so much for coming in last

7

minute and handling it like a boss. Your friendship means more to me than you'll ever know! **Rebeka Christine Perales:** You always make me smile. **Alison Evan-Maxwell:** Thank you for coming in last minute and getting it done like a boss. **Mary Jo Toth:** Your boo-boos are always great! Thank you for everything you do in VIP! **Ella Gram:** You're such a sweet and amazing person! Thank you for your kindness. **Kimmie Lewis:** Your friendship means everything to me. **Tricia Bartley:** Your comments and voice always make me smile! **Kristi Lynn:** Thanks for all your honesty and for joining team M. **Pam Batchelor:** Thanks for all your suggestions. **Jenn Hazen:** Thank you for everything! **Laura Hansen:** I. Love. You. **Patti Correa:** You're amazing! Thank you for everything! **Jennifer Pon:** Thank you for all your feedback and suggestions! You're amazing! **Jen M:** I love all your feedback! Thank you! **Michelle Kubik Follis:** Welcome back! I missed you too! **Deborah E Shipuleski:** Thank you for all your quick honest feedback! **Kaye Blanchard:** Thank you for wanting to join team M! **Beth Morton Conley:** Thank you for everything! **KR Nadelson:** I love you!

To all my author buddies:

T.M. Frazier: I fucking love you, you fucking Ginger.

Jettie Woodruff: You complete me.

Erin Noelle: I. Love. You!

The C.O.P.A Cabana Girls:

I love you!!

<u>To all the bloggers:</u>

A HUGE THANK YOU for all the love and support you have shown me. I have made some amazing friendships with you that I hold dear to my heart. I know that without you I would be nothing!! I cannot THANK YOU enough!! Special thanks to Like A Boss Book Promotions for hosting my tours!

Last but not least.

YOU.

My readers.

THANK YOU!!

Without you…

I would be nothing.

Prologue
Martinez

I leaned back, nonchalantly placing my hands in the pockets of my slacks. Eyeing them up and down with a threatening regard. "You ever held a gun before?" I mocked, cocking my head to the side.

"Please… Martinez… please… just stop…"

I snidely smiled. There was no way in hell I was going to stop. I was just getting fucking started. "Your hands are shaking. First rule of holding a gun. Never let your enemies see your fear. It just makes you a fucking pussy. So, what's your next move? I am right here." I spread my arms out at my sides. Sticking my chest out. "This is your chance to get rid of me. Do it! Pull the fucking trigger! Do it!" I viciously baited. Not giving a flying fuck anymore.

"Stop! Please! Fucking stop!"

"I'm a bad man! I've done unforgivable things. Here's your chance! Fucking take it! Send me straight to fucking Hell! Now!"

I always knew this day would come. I had made so many fucking mistakes throughout my life, but this moment would never be one of them. I lived far longer than I ever thought I would. Always hoping I'd meet my maker from a loving hand, but we don't always get what we want.

I had killed.

I had avenged.

I had loved.

I had destroyed lives and now it was my time to pay for being the Grim fucking Reaper, taking lives that didn't belong to me. I just never thought my life would end like this.

Lying in a pool of my own goddamn blood.

Provoking my assassin to pull the fucking trigger.

Part 1

One

Martinez

"Let's go, Martinez. The girls are waiting for us," my friend Leo stated for the tenth fucking time.

"Alright, hold the fuck up. I'm coming. Besides, you know they'll wait all night for us," I replied with a cocky grin as I walked toward the back door. Careful to make sure the bodyguards and cameras were set up throughout the house didn't see us.

"Alejandro! You're not allowed to leave. Dad warned you. He doesn't like you leaving the house when they're not around, especially without taking a bodyguard with you," Amari scolded while grabbing my arm, stopping me dead in my tracks.

My older sister Amari was always the perfect little angel. I, on the other hand, was the devil. I think my dad was secretly proud when I acted out, but he never voiced it and never let it slide, keeping up pretenses was what he was best at. He raised and molded me to take over his empire since the day I was born, like all the generations of the Martinez men before me. I was fourteen, almost fifteen, but being a kid was never in the cards for me. Which was why I took every opportunity to do whatever the hell I wanted, especially when there wasn't someone constantly on my ass telling me I couldn't. I didn't give a shit if I got grounded. I knew I only had a few years to live a semi-normal life, and I took advantage of it every chance I could get.

Amari was a year-and-a-half older than me, though it was of no importance. She always acted younger than her years. She had been sneaking into my bed ever since I could remember, because every little sound in the night frightened her. I didn't have the luxury of being scared. Fear wasn't a part of the life I was

15

expected to lead. It was only a matter of time until I was the one who frightened her, too.

Exactly the way our father did.

He called it respect, but I knew it was nothing more than intimidation. Amari had always been weak, and it bothered our father in ways I had to make up for. I had to protect her even though I was younger.

"I don't want you getting in trouble, Alejandro," Sophia murmured loud enough for me to hear.

I grinned. Turning my attention away from Amari, my eyes locked with Sophia who was standing at the end of the foyer.

Sophia was my sister's best friend. I always thought their friendship was unconventional because she was my age. Her bright green eyes, pouty lips, and the smell of her long, dark brown hair had been doing things to me since the first time I met her a few years ago. She was from the wrong side of the tracks, so to speak. She attended our New York private school on a scholarship offered to a select number of low-income housing kids with exceptional grades. My sister took to her immediately. She hated the pretentious pricks in our school.

Amari and I had that in common.

Leo and I had been friends since the first day of high school. He was a geeky-ass kid who was getting picked on by all of my so-called friends. One day we were all standing around our lockers before the first bell rang for class, just shooting the shit. The boys were arguing over who got the furthest with Catherine "Big Tits" St. James. I was too focused on watching Sophia trying to reach the top shelf of her locker down the hall, not paying them any mind.

"Well, look what we have here, boys," Jimmy announced. We had gone to school together since we were little. I turned to see who he was talking about. Five lockers down there was a scrawny kid with glasses. He looked like he didn't belong in our school. Jimmy went barreling up to him, knocking the books out of his hands.

"Are you lost? The school for under-privileged kids is on the other side of the city."

Leo ignored him, picking up his books.

The bell rang, warning us to get to class. Jimmy and a few other guys shoved Leo into his locker, shut it, and walked away laughing. Needless to say, Jimmy and the boys were no longer laughing once school let out. I made sure to set them all straight, and ordered them not to fuck with Leo ever again. Or else. There was something about the kid, and to this day I don't know what made me come to his rescue.

After that, he became a permanent fixture in my life. He was still a geeky-ass kid, but it no longer mattered. My friendship was his shield. Nobody would dare to fuck with him anymore. Even at that young of an age, I never pussyfooted around. I meant what I said, and I said what I meant. I never apologized for who I was or my actions. People could take it or leave it. I didn't give a shit. My don't-give-a-fuck attitude only made people want to hangout with me more, when in reality they should have been staying as far away from me as possible.

Everyone knew who my father was, and they feared me because of it.

I had never been a fan of those who preyed on the weak. Maybe it was because I saw so much weakness in my sister. I'd sacrifice everything just to protect her if need be. My father knew Amari wasn't cut from the same cloth, which was why I was never allowed to leave the house when they weren't around. It never made any sense in my eyes. There were always bodyguards everywhere, just waiting to pull the trigger if shit hit the fan. I assumed they were getting paid a fuck-load of money to do a job my father seemed more inclined to give me.

"Amari, they're not going to be back until late. If they even come home at all. They're at someone's initiation or some shit," I replied, pulling my arm out of her grasp.

"Aren't you tired of being grounded all the time? Why can't you just listen for once? It's not that hard," she sassed, waving her hands in the air.

"Just keep your mouth shut. If they come home, you didn't see me."

"I'm a terrible li—"

"Carajo, Amari! Haga lo que le digo pues," I shouted, "*Fuck, Amari! Just do it*," annoyed with her persistent nagging.

17

She sighed, looking away from me.

She hated it when I yelled at her. Our dad did it enough for everyone. He believed in tough love. Hugs and kisses were few and far between. We rarely heard the words "I love you" from his mouth. Our mother was the only one who showed us love, tenderness, and affection. I stepped toward Amari, lightly grabbing her chin, forcing her to look at me again. She peered up at me through her lashes. I knew what this was really about. She worried something would happen to me. She worried constantly about everything. Especially what harm could come to her if I wasn't around.

"I'll be fine. You'll be fine. I promise, you got Dad's new goons here. I won't be back late."

I kissed her forehead, glancing one last time at Sophia before I turned and left. I could tell she wanted to ask where we were going, but she knew better. I winked at her with a sly grin, and she warily smiled. It wasn't until later that night I wished I had never left the house, and by the look on Sophia's face, she felt what my sister might have expected all along.

"You fuck, I'm so late. If my dad catches me, it's my ass he's going to lay out, Leo," I stated, shooting him a death glare.

Those girls were definitely not worth the shit I'd be in if my parents got home before I did. Of course, my mother would try to defend me like she always did, but it wouldn't matter. At the end of the day, what my father said ruled, end of story. The husband's word was the law in Hispanic marriages. The wife was subservient to her husband. She raised the kids, made sure the house was clean, and dinner was on the table every night. Now, add in the fact my father was a crime boss, and you get the picture. He was one of the most feared and hated men in the world, but to my mom, he was God.

He laughed, throwing his head back while we pedaled our bikes as fast as we could.

"You smell that?" Leo replied with a shit-eating grin.

"Smell what?"

"Smells like pussy to me," he chuckled.

"I'm the pussy? Who had to save your sorry ass, once upon a time? I sure as hell wasn't a pussy then, besides, you wouldn't know what pussy smells like if it was sitting on your fucking face."

"Relax, they're not home, it's barely past two in the morning. I've never seen your dad leave a party first. He knows better than to turn his back to anyone," he chuckled. "Alright, bro, this is my street. Talk to you tomorrow."

Leo disappeared into the darkness as I pedaled even harder and faster. Praying I'd make it on time. My heart was beating out of my chest, sweat pooling at my temples. My mind was already racing, imagining every punishment he could bring on me.

I opened the side door of the garage, breathing a sigh of relief when I saw their limo was still gone. Looking down at my watch, I calculated where the cameras would be directed at that time. I had snuck out often enough to know they were on a fifteen-minute rotation. I quietly walked in, making sure none of my dad's meatheads were around. When the coast was clear, I ran up the backstairs, taking three steps at a time toward Amari's bedroom. I wanted to let her know I was home safe, since she probably spent most of the night worrying about me.

"Amari? Sophia?" I called out, lightly knocking on her bedroom door a few times. "I'm home," I whispered, knocking again before opening the door. "I'm coming in. You up?"

More silence.

I looked around the dark room not finding them anywhere. Her bed was still made from this morning. "Where the hell are they?" I asked myself.

Amari hated staying up late, she was always an early riser. Something wasn't right. A disturbing, unsettling feeling I couldn't describe, washed over me. Before I knew what was happening, my body turned, moving on its own accord. I ran out of the room, making my way down the long, narrow hallway toward my bedroom. All I could hear were the sounds of my footsteps echoing off the walls. My shoes pounded into the floor, one right after the other. I couldn't get to my room fast enough.

"Amari!" I was calling out her name before I had even made it into my bedroom. "Amari, where the fuck are you?" I shouted, when I found my room empty, too.

Our house was fucking huge, but we never strayed too far from our bedrooms. They were the only rooms in the house with no cameras watching our every move. At least that's what our mother told us. Who knows if it was true. I ran out of my room like a bat out of Hell, desperately needing to figure out where my sister and Sophia were. If anything bad happened to them, I'd be responsible for it. I'm the one who made the choice to leave them home alone with the bodyguards.

The sick feeling in my stomach intensified with every menacing thought crossing my mind. I ran faster, only stopping to check rooms. The silence was deafening all around me. I never realized how quiet our house was at night, or how every little shadow simply heightened the darkness, lurking in every corner I ran passed. The only sounds that could be heard were resonating off of my body. My adrenaline hammered so fucking hard while every room I looked in turned up empty.

"Amari! Sophia!" I screamed, knowing it was useless. The walls in our house were all soundproof.

I stopped in the living room, hunched over with my hands on my knees, hyperventilating to the point of pain. After checking every last inch of the house, no one was to be found.

No bodyguards.

No Sophia.

No Amari.

Just me.

"What the fuck?" I breathed out, peering around the room in confusion like they were going to suddenly appear out of thin air.

I felt my face pale. All the blood drained from my body, causing shivers to course through me. I shuddered, suddenly cold. The hairs on my arms stood on edge when I realized the only room I hadn't checked was my father's office. We were ordered to never go in there unless he requested our presence. Before I gave it anymore thought, I ran toward the other end of the house. Frantically trying to ignore the nervous and fearful feeling I felt in the pit of my stomach and focus on the task at hand.

My heart pounded so profusely I found it fucking hard to breathe. My mind raced and my chest heaved with each passing moment, escalating with every step bringing me closer to his office. Panic began to set in, and I could no longer control my thoughts from running wild. I anxiously tried to find my resolve.

I was a Martinez.

Not a fucking pussy.

But I was still a kid who was terrified he'd let something happen to his sister and Sophia. There would be no coming back from this. I knew that before I even made it into his office. Everything played out in slow motion like it was a dream. I ran to the door, reached for the handle, turned the knob, and shoved it open. It made a loud thud as it bounced off the back wall. I stopped dead in my tracks when I saw the brutal scene playing out in front of me.

My night quickly turned into my worst fucking nightmare.

Two

Martinez

Two pairs of dark, soulless eyes turned toward my direction as I took in the image that would forever haunt me. In the dim light I could see Sophia thrashing around on the hardwood floor in the middle of the room. Her delicate, small frame held hostage against her will by the two men who were supposed to be protecting us. One bodyguard was pinning her hands to the floor and covering her mouth to muffle her screams. The other hovered above her, straddling her thighs with his slacks hanging down his legs.

Bile immediately rose up my throat, as I was about to witness her innocence being crudely ripped away from her. Her eyes were locked shut as if she was trying to pretend she was somewhere else. Her beautiful face was bright red and swollen with bruises already forming. Tears streamed down her beaten cheeks as she fought to break free. Her shirt was ripped open, revealing her blood-stained, white, lacy bra. One strap torn and hanging down her arm. Her panties and shorts were scrunched down by her ankles, restraining her from making any movement with her legs.

It took me a matter of seconds to look over every last inch of her broken body. It was like I wanted to engrain it into my memory. The bodyguard's eyes stayed focused on me in those moments, and my eyes remained locked on her. Desperately hoping this was all just a bad dream, willing myself to wake the fuck up. Except I knew in my heart it wasn't, and I allowed this to happen.

The bodyguard's hand moved off Sophia's mouth, allowing a devastating scream to escape. I felt the sound pierce deep down within my bones, resonating and making itself home.

"Help me! Someone please help me!" she screeched loud enough to break glass. "Amari! Please help me!"

"Shut the fuck up!" the bodyguard who held back her wrists snapped. "You're asking her to help you?! Stupid, whore! You don't see her? She's so weak and scared, she can't even help herself. Shit, we don't even have to tie her up. I'll let you in on a little secret, she's who we are after, but she's no fun. You, on the other hand, are so feisty. A much better toy to break. But don't worry, her turn is coming soon. After we take care of your pussy ass brother."

I gasped, jerking back. I swear my heart stopped beating when I remembered I still hadn't found my sister. My gaze tore through the room, frantically searching for her in the dark corners of this Hell. It didn't take long for me to find her. She was sitting in the furthest corner of the room with her arms wrapped around her legs, locking them tight against her chest. She looked so tiny and scared, like she was trying to mold herself into the wall and the floor. She shook profusely, but her petrified stare never wavered from Sophia. Blood-stained tears streamed down her bruised face. My eyes quickly scanned over her body, immediately noticing her clothes were still intact. For a second, it gave me a false sense of security they hadn't touched her... yet.

She hadn't even realized I was in the room, which made me think she was in shock. Seeing her in this state gave me the courage I needed to keep going. My stare went back to the men who were frozen in place, both of them trying to figure out what was my next move. I couldn't read the neutral expressions on the bastard's faces. It was as if they didn't have a soul, a conscience, or one fucking ounce of remorse or compassion for what they were doing.

It was the first time in my life I ever witnessed evil in true form. Sophia and Amari's innocence weren't the only things taken that night.

I was no longer a boy.

A kid.

A child.

Rage quickly replaced every feeling, every emotion, and every last thought that crossed my mind was gone in a flash, as if they never existed to begin with.

And all I saw was vengeance.

"Get the fuck off of her," I gritted out through a clenched jaw. My fists tightened to the point of pain by my sides.

Sophia's eyes shot open when she heard my voice resonate through the room, lifting her head off the floor to see me. She started crying harder as she dropped her head back, unable to hold it up for very long.

"What the fuck are you going to do, boy?" the bodyguard hovering over Sophia spewed out, rising to the balls of his feet, tucking his dick back into his pants. I resisted the urge to look at Sophia, disgusted by what I would see between her legs.

"Marco, let her go," he ordered the guy who was holding Sophia's wrists.

Marco complied, releasing his grasp. Sophia scrambled to her hands and knees, crawling as fast as she could over to Amari, who still hadn't moved or made a sound. I released a breath of relief, knowing Sophia was safe for now.

"You made a big mistake walking in here tonight. The fun was just getting fucking started, boy. Wasn't it, John?" Marco mocked, standing alongside the other motherfucker.

I stood taller, not backing down. I was five-foot-nine, one hundred and sixty pounds. I was built like my father and bigger than most guys my age, which gave me an advantage.

"Why don't you just run along, boy," John scoffed out. "Or wait, better yet. Marco grab him, I think we should show this little prick how a real man fucks."

I didn't falter, spitting out, "A real man wouldn't have to rape a girl. But judging by the size of your cock, I can see why women your age won't voluntarily fuck you."

"You little shit," John spewed, walking over to the girls.

I was over to him in four strides, dodging Marco's hands that were trying to get a hold of me. Getting right up in John's face, I snarled, "You touch them one more fucking time, and I'll—"

"What? You'll what? What are you going to do, boy? Your daddy ain't around to save any of your sorry asses. He already

24

called, saying they weren't coming home tonight. Now back the fuck up so I can have a taste of your sister's sweet little pussy."

My fist connected with his jaw before he got the last word out. His head whooshed back, knocking him off balance from my unexpected blow to his face. He stumbled back, holding his chin, before he glared up at me, spitting blood on the floor. Sizing me up for the first time. I had been in kickboxing since I learned how to walk. No one fucked with a Martinez, my father made sure of it.

"You're going to pay for that, you little fucker," he warned, charging toward me but stopped when a shot was fired hitting him right in the leg.

The sound of Amari and Sophia screaming and wailing at the top of their lungs brought my attention to them, cowering in the corner, before I could figure out where the shot came from. They bawled harder and hugged each other tighter, tucking their faces into each other's chests.

John collapsed onto the ground, holding the open wound on his leg that gushed blood onto the floor.

"Motherfucker!" he groaned out in agony.

From the corner of my eye, I saw Marco lifting his hands in the air in a surrendering gesture, backing up slowly. A look of pure fear quickly followed. I turned around, following the direction of his petrified gaze.

"What the fuck?" I breathed out, locking eyes with my father who appeared out of thin air.

I didn't even hear him. He was standing by his office door, still dressed in his tux, with a gun in each hand. One was pointed at Marco, the other at John.

"Tsk, tsk, tsk," he whispered, shaking his head in disappointment. "You haven't been paying attention, boys. What am I paying you so much fucking money for? You two fuck-ups didn't even hear me coming. Oh, yo lo sé," he said, "*Oh, I know.*"

He peered over at the girls with no emotion whatsoever. They both sat there beaten and broken, and he didn't even ask if they were okay. You would think one of them being his own flesh and blood, he would have consoled his child, showed some kind of emotion, but not my father. He stood there like a cold-hearted bastard, as if he didn't give a fuck who they were. He could see what I walked in on. It was staring him blatantly in the face, but he remained calm and collected. Unfazed, like he saw this sort of scene play out in front of him all the time. That's when it hit me like a ton of fucking bricks. This wasn't my dad, this was the crime boss that everybody feared. I had never truly witnessed my father's true nature until this very moment.

I wouldn't learn until later in life you never allowed your enemies to see your weaknesses. You could be burning inside, but had to remain cold and heartless on the outside. Even if your whole life was laid out in front of you, dying.

"Do you like little girls, asshole? Hmm... A usted le gustan las peladitas, cabron?" my father asked, repeating himself and bringing me back to the present. "I asked you a question. Twice, motherfucker. There won't be a third."

Marco lowered his arms. "Sir, we—"

"If you move your hands again, I'll slap the taste out of your fucking mouth. Now do as I say or I'll let the homeboys in the Bronx run a train on your culo. You know what? On second thought, I still might." He let out a throaty laugh that echoed off the office walls.

"Suck my dick, Martinez," John spewed from the floor, spitting blood in my father's direction. "Javier, he sends his regards."

My dad slowly cocked his head to the side with a grin like the name meant something to him.

Was this retaliation for something?

He casually walked over to him. Only stopping when he was a foot away from John's face.

"You like to rape little girls? Raping young girl pussy? Is that your thing? You dirty motherfucker," he didn't falter, kicking him square in the throat. John recoiled, immediately gasping for air, thrashing around not knowing whether to hold his throat or his leg.

Amari and Sophia both let out a scream, taken aback by my father's actions. I stepped forward to go to them, and he pointed his gun in my direction, stopping me dead in my tracks.

"Now is not the time, hijo," he reprimanded, calling me son before turning the gun back on John. "So where were we? Oh yes,

26

you said you wanted me to suck your dick. That's what you said right? For me to suck your cock?"

John whimpered, "No."

My father crouched down to his level, pointing the barrel of both guns to his face.

"What? You didn't say that? You said you wanted me to suck your dick. That's what you said. Are you calling me a liar? I'm a liar? I believe your exact words were, 'Suck my dick, Martinez.' Alejandro, did this piece of shit tell me to suck his dick?"

I stood there nodding my head, unable to find my voice.

"What did he say, hijo?!" yelling at me to answer him.

"He said, 'Suck my dick, Martinez.'"

"That's what I thought." He moved the guns to his cock. "Pull your pants down, John. I'll be nice. Nicer than you were to my daughter and her friend. I promise I won't shoot off your dick. I'll just leave you with one fucking ball. I'll even let you choose. Make a fucking decision. You tell me, right or left?"

"I'm sorry, I'm so fucking sorry," John groaned.

"You know saying sorry is a sign of weakness? Where's the man who wanted to take my daughter and her friend's virtue? Huh? Where did that John go? The one who told me to suck his dick, he's gone? Eh coño?"

Out of nowhere I saw my dad's arm swing straight up behind him, his face not wavering from John's. I blinked, following the direction he was aiming, right as another shot was fired, hitting Marco directly in the fucking forehead. Blowing his brains out the back of his head, causing it to splatter on the floor and the walls.

Time just seemed to stand still, nothing moving, including me. Sour bile burned in the back of my throat, threatening to surface. Blood and death lingered in the air, a scent which would forever haunt me. I had never witnessed someone get murdered. I would remember that image for the rest of my life.

There was no going back, it was now a part of me, burned into my senses, whether I wanted it to be or not.

His dead body fell to the floor with a thud. My father didn't even bother to turn to see what he had just done. He shot a man point blank in the head, executing him without hesitation, without warning, and without any remorse or shame. I envied him at that moment. Seeing him exercise all his power, made me crave it, too, but a part of me was scared and not ready. So many conflicting emotions emerged in a matter of seconds. I still didn't understand my role as a Martinez.

The life I was supposed to lead one day.

The girls' screams echoed off the walls, vibrating through every last fiber of my being. I wanted to move. I wanted to grab my sister and Sophia and run. I wanted to hide, but my feet were glued to the goddamn floor beneath me.

"Man up, son. Man the fuck up," Dad roared while handing me the gun. "One down, one more to go, Alejandro."

I looked from him to the gun in my shaking hands. It was right then and there I knew my life was about to change forever.

"You look me in the eyes when I'm talking to you."

My body began to tremble as I looked into my father's vacant green eyes, trying like hell to control the fear coursing through me.

"This is what we do, hijo. We protect what's ours by any means necessary. No. Matter. What. Family comes first."

I looked back at Amari and Sophia, who were still cowered together like two little girls in the corner. Both of them stared intently at me, waiting. I had never witnessed fear like it before, and I didn't know if it was directed at me or at what they had gone through tonight.

My lips began to tremble as I held back the emotions trying to surface. I wanted the bastard to pay for what he had done to my girls. I wanted him to suffer as they had. I didn't know if that made me the hero or the villain in this story, but in the end, it didn't matter. I knew what I wanted to do. I felt it in my core what I had to do, not for my father, and not for the girls…

For me.

"Eye for an eye, Alejandro. Justice is always made on the fucking street."

John and I locked eyes. For the first time since this nightmare, a sense of calm settled over me. Replacing any doubt or trepidation. The voices of my conscience were silenced. All I could hear was the sound of John's breathing in the distance.

I've always known my fate, but this was the first time I actually wanted to embrace it.

The look in his eyes showed me everything I needed to see.

I raised my gun with a steady hand, causing his eyes to widen, pointing it directly to his forehead.

"You'll burn in Hell for this, boy," John spewed, spitting blood again.

I grinned. "Well then, save me a fucking a seat."

I didn't think twice about it, cocking the gun and pulling the trigger.

Silence.

The girls didn't scream. They didn't make a sound. They just looked at me like they knew John was right. I didn't move. I didn't dare to even breathe. Trying like hell to hold it together. It wasn't until Amari shut her eyes, shaking her head as though it killed her to look at me. I dropped to my knees, slouching over, still holding on to the gun. The realization of what I just did was like a cold bucket of ice being poured over my burning hot body. My father didn't falter, roughly grabbing my chin, making me look him dead in his eyes.

I'll never forget the words that came out of his mouth next.

"You're a Martinez now."

And I was.

Three
Martinez

The next few weeks seemed to drag on, prolonging the nightmares plaguing my mind since I killed someone. It was my fifteenth birthday, and my mom had all of our family and friends over to celebrate. Every birthday my sister and I had turned into a huge, extravagant party, more for our parents than us. We never discussed what happened the night in my father's office. We were forced to move on. The incident, buried along with the bodies, six feet under. In those last few weeks everything changed in my life.

Starting with how my sister looked at me, so callous and cold. Every night I waited for her to come to my room and seek my protection like she always did. But she never came. I don't know if she fucking hated me because I left her that night or because I killed someone while she watched. Either way, there was no turning back.

Not for her.

Not for me.

Not for anyone.

My fate was sealed that night.

We barely spoke to each other, but it wasn't like I had much time to talk to her, anyway.

My father began taking me to his meetings. Business deals were what he called them. I got to see exactly what he did from the time he left till the time he came home and then some. Experiencing another life, another world. None of it even came close to what I thought he did in my mind. When he walked into a room everyone turned and shut their fucking mouths. Waiting for him to sit and speak. He always sat at the head of the table, and no one dared to challenge him for it. It took a lot to know a man, and in the last few weeks, I had learned so much about my father, yet I barely started to understand or comprehend any of it.

When he spoke, everyone listened.

When he moved, everyone parted.

My father was God in a world that was nothing but Hell. The irony was not lost on me.

"Mi amor, aquí tienes," Mom said, "*My love, here you go*," as she handed me her gift.

"Mamá, you didn't have to get me anything. The party was enough."

"Alejandro, what kind of mother would I be if I didn't get mi bebé a gift?" she questioned in her Spanglish which she always spoke.

"I'm not a baby," I simply stated, shaking my head.

She caressed the side of my face with nothing but love and devotion in her eyes. My mom was the strongest woman I'd ever known. Everything my father lacked, my mother made up for. I guess it was why their marriage worked so well. They had the perfect balance.

"You'll always be my baby, Alejandro. Even when you're married and have your own niños, mi bebé para siempre," she added, "*My baby forever*," with a loving smile. "Now open your gift."

I ripped open the wrapping paper and pulled off the cover of a square jewelry box. A black beaded bracelet was placed perfectly in the center.

"It's for protection," she said out of nowhere.

I looked at her confused, not understanding what she meant.

"When we went back home to Colombia this summer, I went to a Santero, a Saint. I had the bracelet blessed for you. Para tu protección," she stated, "*For your protection*."

My family was extremely religious. Like most Colombian people, we were Catholic, both Amari and I were christened as babies, made our first communion and confirmation. Mom was definitely the most religious out of all of us. She went to church often, probably praying for her husband's soul and now mine. She took us to church every Sunday. Sometimes my father would show up, but most of the time not. She always wore a sterling silver cross around her neck, always caressing it while she prayed. In all my years, I'd never seen her take it off.

She called it *her* protection.

With us around her, she needed it more than anyone could ever know.

"I wanted to wait to give it to you on your birthday. You're never to take it off, it will keep you safe, Alejandro."

"Mamá, I don't—" The look on her face stopped me from finishing what I was going to say.

I honestly didn't know what to believe any longer, but I still found myself praying every night for those I loved. If it gave her peace of mind, then who was I to tell her no? I'd keep my word and hold it dear to my heart.

I nodded, smiling. Easing the disappointment on her face. I grabbed the bracelet out of the box, and she helped me put it on my right wrist. She made the sign of the cross on my face and body like she always did.

"Que Dios te bendiga y te acompañe," she whispered, "*May God bless you and always keep you from harm.*" She pulled me into a tight hug, kissing the top of my head. "Now, go enjoy your party. Even though Sophia is not here."

I cocked an eyebrow. Sophia hadn't been around at all. She hadn't returned to school either. I don't know how my father handled the situation with her grandparents and I hadn't asked, knowing I wouldn't get a straight answer.

"Your father took care of it. Give it time."

I nodded again, not knowing how to respond.

The party started to die down, and I was finally able to make my way over to Amari. She was sitting outside by the edge of the pool, her feet dangling in the water.

"Happy birthday, Alejandro," she acknowledged, staring out in front of her without bothering to turn around.

"How did you know it was me?" I asked, standing behind her with my hands tucked in the pockets of my slacks.

"I could smell you from a mile away. You smell like dad. You dress like him now, too," she added in a sad tone.

I peered down at my black button-down shirt and black slacks. We had to wear similar clothes like this for school, but since I had been spending all my free time with my father, I didn't find a reason to change once I got home.

"Do you want to be like him now? Are you not my brother anymore?"

This was the most she had spoken to me in weeks.

"Do you think I have a choice in the matter, Amari? You know who our father is."

"You always have a choice, Alejandro. Whether you want to see it or not, it's there if you look hard enough."

"When I shut my eyes, even if it's only for a few seconds, I still see them."

Her breath hitched and she immediately closed her eyes. My words were too much for her to take.

"I still see you hiding in a corner. Broken and beaten. With dried blood on your face and tears streaming down your cheeks. A look of terror as you watched Sophia, knowing you were next. Your life was hanging by nothing but a thread. You weren't the only one who lost your innocence that night, Amari. The only difference is you can get yours back. I can't."

"Do you regret it?"

Without hesitation, I answered, "No. I would do it again if I had to."

She shook her head, disappointed with my answer. "Two wrongs don't make a right, Alejandro."

I didn't say anything. What could I say to that?

"I don't want to lose you, Alejandro. You're all I have," she murmured, her voice breaking.

I crouched down, kissing the back of her head, letting my lips linger for a few seconds. "I'll always be your brother. I will always protect you, no matter what you think of my choices." And with that I stood, turning to leave.

My father was expecting me. He said we were going to take a ride after the party wrapped up. He still had to give me my gift.

"For now. You're my brother, for now."

I stopped dead in my tracks, feeling her intense gaze on my back.

"Even the Devil was an angel once, Alejandro. It's only a matter of time until you become El Diablo, too."

33

I could feel her stare burning a hole between my shoulder blades, waiting for me to comment. I didn't. I just went back inside, leaving her alone with nothing but the truth that lingered between us.

"Hijo, grab your suit jacket. The limo is waiting outside," Dad ordered, kissing my mom on the lips before heading out the door.

I tried to pretend I didn't see the worry and concern written clear across her face. Instead, I leaned in and kissed her cheek, following my dad to the limo, not looking back. His driver and bodyguards were outside waiting on us. He rode everywhere in a limo. I couldn't remember the last time I ever saw him drive his own car. My mother, on the other hand, refused, saying she didn't come from el barrio in Colombia to be chauffeured around. El barrio was the hood. She was dirt poor growing up, having nothing but the tattered clothes on her back. In a way, I guess you could say my dad saved her.

Bringing her into an extravagant life, where she didn't have to want or need for anything. It was all there for her on a silver platter. Any family she still had in Colombia were taken care of and safe. Not just because she married into money, but she also married into power. The highest authority in the country to be exact.

My father.

They moved to America a few years after they were married. The Martinez men had been doing business in the states for decades. He was the one who decided it was time to relocate and conquer. My sister and I were born in New York and had been traveling around the world with them since we were born.

"You've had your first taste of blood, protecting what was yours, and rightfully so," Dad declared, pulling me away from my thoughts. The limo stopped at our destination, a building located in the center of Manhattan.

"You're a man now, Alejandro. It's time you reaped the benefits of becoming a Martinez."

He opened the door and stepped out of the limo before I had a chance to reply. I followed his lead into the building I didn't recognize, along with his six bodyguards who never left his side. We entered a private elevator that required a slide card to access.

One of the bodyguards swiped the card and punched in a code to the penthouse floor. The doors opened to a huge, fully furnished living room with floor to ceiling bay windows, which overlooked Manhattan.

I stepped off the elevator, passing my dad to walk around the room. There was a kitchen to the left with all stainless steel appliances, and a granite-topped island with ten stools. To the right there was a spiral staircase, which I assumed led to the master suite. The decor was simple, yet elegant, with several pieces of art that looked like they cost a small fortune. There wasn't a thing out of place, everything pristine and in order.

"This is one of my penthouses," Dad answered, reading my mind as I stopped by the window, peering out at the scenic view only Manhattan could provide.

I could physically feel the energy of the city that never sleeps. Taking a deep breath enjoying the feeling coursing through me, absorbing everything around me.

"You're giving me a penthouse for my birthday?" I asked, turning around to look at him.

He arched an eyebrow, nodding to one of his goons to hit the elevator button.

"I'm giving you something way better, hijo."

As if on cue, my attention was drawn to a young woman dressed in a red bra and panties, entering the room with nothing but heels and a bright smile.

"Pussy," he added with a devious grin.

My stare went back to my father, jerking my head back, confused.

"Happy birthday, Alejandro. She's yours for the whole night. You can fuck her three ways from Sunday. I've paid for every hole on that body. I suggest you try each one."

With that, he turned around and left. Leaving two bodyguards to stand by the door. I turned my attention back to the blonde who was now sitting on the couch like the whore that she was. The bra and panties she wore left nothing to the imagination, her tits lifted high to accentuate her small waist and luscious ass. Her pouty red lips made me immediately want to stick my cock in between them. It was as if her body was made just to fuck.

35

Her blonde hair cascaded down the sides of her face and her body shined bright against the dim lighting of the room. Her creamy white skin looked as inviting as her legs that were spread wide open as she leaned back into the cushions.

Waiting.

We locked eyes.

Her sultry blue eyes scanned me over as she licked her lips ever so slightly, making my cock twitch. By the look on her face, she liked what she saw.

The feeling was very fucking mutual.

"You look a lot older than fifteen," she said, breaking the silence with her fuck me eyes. "Your daddy paid a lot of money to have me here tonight. We have more in common than you think, Alejandro. I'm a prodigy too. One day, I'll be the Madam and you'll be God."

I narrowed my eyes at her, not understanding.

"I'm a VIP. Very Important Pussy. I'm the best you will ever fucking taste, and I'm going to show you the time of your life, birthday boy. So, the question really is, what hole do you want to fuck me in first?" she rasped, sucking in her lower lip.

I slowly made my way over to her, just out of reach. One hand placed in my pocket, trying to conceal my excitement, and the other rubbing my chin, contemplating my next move. Taking in every last inch of her body, right down to her exposed pussy. It was my turn to lick my lips, desperately wanting to drop to my knees and devour it.

"You don't say much, do you?" she asked, bringing my gaze back to hers.

"What's your name?"

"Anything you want it to be."

"That's not what I asked."

She smirked. "Lilith. My name is Lilith."

"How appropriate. How old are you, Lilith?"

"Old enough. Besides a lady never tells her age."

"Well then, it's a good thing you're not a lady," I scoffed, tilting my head. Trying to guess.

She held back a smile. "I'm a few years older than you. I think we're going to be very good friends one day, Alejandro," she purred, getting onto her hands and knees and crawling toward me.

She peered up at me through her long, dark lashes and although she was gorgeous, she wasn't who I wanted her to be. But who was I to stop her when she pulled out my cock and deep throated it like the goddamn pro she was. Leaving a ring of bright red lipstick around my shaft.

I spent the rest of the night fucking her in every possible position known to man. I lost my virginity to a whore, all because my father was proud of me for murdering a man. If that wasn't fucked up…

Then I don't know what is.

Four
Martinez

"Amari? You up here?" I called out, climbing up the ladder to the attic.

We used to play up there when we were kids, and as we got older, it turned into a safe place to escape life. Even if only for a few minutes. It was our safe haven.

They say time heals all wounds, and I began to believe it. Six months passed since my birthday, and over the last few weeks, Amari started feeling comfortable enough to be around me again. Casually starting conversations with me that weren't forced, asking me for help on her homework, and even coming into my room to watch movies together. Little things like that gave me hope that maybe one day she would look at me the way she used to.

With love.

She was leaning against the far wall, looking out the window. A daisy hung from her fingertips, with its pedals scattered by her feet. It had been her favorite flower since we were kids.

"He loves me, he loves me not," I heard her whisper.

I didn't need to ask who she was thinking of, it was Michael, a white-ass boy we went to school with all our lives. Her first real crush. She had loved him for as long as I could remember. Blushing like a little schoolgirl anytime he acknowledged her. They had officially been together a year, much to my father's dismay. It took him years to finally accept that Amari wouldn't date any of the guys he kept bringing around for her.

We all knew he wanted her to have an arranged marriage. Our dad didn't care if his daughter was going to be loved, or if her husband was going to be faithful. No, none of that mattered. Our dad cared about what they could offer our *family*. More power, more territories, more soldiers.

More, more, more.

Our mom constantly reminded him that he married for love, and he needed to give Amari and I the same chance. After years of constantly going back and forth with it, she was finally allowed to start dating Michael.

"Hey," she greeted as I sat down next to her, leaning forward to rest my arms on my knees.

I handed her another daisy from the vase next to me. She smiled, grabbing it out of my hand to twirl it around her fingers. Her smile quickly faded as she watched the daisy dance in her hand. Silence filled the space between us.

"Why the sad face?"

"We're not kids anymore, are we, Alejandro?" she asked, looking back up at me.

"Were we ever?"

"I'd like to believe so. You used to smile, laugh, and joke around. Now, you're so serious all the time. It's like you went from being fifteen to fifty in a matter of months. Feels like it's been forever since I've seen you happy. Where's my brother? Where did he go?"

I met her gaze for a few seconds before deciding to look out in front of me. Avoiding the pain in her eyes.

"I'm with you right now."

"That doesn't answer my question."

"It sounded more like a statement to me, Amari."

"Dad let you off his leash?"

I grinned, glancing over at her, laughing silently to myself.

She smiled, nudging my shoulder. "There he is. There's Alejandro."

"What are you doing up here?" I asked, changing the subject. "Where is your douchebag of a boyfriend?"

She shrugged, not paying any mind to my name-calling. She was used to it. No one would ever be good enough for my sister. Especially some pussy gringo guy.

"Michael and I are... I don't know. We're fighting, I guess. And no... I don't need you to go rough him up."

39

"Did I say a word?" I responded with my hands surrendered in the air.

"Don't give me that look, brother. I know it works on your little hussies, but it doesn't work with me. Have you talked to Sophia?"

"We were discussing Michael," I simply stated.

"I don't want to tell you. I don't want you to hate him anymore than you already do."

"Whether you tell me or not, I'll find out. So, how about you save me the time and spit it out already?"

She rolled her eyes at me knowing I was right. I had never cared for Michael. Quite frankly, I wish the fucker would disappear. I had seen him staring at Sophia more times than I cared to count. The fact that he would disrespect my sister in front of her fucking face made it easy for me to dislike him. I never said anything to Amari because she was oblivious to it, and the last thing I wanted was to lose my sister over some asshole.

She sighed. "Do you promise to keep your cool? You won't say anything to him? Or hurt him?"

I nodded, even though I was lying. If he hurt her, I would break his fucking face without any hesitation.

"You're lying. I don't believe you."

"My word is all I have, Amari."

She bit her lip, contemplating if she should tell me or not. She shook her head. "Fine... we were hanging out after the football game last night, and this guy from another school started talking to me while Michael was shooting the shit with his boys. So—"

"He left you by yourself?" I interrupted, putting my hand out to stop her. Needing clarification.

"No. What? He was mad because I was talking with another guy. We got into a huge fight over it. He's pissed at me. I don't know what to do to make it better. I told him we were just talking. It didn't mean anything, but he says he could tell I was flirting or some shit like that. I don't want Michael thinking I'm a slut or a cock tease."

"One, he shouldn't have left you by yourself if he's that insecure. Two, if he called you a slut, I will fucking rip his—"

"Oh my God, he didn't leave me by myself. We were at a party. See, this is why I didn't want to talk to you about it. You're just going to put all the blame on him. You're supposed to be helping me, not pointing fingers."

"I could break his fingers. But, instead I'm here just listening to you."

"Alejandro…"

"Amari, don't whine. It's fucking annoying," I scoffed, pissed off that she was defending him.

She narrowed her eyes at me. "You know, for someone who claims to be a 'take charge' kind of guy, you're still number two and you sure are pussyfooting around—"

"Pussyfooting? The only thing I do with pussy is fuck it. You want me to tell you what I'm thinking right now? My opinion? Because, sweetheart, you're not going to like it."

"You're vile," she spat, getting up from where we sat. I followed suit, not backing down.

"I'm honest. Your boyfriend is an insecure little bitch, who would rather call you a slut than walk over to you and claim what he thinks is his. He wants to fuck you, Amari. And the fact that he's acting so possessive can only mean one thing. You haven't spread your legs for him, yet."

Her eyes widened from my revelation of her truth.

"How about that for honesty?"

She shook her head, backing away from me. I grabbed her wrist stopping her.

"Don't you dare walk away from me. Words, Amari. Fucking speak."

"Let go of me," she gritted out, trying to tear her arm out of my grasp. "You think you're so high and mighty, Alejandro! But here you are, Dad's lapdog. Marching in line with every last thing he says. You're nothing but *his* bitch."

"At least I'm not weak, Amari," I countered, letting her go.

She didn't falter. "I'd rather be weak than be condemned to this life of hell. I can't wait until I'm old enough to leave. I want nothing to do with this life. I will be out that door and out of this purgatory as soon as I fucking can."

41

"With Michael?" I mocked in a condescending tone, standing close to her. "You think he can protect you? From. Me? Your own flesh and blood. I'll always be your brother, and I'm not going anywhere. Even *if* you think you are."

Her chest rose and descended with each word that left my mouth.

"I'm not scared of you, Alejandro. I know who you really are, in here," she paused, placing her hand over my heart. "So stop pretending like I don't. You don't intimidate me. You need to worry about your own life and stay the hell out of mine. You've made your own choices, now you need to let me make mine. Maybe it's time you stopped *pussyfooting* around with what's been right in your goddamn face for a long time. How about you claim what you want to be yours? Since it's so easy for you—"

"Enough, Amari," I ordered, putting my hand out in front of me. She shoved it away from her face.

"She's waiting for you. You know that, right? She thinks you're her fucking hero, her savior ever since that night. She's loved you since the first day she laid eyes on you, and I'm certain the feeling is mutual. Maybe it's time for you to grow some balls and actually do something about it. She's going to be here in a few minutes."

"Get the fuck out of my face!"

"Truth hurts, doesn't it, brother?" She smiled before turning around to leave, never looking back.

I stood there alone for I don't know how long, contemplating everything she had just said. Taking a few deep breaths, trying not to let my temper get the best of me. It was a Martinez trait. We could go from zero to sixty in a matter of seconds. My father already warned me on several occasions that I needed to learn how to keep my emotions in check. Protecting what's mine without showing any weakness. Never backing down. It only took one wrong move in this life to end up with a bullet in your goddamn head.

Your enemies couldn't hurt you if they didn't know what you're feeling. What you're thinking.

It was the code of life.

A very thin fucking line between being dead, or alive.

I took another deep breath as an unrecognizable feeling washed over me. It was a strong force, a pull drawing me, making me gravitate toward the window. My hands securely placed in the pockets of my slacks, rubbing my fingers together. A calming gesture I had acquired somewhere along the way. I felt her before I saw her.

Sophia.

She started coming around more in the last month. I had seen her a few times in school between classes, always struggling with her fucking locker. She'd caught me staring at her on more than one occasion and would smile shyly at me from a distance. I'd always look away, never acknowledging her, turning and walking in the opposite direction.

I wanted to remember the way she used to look at me, rather than the way she looked at me now.

She was in the daisy field behind our house. Amari was nowhere to be found, but I assumed she was there for her. There was no taking my eyes off her. I couldn't, and I didn't fucking want to. She was breathtakingly beautiful, sitting there in a teal sundress. Her long legs placed out in front of her, leaning back on her hands for support. Her dark brown hair gleamed in the rays of the sun, gently blowing in the breeze. Her soft, creamy skin flawless. I could see her bright green eyes shining from the distance between us. She looked like a dream.

My dream.

Before I could give it any thought, I went to her. Taking the attic ladder two steps at a time. Hoping she was still sitting there alone by the time I got downstairs. She didn't turn toward me or even acknowledge that I was there. She was in her own little world. A world I desperately wanted to become a part of. I sat down beside her, gazing at the side of her beautiful face. Willing her to say something, but her eyes remained looking front and center toward the Manhattan Bridge in the distance, while mine remained on her.

"It's been a while," she said loud enough for me to hear, breaking the silence. Her tone laced with nothing but worry. "Your sister let me in. She said to go out back and you would find me. I know what you're thinking, but I'm not here for Amari, I'm here for you."

"Why?" I found myself asking, holding back the desire to reach over and touch her, knowing it would only frighten her.

"You never gave me a chance to say thank you after that horrible night. They were about to rape me and God knows what else. It has taken me months to wrap my head around it. I've been trying to heal, both physically and mentally. When you found us, I remember thinking God sent us an angel. You saved my life, Alejandro," she paused, letting her words linger. "I can't begin to tell you how grateful I am. Thank you for—"

"Now, tell me why you're really here," I interrupted, needing to know.

This was all very touching, but I was tired of the bullshit. I had enough of that in my life.

She immediately turned to look at me, locking eyes. Her intense gaze lit me on fire in a way I hadn't ever experienced before. I never wanted to kiss someone as much as I did her at that moment. There were so many what ifs racing through my mind in an instant, so many consequences and scenarios that could happen, so many fucking choices that could be right or wrong. She needed to stay away from me. That was the right thing to do. I was no good for her.

She looked at me as a savior, her hero, when I was anything but those things.

I reached over and caressed the side of her face. She leaned into my embrace like she had been waiting for me to do it since the second I sat down beside her. My thumb moved toward her pouty lips, rubbing off the lipstick that she wore for me.

I didn't want her to pretend to be anything but what she was. She closed her eyes, melting into my touch.

Her breathing hitched when I pulled on her bottom lip. My hand suddenly moved to grip the back of her neck and bring her toward me.

I knew this was wrong.

I knew I should have stopped.

I knew there was no coming back from this.

I gently pecked her lips, beckoning them to open for me. She did, releasing a soft moan when she felt my tongue in her mouth.

See, I also knew I was going to Hell.

I just never imagined…

I would be taking her with me.

Five
Martinez

"How many assault rifles are in the crates?" Dad asked the black-market arms broker during a meeting at one of his warehouses downtown.

He had me attend more and more meetings over the last year, molding me into the prodigal son. Always reminding me that this would all be mine one day.

As if I could forget.

We all sat around a rectangular mahogany table in the middle of a wide-open space. It looked like a scene from a mobster movie. My dad was at the head of the table, of course, and I was sitting beside him. The two arms brokers were sitting across from me, with smug looks on their faces. There were three bodyguards behind my dad, and one behind me. Two more stood watch by the door.

If the two motherfuckers tried to pull anything, they wouldn't be walking out of there alive.

"Four to five," he replied in a thick Russian accent.

"It's either four or it's five. Which one is it? I don't have time for your bullshit."

"Usually four."

"Usted lo que esta dicendo es…" Dad snapped, "*So what you're saying…* is that you were trying to fuck me when you already knew it was four. You just wanted me to pay for five?"

"No, that's—"

He put his hand up in the air, silencing him. "That wasn't a question. My reputation speaks for itself. Would you like me to remind you what I'm known for, hijos de putas?" Dad sneered, "*Son of bitches.*"

The arms brokers looked at each other suspiciously then back at my dad. By the look on their faces they wanted to tell him to go fuck himself, but they knew better. Dad sat there with his head cocked to the side, sizing the men up. Lazily spinning the Glock sitting in front of him like a roulette wheel. Stopping it every time it pointed to the Russians.

"I want a thousand rounds of ammunition for each of those rifles."

"We can do five hundred."

He didn't falter, arguing, "If I wanted five hundred, I would have said five hundred. Four assault rifles per crate. I want a hundred crates. I'll pay you two thousand a crate, five hundred per rifle and fifty thousand for the ammo. That's two hundred and fifty thousand total."

"That's too low. We need—"

The gun spun one last time and before I knew it he had it off the table, holding it casually out in front of him instead.

"The crates need safe transportation until offload at the shipping port downtown. I'll pay you half now, half when they get delivered."

"Let's nego—"

"If you want to negotiate then get the fuck out of my office, pedazos de mierda," Dad roared, "*Pieces of shit.*"

"We take high risk doing this and you're offering—"

"Quarter of a million. It's an offer you shouldn't refuse. Your risk is well compensated. These are wholesale rifles. I'm moving them onto the streets. The serial numbers need to be shaved off so it's going to cost me money. If you don't want to take the deal, I can reach out to the Albanians. You're not the only pendejos I can buy from, take or leave it. But next time you try to come in here, don't waste my fucking time with bullshit excuses. We're not selling Girl Scout cookies, motherfuckers. We're in the business of making things happen. Either you make it happen, or I'll find someone who will."

The arms broker cleared his throat. "Right... we will have them delivered next week."

My dad pounded his hand that was holding the gun on the table. The three bodyguards behind him stepped forward.

"Thursday," he gritted out.

Which was three days from today then he casually stood up, buttoning his suit jacket. I followed suit. From the sound of things the meeting was over.

They nodded, clenching their jaws. "Thursday, amigo."

My father shook his head with a cocky grin. "I'm not your friend."

Grabbing the briefcase that was under the table, Dad placed it out in front of them. He slid open the locks, revealing stacks of hundred dollar bills perfectly placed in a row. Filling the entire briefcase from top to bottom.

"Since you think I'm your amigo, I'm assuming you don't need to count it," Dad crudely mocked, shutting the briefcase and sliding it across the table. The arms broker intercepted it.

"You interested in the women we picked up? I have a mother and daughter, beautiful women with big tits and voluptuous asses. A few other women as well, all young. Fresh. We had our go with them. They're ready to be transported. If you're—"

"No," Dad cut him off without missing a beat.

I narrowed my eyes in confusion at the sick fucks sitting in front of me.

"Are you sure? They make good business. Make you a lot of money for—"

"Did I fucking stutter? Take your money and get the fuck out. My men will see you on Thursday."

"How will we—"

"They'll know."

They stood up. I watched them leave without so much as a second glance.

"Say it," Dad ordered, reading me like a goddamn book as soon as the doors closed behind them.

"You let them take those women?"

"I didn't let them do shit. I don't traffic women, Alejandro. But some of the men I know do. Everyone has a mother or a child. Those are two things that I don't fuck with. You understand me?"

I peered down at the table. "Yes."

My mind was spinning at what was going to happen to those women. All I could think of was Amari and Sophia, I would

48

fucking kill anyone if they tried to take them. I proved that to be true already.

"You look me in the eyes when I'm talking to you, hijo. My patience is wearing very thin with having to remind you."

I looked up, staring into his dark, cold, daunting eyes that never showed any emotion. There were times like these where all I wanted was to know what he was thinking, what he was feeling.

Especially, to know whether he loved me or not. Always feeling as though I was just another card that he brought to the table.

Power.

"Some people may never like me, and I will never give a fuck. Everything I do, I do it for all of you. At the end of the day, family is all that matters."

I narrowed my eyes at him, taking in his words.

"Respect is not given, it's earned. Until that day, you will look me in the eyes when I'm talking to you. One day you'll stand where I am, and you'll thank me for making you who you are."

We rode home in silence. I stared out the limo window the whole way home, contemplating everything I had learned that day. When we got home my dad went straight to his office like he always did, and I headed up to my room. I spent the rest of the night staring at the ceiling, thinking about my life and how Sophia fit into it. She was never far from my thoughts. She knew who my family was. What the future held for me. We didn't discuss it, but we didn't have to. The truth was blatantly staring us in the face. Except when I was with her, I didn't want to be anywhere else. It was like living a double life. Sophia's Alejandro, the sixteen-year-old kid, and Alejandro Martinez, son of the notorious crime boss.

Destined to take over one day.

Over the last year, Sophia and I had gotten closer. Close in ways I never imagined could be possible. I had pussy thrown at me left and right. Women literally threw themselves on my dick when they saw me walking in with my father. That's all it took for them to want to get on their knees and suck my cock.

All I wanted was Sophia.

No one else existed in my eyes. She was there when I needed her, and even when I didn't. I tried to keep that part of my life

49

private from my father. I knew he was becoming suspicious, since I never took those women up on their offers like I had before. Fucking every single one of them without thinking twice about it. Now I just worried that he would try to take her away from me.

He couldn't.

There wasn't a chance in Hell I'd ever let him. She was mine. End of story.

A few days later I finally had some down time and got to spend some alone time with Sophia. My face turned into the palm of her hand and I softly kissed it. We were lying on my bed, paying no attention to the movie playing in the background. My parents were gone for the night. It was their anniversary, and my dad took my mom out. Ever since the incident with John and Marco, Dad was extra diligent with whom he hired to protect us. There were always extra bodyguards on staff now, specifically around me. Dad said I had become a target, enemies craving to put a bullet in my fucking head the second I stepped foot into a meeting with him.

I started to appreciate life, or whatever the fuck I was living because nothing was guaranteed.

Especially my life.

Sophia came over for a sleepover with Amari, and Michael stopped by shortly after. Much to my fucking disapproval.

In the eyes of Sophia's grandparents, my father was her savior. I don't know what bullshit story he told them about what happened that night, and I didn't give a flying fuck because my girl was in my bed.

"You look tired," she rasped, scratching my head that was lying on her lap. "Your dad is working you too hard."

I slowly turned my face in her lap, nuzzling my nose along her inner thigh. I peered up at her as I wrapped my arms around her waist. In one swift move, I tugged her tiny frame toward me, making her squeal. I lightly brought my body on top of her, supporting my weight with my arms on either side of her face. My mouth was now inches away from hers.

"I don't want to talk about my dad, cariño."

She smirked, as I gently brushed my lips back and forth along her mouth. Loving the feel of her lips against mine.

So soft.

So warm.

So fucking mine.

"Oh yeah? Then what do you want to talk about?"

"Who said I wanted to talk?" I rasped, working my way down her neck. Wanting to feel her pulse beating against my lips.

To this day I was still so goddamn grateful she was alive. I stopped on the spot right under her ear that made her go fucking crazy. Moving her hair to the other side of her neck, never letting up on my caresses on her skin. I could feel the effect I was having on her, and she hadn't stopped me, yet.

"Alejandro…" she moaned.

My heart sped up, and my cock twitched, hearing my name roll off her tongue. I had never heard that tone come from her before. Sophia had always been a good little girl, pure and innocent. That didn't stop me from wanting to be the first guy to feel her from the inside, taste every last inch of her perfect body. Make her come on my cock and beg me to stop.

We hadn't done anything more than kiss. I was patient, but my dick was eager to sink into her sweet pussy. I would never pressure her into anything she wasn't ready for, but that didn't mean I couldn't drive her insane with need. Taking her to the edge, getting her nice and fucking wet.

I may have been falling in love with her, but I wasn't a goddamn saint.

I was a man.

I had needs, and I needed *her*.

"What, baby?"

I sensually kissed down her neck to her collarbone, working my way down closer to her breasts. Going right for her hard nipple that was poking through her slim cotton tank top. I wanted nothing more than to take her tits in my mouth, and make her come from that sensation alone. She knew better than to come into my bed without wearing a bra.

"You need to stop," she purred, arching her back off my bed.

"No, I don't," I spoke honestly, continuing my descent.

Her chest was rising and falling with every movement of my lips getting closer to her nipple.

"We shouldn't do this."

"Is that right, cariño?"

I lightly flicked her nipple with my tongue through her tank, grinning as I peered up at her. She was coming undone beneath me, soft moans escaping her pouty lips. I grabbed her wrists with one hand and placed them gently above her head. My other hand working its way down her torso to her hip, as I grinded my hard cock right against her sensitive pussy. Pushing her further to the edge.

"You're so fucking beautiful," I groaned, desperately needing to take what I wanted to be mine.

Her mouth parted and she licked her lips as I slowly pulled down her tank top. The smell and feel of her was all around me, making me burn with desire to claim every last fucking inch of her. I had done way more than any sixteen-year-old should have even known about, but it never felt like that. With her.

Not even close.

Not one time.

I wanted to capture this moment, and hold onto it for as long as I could. I wanted to remember her just like this.

For me.

Mine.

And I couldn't hold back any longer. "I love you, Sophia. You own me. I'm yours. Para siempre," I confessed, "*Forever.*"

She lifted her head off my pillow. Her lust-filled gaze was quickly replaced by shock as her eyes widened, looking past me toward my bedroom door. I turned to see what ruined our moment. Coming face to face with Michael who was standing in the hallway.

Watching.

Six

Martinez

"Alejandro, my office. Ahora!" Dad ordered, "*Now!*" In a tone I didn't appreciate.

He walked right past the dining room, not even acknowledging any of us who had been waiting for him to come home to eat. Mom had invited Sophia and Michael over for dinner. She had been slaving away all day, cooking my father's favorite damn meal. He didn't so much as look in her direction to say a simple hello or thank you. He just stormed in, too pissed off at God-knows-what, and I was about to get the wrath.

Mom and Amari glanced at each other and then back at me. Their worried expressions mirroring one another. I simply scooted my chair back and calmly stood, smiling. Reaching over the table, I squeezed my mom's hand in a loving gesture before excusing myself.

No one said a word, but they didn't have to. Their faces spoke for themselves.

When I walked into his office, he was sitting behind his desk. His arms set out in front of him with his head cocked to the side, waiting to unleash his fury on me.

He nodded toward the door. I understood his silent gesture to close it behind me. I did, allowing it to slam a little, earning me a glare I used to fear. I casually walked over and took a seat in one of the chairs in front of his desk. Leaning forward, I placed my arms on my legs, clasping my hands together in front of me. Looking him dead in the eyes.

I arched an eyebrow, *waiting*.

"I'm going to ask you this one fucking time, Alejandro. One time," he emphasized, holding his finger out in front of him. "Did you think I wouldn't find out about Sophia?"

"I don't—"

"I highly suggest you don't fucking lie to me. I'm giving you a warning because you're my son."

I swallowed, hard. Contemplating my next move. If I showed him fear. If I gave him what he wanted, what he expected, I would forever be in his goddamn grasp.

Under his control till the day he dies.

It was *now* or *never*.

I leaned back into my chair, folding my arms over my chest, not backing down.

"Since when do you care who I'm fucking, old man?" I countered, laying all my cards out perfectly on the table.

It was the only game my father played. And I was prepared to call his bluff. Hoping like hell that he wouldn't call me out on mine.

His eyes lit up, it was quick but I saw it. He grinned, leaning back in his chair. "If you were just fucking her, then you wouldn't be sitting in front of me with a shit-eating grin on your face."

"I thought you wanted me to enjoy pussy. Wasn't that the whole point of getting me a whore?"

"Carajo," he breathed out, "*Fuck*," with an expression I had never seen before. "You love her?" he stated as a question, shaking his head in disappointment. "You fucking love her…"

I knew it wouldn't take him long to figure it out. I didn't have to tell him the truth. He could smell it on me.

"It's kind of a coincidence, don't you think? Girl from the wrong side of the tracks makes rich, powerful boy fall in—"

"She didn't fucking make me do anything," I gritted out through a clenched jaw, cutting him off.

Before I even got the last word out, his chair flew out from underneath him, crashing into the wall with a thud. His fist slammed against the desk, making me jump.

"You stupid, son of a bitch! The change in your eyes, your composure, the sudden drop of your fucking balls talking to me like that. To me. Your father. You want to bring her into this life?

54

Then you better learn how to fucking hide those emotions, hijo. I can see straight through you. I can see her behind your eyes. I can feel her coursing through your bloodstream. It's pouring out of you. She's your weakness, your fucking death sentence. She would be the first thing I would use against you. Do you think she's strong enough to handle our lifestyle? Your future."

I didn't falter. I couldn't. If I did, I would lose.

Her.

"Is that why you tried to kill her?" I viciously spewed, finally saying what I had been thinking since that night.

"You think I'm capable of that? Do I need to remind you that my own daughter was there that night?"

"It was pretty convenient that Amari was barely touched. Just roughed up a little. Sophia, on the other hand, was two seconds from being raped and beaten to death. So, yes, I think you're capable of anything."

"Is that right?"

"Yeah, that's right."

He casually nodded, rounding his desk to walk around the room. The silence was deafening all around us, every step he took I expected him to lash out. Yell, threaten, or punish me, but his silence was eerier than his rage. I followed his every movement, feeling as if each step brought me closer to my demise.

He spun, locking eyes with me. Placing his hands in his pockets casually. "I paid all of that girl's medical expenses. I made sure her grandparents wouldn't need or want for anything for the rest of their lives. Including getting them papers, did you know they were illegal immigrants? I didn't stop them from going to the cops, the only lie I told was that someone broke in. I'm even paying for her college. She's no longer a scholarship student. I gave another person the opportunity to get an education at the school you and your sister don't give a shit about."

I scoffed, "Hush money? That's supposed to impress me? Come on, old man, you can do better than that."

He grinned, shaking his head. "Not enough, eh? How about the two men's bodies that I personally lit on fire, not leaving a trace of their fucking lives on this earth. This is a dangerous time for our family. I expect retaliation from Javier's side. You think it's the best time to bring a girlfriend into your life? If you love her so much, then you would let her go. It's the right thing to do."

I stood, placing my hands in my pockets, mirroring his demeanor. Getting right up in his face, I argued, "You wouldn't know the right thing to do if it slapped you in the fucking face and said hello. You're telling me that you had no idea who those men were? Because I know for a fact that you pretty much make your men bend over and cough before you hire them. So, you can see how I find your story hard to believe."

I would never forget the next words that came out of my father's mouth for the rest of my life. It was the first, but not the last, time that I witnessed...

Humanity.

His eyes glazed over with so much fucking emotion that it almost knocked me on my ass.

"I made a mistake, Alejandro," he confessed, bowing his head in shame.

I jerked back, the impact of his words too much for me to take.

"But I took care of it, hijo. I fucking took care of it. The dead can't talk, and I made damn sure of it."

I was about to say something about his confession, but he cleared his throat, looking back up into my eyes. If I had blinked, I would have missed it. That was how quick his ironclad guard came back into its usual place. Once again the hard ass he always was, locking up his emotions as if they never existed to begin with.

He patted my back, turning to leave his office, not saying another word.

"You might have laid my path, but you do not tell me who I can love," I declared, stopping him dead in his tracks. "That's my choice. And my choice is *her*."

There was nothing left to say, it was all burned to ashes.

Exactly like their bodies.

I didn't give him a chance to respond, wanting to have the last word. I left him standing there with nothing but the truth I'd just warned.

All eyes were on me when we entered the dining room, probably shocked to see that I came back in one piece. It was as if they had all been holding their breath the entire time I was gone.

My dad walked over to my mom, kissed her on the cheek before taking his seat at the head of the table.

Sophia gave me a reassuring smile as I pulled out my chair. She was so fucking beautiful. I didn't give it a second thought. I was over to her in four strides, grabbing the sides of her face. Kissing her deep for the first time in front of everyone. Needing to stake my claim.

To show my father.

And Michael.

That I didn't give a flying fuck what they wanted.

I took Sophia home later after we watched a movie. Heading back, hoping to catch the motherfucker before he left my house, I stood by Michael's car, counting the minutes until I saw his goddamn face. Wanting nothing more than to lay him the fuck out. But out of respect for my sister, I would give him one fucking warning.

Just one.

"Well, look who it is? The prodigal son," Michael mocked, walking down the driveway toward me. "What the fuck do you want, Martinez? Why are you waiting for me?"

I didn't hesitate, getting right up in his face, slightly pushing him back. He stammered a little, but didn't waver much.

"I know it was you, motherfucker. You went to my father like the fucking bitch that you are. Man up. Man the fuck up and tell me to my face that you're not the one who told him about Sophia and me," I sneered, my hands balling into fists at my sides. Itching to knock the fucking grin off his face.

He chuckled, nodding, "Fuck you, asshole. I don't want your sloppy seconds. I got a girl already. You may know her, she's your fucking sister."

"You got a dick," I spit out, grabbing him by the shirt, and pushing him up against my car. "I see the way you look at Sophia. I see the way you've always looked at her. You're lucky I don't break your fucking legs for disrespecting my sister, every time your wandering eyes land on *my* girl," I gritted out. "And if you pull that peeping Tom bullshit again, next thing you'll be looking at is the ceiling at your goddamn hospital room."

57

"I don't know what you're talking about. I didn't tell your dad shit. Maybe you should try to keep your dick in your pants, and he wouldn't fucking notice." He shrugged me off, starting to walk away toward his car.

"Jealous?" I yelled, stopping him in his tracks.

He ran his hands through his hair in a frustrated gesture, before walking back over to me, shoving his finger into my chest.

"You're no good for her, man. She's a good girl. All you're going to do is bring her down with you. I'm trying to save her from your hell. Exactly the way I'm trying to save your sister—" he pointed to the house, "I'm the good guy here."

"You're a fucking wolf in sheep's clothing. I can't make you stay away from Amari, but I sure as fuck will make you hurt if you so much as upset my sister. It's only a matter of time until she sees through you. I hope for your sake it's sooner rather than later."

"Is that a threat, Martinez?"

"No, motherfucker. I will put a bullet in your fucking head without blinking an eye. That's a threat. Stay away from Sophia, and start looking at my sister like she's the only one you really want to fuck. You claim to love Amari, then fucking show me your worth."

His chest heaved. The air was so thick between us he stepped back and away from me. Backing down like the pussy he was.

"I love your sister. I love her more than anything. Don't misinterpret my concern for Sophia for something that it's not. You don't know me, Martinez. I know who you—"

"You don't know shit about shit."

"I know your sister is scared of you. How long do you think it's going to take until Sophia is too?"

"Amari is scared of everything. That doesn't mean shit to me. You let me worry about Sophia. You keep my father out of this. She is mine. Do you hear me? *Mine*. You don't get to tell on me like a little puta, then walk away with your dick tucked between your legs for trying to be a boy scout."

"For the last time, I didn't say shit to your dad. Why do you automatically assume it's me? I'm not the only one that knows," he said, stepping toward me again.

I knew what he was insinuating, and I couldn't hold back any longer. I gripped the front of his shirt, tugging him toward me. My face was now inches away from his.

"You have some brass fucking balls, throwing my sister in the line of fire to save your sorry ass. Amari wouldn't betray me. Neither would my mother. It's called loyalty, you fuck. You seem to lack that fucking trait." I let go, glaring him up and down. "I won't warn you again."

And I wouldn't.

Seven

Martinez

"You ready, cariño?"

Sophia sighed, looking at me through the full-length mirror in front of her.

"You are the most impatient man in the world. Do you know that?" she lamented, rolling her eyes as she continued to apply her lipstick, not paying me any mind.

I fucking hated that shit, and she knew it.

She was naturally beautiful.

I was over to her in three strides, grabbing her wrist, and turning her to face me. "You sassing me, baby?" I asked, wiping off the lipstick she'd just applied.

She rolled her eyes at me again as my hands inched toward her ass. "It's not sass when it's true," she mocked.

I spanked her hard and grabbed her ass, making her yelp. "Ow! Don't! That stung."

I grinned as she pushed against my chest, trying to get out of my grasp. It was no use. She wasn't going anywhere unless I wanted her to, but it was still entertaining as fuck to watch her try.

"It's my birthday. I'm allowed to do whatever the fuck I want today."

"What's your excuse for the rest of the year?" she giggled as I slowly moved my hands near her inner thighs. It didn't take much to make her squirm, she was sensitive everywhere. I made sure to touch her every chance I got, just to hear her laugh.

She tried to swat my hands away. "Stop, that tickles." Thrashing and throwing her head back with laughter.

She gasped when I suddenly lifted her up, leaning her back against the wall with a slight thud. Wrapping her legs around my waist and her arms around my neck for support. She bit her lip as I stared into her big green eyes that I knew held my future.

"For someone who is so impatient, you sure are making it hard for me to get ready. I thought you wanted to go?" she rasped as I kissed along the pulse of her neck. Triggering a small moan to escape her lips.

"Everything I want, everything I need, is right here in my arms," I said, continuing my assault. Kissing every spot I knew that drove her crazy.

She was wearing a low cut tank that I wanted nothing more than to rip the fuck off. Her breathing hitched when I reached the top of her cleavage that was on full display. All I knew was that when her body was pressed up against mine, it took every ounce of strength I had to not go balls deep in her sweet pussy. We had messed around a few times, but I kept with the PG-13 bullshit for the most part.

She wasn't ready for what I so desperately wanted to do to her. Not yet.

I deliberately pushed my hard cock against her core so she could feel my need for her. Continuing my descent, I took it a step further. My hands started to roam from her hip up her side, grazing her tit, causing another moan to escape her mouth.

"Shhh... your grandparents are home," I groaned, rubbing my cock along her heat again. Making her legs wrap tighter around my waist.

She wanted to feel every inch of our contact.

My hands worked their way under her tank, the need to feel her soft skin against my calloused fingers won. I peered into her eyes. Our connection had always been flawless and easy. It was never a burden or an obligation to be with her. If anything, she was my salvation. The only good thing I had in my life.

Love and desperation.

Longing and guilt.

My feelings were so torn that I questioned my resolve to not take her up against the wall right then and there.

When her small, delicate hands started moving from my neck down to my chest, I instantly grabbed her wrists, bringing them above her head. Holding them tight in my grasp.

"Did I say you could touch me?" I taunted, brushing my lips lightly over hers.

She shook her head no, her nose grazing mine. "Well, I don't remember saying you could touch me," she countered, angling her head, trying to kiss me.

I chuckled against her mouth. "When you own something, you can touch it whenever you want. You belong to me, cariño," I breathed out, pecking her lips. Giving her what she wanted.

"Your heart belongs to me, doesn't it?" she simply replied.

"Mmm hmm…" I deepened our kiss, getting lost in the feeling of her velvety tongue.

She pulled away first, and I immediately missed her lips. Smirking up at me through her lashes, she purred, "And so do your balls, buddy." Tearing one of her hands free from my grasp, she reached for my boys.

I intercepted it, kissing her palm before claiming her mouth again. Slow, deep and passionate. "No, sweetheart," I coaxed in between kissing.

Without warning, I released her hands and stepped back. Causing her to fall to her feet unexpectedly. She whimpered from the loss of my touch. Glaring at me as she adjusted her clothes.

I spoke with conviction, "Those are still fucking mine. Now grab your shit. Let's go. I have the worst case of blue balls known to mankind."

And with that I walked away, hearing her laugh from a distance.

We said our goodbyes to her grandparents. She told them she was staying with my sister for the weekend and would be back on Sunday. I threw her overnight bag in the trunk of my car and opened the passenger door for her.

"I have a surprise for your birthday," she announced as I backed out of the driveway.

"Is that right?"

She nodded her head, gazing out her window, blushing. "Yup. Head downtown."

I fucking hated surprises. In the world I lived in, surprises were never a good thing. But I would let her have it this one time because the simple flush of her cheeks made my cock twitch, wanting to know what else would cause her to blush like that.

We rode in comfortable silence while I held her hand in my lap. Bringing it up to my lips every so often, gently caressing it. The feeling of her soft, smooth, silky flesh in my mouth was one of my favorite sensations. I loved to feel her. Her vanilla and honey scent that always lingered around her drove me mad, it was like a direct signal to my fucking cock.

I had been arguing with my parents for weeks about not wanting to make an ordeal out of my seventeenth birthday. Of course, they didn't listen. Especially since it landed on a weekend. I was able to convince my mom to throw the party the day after my actual birthday so that I could spend the day with Sophia. She reluctantly agreed.

"Make a right into that parking lot."

"Why am I parking at the Hyatt, cariño?" I asked, glancing over at her.

She shrugged, turning to look at me with a huge smile on her face. "Just park the car, buddy. I got it under control."

I cocked an eyebrow with a stern expression.

"Please," she added with a pouty lip.

I shook my head, chuckling. Throwing the stick shift of my 67' SS Chevelle into neutral, I pulled the parking brake, popped open the trunk, and got out. Ever since I could remember, I had a thing for old muscle cars. The Chevelle was my birthday gift from my parents last year. They replaced the engine to a 396 this year.

Sophia reached for her bag but wasn't quick enough. I took the strap and threw it over my shoulder. Grabbing her hand, I started to walk in.

She led us to the elevator, not bothering to stop at the front desk. She wasn't fucking around when she said she had everything taken care of. The elevator pinged when we reached the top floor, and the doors slid open. She pulled out a room key and led me down the hallway to room 2406.

"Close your eyes."

I didn't.

"Oh, come on. Don't you trust me? I promise I won't steal your virtue. We don't have to do anything you don't want to, baby," she teased in a sarcastic tone I didn't fucking appreciate.

Narrowing my eyes at her, I stated, "Aren't you cute. You better watch it, sweetheart. You may end up with a surprise of your own with that sassy little mouth of yours," I stated, gesturing to my cock.

She bit her lip, looking up at me through her lashes. Something gleamed in her eyes I'd never seen before. Without turning, she pushed down the handle and the door clicked opened. I would be lying if I said I wasn't completely captivated by her and where this was possibly leading. She grabbed my hand and walked backward never taking her gaze off mine. Both of us lost in our own thoughts as we walked through the foyer of the suite and into the living room.

I didn't pay any mind to our surroundings, just following Sophia to wherever the fuck she led me.

"How did you get this room?"

"Amari," she simply stated. "She helped me plan all of this." Gesturing around the room.

"And what exactly is this?"

As if on cue, we walked into the bedroom. The shades were drawn, but the sliding glass door to my right was open, allowing a warm breeze to surround us. Dropping her hand, I walked around the room taking in the scattered rose petals on the floor and bed. The lit candles on the nightstands and dresser only emphasized the romantic allure to what she had done.

For the first time in my life, I was speechless. I followed the rose petals that led out to the balcony. Finding a table set up for two, placed perfectly by the railing, with more candles illuminating the small space. A stunning view of Manhattan shined bright behind it.

I stood there for a few minutes lost in my thoughts. My emotions that I was supposed to keep in check at all times were getting the best of me. The thought she had put into this night, made me love her just a little bit more. I couldn't hold back the feeling that she was the one for me.

My girl.

I pulled back the drapes to walk inside. "Sophia, this is—" I stopped dead in my tracks when I saw her.

She was wearing one of my white collared, button-down shirts. Leaving it slightly unbuttoned, faintly exposing her breasts and stomach. There was a red ribbon tied around her waist, holding my shirt in place. She sat in the center of the king-sized bed with her legs tucked underneath her, looking so fucking tiny. Her hair cascading down the sides of her face and body. The soft flicker of light from the candles danced off her creamy smooth skin.

She was breathtaking.

In all my life, I had never seen anything so fucking beautiful before. And I knew right then and there.

I was done for.

Eight

Martinez

I leaned my shoulder against the sliding door frame with my arms folded over my chest. Cocking my head to the side, soaking up every last inch of her body.

A memory I would cherish and take to my grave.

Grinning, I rasped, "Is it bedtime, cariño?"

"Why don't you come here and unwrap your present, birthday boy? I can guarantee sleep will be the last thing on your mind," she purred, patting the bed.

I didn't need to be told twice. I pushed off the door frame with precise and calculated strides, till I was standing at the edge of the bed. Hovering above her half-naked body. She brought her legs out in front of her in a submitting gesture. Her eyes dilated, waiting for my next move.

I slowly leaned forward, never taking my eyes off hers. With one swift movement, I grabbed her ankles and tugged her toward me. She came effortlessly, breathless and dazed. Caught off guard by the turn of events. I ran my hands up her long legs, leaving goose bumps in their wake. Wanting to feel her in every possible way.

"Is this what you want? Is that why you brought me here tonight? To fuck you? Because once I'm inside you, I won't hold back. I won't stop until I have explored every last inch of your body," I admitted, needing her to know what she was getting herself into. "I don't make love, Sophia. I fuck. I fuck long. I fuck hard. I want to fuck you. It's taking every ounce of restraint inside of me right now to not take you like that. It's all I know. I've never made love, baby. But I want to… with you."

Every fiber of my being raged to touch her, but my heart was in my throat. My pulse quickened, waiting for her to say something, anything. Terrified that I had scared her.

Sophia was the last person in the world that I wanted afraid of me.

She licked her lips, slowly getting on her knees at the edge of the bed, inches away from where I stood. Our eyes never wavered from one another as she reached over to touch my heart that I swear was beating a mile a minute.

"I know you won't hurt me. I trust you with my life, Alejandro. I love you."

That was the first time she'd said those three words to me. I never repeated them after the moment was lost that night in my room.

Not finding another time to relive it.

"I don't know what tomorrow will bring, Sophia. Nothing in my life is guaranteed. I don't know what kind of life I can offer you. Or what kind of man I'll turn into. All I know is that I love you, and I'll protect you with my life. Taking my last breath if I have to."

Her eyes watered and her lip trembled from the truth of our love story.

"I can't imagine my life without you. I'd rather die than live a day without seeing your beautiful face. I need you, and that's a terrifying thing for a man like me. I shouldn't bring you into this life, into this world, but I can't let you go. I won't. You're the only thing that makes sense to me, the only thing that's just for me and no one else. I'm not going to stand here and bullshit you. I'm not a good man, Sophia, but you make me want to be one."

Tears slid down her face as she took in every last word that came out of my mouth. Using my thumbs, I wiped her tears away. Holding my whole life between my hands.

"I want to marry you as soon as we graduate. I want you to carry my last name and claim you as mine." I caressed the sides of her face, seeing myself in her glossy eyes. "You don't have to answer now, cariño. I just needed you to know that I'm not going anywhere. *Mi vida es tuya*," I honestly spoke, "*My life is yours*."

67

She didn't say a word, but she didn't need to. Her eyes showed me everything I needed to hear. Wanting to live in the moment with her, I didn't falter, slowly pulling at the ends of the ribbon that were securing my shirt. Undoing them and letting it fall to the bed. My dress shirt fell to the sides, baring her perfect fucking body. I took her in for the first time with a predatory regard, from her perky breasts, to her small waist, and narrow hips. Letting my eyes linger before moving down to where I wanted to look the most.

Her slender thighs exposed her tight, tucked, pussy lips that had a landing strip at the top.

"Jesus Christ, you're so fucking beautiful." I peered up into her eyes, and she shyly smiled. Her cheeks turned my favorite shade of red.

Never breaking eye contact, I brought my hand up to my mouth, licking my index and middle fingers. Making them wet before I placed them on her pussy. She gasped when I pulled back her hood to expose her clit. A deep growl escaped from within my core.

I roughly gripped the back of her neck and tugged her toward me, my mouth colliding with hers. Her lips parted against mine as I worked her nub in ways that had her legs spreading wider and her hips rocking against my hand. Clutching the back of her neck, I brought us closer, but not nearly close enough. I slipped my tongue into her waiting mouth, I wanted no space or distance between us. Savoring every last touch, every last push and pull, every last movement of my fingers against her pussy. My lips against her mouth.

As if she was made just for me.

Only me.

Her body started to tremble as she threw her head back. Breaking our kiss, our connection. I knew she was close. Her hooded glare crippled me in ways I never thought possible. My balls ached to be inside her. She hadn't even touched my cock yet, and I could feel her all over.

So intense.

So consuming.

So mind-blowing

"That feel good, cariño?" I huskily murmured.

"Please don't stop," she begged, leaning into my touch. Placing her hands on my shoulders for support.

Grinning, I moved her clit side-to-side. "Don't stop what? What don't you want me to stop?"

"That. What you're doing... please..."

"Here?" I baited, changing the angle of my fingers.

"Yes..." she moaned, coming apart as her eyes rolled to the back of her head.

Not giving her a chance to recover, I roughly pulled her legs out from beneath her, dropping her back to the bed.

She yelped, surprised.

My arms wrapped around her thighs and I tugged her toward me, bringing her ass near the edge of the bed. I immediately dropped to my knees, placing her legs on my shoulders, burying my face in her perfect pink pussy that I've done nothing but dream about. She squirmed as I licked her from her opening to her clit, sucking hard before going back to her opening to fuck her with my tongue. Her back arched off the bed, wanting more and I readily obliged.

She was my new favorite goddamn flavor.

I couldn't take it anymore. My dick throbbed against my slacks. I unbuckled my belt, letting my pants fall to the floor. Fisting my hard cock in the palm of my hand as it sprang free. Jerking myself off, while I continued to make love to her with my mouth. Bringing us both to the brink of coming undone.

"Fuck..." she panted in a heady tone, bringing my attention back up to her.

She was leaning up on her elbows and staring with wide eyes, watching me devour her as I simultaneously stroked my cock. Her intense stare set my already burning body on fucking fire.

When her legs began to shake, and her eyes shuttered, I knew she was close again. I didn't falter, easing my middle finger into her opening. I needed to get her ready to take my dick. The last thing I wanted to do was hurt her. There was no way in hell she could take all of me if I didn't. Her body instantly locked up when she felt my finger.

69

I sucked on her clit harder, moving my head side-to-side and up-and-down, until her body sank into the mattress, and her thighs loosened up. Slowly pushing my finger in deeper, going right for her g-spot. She was so fucking tight, her climax only making her tighter.

She whimpered at the sudden intrusion. The pain mixed in with the pleasure had my cock aching to be inside of her.

"Almost there, baby," I groaned, licking her clit. "I'm going right fucking here…"

She loudly moaned when I pressed against her g-spot, squeezing her legs together from the new sensation.

"Oh, God! I can't… I can't…"

"Relax, I'll take care of you. Just let go, cariño."

"It's too much… oh my God…"

Her body was shaking so fucking bad that I had to let go of my cock and lock my arm around her legs, holding her in place.

Seconds later she came hard, screaming out my goddamn name.

Flicking my tongue one last time on her clit, I let her ride out her orgasm on my face until her body went lax. I stood, licking her orgasm from my lips. Savoring the taste of her. Her eyes instantly widened when she saw my hard cock for the first time.

"Alejandro, that thing will never fi—"

"It will," I interrupted, trying to ease her mind while I unbuttoned my shirt, grinning down at her.

"It's going to kill m—"

"It won't." I threw it on the chair.

"Are you pos—"

"I am." Kicking off my shoes and slacks that were now bunched up at my ankles, grabbing my wallet before tossing them aside too.

"We don't need that," she informed me when she saw me pulling out a condom. "I'm on the pill. And I trust you."

I grinned again, crawling up her body. Kissing her skin as I made my way to her face. I caged her in with my arms, reassuring her, "I'll always take care of you. When you're with me, Sophia, you let me worry about everything," I whispered, against her lips.

The second my tongue touched hers, it turned into its own moment, its own creation. We were in our own world. My legs spread hers, readily laying in between them, placing all my weight on my arms that were cradling her face.

I peered deep into her eyes, murmuring, "I've never gone raw before."

She beamed, her smile lighting up her entire face. It was so fucking contagious. I couldn't help but smile back at her. I started placing soft kisses down her cleavage and toward her nipple while still looking up at her. Wanting to witness the effect I had. I sucked her nipple into my mouth, swirling my tongue as my hand caressed her other breast, leaving her breathless beneath me.

Placing the tip of my dick at her opening, I gently bit down on her nipple, giving her exactly what she craved.

"Te amo," I whispered, "*I love you.*" Needing her to hear it.

"I love you, too," she repeated, moving her hips, beckoning me to keep going. I lowered my hand toward her clit, playing with her already over-stimulated nub. Slowly easing my way inside her.

"Hmm..."

"Are you okay?" I groaned into her mouth.

She nodded, trying to catch her bearings as I pushed in further and deeper. Nothing compared or even came close to the feeling of Sophia. To the sensations that only she stirred within me. Slowly I pushed in inch-by-inch, letting her pussy adjust to my cock. Thrusting through her barrier till I was balls deep.

A throaty moan escaped my lips as she whimpered in pain.

"You're mine, Sophia," I huskily reminded, causing her to smile through the discomfort.

I took a moment when I was fully inside her, cherishing the feel of her for the first time, not stopping the friction of my fingers against her clit. I gradually started driving in and out, rubbing my fingers faster and with more determination. Her body began moving in perfect sync with mine as I grabbed her ass, pushing her further and further down my shaft.

She was so fucking tight, so fucking wet, and so fucking perfect.

71

I kissed her again, savoring the silky feel of my mouth claiming what was mine. Before resting my forehead on hers, thrusting a little faster.

A little deeper.

A little harder.

Her back arched off the bed in a frenzy from the pain and pleasure of it all. It didn't take long until she started matching my thrusts, grinding her hips with mine. Her legs opening wider for me.

"I want to fuck you so hard right now, baby. I want you to feel me in the morning. I want you to feel me all fucking day, but you're so tight and I'm holding back as much as I can," I growled.

She didn't say anything, just lifted her hips. Making a silent plea to take it further. Positioning my knee higher, her leg inclined with mine. Her breathing elevated, and I knew I was hitting her g-spot better from that angle. I grabbed the back of her neck to keep our eyes locked. My forehead hovered above hers as we caught our breaths, trying to find a unified rhythm. I once again brought her lips to meet mine. Pushing my tongue in, claiming every last goddamn inch of her.

My movements became harder and rougher, her body responding to everything I was giving her.

Everything I was taking…

Her eyes dilated in pleasure, but also in pain. I immediately lapped at her breasts unable to get enough of her, and wanting to take her mind off the sting and focus on the ecstasy. Moving back up to her face, our mouths were now parted as we both panted profusely, unable to control the movements of our bodies.

"Oh, God… I'm going… I think I'm going to come…"

I thrust faster, moving my fingers hastily.

"Yes… Alejandro… Yes…" she breathed out, climaxing all down my shaft, taking me right over the edge with her.

I came so fucking hard inside her, kissing her passionately and holding her tighter till there was nothing left inside of me.

"Te amo, cariño."

We stayed like that for I don't know how long. Enjoying the feel of our skin on skin contact for the first time. I kissed all around her face, her neck, back up to her face again.

She was mine.
For the rest of my life, I would never let her go.

And I didn't.

Nine

Martinez

In the last year and a half, Sophia really became part of our family. She even helped my mom plan my eighteenth birthday party a few months ago. They went everywhere together for weeks, making sure they had the perfect cake, food, and entertainment. I think my mom saw her more than I did. The party was a fucking shit-show. My mom wanted it to be extra special because I was officially an adult now. A man was what she called me, no longer her baby.

She and Sophia had gotten close in the last year. They loved each other. And since Sophia had lost her mother at a young age, my mom took her under her wing. Sophia was interested in things Amari didn't give a fuck about, and my mom took advantage of that any chance she could get. She taught Sophia how to cook all my favorite meals, what kind of Spanish spices she needed to have at all times, and other random shit, like how to fold my clothes.

It was how she took care of my father, and if she was trying to mold Sophia to be anything like her, then who the fuck was I to complain?

I let her have that.

I think she tried to pretend like I hadn't seen the things I had. As if my father wasn't showing me more and more violence as the days went on. How the world really wasn't a good fucking place. Seeing bloodshed had become the norm for me. My mom, Sophia, and Amari all looked the other way when I came home with bloody, cut up knuckles or blood-stained shirts.

My father had his dirty hands in everything from drugs to guns to clubs. He was the definition of organized crime, and there was very little that he didn't own and operate. Politicians, police, FBI agents, they were all corrupt and all in his pocket. Not a damn thing could be traced back to him. He'd built a motherfucking empire on nothing but shady-ass shit.

The darkness that was all around our family only dragged me further and further into the abyss.

Mom didn't acknowledge the present he handed me on my birthday, wanting nothing to do with it. Two matching 9mm Glocks with a harness that I was to wear under my suit jacket at all times. Never being allowed to leave the house without being strapped. Sophia wasn't too happy about it either, but didn't say a word to me. She knew what kind of life I was leading. The look on her face spoke volumes the first time she put her arms around me and felt the guns between us.

The irony was not lost on me.

A few weeks before our graduation, I took Sophia back to that same room where I took her virginity. Following through with my promise, I never gave her a ring so I had to redeem myself. I wanted her to know I was serious. Last time she never gave me an answer, her agreement was left unspoken, but I needed to hear the word, "Yes." She excitedly agreed as I put a white gold infinity ring on her finger. Making her another promise that I would replace it with a diamond after we told my father we were engaged. I didn't want to have to answer to him so soon. I just wanted to enjoy our engagement for as long as I could.

There was no hiding it from my mother. She noticed her finger with the sparkling band as soon as we walked in. All she did was smile to herself as she strolled away from us. I knew we had her blessing. It wasn't her I was worried about.

When I put the ring on Sophia's finger I also promised her that she didn't have to do a damn thing once she was my wife. I would take care of us.

She said all she wanted was a family.

I let her know that I would gladly make that happen the night of our wedding, if that's what she wanted. Prom was in a few weeks and graduation wasn't far behind that. I couldn't wait to get the fuck out of school. I wasn't going to college, that much was a given. I don't even know why I bothered finishing high school, other than because it made my mom happy. She wanted my diploma to hang right next to Amari's on the wall or some shit. Amari graduated last year along with Michael. I thought about what she said a few years ago in the attic, all the time. About getting the hell out of here as soon as she graduated and was old enough.

She was still living at home nearly a year later. I was hopeful that maybe she accepted this was her life and at the end of the day...

We were her family.

"Alejandro Eduardo Martinez de la Cruz!" Mom shouted my whole name, pulling me away from my thoughts. She walked right over and stood in front of the television. Yelling with her hands in the air. "Tu le dijistes a Sophia que no sabes bailar?" she roared, adding, "*You told Sophia that you don't know how to dance?*"

Fuck.

Sophia had been busting my balls about wedding songs and mother/son songs. I finally just said I didn't know how to dance and she could choose whatever she wanted to get her off my ass.

"Mamá, estoy viendo una película," I replied, "*I'm watching a movie.*" Moving my head to see around her with a stern expression. "Not right now."

She didn't falter, immediately turning around to shut it off. From the corner of my eye, I caught Sophia giggling in the archway, her hands over her mouth as she watched my mom reprimand me.

"What's so funny, cariño?"

Her head fell back with laughter. She was definitely going to pay for this later.

"I taught you cómo bailar, to dance, by the time you were standing," Mom reminded in an authoritative tone with a hand on her hip and the other out in front of her, waving a finger in that Hispanic mom way.

If this were anyone else but my mother, I would have never allowed it.

"Why did you lie to Sophia?"

She didn't give me a chance to explain before continuing her outburst.

"You know how to dance to everything, especially salsa and merengue. I made sure of it." She patted her chest, moving toward the receiver in the corner of the room.

I knew exactly what she was going to do, and I dreaded every last fucking second of it. Sophia couldn't stop giggling and gave up on trying to hide it. Leaning against the archway with her arms crossed over her chest, enjoying the show.

"Mi Gente" by Héctor Lavoe blared through the speakers, one of her favorite songs. I took a deep breath, trying to calm the anticipation of where this was leading. She strutted her way over to me, moving her body to the rhythm of the salsa song.

"Ven," she said, "*Come*." Reaching her hands out for me.

"Mamá…" I warned.

"You don't tell me no. Ven," she repeated, pulling me toward her. "Show Sophia how you move. Make your mamá proud." She placed one hand on my shoulder and the other out to the side, waiting for me to get into position. "Ready?"

"I guess I have to be," I retorted, stepping closer, taking my mother's hand and wrapping the other around her upper back.

We began to move. I stepped forward as she stepped back and then vice versa. My hips swayed with the beat of the music, doing a basic rock step. Repeating it a few more times, getting used to the movement until we found our synchronized pattern. I took the lead, grabbing her right hand bringing her around in an underarm turn, while our feet kept the basic rhythm going.

It didn't take long for us to lose ourselves in the music, almost forgetting Sophia was watching.

We moved effortlessly around the living room. I brought our arms up into a cross-arm turn, spinning her and then myself, always returning to our basic hold. Our feet never missing a beat as I brought her across my body, spinning her three times across the floor toward Sophia. She stood there, watching our every move with lust in her eyes. I spun my mom one last time and eased her into a dip, taking her by surprise. Causing her to bust out laughing. It was the second best sound in the world. I loved seeing her like this, so carefree.

I locked eyes with Sophia as I brought my mom up, hugging her to my chest. Kissing her head before letting her go.

Mom danced toward Sophia who took a few steps back, putting her hands out in front of her. Shaking her head no. "I don't know how to dance to this," she laughed out.

"Ven, *come*," she insisted, grabbing Sophia's hands and tugging her toward her. "You learn. You need to dance like this at your wedding." Mom winked, spinning her in my direction, letting her fall into my arms. Sophia's face paled, shocked by my mother's mention of a wedding. "Alejandro will teach you. Show her, Alejandro. I want to go get a camera to take pictures."

"No, Mamá. No camera. I think you have embarrassed me enough for one day."

"Go on, teach her. I'll be right back." She was a very persistent woman who went after what she wanted.

"Muy bien, cariño," I praised, "*Good job*," when I brought her against my chest. Loving the feel of her in my arms. I could never get enough of it.

"I can't believe she's okay with this. Us getting married so young?" she questioned with worry in her eyes.

"She married my dad when she was barely seventeen. My grandparents had to sign papers in order for them to have a ceremony. My father is twenty years older than her."

Her eyes widened in disbelief.

"She loves you, Sophia. It's hard not to. She would be pleased to call you her daughter."

She smiled.

I placed her left arm on my shoulder, my hand wrapped around her back, our other hands entwined at our sides. She gasped when I unexpectedly brought my right leg in between hers so she was pretty much straddling my thigh.

I wanted no distance between us.

"I don't remember you and your mom dancing this close, buddy. You're invading my personal space."

"Is that right?" I lifted my leg a little higher, brushing her inner thighs, inches away from her pussy, feeling her heat.

I grinned, forewarning, "Hold on tight."

"Wha—"

I led us around in fast circles, grinding my hips against hers. Pausing only when the music allowed it. I twirled her around and brought her back toward me, our chests colliding.

"Whoa," she breathed out.

"Good girl."

I repeated the same steps a few times till she caught on, and I could show her new ones. She was smiling and laughing the entire time, breathless. Her face was so goddamn beautiful as I showed her basic salsa steps, and how to sway her luscious ass to the music. Never thinking that I would actually enjoy doing this with her.

I hated dancing, but dancing with her, I fucking loved.

"Mira los!" Mom yelled, *"Look at you."* Snapping picture after picture with her camera until I excused myself. I could see my mom wanted a private moment with my girl.

"Sophia," Mom rasped, holding my world in between her hands.

I stood by the archway, leaning against the wall with my hands in my pockets, they hadn't noticed I was still there. The music continued floating through the air as my mom and Sophia stood face to face.

"You brought life into my son. You brought light and love into his heart. You're an angel. I have never seen him like this before. This world, Sophia… It's very hard. It is so easy to slip into the darkness. I have seen my husband turn into a man I don't know. There are some days—" She stopped herself from what she was going to say.

I lowered my eyebrows, confused. Caught off guard by what she just shared.

"I can't save my baby from it. As much as I wish I could… I can't. It's out of my hands now. It's in yours. You love him. You love him with all your heart. Always. You show him that light that lives inside of you. You never let the darkness into your home. There's no going back once it's there. Do you understand me?"

Sophia frowned, nodding. Her eyes filling with tears.

"Promise me. Promise me," Mom repeated, her voice breaking.

"I promise, Mrs. Martinez."

"No more of this Mrs. Martinez nonsense anymore. You can call me Mamá. You're family now."

Mom breathed a sigh of relief and kissed her forehead. We spent the rest of the afternoon dancing, laughing, and enjoying each other's company. It was one of the happiest days of my life.

I couldn't stop thinking about what my mother said. Never realizing that those words would forever haunt me.

Ten

Martinez

Guests filled the banquet hall for our engagement party. Everyone was dancing, talking, and enjoying the night that probably cost my parents a small fortune.

The clinking of a glass rang through the room. "Ladies and gentleman, can I have your attention for just a minute. As the best man, I'd like to make a toast to the happy couple," Leo announced, standing up from his seat. "I've known Martinez since we were twelve years old, and he saved my ass on the first day of school. We have been friends ever since," he chuckled, winking at me. "He was a cocky son of a bitch back then, and as you all know, not much has changed."

The room broke out in laughter, Sophia nodding in agreement.

"I've never seen him, the way he is Sophia, with anyone else. I couldn't be happier for him. You have finally met your match. Sophia, have fun with him, and I wish you the best of luck." He nodded toward us, and I flicked him off. "Everyone please raise your glasses and help me wish this beautiful couple a lifetime of happiness. Salute." Leo raised his glass, and our guests followed suit, all wishing us the best.

"Wow, I can't believe you know all these people. Is our wedding going to be this big, too?" Sophia whispered to me with astonishment.

I shook my head, letting out a small chuckle from the look on her face. Pulling her into a tight hug and kissing her head. "If my mother has anything to do with it," I replied, drawing back. Glancing at the side of her face as she continued to take in the sea of family, friends, associates, and enemies.

My father always kept his friends close, but his enemies closer. It was another mentality that kept you alive. We finally told him we were getting married a few days after we graduated three months ago. He took the news of our engagement better than we expected. Catching us all off guard when he offered us his blessing. It wasn't as if I would have given him a choice in the matter if he hadn't.

Mom insisted on stealing Sophia, walking with her around the room at our party, introducing her to everyone. She was the belle of the ball who had all of my mom's rich bitch friends hanging on every word she said. Kissing her ass, knowing who she was to me. A part of me knew that as much as Sophia was scared of this life, she was also secretly drawn to it. It was hard not to be. From an outsider looking in it was a glamorous life.

When in reality it was Hell on Earth.

Once I finally got Sophia back from my mom, I took her out on the dance floor. Holding her tight, humming the soft melody in her ear.

"I can't believe you made me think that I lost my ring." She peered down at the three-karat diamond that I had added to her infinity ring. Setting the stone right in the center of the symbol.

I surprised her with it that morning, and she spent the rest of the day thanking me for it.

"I'm still shocked your dad reacted so calmly to our engagement. Maybe he isn't so bad, Alejandro," she admitted out of nowhere.

As soon as those words left her mouth, I stopped dancing. "Look at me," I ordered in a harsh tone. "He's the Devil, Sophia. He's the goddamn Devil. I never want you thinking he's anything but."

She lowered her eyebrows. "And you? What does that make you?"

"Next in line," I replied without hesitation, starting to move with her again.

She grimaced, following my lead. "Are you going to change when you take over? Am I not going to know who you are anymore?" she finally asked what had been plaguing her since the day she made my mom that promise.

82

I would be lying if I said I hadn't noticed a change in her after that day.

More questions in her eyes.

More worry in her tone.

More uncertainty in her actions.

More. More. More.

I grazed her cheek with the back of my fingers, getting her to relax. Promising myself right then and there I would never lie to her.

"You look beautiful, cariño."

"You didn't answer my question."

"You shouldn't ask questions you really don't want the answers to."

She jerked back, hurt, taking a step away from me.

"I am who I am, Sophia."

She didn't falter, blurting, "Have you killed anyone else, Alejandro? I mean since that night. Is there anymore blood on your hands?"

"What I do is none of your concern."

"So that's a yes," she huffed, shaking her head in disbelief.

"It's not a no."

She backed further away from me, my statement causing her to shudder. For the first time, she looked at me as if she didn't know me. A glare of disgust spread over her face. It killed me not to lie her. I hated that I couldn't tell her what she wanted to hear. It would have been easy to pull her into my arms and relieve her worry.

I wasn't made like that.

I may have been a lot of things.

But a liar wasn't one of them.

She turned her back on me, wrapping her arms around herself in a comforting gesture. Needing to get away from the truth that was blatantly staring her in the face.

Me.

I allowed her the space she needed, even though I fucking hated it. I ran my hands through my hair in a frustrated gesture, locking eyes with my father across the room. He was smoking a cigar with his associates standing around him. Lifting his glass of whiskey out in front of him in a congratulations gesture.

I grabbed a glass off the table in front of me, nodding, returning the sentiment. I swiftly downed the contents before turning to leave. Desperately needing to get some air and space of my own. Feeling as though the room was closing in on me. I needed to clear my head from the fear that I felt in my heart and the thoughts that cluttered my mind.

My present and my future colliding.

I grabbed a bottle of bourbon from the bar and left. Taking a swig as soon as I walked outside the back entrance of the banquet hall. I wanted to be alone. I wanted to drown my sorrows. I wanted to get lost in my own thoughts.

My own compulsions.

My own Hell.

The fiery liquid burned as I took another swig, welcoming the pain that resonated in my chest. I wanted to pretend like the last ten minutes didn't fucking happen. Like my whole world hadn't crashed down around me with a look I never wanted to experience again. I knew it was only a matter of time before Sophia would want answers I couldn't provide.

Soon, her whole life would be changing, and not for the better. I made that decision. No one else but me. Michael's words haunted me with each step on the gravel that took me away from my own party. Not giving a fuck where I was going, just walking aimlessly. Trying, hoping, praying that I was doing the right thing.

That loving her wouldn't be her destruction.

Never realizing that it might be mine.

I turned back around searching the wooded area that surrounded me, suddenly feeling the loss of her light she always brought into my life. Out of the corner of my eyes I saw shadows in the distance. It took me a second to realize it was my mom. She was standing in front of her bodyguard Roberto in a gazebo. I stepped closer to get a better view, and it was then I noticed she looked pissed.

Nothing like the vibrant, radiant woman she had been all night.

Gone was the smile and happy demeanor.

She threw her hands up in the air, furiously shaking her head. Pointing toward the hall, she exaggerated her words.

Saying something I couldn't make out. The expression on her face had my mind racing. Roberto said something with a look of remorse, causing her to tense and turn her back to him. She stared off into the distance with her arms crossed over her chest.

I was about to make my way toward them when I heard Sophia calling my name. I turned around as she was walking up to me.

"Hey…" she breathed out. "I've been looking all over for you. I thought you had left me here."

"Never."

She smiled. "I'm sorry, Alejandro. I didn't… I mean I wasn't trying… it's just…" she paused, sighing. Trying to gather her thoughts when mine were still on my mother.

"I guess I'm just learning my role in all this. In your life," she spoke, bringing my attention back to her.

"You'll be my wife. The most important person in my life. Nothing will ever change that."

"It's not that simple."

"You're making it harder. Baby, we are different. What we have is different." I stepped toward her, taking her face in my hands.

"I don't want to lose you. I don't want you to change. I love you. For the man you are now. Do you understand?" Tears threatened in her eyes.

"I don't have a choice, Sophia. Do you understand?" I countered, letting her go.

She nodded, reaching up to wrap her arms around my neck. I leaned forward taking her into my arms.

"Yes. I don't want to fight. You do enough of that for the both of us," she chuckled, trying to break the tension between us. Our fight was over.

For now.

"Te amo," I murmured against her ear, "*I love you.*"

"I love you, too. Come on. Let's go back to our party." She pulled away, grabbing my hand.

When I looked over my shoulder toward the gazebo, they were gone.

I spent the next week thinking about what I witnessed. Watching my mom walk around, going on with her daily life like nothing was wrong. Even though I knew otherwise. On several occasions, I walked in on her and my father whispering to each other, having intense conversations. They never fought. Something wasn't right, and they sure as hell weren't telling Amari and me.

One afternoon Sophia, my mom, and Amari decided they were going to start looking around for wedding locations. I took the opportunity to talk to my father. Determined to get some answers to what the fuck was going on with my mom.

"Come in," Dad announced after I knocked on his office door.

"Do you have a few minutes?" I asked, peeking my head inside.

He gestured with his hand for me to enter and for his bodyguard to step out. I closed the door behind him wanting some privacy. Taking a seat in one of the chairs in front of his desk, where he was sitting with piles of paperwork in front of him.

"Everything go okay with the Italians?" he questioned, looking over the documents not paying me any mind.

"I handled it," I simply stated, leaning back in the chair, eyeing him.

"Good. Then what's this about?"

"Is there something you're not telling me?"

He peered up from his paperwork, placing the stack back onto his desk. "Care to elaborate?"

"I saw Mom upset at the engagement party. What the hell is going on?"

He scoffed, "Your mother gets overwhelmed about everything. You're getting married, Alejandro. It was a hard day for her. Her little boy is becoming a man. Accomplishing another major milestone. She knows you're leaving soon. Amari will probably be next with how things seem to be going with her and Michael."

"I'm not blind. I know what I saw. Has something happened? Is Mom in danger?"

"She's always in danger. It's part of being a Martinez."

"No shit. I've seen you guys whispering. You're hiding something. Is she sick? If she's sick, you need to tell me. There—"

"I don't need to do anything, Alejandro."

I narrowed my eyes at him with a sincere expression. "I'm here out of concern for my mother."

He took a deep breath, contemplating what he was going to say. "I have it taken care of. Javier is... I'm handling it."

"It's been almost four years. Four fucking years, and that motherfucker is still walking. He should have been taken care of already. What the fuck is the hold up?"

"Are you questioning my authority?" he spewed, eyeing me up and down.

"When it comes to my mother's safety, I would question Jesus Christ's authority."

He slammed his fists on the desk, gritting out, "I would never let anything happen to your mother. My wife. Do you hear me? Don't ever disrespect me by insinuating that I would."

I immediately stood, leaning forward. Placing my hands on the desk, I looked him dead in the eyes and spoke with conviction, "If you don't put a fucking bullet in his head, I will."

And I meant every last word.

Eleven

Martinez

"Are you ready?" Amari asked, as she took a seat next to Sophia, who had a spread of bridal magazines laid out on the kitchen island. She had immersed herself in gowns, centerpieces, and decor for the past hour. Color coding and organizing what she liked and didn't.

"Why am I going to this again?" I asked, annoyed. They were dragging me along with them to do wedding shit. "Women are supposed to be the ones that handle all this. I did my job. I proposed and put the ring on her finger."

"That was a very sexist response, brother," she replied, flipping pages. Pointing out what she liked.

"Call it what you want. I'm the odd man out. Last time I checked, I had a dick, Amari."

Sophia laughed, and my sister rolled her eyes.

"Alejandro, you're a picky eater. You need to come try the food for the reception. Then we have the cake tasting at two o'clock. After that, you can go back to not caring about our wedding," Sophia added still not looking up from her damn bridal magazine.

"Baby, it's not like I don't care about the wedding. I just care about the wedding night and the honeymoon more. I offered to help you pick out your lingerie. That has to count for something, right?"

"You care about the sex," Amari chimed in.

"So romantic," Sophia added, shutting her magazine and grabbing her purse to leave.

"I'm a man," I shrugged, grabbing Sophia by the waist and pulling her into my side.

"You're a pig. Michael would never—"

"Michael's a fucking pussy."

Sophia smacked me on the chest and Amari rolled her eyes again, standing up. "On that note. Let's go. Mamá is going to meet us downtown after her doctor's appointment. If we're late, it's your balls on the line because you know I'm going to blame it on you."

The limo that my dad insisted I needed to start using was waiting for us outside, along with five bodyguards.

"Are they always going to be with us?" Sophia whispered at my side. Even after all these years, the men protecting us still scared the shit out of her. Permanently scarred from *that* night.

Amari peered over her shoulder, blurting, "Get used to it. Knowing Alejandro, you'll have more than necessary."

I glared at her and she smiled, getting into the limo first. By the time we made it downtown, we were running late for our appointment.

"Relax, Mamá isn't even here yet. Her car isn't in the parking lot," I announced, stepping out of the limo.

They both looked around the lot. "How did you know that? We just got here," Sophia stated, glancing back at me.

"I'm always aware of my surroundings, baby. Let's go." I nodded toward the guards to do their checks and led the way toward the garage elevator.

Amari stopped as the doors opened. "Maybe we should wait for her. She gets lost everywhere, Alejandro. You know she has no sense of direction," she reminded. "I bet that's why she's late. She probably gave Roberto the wrong address."

She was notorious for getting turned around, especially when she was out on her own.

"I don't want to miss this appointment," Sophia whined, pulling on my hand to go. "We're already so late. We had to schedule this weeks ago and—"

"Cariño, you know I hate it when you fucking whine like that." I pulled her toward me, wrapping my arms around her waist.

Elegant Edge catered to the rich and famous. The building had a private entrance and parking located in the back alley. Privacy was a must when it came to celebrity and high-end weddings. My mom always wanted the best for her children, no matter what the cost.

"Relax. We won't miss the appointment, I'll make sure of it. But Amari is right. We should probably wait for her."

She smiled, looking up at me adoringly. "Oh yeah? You think your blue eyes and devilish grin work on every woman, huh?"

"I know it does." I grinned just to prove my point. Whispering in her ear, "The best two out of my three attributes."

"What's the third?"

"My cock," I responded, rubbing my dick against her just to prove my point again.

"Alejandro." She blushed, slapping my chest. Trying to push me away.

I held her tighter, chuckling, "I love you."

"Alright, you two love birds," Amari interrupted, bringing our attention to her. "There's Mamá's car." She gestured behind us.

We all turned to see Roberto driving up the back alley with Mamá in the back seat, waving and pointing in our direction as we came into view. I could see her smile. We all could. In her excitement, she was about to forgo protocol, opening the door without her guard next to her.

I would remember the next turn of events for the rest of my life.

My father once told me that Martinez men didn't hold onto memories in our minds. They were burned deep within our souls where they laid dormant. I never understood what he meant by that until now. Except this was one of those scenes that no matter how hard I tried, how much I sacrificed, how long I prayed, I would never be able to forget. It would eternally haunt me. My mind would be forever branded. My heart forever broken. My future immorally damned.

The moment where a part of me died.

A black SUV with pitch-black tinted windows came up from behind my mom's car in the alleyway, heading toward us. Out of nowhere a matching SUV skidded out from the side street to the left. Pulling up in front of Roberto, causing him to slam on the brakes. Blocking the way to the garage, but not our view. The windows of the SUV in front of them rolled down, exposing two rifles. Roberto sprang into action, throwing his body over my mother.

The rest played out in slow motion. A nightmare that would eternally haunt me. I'll never forget the look on my mom's face as gunshots rang out. Her worry-free smile quickly turned into a look of pure horror. As if she knew it was the moment she was going to die.

Her time had come.

An inevitable day she had been expecting all her life. Knowing all along the consequence of loving a Martinez man.

"NO!" I shouted with everything in me as the sound of shots ricocheted off metal and glass, ringing as screams echoed in the alley.

Bullets flying everywhere, decorating the car with holes.

Two bodyguards tackled Amari to the ground, guarding her. While I simultaneously picked Sophia up into my arms, throwing her onto the rough pavement behind a parked car. Tucking her head against my chest, as my hands skinned against the asphalt, breaking our fall. Shielding her body with mine. Seconds later we felt the weight of my bodyguards on top of us. The air filled with rapid fire rumbling from afar, with Sophia and Amari screaming and crying all at once. She shook so fucking bad in my arms, her body convulsing with fear.

"Take her!" I ordered, shoving the men off me. "You guard her with your fucking life! Do you understand me!? With your fucking life!"

They nodded as Sophia forcefully shook her head. "No! No! Don't go! Please! Don't go! Don't leave me!" she bawled, clutching onto me like her life depended on it.

"Grab her, now! Get them out of here!" I ordered, ripping her off of me.

They roughly tore her out of my arms, kicking and screaming, giving the men one hell of a fight. Her face was a blank canvas, but her eyes portrayed her pain.

I affirmed, "Te amo! Vamos!" As the guards rushed the girls into the elevator to take cover. Hearing Sophia's pleas not to go as the doors closed.

Standing without a second thought, I nodded toward the three guards who stayed behind with me. Instantly yanking my guns from the holsters inside my suit jacket. We sprinted down the parking lot, hauling ass toward the vehicles. Immediately opening fire, lacing the SUV's. Bullets recoiled off the steel, breaking through the tinted glass.

Four men opened fire back at us, hitting one of my men several times in the chest. Knocking him to the ground, instantly dead. The other two tried to cover me as best as they could, but an endless stream of bullets kept coming at us from all directions. I felt a burning sting graze my shoulder and then again at the side of my stomach. Blood flying everywhere, not knowing if it was theirs or mine.

Adrenaline coursed through my veins, throbbing through my bloodstream. Taking over every inch of my body. My heart pounded against my chest as I tried to make my way over to my mother. Praying that she'd be alive under Roberto's stilled body. My vision tunneled, seeing nothing but red the closer I got to her car.

"Fuck, boss! You've been hit!" the guard to my right shouted as we took cover behind a nearby van. Bullets still flying in every direction.

I looked down at my body trying to figure out where I'd been hit. Blood was seeping through my white shirt. "Fuck it! I'm fine!" I roared, reloading my gun. Only having enough bullets for one more round. Tossing my other pistol to the ground, I stood, still taking cover behind the van. I took my left hand and applied pressure to my side.

"Boss, let us—"

"Shut the fuck up. Let's go!"

Shot after shot erupted from our hands. It was one right after the other, merciless images of death, the smell of blood all around us as souls were being dragged straight down to fucking Hell. Sirens could be heard in the distance, causing the SUV's to immediately cease fire and skid off in opposite directions. Though it didn't matter. It would take the cops fucking forever to figure out our exact location. Tall, brick buildings surrounded the back alley, causing the noise to echo from all directions.

Making it harder to pinpoint where the bullets and chaos came from.

"Boss! Wait!"

I ran.

I ran so fucking fast, ignoring the sharp pain in my side and the blood I was losing in the process. I darted toward her car not giving a flying fuck if my life was still in danger. Only needing to get to her as fast as I could. No matter what the cost.

It was my life or hers.

I. Choose. Hers.

Twelve
Martinez

When I came upon the mangled metal, I instantly saw Roberto's dead body slouched over the back seat. I couldn't see my mother's small frame, panic and fear immediately assaulted my senses. Sinking deep into my pores before I even had the car door open.

"Please God! Please! Please God!" I begged to the Lord above as I swung open the door. Knowing that I had no right asking the Heavens above to help a man like me.

This was my fault.

I did this.

No one else but me.

She was an innocent soul in all of this mayhem. Getting caught in the crossfire of the life the Martinez men led. Being punished for the choices we made. The lives we had taken. Our daily struggles between good versus evil, when evil always won in the end.

She was the only love I had known for most of my life. The only light that surrounded the darkness that lived within us. I prayed to God, the saints, and the angels that they would see everything she stood for. That they would know she didn't deserve this. That this wasn't the way she was supposed to die, through an act of vengeance meant for my father and me. I prayed they would give her mercy for her kind heart, her pure spirit, and undying devotion and love to the men in her life. Even though we didn't deserve it.

I threw off Roberto's limp body, finding my mother beneath him on the floorboard, gasping for air. Desperately clutching onto the cross necklace that she never took off her neck. Her protection.

94

Her body seized uncontrollably with every forced breath that escaped her chest.

"Jesus Christ," I pleaded, not knowing where to touch her, hold her, or comfort her.

There was blood everywhere, splattered on every surface of the car. Her clothes drenched in red. I couldn't tell if it was hers or his.

Probably both.

"Mamá," I murmured, finding it hard to breathe, struggling to keep going when all I wanted to do was die along with her. My heart broke into a thousand pieces. Falling upon the massacre in front of me.

Tearing apart.

Dying.

Experiencing pain and agony like I never had before.

I reached for her, grabbing her cold hand in a comforting gesture. A whimper escaped her lips. Her eyes shut from the excruciating pain I was sure she was experiencing.

"Mamá, it's okay. I'm here. Your baby boy is here. You're going to be okay," I bawled, my voice breaking. "But goddamn it, you stay with me. Do you hear me? You stay with me! I'm here. I'm here, Mamá! I'm fucking here!"

I gently wrapped my arms around her upper torso, pulling her broken body away from the wreckage. Being careful not to cause her more distress. An unceasing amount of blood gushed from her chest and stomach. Seeping into every last fiber of my being. I slid down the side of the car as my legs gave out on me, ignoring the sting of my own wounds, leaning against it as I held my dying mother in my arms.

My soul drenched with guilt.

"Mamá, no! Please God! Please! Somebody help us! Somebody please help us! She's dying! She's fucking dying!" I screamed bloody murder. Uncontrollable tears streamed down my face, falling on her body beneath me. Shuddering, my body shook as profusely as hers. I held her so tight, so close to my fucking heart. Needing to feel her heartbeat against my chest. Reminding her how much I loved her, and how fucking sorry I was.

"Alejandro..." She coughed up blood, her body convulsing in my arms.

I held her closer, kissing all over her bloody face. "Shhh... Mamá... shhh... it's okay..." I cried with trembling lips. Caressing her face with the knuckles of my hand.

"I love you, mi bebe para siempre," she quivered, "*My baby forever.*"

I shivered, my chest locking up, hyperventilating from bawling so fucking hard. My eyes blurred with tears, barely allowing me to see her face.

"I'll never see you get married. I'll never get to see your babies and spoil them," she choked out, struggling to place her hand over my heart. "You protect and take care of your sister, and I'll always protect and take care of you. I'll always be with you, mi bebe. He-here," she said between gasps, setting her hand on my heart.

I fervently nodded, taking her hand. Kissing it. Letting my trembling lips linger along her barely beating pulse.

Chaos was all around us. Bodyguards held in their earpieces, yelling orders. Bystanders still ducked behind cars. Sirens were getting closer and closer.

"Somebody help me! Please! Someone fucking help me!" I looked back down at her, grabbing the back of her head, holding her right against my chest. Trying to keep her body from shaking while it shattered in my arms. She trembled faster and harder, vibrating against my core. Tucking her face under my chin, I cradled her in my shaking embrace. Rocking her back and forth. "You're going to be okay, Mamá. The bodyguards. They're getting help. Help is on the way. You hear those sirens. They're coming... You're fine. You're going to be okay. Just hold on, okay... Please, Mamá. I'm begging you. Just hold on... Please don't leave me... Don't leave me... I love you... I love you so much. Please! Please God... Don't do this. Don't do this to me!"

She sucked in a few breaths, gasping for more air.

"Shhh... I got you. It's okay... you're going to be okay..." I closed my eyes, remembering the last time I saw her happy. We were dancing with Sophia. She was laughing. She was smiling. She was breathing. She was so full of life. I didn't know how to

96

comfort her so I started humming her favorite lullaby, the very one she used to sing to us when we were kids, "Me Niños Bonitos."

Her body went lax.

I was losing her.

"Mamá," I whispered, my body suddenly shaking profusely. "Mamá," I repeated, slowly pulling her away from my chest.

Her mouth was hanging open and her eyes no longer held the light they used to.

I shut my eyes, clutching her tight in my grasp along my chest. "NO! NO! NO!" I screamed till my throat burned and my chest ached. Bawling like a newborn baby. "NO! NO! PLEASE, GOD, NO! TAKE ME! FUCKING TAKE ME! I'M HERE! TAKE ME!"

I was at a loss.

Silently cursing God. Hoping that this was a nightmare I would soon wake up from. A God-awful fucking dream.

Something…

Anything…

Other than what was actually happening.

I laid her down on the pavement. Pinching her nose closed and breathing into her blue lips. Her chest rose. "One, two, three," I pumped my hands against her blood-soaked chest. "No! Stay with me! Fucking stay with me!" Blowing into her mouth again. "One, two, three. No! No! No!" I sobbed, my body convulsing as I took in the body of my dead mother in front of me.

Bowing my head in shame.

At that moment, I would have sold my soul to the Devil if it meant that it would bring her back. I sat up on my knees, looking up at the sky with my hands out in front of me.

"I HATE YOU! DO YOU FUCKING HEAR ME! I FUCKING HATE YOU!" I bellowed to the Lord above for taking my mother away from me.

I took in my surroundings. Through my tunneled vision, I saw shadowy figures running toward the scene. Yelling incoherent words. Out of the corner of my eyes I saw Amari and Sophia come into focus. Amari was fighting off the guards, trying to run toward me. Sophia stood frozen in place, in shock. The roles from that night so many years ago were now reversed.

"Alejandro! What are you doing?! Fucking save her! Do something! You're letting her die! You better not let her die," she screamed, flailing in the guard's arms. Reaching her hands out, pleading. "Please don't let her die! You need to do something! Bring her back! Bring her fucking back!" she hysterically wailed, escaping the guard's grasp and falling to her knees. Breaking down in front of me.

My stomach dropped. My heart was now in my throat, bile rising, but I swallowed it back down. Sophia had a look of horror on her face, taking in the gore that looked like a scene out of a horror film. Amari continued to sob so fucking hard, her fragile frame heaving for breath. I couldn't move, I couldn't go comfort them. I couldn't look them in the eyes, knowing I failed them.

Knowing I failed my mother.

All I could do was mouth "I'm so sorry," from a distance, burying my face in my hands. The memory of their distraught faces added to the images that would forever haunt me. There wouldn't be one day where I wouldn't remember them like that.

Falling apart in front of me.

Not. One. Day.

I sucked in air, my chest heaving from my own sobs. A sound so foreign, yet so real. My heart hurt, and I felt a pain I'd never in my life felt before, a part of me gone.

"Mamá," I whimpered one last time, peering back at her through a cloud of tears, through a branded memory burning painfully deep in my soul.

"I promise you they will pay for this. I will make them pay," I whispered in her ear as I softly closed her eyes and did the sign of the cross over her beautiful lifeless face. The way she'd done a million times to me, kissing her forehead one last time.

I wanted to scream at the top of my lungs through the dark streets, I wanted to die, and… I wanted what all Martinez men wanted.

Revenge.

The feel of blood on my hands that wasn't my mother's.

She wasn't the only one who died that day…

We all did, too.

Thirteen

Martinez

"How many guards are outside?" I asked, getting the security handled before the mass.

"We have fifteen set up in the front of the church, ten in the back, and five at each side entrance," Victor, my head of security replied.

"No press is to get past those gates. Do you understand me? If they do, it's your ass," I ordered, pointing a finger in his face.

He nodded, not taking my warning lightly. The past week had been a fucking shit-storm. Between the newspapers, news stations, reporters, and cops wanting answers in regards to the shooting. Our lawyers were working day and night to get this problem out of the public eye.

Fucking failing at doing so.

I was the last one from our immediate family to arrive at the church. Sophia, Amari, and Michael drove together, escorted by bodyguards. My father came with his men, saying he had some stuff to take care of before the mass. I spent the entire week planning the wake, funeral, and reception that would follow at our house. We were all watching our asses, more so now than ever before. The Martinez name was being thrown in the line of fire for the first time. My father handled the business, making sure to keep everything in order while everything around us seemed like it was falling apart.

He looked like he had aged twenty years overnight, the loss of his wife almost too much for him to bear. It was the first time I ever felt sympathy for him. An emotion I wasn't used to when it came to my father.

I walked into the empty cathedral, needing a minute to sit before the guests started to arrive. My shoes echoed off the tile beneath me, mimicking my heart, as I walked over to the last set of pews. Wanting to be the furthest away from my mother's body as possible. She was lying in an elegant red mahogany coffin beside the podium.

In the last two days, family and friends paid their condolences, saying their goodbyes to the body that lay resting. I hadn't made it up to see her yet. A part of me wanting to remember the woman that used to be so full of life, not the unrecognizable one laying there lifeless.

I watched from afar.

The image of her dead body was the only thing that I saw in my mind every day. I felt like I hadn't slept since the day she died in my arms. I was emotionally and mentally drained, my body physically spent. I just kept moving like I was on autopilot.

If I stopped, I wouldn't have been able to get back up.

"Hey," Sophia announced, coming up behind me. Rubbing my back as I blankly stared out in front of me. "You look exhausted. Have you been sleeping? At all? Even if it's just for a few minutes? You were shot, twice. You need to rest. When was the last time you took your medications? You're going to get an infection if you don't start taking care of yourself."

"Where is Amari?" I replied, ignoring her questions. I suffered minor wounds during the altercation. Just a few grazes to my shoulder and the side of my stomach. A few stitches, some medication, and I was good to go. My body would heal with time, but my heart was never going to mend itself.

Sophia sighed. "She's in one of the backrooms with Michael. A few of your family members just arrived. Do you need me to get—"

"Make sure Amari eats today. She looked as pale as a ghost all day yesterday. I don't trust Michael to look after her."

"What about you? Huh? You need to let me take care of you, too. You're not made of steel, Alejandro. It's okay to grieve."

I glanced up at her, taking her in. "Thank you for looking so beautiful for me today."

"Babe…" She came around and crouched down in front of me. Placing her hands on my knees for support, looking me straight in the eyes. "It's okay to talk to me. I was there, too. I can't imagine what you're going through, but you can't close off like this. You can't shut down, Alejandro. It's not healthy. I'm here. You can—"

I placed my thumb over her lips, silencing her. "No more talking, cariño. That's not what I need right now." Rubbing my thumb along her pouty lips, I wiped off her lipstick.

"Ale—" The doors opened from behind us, guests began to arrive for the mass that was taking place before the funeral. I welcomed the interruption, knowing where this conversation was going.

I stood, bringing Sophia up with me, wrapping my arm around her lower back. Nodding my head toward the associates that just walked in. We made our way toward Amari in the congregation room of the church. She was sitting on a chair with Michael crouched in front of her, peering down. Her skin much paler than it was this morning.

"Carajo, Amari. You need to eat," I stated in a harsher tone than I intended. Grabbing her forearm, pulling her to stand in front of me. I lifted her chin with my finger so she would look at me. "Do you understand me? You need to eat."

Tears streamed down her sunken face, murmuring, "I can't do this, Alejandro. I can't go in there and say goodbye. I'm not strong like you, I have never been. My heart is filled with so much pain. I can't breathe. I feel like I can't fucking breathe."

Michael tried to pry her out of my arms, stepping in like he actually gave a fuck about her feelings. I glared at him with a warning. His jaw clenched, rubbing her back instead.

"I will be there with you, Amari. You can lean on me. I promise to hold you up. You need to promise me you will eat. Let me worry about everything else. Okay?"

"Is she really gone? This isn't just a nightmare that we're going to wake up from? This is really happening? She's dead, and I didn't even get to say goodbye? Please… tell me it's just a cruel joke. I keep thinking that any second now she's going to walk though those doors and tell us it was all a bad joke. That this isn't

101

real. Please… Alejandro… I beg you… tell me this isn't real," she bellowed, her lips trembling.

I held her face between my hands, and it was like looking into my mother's eyes. "I wish I could wake up, too. I wish I could lie to you and tell you everything is going to be okay. But this is life, Amari. There are no guarantees, no promises of tomorrow. We have today. And today we have to say goodbye to our light. Our beloved mother." I kissed her forehead, bringing her into my arms. She melted against me.

Sophia wrapped her arms around her waist in a comforting gesture, watching me while I was comforting my grieving sister.

Our father and the priest walked in to tell us it was time to go. Amari looked up from my chest and wiped her face, walking over to Michael. Dad went to reach for her, but she jerked back from his grasp with a look I couldn't quite place. Catching all of us off guard by her drastic change in demeanor toward him. If looks could kill, this would be my father's funeral, not my mother's. He cleared his throat, slightly bowing his head, leading the way out the door.

Amari tucked her body into the nook of Michael's arm and walked out. I grabbed Sophia's hand and brought it up to my lips as we headed in the same direction. All of us walked in together through the side entrance of the cathedral. Following the priest toward the altar and taking a seat in the first row, closest to the casket.

I tried to pretend that it didn't bother me, as if I wasn't dying inside. I ignored the sermon that the priest recited, every verse read by family, every memory her friends shared.

Getting lost in the abyss that now resided in my soul.

My father stood, bringing my attention back to the present as he made his way up to the podium to say his eulogy. He peered out at the crowd of people with a devastated expression. Every row in the cathedral was packed with everyone who loved our mother.

Even that didn't grant me peace.

He bowed his head for a few seconds, needing to gain his composure. "Adriana, my wife, was the love of my life. My past, my present, and she would have been my future," he announced, looking back up.

102

As soon as the words left his mouth, I felt Amari tense beside me.

"Before I begin, I would like to thank you all for coming here today to honor and celebrate the accomplishments of my wife. Thank you for the sympathy and support you have shown my children and me during our time of need. I can't begin to tell you how much I wish my wife were here. Standing right here by my side, witnessing how loved she really was."

Amari scoffed out, "Unbelievable" under her breath.

"I spent twenty-two wonderful, blissful years married to the woman who was my soul mate. She was only thirty-nine years old and had so much more life to live. I never imagined I would be a widower at fifty-eight years old, having to spend the rest of my life alone when we should be spending it together. I vowed to always keep her safe. To always protect her."

"Liar," Amari blurted a little too loud, catching the attention of the people sitting around us.

"Amari," I warned, looking over at her. She scowled, narrowing her eyes at me as he continued his speech. "Enough," I added in a demanding tone. She just shook her head with a disgusted look on her face. Peering back at our father.

"I know my wife is looking down on us today with nothing but love in her eyes. Thankful for the years we shared and the children we made. Proud to have called us her family. To have—"

"Jesus… I'm sorry, Mamá. Please forgive me, but I can't listen to this any longer," Amari interrupted, standing abruptly, pushing her way out of the pew. Immediately making her way toward the side exit.

I stood, trying to grab her arm, but I was too late, she was out of reach. "Amari," I called out after her.

"Please, forgive my daughter. She is hurting badly. She not only lost her mother, but her best friend, and we all grieve in different ways."

Amari stopped dead in her tracks, her body stirring with emotions she couldn't control. Her chest heaved as her hands worked into fists at her sides. As if reading my mind, Michael stood to go comfort her. He wrapped an arm around her waist, leading her to the door. She leaned into his embrace, breaking down as they left together.

Never looking back.

My father nodded to one of the guards to follow them out, and then locked eyes with me. Both of us concerned about Amari's outburst, not knowing what fueled it. I sat back down and he continued with his eulogy. Sharing memories of the love he had for a woman he would never see again. At one point he had to stop, bowing his head on the verge of shutting down. He pushed on, and with each word that left his mouth, my heart broke for him a little more.

The rest of the service went on without a problem, filled with nothing but sadness and tears. Amari was already in the limo when we walked out, waiting for us to go to the cemetery to officially lay our mother to rest.

We drove in silence, all of us lost in our own thoughts. Staring out the windows as the rain came down mimicking everyone's despair.

"Alejandro, it's okay to cry," Sophia whispered, rubbing my back as we stood in front of her grave.

I reached over and held her hand, squeezing it in reassurance. Watching through my dark sunglasses as they lowered my mother into the ground. My father was the first to throw a single white rose onto the coffin. Making the sign of the cross, walking away from his wife for the last time. Tears running down his face as he got in his limo.

I wrapped my arm around Amari, supporting her as we each threw in another two white roses. Sophia and Michael followed. Amari was physically falling apart in my arms, and I couldn't do anything to take away her pain. I couldn't bring back our mother. Her eyes held so much sadness, anger and disgust, all mixed together.

Not knowing who it was for.

By the time we made it back to the house, it was packed with mostly everyone who had attended the funeral. If Amari heard "I'm so sorry" one more fucking time, she was going to lose it. She was hanging on by a thread that was ready to snap at any second. I paid close attention to her the entire afternoon, making

104

sure that Sophia or I were near her at all times. Making her eat and be somewhat social. When all she wanted to do was go up to her room and drown in her sorrow.

I wish I could tell you I was expecting what happened next…

But I didn't.

Not for one goddamn second.

"I'm so sorry for your loss," the wife of one of my father's associates consoled him. "I can only imagine what you're going through."

"I loved my wife with everything inside of me. A part of me doesn't even know how I am going to keep going. She was my everything. I promised her that I would always protect her—"

"Liar!" Amari shouted, slipping out of my grasp. Going right for my father.

Fuck.

"You did this! You're the reason that she's dead!"

Dad jerked back, her accusation almost knocking him on his ass. An immediate eerie silence filled the room that was packed with guests. All eyes were on them. I didn't falter. I was over to her in a heartbeat, gripping her arm but she roughly tore out of my grasp.

"Amari, I understand you're hurting—"

"You don't understand," she interrupted him. "You know nothing. You think you do. You think you have everything under control with your holier-than-thou persona. All you do is hurt people! You have no respect for anyone or anything! You will do anything to make people fear you! Look where that has gotten you. It should have been you we were burying today, not her. This is all your fault! You're nothing but the Devil trying to pretend that he's God," she gritted out through a clenched jaw, her fists balling at her sides.

My father stood there, his chest rising and falling. Trying to remain calm in front of everyone. "Amari, now is not the time—"

"To what? To call you out on your bullshit and lies! That's all you fucking care about!"

"Amari," I murmured, grabbing her arm again. Yanking her toward me. "That's enough."

105

She peered up at me with hurt and fury blazing in her eyes. "Fuck. You. Alejandro. You're a part of this, too! Dad's little puppet. You're both to blame for MY mother's death. You both brought evil into our lives. Do you know how much it kills me to say that to you, Alejandro? You're my brother, and I love you more than anything in this world, but all I want to do is hate you right now! He may be the reason she's dead, but you're going to be just like him. The Devil in the making, and it makes me fucking sick! Our mother lost her life because of her love for him! She's dead, Alejandro. Do you understand that? She's fucking dead! And her blood is on both of your hands."

I swallowed hard, knowing everything she was saying was true.

"I hope for Sophia's sake you walk away from this asshole, and show her a life full of love. Not a life where you'll always be looking over your shoulder, waiting for bullets to fly. Waiting for death to come for you. Or she's the next woman you're dragging out of a car."

Sophia and I locked eyes from across the room. She was the first to break our connection, the truth in my sister's words taking residence in her mind.

Amari's intense glare turned back to our father. He put his hand up in the air in a surrendering gesture only fueling Amari's rage.

"I love you, Amari. I'm so sorry. But you lashing out like this isn't going to change anything. I'm your father and that's never going to change. You will always be my daughter, whether you like it or not. You're a Martinez. I understand you're hurting, but breaking up our family isn't the answer, you—"

Before he even got all his words out, she charged at him, screaming. The guests, including Sophia, stood there, horrified at the scene Amari was causing. I immediately sprang into action, holding her back.

"YOU KILLED HER, YOU MOTHERFUCKER! There is no more family, she was the bond that kept us all together and now she's gone. This is your fault! And I fucking hate you for it! This life! This Hell! I'm done. Do you understand me? Fucking done!

106

I'm leaving, and I don't ever want to see you again!" She thrashed around in my arms, wanting to hit him.

Needing to hurt him.

"I HATE YOU! I HATE EVERYTHING YOU STAND FOR! YOU'RE DEAD TO ME! MY FATHER DIED THE DAY MY MOTHER WAS MURDERED!"

I hauled her out of the room, kicking and screaming. Putting up one hell of a fight to go after him. Whipping her body around trying to get out of my grasp.

"Jesus Christ, Amari! That's enough," I roared once we were outside and away from prying ears. Sophia and Michael not too far behind us.

She spun, facing me. "Let me go," she gritted, pulling her arm out of my grasp. Pushing me in the chest with all her strength.

I barely wavered.

"You're an asshole! How could you do that to me! How could you take his side after everything he's done! You know I'm right! Or is your conscience too fucking scared to admit it out loud?!" she yelled, shoving me over and over again.

I let her take out all her aggression on me.

I deserved it.

I deserved everything.

"Amari, calm the fuck down," I reasoned, only pissing her off more. Grabbing her by the wrists, halting her assault.

"Why didn't you do something?! Why didn't you save her?! How could you just let her die like that?!" she sobbed, breaking free, shoving me the closer I tried to come toward her.

"Amari, I'm sorry. I'm so fucking sorry. I did everything I could. Don't you think I would switch places with her if I could?"

Her eyes blurred with nothing but tears, and my body twisted with the longing to fall apart. To finally let out all my emotions that were wreaking havoc on my soul.

"She's gone! She's fucking gone! I hate you! I hate you!" she yelled over and over to let it sink into my pores and make it become a part of me.

Making me truly believe it, truly know that this was the end.

"Amari, I'll make it right. I promise you I'll make it fucking right. Look at me. It's me, your brother."

107

She crumbled to the ground, taking me along with her. I dropped to my knees, ignoring the sting, which was minor compared to the pain in my heart. The devastation in my soul. I broke her fall as her body hunched over. Shattering into pieces in my hands, slipping through my fingers.

"I'm so fucking sorry… please… you have to forgive me… I can't lose you, too…" I murmured, my voice breaking.

Sophia and Michael just stood there, watching the two loves of their lives, breaking.

She let me take her in my arms, her head buried in my chest. Her body lying in between my legs.

"I feel like I'm dying… I feel like a part of me is dead, and I'm never going to get it back. I don't want to hate you, but I can't forgive you. I don't know what to do, Alejandro. Nothing is going to bring her back," she sobbed uncontrollably.

"Shhh… it's okay," I whispered, rocking her back and forth. "Shhh… I'm here. I'm here, Amari," I reassured her at a loss for anything else to say or do.

Our lives would forever change after that day.

Especially mine.

Fourteen
Martinez

The limo pulled into the driveway just after five in the evening. It had been a few days since the funeral, and I was trying to play catch up and get everything back in order. I couldn't even remember the last time I had a good night's sleep.

I was so fucking exhausted.

I stepped out of the limo, noticing Sophia's car was parked behind Michael's. That motherfucker was around more and more lately, consoling my sister, but I knew he had other intentions. I hadn't seen Sophia much since the funeral, too busy dealing with worried business associates, and dodging the media that still lingered around like savages. The wedding plans were put on hold, the ceremony postponed as of now. We all needed time to heal and grieve. Neither one of us wanted to relive the painful memory that was now associated with my mother's death.

I walked inside the house and headed straight for my bedroom, looking for Sophia. Sometimes she'd curl up on my bed and wait for me in there, or before my mom passed, she would be in the kitchen cooking with her. My chest tightened at the thought, remembering how many times I would lean against the door frame just to watch without them knowing. Loving their banter and the way they were around each other.

Memories I would cherish till the day I died.

"Cariño," I called out, rounding the corner into my bedroom, expecting her to be waiting for me. "Sophia?" She was nowhere to be found.

I took off my suit jacket, along with the holster. Placing my guns on the nightstand and throwing the jacket on the bed. I made my way toward Amari's room, figuring that she would be in there.

Maybe hanging out with my sister who I hadn't seen much of either. Giving her the space she obviously needed. She stayed at Michael's more often than not, avoiding my father, and the memories of our mother that would always linger in the house.

"Sophia, you need to listen to me," I heard Michael say from down the hallway. "I'm only trying to protect you."

I stopped just shy of the door, wanting to hear where this was leading.

"Michael, I—"

"Do you really want this life? A life where bodyguards are constantly surrounding you because your life is always in danger? Waking up every morning not knowing if it's your last? What about your kids? Huh? You want to risk their lives, too? Do you want to spend the rest of your life married to a criminal? Because make no mistake, Sophia, under the fancy suits and expensive façade, that's what he will always be. A notorious gangster. Do you want to know where your love for him is going to lead you? Six-feet underground, right next to his mother. You need to go, you—"

I slowly clapped my hands, walking in. Snidely laughing, "Well, that was quite a goddamn speech, motherfucker. Next time you so much as mention my mother, I promise you, it will be *you* that's six feet under."

He narrowed his eyes at me, not backing down. "I'm not scared of you, Martinez."

I chuckled, "That much is clear."

"I'm trying to protect her. Save her fucking life, unlike you, who couldn't even save your mother's."

"You motherfucker." My fist connected with his jaw before he even saw it coming.

He stumbled a little, catching himself on the nightstand. Standing up and grabbing his jaw, adjusting it side to side. "You son of a bitch." He charged me, ramming his shoulder into my torso, taking me to the ground. Sophia shrieked, immediately yelling at us to stop. Standing back watching two grown men have it out. I instantly fought back, wrestling around on the hardwood floor for a few minutes, each of us trying to get the upper hand. He was able to get on top of me, getting in a few hits to my face.

110

"You're just proving my point, Martinez. That's how you handle everything, isn't it? Violence is all you know," he spewed, pushing the side of my face into the floor. "That's the life you want for your girl? Is that what you're going to teach your kids? Huh? You're an animal. And it's only a matter of time until it costs you Sophia."

"And it was only a matter of time until I fucked you up." I hit him in the gut, and he fell forward. I flipped us over, locking him in with my weight. "I've warned you more than once." I hit him. "Unlike my sister, I know what the fuck you want and it's not her!" I punched him again. "You don't want to fuck with me, or what's mine." I hit him twice more. "You sorry ass motherfucker. Spitting your bullshit lies in my goddamn face. You're lucky I don't put a bullet in your fucking head right now."

"I love Amari," he yelled, blocking another blow.

"Alejandro, stop!" Amari shouted, trying to pull me away. "Please stop! I'm pregnant!"

I froze. Our labored breaths were the only sound in the room. I removed myself from him, our intense, crazed stares never faltered. I stood up, needing to take a few steps back to collect myself. She immediately got down on her knees in front of him, taking his bloody face between her hands. Comforting the piece of shit.

"Are you fucking kidding me? You go to him?" I seethed.

She glared up at me. There was no love for me in her eyes. Nothing.

"Jesus Christ, Alejandro, he's on the ground, you're standing. You insensitive prick."

Sophia rushed over to me, trying to tend to my wounds. I pushed her hands away, not needing to be fucking babied. "I'm fine!" I yelled, startling her. "When?" I retorted, only glaring at Amari, not having any patience left in my body.

"You want to talk about this now? Are you serious?"

"How far?" I snarled through gritted teeth.

She looked down at Michael and then back at me. "A little over three months. It's why I've been so pale and not eating. Morning sickness has kicked my ass. I can't keep anything down.

We wanted to wait until I was past the first trimester to tell anyone. I was going—"

"Did Mamá know?" I interrupted her, needing to know.

She shook her head no. "We were going to tell everyone the day sh-, the day she was murdered," she announced, choking back tears. "I told her we had a surprise for her after your wedding appointments. It's probably why she was so happy when she saw us. You know her, she knew everything before we even told her."

I ran my hands through my hair in a frustrated gesture, wanting to tear it the fuck out. I turned away from her, looking back at Sophia. "Did you know about this?"

She just stood there looking at me, silently confirming what I feared. Michael grabbed Amari's hand and she helped him up, putting his arm around her neck and leaning on her for support.

Fucking pussy.

"This ends now, Alejandro. He's just trying to protect her. You should be thanking him, not trying to fight him."

"Are you that fucking blind?"

"It doesn't matter anymore," Amari paused to let her words sink in. "I'm pregnant, and we are getting married," she revealed, almost knocking me on my ass. "Michael asked me to marry him, and I said yes. We're leaving, and there is nothing you can say or do about it."

It was like blow, after blow, after fucking blow to my heart.

I almost fell to the ground, stunned. Watching as she helped the piece of shit sit on the bed. Turning back around to face me again.

"You're going to be an uncle. I think it's a girl," Amari nervously laughed, trying to lessen the tension that filled the room. The air was so fucking thick I could barely breathe. Suffocating in the truth that surrounded us.

"If it is, we're naming her Daisy."

"Jesus Christ," I whispered to myself, attempting to take everything in. The room felt as though it was caving in on me. I took a few deep breaths, trying to calm the fury within me. Wanting nothing more than to take out the son of a bitch who got her pregnant and put a fucking bullet in his goddamn head.

"I can't stay here anymore. There's nothing left for me. I need to move on with my life, raise a family. Get a house where my babies will be safe. Where my family won't live in fear," she added.

"What about me? Huh?"

"You'll always be my brother, Alejandro. If you want to be in our lives, you're always welcome. But you're going to have to accept Michael as part of mine. He's the father of your niece or nephew. We're all family now."

I was over to Michael in three strides without giving it a second thought. Getting right up in his face. Grabbing the front of his shirt, jerking him up and toward me.

"Alejandro!" Amari tugged at my shoulder, trying to stop me, but I didn't pay her any mind. Too focused on my task at hand.

"You take care of my sister and that baby. Do you understand me? This is the last time I will ever grant you another warning. You protect them with your life. You treat and respect her like she fucking deserves. All I need is a reason... Give me one reason, motherfucker. I don't care who the fuck you are, or what you mean to Amari," I gritted out through a clenched jaw. "I will lay you the fuck out, and not think twice about it."

I shoved him off. He lost his balance, stammering to sit back on the bed to regain his composure. "They're my life. I love your sister and that baby more than anything," Michael declared his love and devotion. Complete and utter bullshit.

I shook my head, slowly stepping away, needing to get the fuck out of the room before I did something I would regret. Sophia trailed closely behind as I furiously made my way back into my room. Shutting the door behind her, I paced around the room with my feet moving on their own accord. Fueled by uncontrollable rage, burning a hole in the floor beneath me. Each stride only added to the tension I felt in my core, throbbing through my veins, producing a piercing sting in my mind.

"Alejan—"

I put my hand out, silencing her as I continued to pace around the room. "Don't."

"Let me just—"

"I'm fucking warning you, Sophia. Not. Right. Now."

"You're warning me? What, am I next?"

I stopped dead in my tracks, glaring at her. Cocking my head to the side, I scoffed out, "Let's just say I wouldn't take my warning lightly. I want nothing more than to take my goddamn anger out on your sweet little ass right now. But contrary to what you seem to think about me now, I'm not a fucking monster."

She jerked back, hurt.

I didn't falter. "Is that all it takes for you to turn on me? Because I'll tell you right now, Michael is a dime a dozen, sweetheart. There will be a Michael around, lurking in the corner, trying to make you turn against me. Especially after you carry my name."

She grimaced.

I raised an eyebrow, stepping toward her, causing her to back away until she hit the wall with a thud. I caged her in with my arms, eyeing her up and down.

"Since when do you want me to fight your battles?" she asked not backing down.

"You didn't say one word in there, Sophia. Not one fucking word. I don't need you to fight my battles. I need you to fight for our love."

I saw doubt in her eyes for the first time. She didn't even try to hide it. And that look alone almost brought me to my knees. I pushed off the wall, slowly backing away from her. My father's words from not so long ago coming back to haunt me.

"Do you think she's strong enough to handle our lifestyle? Your future."

I shook my head, ridding myself of doubts and memories as she reached for me, immediately realizing her mistake.

I shoved away her embrace, roughly grabbing her chin instead and spoke with conviction, "Actions will always speak louder than words, cariño, and yours just spoke fucking volumes." I let go of her and walked away, leaving her to wallow in the doubt that I knew was now implanted in her head.

I went up to the attic of the only home I'd ever known, feeling more alone than I'd ever felt before. Contemplating if this was the life that I was destined to lead.

No family.

114

No love.

No God.

Only darkness.

I sat there for what felt like hours, lost in the depths of my mind. A menacing place I didn't like to frequent very often.

I felt her presence before she even sat down next to me. Amari took a deep breath, whispering, "I knew I'd find you up here." She stared out ahead, gathering her thoughts with what she wanted to say to me. Already knowing this was going to be one of our last conversations for who knows how long. "I have loved Michael all my life. He's the only future I ever wanted. I've ever needed. I've always known he was my way out. A baby would just seal us together, forever."

I glanced at her, narrowing my eyes as I processed her words and what she was implying.

"Michael is a good man. Contrary to what you think, he will be an amazing husband and father. No one will take him away from me. He's mine now."

We locked eyes.

"I love you, Alejandro. You'll always be my brother, no matter what. I'll always be a Martinez, and with that name comes purgatory. I need you to promise me something."

"Anything," I simply stated, breaking my silence.

"If something were to happen to Michael and I… I need you to promise me, to swear to me on your life that you will step up and raise our child as your own."

"Amari—"

She stopped me, putting her index finger to my mouth. "Promise me."

"Why me? You're running away from this life and yet you trust me with your child?"

"Michael's parents are old, and he's an only child. You're the only family I have. The evil you know is better than the evil you don't."

I nodded, murmuring, "I promise," as I leaned forward to kiss the top of her head. I allowed my lips to linger for a few seconds. "Nothing will ever happen to you."

She lovingly smiled. "I have to go. Michael is waiting for me." Getting up, she went to the stairs without a second glance.

Walking away from her past to be with her future. Vanishing right before my eyes.

I needed to get the fuck out of there. I didn't know where I was going, but I needed to clear the thoughts that were pushing me deeper and deeper down the black hole of life. I grabbed my keys and wallet from the kitchen counter and headed toward the front of the house, passing my father's office on the way out. His door was slightly ajar, and I could hear voices on the other side.

"She got what she deserved," Dad laughed, causing me to abruptly stop.

I thought the moment my mother took her last breath would forever haunt me, an image that was carved into my mind till the day I die. But the next words out of my father's mouth killed me completely.

"Sorry for taking so long to contact you, I had a lot of heat on my shoulders, but I just want to thank you for taking care of business. They both got what they deserved. The bitch should have known better than to betray me. She came from nothing, she had no clothes on her back, and I gave her everything she yearned for. And she paid me back by fucking her bodyguard? The puta deserved every last bullet she got," he confessed, with nothing but amusement in his voice.

Destroying the last part of my humanity and my soul.

116

Fifteen
Martinez

A lot had changed in the last few months. Amari and Michael left a few days after our altercation, leaving behind all the bad memories, including me. She left without saying goodbye. Not so much as a note to tell me where they were going. But I had my ways to keep tabs on them. They were living in Washington, playing fucking house. Amari was a housewife who devoted her hours to charity work, and Michael got a job with an import/export company. My father didn't even bat an eye when I told him they got married at a courthouse while he was handling business in Colombia. I never spoke of the day I learned the truth. I let him go on pretending to be a grieving widower and me a devoted son. Even though I wanted nothing more than to end him.

I moved into my own penthouse in Manhattan, similar to the one my father owned. The whole top floor was mine. I wanted privacy now more than ever. It was a spacious seven-thousand-square-foot penthouse that overlooked the Brooklyn Bridge. Floor-to-ceiling windows lined the east wall with French doors that opened to a private balcony. I spent most of my time sitting out there, breathing in the city that never slept.

Exactly like me.

They say your body gets used to whatever it's given. It's our natural form of survival. Adaptation in its truest form. I was lucky if I slept two to three hours a night, never fully reaching the deep sleep phase. The faintest sounds woke me during the night. I was always looking over my shoulder, unable to trust anyone in this life.

Including my father.

I spent hours in my office working just to keep myself moving, much like him.

The irony was not lost on me.

Distance was supposed to make the heart grow fonder, and that was proving to be true. At least in my case, I couldn't speak for Sophia. I fucking missed her like crazy. She was my world, the air I needed to breathe. She had been distant lately, but I refused to let my mind ponder the reasons behind her behavior, the thought almost too much for me to bear. Deep down I knew what Michael told her changed us, but I decided that if I wanted us to get back on track, then I had to fight for my girl.

I told her to meet me at my place one evening. She'd only been there a handful of times, but never stayed for too long, always with an excuse of why she had to go. I wanted her to move in. I wanted us to get married, but I also knew she needed time. After all the loss I had experienced these past few months, I wanted her next to me. I needed to know she loved me for who I was. Wanting nothing more than to hold her in my arms every night and wake up to her beautiful face every morning.

I ordered dinner from her favorite restaurant downtown, making sure to get everything she loved off the menu and then some. I even went the extra mile and had someone come in and decorate the dining room and bedroom with all kinds of romantic shit women loved. Hoping that this night would be a new starting point for us.

A new beginning.

When the bodyguard let her in, I took in her thinning frame. She looked as exhausted as I felt, but God, she was still so fucking beautiful, so completely breathtaking. I leaned against the wall in the shadows, wanting a few seconds to look at her without her knowing. Her dark brown hair was down and flowing with the light breeze that cascaded through the room from the balcony doors being open. She wore a cream-colored dress that hit just above her knees, with matching heels. I watched her with a predatory regard as she gazed around the room looking for me.

"Hey," she breathed out, visibly nervous when she found me.

I smiled for what felt like the first time in weeks. "Come here."

She made her way over to me, her dress flowing with every step that brought her closer. I watched the way she moved, the way her body swayed with each step she took, the way her scent assaulted my senses. I couldn't fucking help myself, I reached out instantly taking her into my arms when she was within reach, holding her as tight as I could. Breathing her in, cherishing the feel of her against me again.

"God, you feel so damn good."

She melted into my arms.

We stayed lost in each other for I don't know how long, chest-to-chest feeling our hearts beating as one. I grabbed the sides of her face, needing to kiss her. Wanting to devour her. She looked deep into my eyes, intently searching for something in my stare. Looking for a trace of the man I used to be. Trying to find signs of the man she fell in love with, the remnants of who we were once upon a time. I had never seen her look at me like that before.

Longing.

I slowly moved my thumbs along the edge of her face, tracing her cheeks from side to side. Soaking up the feel of her skin against my fingertips. Ever so softly brushing my lips against the shell of her ear, remembering how she used to feel. Pulling back, our eyes connected again. She licked her lips as I brushed my finger down her chin to her neck, stopping to caress her beating pulse on the side of her throat. Feeling the effect she always had on me. I made my way down to her chest, breaking eye contact, and focusing on her heart that I hoped still belonged to me. Caressing my fingers along it, sending shivers that shook her core.

Her heart was now beating a mile a minute, nothing compared to my steady beat. She gazed up into my eyes with a glazed look in hers. They had changed from what I saw only a few seconds ago. She looked down at my lips, taking a deep breath, stepping closer to me, leaving no space between us. Her hand settled on the side of my neck, standing on the tips of her toes with our eyes still locked, she leaned in, tenderly placing her lips on mine.

Our mouths moved together as if they were made for each other, our lips starving for affection. I felt like I hadn't kissed her in fucking forever. I didn't waver, picking her up by her ass,

119

wrapping her legs around my waist. I walked us toward my bedroom, never breaking our intense kiss.

As soon as I laid her down on my bed, she reached her arms up above her head. Waiting for my next move.

Lowering my frame on hers, I grasped her hands, caging her in with my arms. Her heartbeat drastically accelerated, and I swear it echoed through the room.

"Te amo, cariño."

She took in my words for a few seconds, relaxing her body underneath mine. I reached for the hem of her dress, pulling it over her head. Leaving her in just her panties that I proceeded to tear off her luscious ass. She watched with hooded eyes as I undressed and crawled over to her again, placing my body right where it belonged.

On top of hers.

I could feel her thoughts raging war in her mind. She immediately shut her eyes when she realized they were telling me everything that maybe she couldn't.

"Open your eyes, Sophia," I murmured so low she could barely hear me.

She swallowed hard before opening them again. Her eyes were filled with unshed tears. Seeing her like this was my undoing, I couldn't take it anymore. I gripped the sides of her face.

"I'm so fucking sorry, baby," I breathed out against her lips. "I can't change what we have been through these last few months. I can't take back everything I wish you hadn't seen. I don't ever want you to be scared of me. I would never hurt you. I would die before I could ever fucking hurt you." I kissed her lips, her cheeks, the tip of her nose, and all over her face as I slowly moved my hand down her neck. "Do you understand me? You're the only light I have left in my life. My salvation," I urged and she nodded, claiming my lips with hers, keeping our eyes wide open.

I rubbed along her smooth skin, trailing my fingers over her naked body. My forehead resting on hers as I slowly moved my hand back and forth, caressing her in a way I used to. How I knew she loved. Wanting to bring back the passion between us. Ignite our flame that started to burn out weeks ago.

"You're all I ever wanted," I exhaled as she inhaled. It was like we were breathing for one another. "There's my girl," I groaned, positioning myself at her opening. I started to ease in, thinking how much I missed her sweet pussy, once again claiming what was mine.

She froze, pushing me off her. "I can't do this," she snapped out of nowhere with a cold and detached voice, making me jerk back, stunned.

"The fuck?" was all I could manage to say.

She continued to try to push me off her. "I can't, Alejandro. Please, I can't do this." She shoved me with her hands, scooting out from under me. Leaving me wondering what the hell just happened.

She grabbed her dress off the floor and threw it on, immediately rushing out of the room, getting away from me as fast as possible. Ignoring my plea for her not to go. I found my slacks and quickly slid them on, not bothering with a shirt. I rushed after her, needing to stop her from walking out on me. There was no way in hell I was going to let her leave here without telling me what the fuck was going on.

Stopping dead in my tracks, I saw her standing in the dining room. A look of horror spread across her face as she took in every last detail of the night we were supposed to have. The food was all laid out perfectly on the table, champagne still chilling in a bucket of ice, candles spread out all over the room, adding to the romantic allure.

"What the fuck was that, Sophia?"

She cringed, stepping away from me, surrendering her hands to stop me. "I can't believe you did all this. Fuck..." She grabbed onto the back of the chair in front of her for support. Looking up at me through tear-filled eyes. "I can't do this anymore."

"Can't do what exactly? What can't you fucking do?"

"Us." She gestured between the two of us. "This."

I jerked back like she had hit me. "You don't mean that," I stated, stepping toward her again.

"Stop! I can't pretend anymore. It's too real. Your life. This life you were born to lead. It's too fucking real. I was almost raped. I thought you were my hero, my savior, when all along you were the reason," she spewed, causing me to step back, narrowing my eyes at her with the realization of her words. "I watched your mother take her last breath as she died in your arms. Murdered in cold blood. I watched your sister leave the only family she has behind. Running away from this life, instead of embracing it. I've seen the blood on your shirts and knuckles, I've seen the guns you carry on you all the time. I'm not stupid, nor can I continue to pretend to look the other way, Alejandro. I've seen you change from the boy I once knew, to a man I hardly recognize. You are slowly turning into your father and that's a scary thing to watch. Michael was right. I don't know you at all. I know the boy I fell head over heels for as a girl. But I don't know the man who is standing right here in front of me. You're a fucking stranger."

"I saved your fucking life that night, so don't you dare throw that in my face. I didn't want to love you. I tried to stay away, knowing that one day you'd bring me to my knees. And here I am begging you like a goddamn pussy not to fucking leave like a scared little girl. You came to me, not the other way around, sweetheart. I have fucking given you everything! Everything you have wanted or needed. Did you ever really love me, Sophia? Or was this a game to you? Were you dreaming of a fairytale and reality was too much for you to handle? I guess my old man was right about you after all."

"Fuck you!" she roared, turning to leave.

I caught her by the wrist, spinning her around to face me. "We are not done. No one walks out on me. Do you understand me? No one!"

"Let go of me!" She struggled to get away from me, pounding her fists on my chest.

"I. Love. You," I emphasized each word, needing her to understand, needing to get through to her. "I'm still the same man, cariño. I'm the man who you're supposed to spend the rest of your life with."

She winced, like it physically hurt her to hear me say those words. Giving up on the fight, bowing her head in shame, and letting tears stream down her perfect face. I let her go. She clutched onto the ring I placed on her finger months ago.

Our future.

"I'm so sorry, Alejandro," she wallowed, slipping the ring off her finger.

Stepping away from her, I shook my head. "Don't fucking do this."

She peered up at me through her tear-soaked lashes. "You did this." For the first time it was as if I was staring back at a stranger.

My Sophia was gone.

She wasn't the woman I loved with every last fiber of my being.

She reached over to take my hand in hers. Gently placing the ring in my palm and closing my fingers around it. Before releasing it, she brought my hand up to her lips and whispered, "I can't." Turning her back to me, she headed for the door.

I was over to her in one stride, grabbing her shoulder to turn her to face me again. Pulling the hair away from her face to look deep into her eyes.

I spoke with conviction, "Don't you see? Don't you see that I can't live without you? That I can't breathe without you?" I urged, hanging on by a thread. "That I'm nothing without you."

I could sense her resolve breaking, and I couldn't take it anymore. Tears slid down my face, mirroring hers. "Please," I added in a voice I didn't recognize.

She didn't waver. "If I asked you to choose me. To. Choose. Us. Would you?"

"My heart would choose you. Us. But that doesn't change the fact that I'm a Martinez. There is no getting past that, it's me."

She nodded her head, slipping out of my hands. "I know. Which is why I would never ask you to do that." I reached for her one last time, but she swiftly moved back, shaking her head and walking to the door. It took everything I had in me not to go to her. She looked broken. I had broken her, and now there was no going back.

I had to let her go.

She turned, grabbing the door handle, pausing. For a second I thought she was coming back to me, for a moment I thought our love had prevailed.

That this wasn't the end of our love story.

"Please take care of yourself. I know it's stupid for me to say that, but I can't help it. I'll always love you. I just can't die with you. Goodbye, Alejandro," she said as she opened the door and walked out of my life just like that.

Leaving me to walk through life without her by my side, taking my whole world with her. It was then I finally understood who Alejandro Martinez was born to be. I lost everything that ever mattered to me. My mom, my sister, and now my girl. Everyone I cared for, everyone I loved, had vanished.

They were all forever etched into my soul, a part of me that I would never be able to detach myself from. The truth of my life swallowed me whole. I screamed out my frustration, unleashing the rage and wrath I no longer had any control over. It pounded into me as furiously as Sophia's last words.

"Goodbye, Alejandro."

I slowly turned around, looking at the dining room table. Holding the possibility of our future in my hand. I lunged forward, clearing all the contents off the table, to the floor. The sounds of the glass crashing onto the hardwood was mocking me… my heart shattering the exact same way.

It was everywhere and all around me.

I couldn't run.

I couldn't escape.

I had no one.

I kept moving because I knew once I stopped I would crash, and possibly never get back up again. I darted around the dining room, my feet stomping with every step, leaving a path of destruction in their wake. Throwing candles, dishware, and chairs. Flipping the goddamn table. I went after anything I could find, demolishing the perfect night.

"I fucking hate you! I fucking hate you!" I yelled, punching the fucking mirror that I caught my reflection in. Not even flinching from the pain. I repeated that mantra over and over, letting it sink into my pores, and making it become a part of me. Destroying everything in my path, the future I would never have.

I pulled my hair back, taking in the destructive scene before me. "Jesus Christ, get yourself together, you fucking pussy," I rasped, making my way to the bar. Taking four swigs of whiskey from the head, not bothering with a glass, and repeating it several times until the bottle was empty, and I felt nothing but the burn through my body.

I couldn't take it anymore. I grabbed another bottle, wanting to drown myself in the amber liquid. Leaning my whole body against the wall, I started sliding down, wallowing in the despair of what my life had become. I don't know how long I sat there, drinking my fucking life away when I heard the front door open, footsteps coming my way.

"Sophia?" I slurred.

A part of me hoped that it was somebody that was coming to put a bullet in my fucking head. Putting me out of my goddamn misery.

"Fuck," I heard Leo announce as he hovered above me, reaching for my arm. "Get up, motherfucker. Get up!"

I took another swig of the bottle before he pried it out of my bloody hands. "Jesus, are you trying to have yourself admitted to the hospital? The entire bottle is almost gone. I'm not holding your hair back if you throw up, princess."

"Fuck you," I groaned, my head swaying.

"Come on, you need a cold fucking shower, then you need to pass the fuck out," he ordered, placing my arm over his shoulder as he stood me up as I rocked to stay upright.

"She's gone… Leo… she's fucking gone…"

"I know, man. I know. She called me."

"Everyone is gone…" I struggled to get out as we walked toward my room.

"You just keep fucking moving. Tomorrow is another day, brother." He laid me down on my bed.

I saw my dying mother in my arms.

I saw my sister leaving me.

I saw Sophia saying goodbye.

Before I passed the fuck out. Knowing I would wake up another man because the Devil…

Had won.

Sixteen
Martinez

"Alejandro," Dad greeted as I walked into his office. Not bothering to get up.

He was sitting at the head of the rectangle table at the far end of the room. Antonio, a new associate from Panama that we were about to use for the first time, was sitting across from him. I spent the last week in his territory, making sure they knew we meant business and they were aware of how we handled ourselves.

I didn't acknowledge him.

There was something about the fucking prick that rubbed me the wrong way immediately. The last thing I needed was to babysit another incompetent asshole who thought with his dick and not his head. My plate was already full. I didn't need any more shit piling up. Although, I had to give him some credit, the man had some brass fucking balls for sitting parallel to my father. I would be lying if I said I didn't want to shake his goddamn hand for it. I'm sure my dad loved that.

A power struggle at its fucking finest.

I wasn't a take-charge kind of man.

I was in charge.

End of fucking story.

I had proved myself to my piece of shit father more and more as the months passed. I unbuttoned my suit jacket as I sat down next to my dad. Making myself comfortable before heading the meeting.

"I paid off everyone that needed to keep their goddamn mouths shut, and the remaining were silenced… permanently," I informed, breaking the silence since I barged into the room.

"Antonio, this is—"

"I know who he is," he interrupted my father, leaning forward on the table with his hands placed out in front of him. "Your reputation precedes you, Martinez. Quite the Devil, huh?"

I grinned, tapping my fingers on the table one right after the other. "I've been called worse things by better people."

He narrowed his eyes at me, cocking his head to the side.

Waiting.

I knew what he was trying to do. I learned from an early age how to read people. Who was lying, who was pretending, who was bluffing, and who was just full of fucking shit. A person's body language always told me their story.

Some of it was instinctual.

Some of it was bred.

Some of it was learned.

Most of it was bullshit.

"Your father was telling me that you're going to be taking over soon. You think you can handle it?"

"Handle it?" I questioned, smiling. Leaning back, I reached down to grab my dick. "I'll handle it like I handle my fucking cock. Assertive."

My dad chuckled, sitting back with his arms crossed over his chest, an amused expression on his face.

Antonio jerked back, clearing his throat from my brutal honest response. Stammering, "I'm just saying... that's quite an accomplishment for someone so young."

"I'm just saying," I mocked in a condescending tone. "If I wanted your fucking opinion, I'd ask for it."

"I—"

I didn't give him a chance to reply, grabbing the folder that was sitting in front of him. I went over his proposal and leaned back into my chair, flicking the documents in his direction. Scoffing out, "What the fuck am I supposed to do with these? Wipe my ass with them?"

"That's the best I can do. We're taking a huge risk transporting that amount of cocaine into the U.S. It's going to cost you. I need to protect my men."

"Huh? Did you feel that?" I sat forward. "I actually almost gave a flying fuck about your men or your risks. Do I need to remind you that you work for me? Not the other way around. You don't set the rules, I do. When I say I need something, and I mean anything, including what the price per kilo will be, then you go and fetch, doggie."

He slammed his closed fist on the table, rattling the glasses. "I am the best! How dare you?!" Fury written all over his face.

"That's nice, now be a good boy and use your inside voice." Cocking my head to the side. "I know people who can make your life easier, or they can make it harder. I can slam my fists on tables too, like a fucking pussy. Want to see who can make it move more?" I threatened. "Now, if you could so kindly tell your goons to lower the guns that are pointing at me and my father under the table, I would really fucking appreciate it."

His eyes narrowed, giving me a smug look before nodding to his men. They retracted their weapons and placed them on the table.

"Gentleman," I declared, setting my elbows on the table with my hands in a prayer gesture. "We're not here to argue. I'm simply explaining why I'm right. Either you make it happen, Antonio, or you can go suck the dick you rode in on. Your choice."

I could feel my father's pride radiating off of him, burning a hole in my side. He slapped my shoulder and laughed, adding, "And that's how he handles it, Antonio."

Antonio instantly stood, the chair scrapping across the hardwood floor.

Facial expressions always revealed a lot about a person. Feelings truly were a bitch to hide. Energy of any form was communicated through a person's gaze. In this line of business, it was all about looking for the signs.

Nothing more.

Nothing less.

The longer you were around someone, the more you learned about them. You never even had to know their goddamn name.

"I'll have a new proposal drawn up," he caved, exactly how I knew he would.

"Great, now go lay down by your bowl," I ridiculed, enjoying every fucking second of it.

He stood taller, inhaling deeply.

I smiled not paying him any mind, nodding toward the door for them to get the fuck out of my face. He understood my silent order and left without so much as another word.

"Well, nice to see you too, hijo," Dad's voice boomed, bringing my attention to him.

"You're welcome," I replied, ignoring his endearment. I stood, grabbing his glass.

It was tradition to have a drink together after a business meeting, especially one that went in our favor. Turning my back to him, I made my way over to his wet bar at the other end of the room, pouring two glasses of scotch.

"I'm getting old, Alejandro. Your mother's death… it's… taken a toll on me. I know you will make me proud, carrying on the Martinez name. You've done well, hijo. They're already calling you El Diablo, The Devil. Twenty years old and already fucking feared. I couldn't be more pleased to call you my son."

The mere mention of my mother made me physically cringe, knowing the truth. I took in his words, turning with our drinks in hand, before walking back over to him again. I set his drink down in front of him, taking my seat at the other side of the table. Exactly where Antonio was sitting only minutes ago, causing him to narrow his eyes at me. It was the first time in all these years I ever sat parallel to him.

Lifting my glass, I nodded my chin toward him, a silent toast before downing the fiery liquid in one gulp. Setting my glass down on the table with a thud. He followed suit, taking it down like it was a glass of fucking water.

"Did you ever really love her?" I asked out of nowhere, catching him by surprise.

He lowered his eyebrows, confused.

I stood from my chair again, needing to get away from him. Since I found out the truth, I had distanced myself from him, spending very little time in his presence. Even sharing the air that he breathed made me fucking sick. I paced around the room, waiting for him to answer my question. Knowing I would never get an honest response.

That wasn't how my father was made.

I stopped at his desk, running my fingers along the mahogany wood. Staring at the pictures of my mother and Amari in the corner, shoved away, like the truth.

"Is this where you made the call to seal my mother's fate?" I sat down in his chair, putting my feet up on his desk. He watched my every move with nothing but a guarded stare. I lit a cigar, taking a few deep puffs, blowing precise smoke rings into the thick air. "So tell me. Did you murder her because she was having an affair with Roberto? Or because she was pregnant with his baby?"

"Hijo—"

I glared at him. "You lost the fucking right to call me that the day you murdered my mother and had me fucking watch. Not giving a fuck that Amari was there. Tell me, did it ever cross your mind that she could have been killed, too?"

"Mi familia lo es todo para mi," he clenched out, "*My family is everything to me.*"

I reached into the pocket of my suit jacket, pulling out a folded piece of paper I spent hours, even days, staring at. Memorizing every last goddamn word written. The edges so worn from my bleeding grasp.

I threw it at him. Landing in the space between us.

"I thought you didn't get an autopsy. Isn't that what you told us? That we didn't need to get one? That she was a victim of retaliation on you? On us? Or do you not remember the fucking lies you tell anymore?"

He grimaced, still sitting where I left him at the table. "I would never hurt my wife. The mother of my children."

"No, you just had someone else do it for you. Are we even your kids?"

"Get the fuck out of my office, Alejandro!" he roared, the vein on his forehead pulsating.

"She loved you. She gave you everything, old man. She cheated on you because you're a miserable fuck, who treated her like shit. I'm surprised it took her that long. Kinda makes me wonder if Roberto was the only one. I don't blame my mother at all. Life is full of disappointments, and you're one of them."

"You despise me, don't you? Is that what this is about?"

130

"You know, I probably would. If I gave you any thought at all. You know what comes to mind when I do think about you, though? My mother dying in my arms, fighting to fucking breathe. She didn't say one goddamn word about you as she shook in my arms. You weren't even a thought in her mind in the last minutes of her life. Like you didn't even exist in her world. She did whisper his name though," I lied, just to hurt him.

"Alejandro," he coaxed, his mouth contorting, struggling to breathe. Sweat pooled at his temples as his now bloodshot eyes protruded out. His tan face quickly turned a reddish, blue hue, oxygen being cut off more and more. His chest heaved as he was trying to beg for help.

My help.

He wilted over in his chair, placing his head between his knees, clenching his chest with his right hand. Gasping for air that wasn't available for the taking. I watched with fascinated eyes, not moving an inch to help the son of a bitch.

"I wonder if she thought about him when she was with you?"

With wide eyes, he patted his hand against his chest. "Hijo, I think… I think… I'm having a heart attack," he stuttered.

"I wonder if she ever wanted to call out his name when you were together?"

"You... know... nothing..." he drawled, gasping. Having a hard time getting his words out.

I didn't falter. "Picturing his face when she told you she loved you," I viciously spewed.

"Mother... fucker. Who do you... think you... are?" he questioned, dry heaving.

"I know one thing, she probably fucking hated you. Like mother, like daughter. Amari couldn't get away from you fast enough. Is that why you had Mom murdered? Couldn't handle that she found someone newer and younger, replacing you, you miserable fuck. Picture it, Roberto balls deep in your wife, in your house, in your bed, while you were off fucking people over," I snidely chuckled.

"Call 911, you ungrateful... bastard, I can't... No puedo..." he whimpered, sweating profusely now. "My heart…" He grabbed his

131

chest, trying to stand to reach the phone receiver in front of him. Inching his fingers closer and closer until his body betrayed him.

"So close, yet so far away." I clapped my hands, then took another puff of my cigar. Blowing smoke toward him. Making him cough.

His legs gave out and his body slid off the table backward, falling to the ground. His glass followed, shattering into a million pieces below him. He landed on his back, head bouncing off the floor, convulsing uncontrollably.

Stubbing the cigar out in the ashtray, I sat back watching him seize on the ground and enjoying every last fucking second of it. Letting him feel the spasms of his heart pumping hard through his body. His veins protruding, losing circulation. Spit forming near his mouth, as his back arched off the floor choking on his own saliva.

His body betraying him like he betrayed my mother.

I finally pushed off the desk, stepping toward him, each stride more determined than the last.

Crouching down, close to his face, I growled, "The dead can't talk, old man." Throwing his own words back at him. Wanting him to remember the day he set my life in motion.

The day he damned me.

"Please… help me…" he muffled so low I could barely hear him, placing his hand over his heart.

"Like you helped my mother?" I didn't falter, gripping onto his throat, squeezing lightly. Cutting off more of his air supply.

His eyes widened in fear. I would remember the look on his face for the rest of my life. Another memory that would forever haunt me until the day I died. I held him down, pinning him to the floor by his throat, feeling it constrict under my fingers. I wanted him to feel everything as I choked the life out of him, slowly. Wanting him to feel the pain as he took his last breaths. Hoping that his life was flashing before his eyes.

I needed to witness him struggle like my mother did, fighting for his life.

I leaned forward, getting as close as I could to his ear, staring him dead in the eyes. I spoke with conviction, "This was for my mother."

His eyes glazed over, the realization that this was my retaliation. My revenge for my mother's death. My vengeance on making it right by murdering him.

His son was his demise.

"Eye for eye, motherfucker." I gripped his throat as hard as I fucking could. His body convulsed, legs, arms shaking uncontrollably and all over the place. "May you burn in Hell," was the last thing I gritted out before his eyes rolled to the back of his head, and he was dead.

Letting go of his throat, I stood. Taking him in one last time, making sure he was really gone. Nudging him with my foot, rolling him over so I wouldn't have to look at his fucking face again. I didn't close his eyes or make the sign of the cross, I never wanted his goddamn soul to rest.

I took a deep breath, immediately feeling a sense of peace since my mother died. I walked over to where the autopsy report laid on the floor, picking it up and placing it on his back. Along with the Pentobarbital that was inside of my suit jacket.

Forever condemned.

"Come and clean up this fucking mess. It's done," I ordered to one of my men on the phone.

And I left.

El Diablo never once looking back.

Seventeen
Martinez

"We have a problem," Esteban stated, barging into my office without knocking, forcing my attention to him.

The days turned into weeks, weeks turned into months, and one year bled into the next. I was twenty-four years old and I was Lucifer himself, leading the way to Hell. Almost a year after I took care of my father, I met Esteban at one of my strip clubs downtown.

Let's just say he wasn't enjoying the entertainment.

I was talking to my men, when we heard a little girl scream, *"Stop! Don't hurt him."* My men tried to step in and intervene, but I put my hand out in front of their chests, stopping them. I pulled out a cigarette instead, leaned against the brick wall behind my strip club and watched. Esteban was getting his ass kicked by three junkies in my alley. He was homeless at the time, rummaging through the dumpster for food. Sleeping under overpasses or in alleyways. He was a scrappy little fucker but he could handle his own.

Taking as much as he was giving.

Out of the corner of my eye, I saw a little figure cowering in the shadows. I walked toward her, picking her up and placing her in my arms. She had bright green eyes and long dark hair, she couldn't have been older than four.

"Where the Hell did you come from?" I asked her.

"A...lex...a," she stuttered, bowing her head. I could barely understand her baby gibberish. Tears poured down her porcelain skin, terrified at the scene unfolding in front of her. Nothing a little girl should be witnessing.

"Lex, hasn't your mama told you about the monsters that lurk in the dark?"

Her eyes widened with fear.

"I'm one of those monsters," I whispered into her ear.

Esteban tried to watch the whole scene unfold, making it harder for him to defend himself. To make a long story short, my men stopped the fight, Esteban was the only one that stayed behind, worried for the little girl.

I respected that.

I asked him if he wanted a job, and he happily obliged. After bullshitting for a few minutes, I handed him the kid and told him to find her fucking parents. I didn't have time to babysit.

He'd been working for me ever since.

I peered up at him, narrowing my eyes. "Congratulations. Did you forget how to fucking knock?" The blonde's head that was sucking my cock tried to look up, but I pushed her back down. "Did I say you could stop?" She gagged, taking my dick all the way to the back of her throat.

"I... I was... it didn't..." Esteban stuttered, watching her mouth stroke me up and down, my grip never moving from the back of her head.

My cell phone rang with an unknown number appearing on the screen. "I need to take this."

"I need—"

"I don't know why you think I fucking care, Esteban. Now turn around, man the fuck up, and take care of the problem."

"Alej—"

"Go outside, and play hide and go fuck yourself. I need to take this call," I ordered in a demanding tone. "Ahora!"

Patience was never part of my nature, especially now.

"Did I fucking stutter?"

He finally nodded, turned and left.

I shoved the blonde's head away, causing her to fall on her ass with a thud. "That means you too, sweetheart."

"What the fuck?" she seethed.

"No shit. With lips like yours I thought you'd be a goddamn pro."

"Who the fuck do you think you are talking to me like that? I'm the best."

"The best thing to ever come out of your mouth was my cock. Now get the fuck out."

"You're an asshole!"

"If I wanted a *come*back, I'd ask you to spit."

She stomped her way toward the door, like I gave a fuck. "Martinez," I answered the phone as soon as she slammed the door shut behind her.

"Alejandro Martinez?" the woman on the other end inquired.

"This is him," I responded, annoyed.

"I'm calling from Sibley Memorial Hospital. There's been a car accident. You're the contact in case of emergency for Michael and Amari Mitchell. We need for you to come in as soon as possible."

"What? What do you mean? Where's Amari? Is she okay?" My heart sped up, beating out of my chest. Panic setting in.

"Sir, calm down. All I can tell you over the phone is that we need you to come in. We're legally bound not to disclose any information over the phone, Sir."

"Please…" I begged in a voice I didn't recognize. "Where is the little girl? Daisy, their daughter. The least you could do is tell me that. Where is Daisy?"

"She's here too. I'd advise you to come immediately. The nurses will inform you once you've arrived."

"Ma'am, with all due respect I need to talk to my fucking sister," I gritted through a clenched jaw, trying not to flip the fuck out on her.

"Mr. Martinez, it's important that you get on the next flight out. That's all I can say."

I ended the call, dialing one of my men I had watching them. "What the fuck?"

"Boss," he answered. "It's bad. It's really fucking bad. I was just about to call you."

"Are they alive?"

"Boss, I—"

"Are they fucking alive?"

"Daisy is. I'm sor—" I hung up.

136

The picture of Daisy lying on Amari's chest when she was born, sat on the corner of my desk, mocking me. She was looking down at her newborn daughter adoringly, already a devoted mother. Daisy was the first and last baby I'd ever held. I hadn't seen either one of them since that day, six years ago.

I loved Daisy instantly, which was such a foreign emotion for me. I hadn't felt love in such a long time. I didn't even think I was capable of feeling it any more. I held her tiny frame against my chest, cradling her in my arms. Rubbing her chubby baby fingers, as I stared into her beautiful eyes. Memorizing the feel of her soft skin and baby scent. The need to protect her was so overpowering for someone I'd only just met for the first time. A primal urge to keep her safe took over, and I would stop at nothing to keep my niece away from harm.

Exactly how I would her mother.

No matter what the cost.

It was then I realized I didn't fit into Amari's life. Knowing I could bring danger into the lives of the only family members I had left, was too much for me to bear.

I stayed away to keep them safe.

My feet moved on their accord toward the wet bar in the corner of my office, downing the amber liquid without thinking twice about it. No glass needed. Bringing the bottle away from my mouth, I hurled it across the room. Watching as it shattered against the wall, falling into shards on the hardwood floor. My stomach churned and my mind reeled. My body couldn't move fast enough around the room, pushing over everything that was in my immediate sight. Throwing and swinging at anything I could find, screaming at the top of my lungs over and over again, until my throat burned raw. And my chest heaved.

Seconds, minutes, hours later, everything blended together, and I just stood there taking in the results of my destruction. My body propelled itself upward while panting and heaving, every breath harder to take than the one before.

How did this fucking happen?

I was supposed to protect her.

Beating myself up inside.

I blinked and I was sitting in my airplane, flying toward Washington. Contemplating my life.

I've killed.

I've tortured.

Innocent lives had paid the price. My price. Just to prove a fucking point, to rise above everyone and everything. Even God wasn't safe from me. I was a ruthless motherfucker who didn't take no for an answer. No one crossed me and lived to tell the tale. I had no respect or loyalty to anyone but myself.

Not once did I ever think about the pain I was inflicting. The consequences of my actions would be the biggest regrets of my life.

Everything progressed in slow motion, seconds turned to minutes, and minutes turned to hours. The ding to my voicemail broke the silence around me. The screen lit up as it had for the past two days. Notifying me I had one missed call and one unheard voicemail that stuck out from all the rest.

My sister's.

I wasn't sure what I felt at that moment, fear maybe, panic, confusion. Remembering I hit ignore to Amari's phone call two days ago, always too busy to take a few minutes out of my fucked up life to talk to her. My adrenaline was racing, my body felt stiff, and my hands were shaking. I suddenly felt bile rising in my throat, and fought back the urge to heave.

Taking a few deep breaths, I hit the voicemail button, deleting message after message until I got to hers.

"Shit! Oh, crap, Daisy, don't repeat that," Amari's voice filled the air. "I didn't mean to call you, stupid fat fingers hitting the wrong numbers. I was trying to reach Michael. Daisy and I are stuck on the side of the road, and it looks like it might start pouring any second now. Anyway, I don't know why I'm telling you all this, it's not like you care." Her bitter tone bit me like a snake in the night.

My vision blurred, not being able to see anything in front of me. *Was I crying?*

"It would be nice to just hear from you from time to time. You're still my brother, no matter what. I love you, Alejandro. I'm still here. Maybe you need to hear it from me to remember that. Hopefully we will talk soon. Be safe." The line went silent.

The only words that registered were…

"I'm still here."

My hand fell away from my ear, still holding the phone. Not bothering to hit the end button, staring at the screen while my mind was stuck on one phrase.

"I'm still here."

It was an endless phrase that repeated itself over and over in my head, a cycle that I couldn't stop, over and over again.

"I'm still here."

I couldn't move. I couldn't feel. I couldn't talk.

I was numb.

The darkness settled all around me. Memories of Amari and I came flooding into my mind. From our childhood to the day she walked out of my life, and everything in between. Little mental souvenirs of our time together. I sat there until my body couldn't take it anymore. I sat there until I felt like there was nothing left of me.

Knowing I would be nothing after this. A shell of the man I used to be. I was an abstract painting and a kaleidoscope of pain. I lived everyday with constant reminders of mistakes and regrets, the things I could never change…

The past.

The present.

The future.

Then.

Now.

Forever.

The relentless torture of love and hate.

The distant memory of the boy I was, and the ruthless man I'd become.

The next thing I knew, I was walking toward the morgue in the hospital to identify their bodies. My heart pounded against my chest, ringing in my ears as they pulled back the locker that held my sister's body. Nothing could have prepared me for what I was about to see. The woman that was lying there, no longer full of life, laughter, or love.

No longer full of anything.

I leaned forward, kissing her forehead, expecting to feel her warmth. Instead all I got was her freezing cold skin against my lips. "Peace, I leave with you. My peace I give you," I whispered the bible verse, making the sign of the cross over her body.

I nodded to the coroner, unable to find the words to say this was Amari. Holding back the desire to fall apart and die right along with her. I couldn't, her baby girl needed someone, and I'd made her a promise a long time ago, a promise I intended to keep. I left the morgue without looking back. The hospital where I held Daisy as a newborn, welcoming her into the cruel world, was now the same hospital I said goodbye to her mother.

My beloved sister.

I walked into Daisy's hospital room, her tiny frame hooked up to several machines, as she laid unconscious in her hospital bed. The beeping sound of the heart monitor and the rhythmic hissing sound of the ventilator echoed all around me. Filling me with some kind of hope. She looked so small and delicate holding her favorite blanket, the one I had sent to Amari for Daisy's first birthday. I may not have kept in touch, but I never missed my niece's birthdays or holidays.

I pulled up a chair beside her bed and took a seat. Taking in her beautiful face that reminded me so much of Amari's. Reaching for her hand, I lifted it and placed it in my grasp. My hands so big compared to hers, they swallowed them whole. I leaned over, bowing my head in shame over her broken, bruised, cut up body.

"I'm so sorry, peladita. I didn't want this for you. I'm so fucking sorry," I sobbed, laying my forehead on our joined hands.

This would be the last time I cried for the rest of my life.

The last time I would apologize to anyone.

Saying goodbye to my sister was the final farewell to what was left of my heart and soul. I was now hollow inside. It was easier that way, I needed to turn off my humanity. No longer wanting to feel anything.

After this…
There was nothing left of me.

Part 2

Eighteen
Lexi

"Alright, little lady Lexi, this is your stop," my bus driver, Anna called out. Peering up at me through the mirror above her head.

I stood, walking down the aisle, passing all the kids I went to school with. Ignoring the hateful glares I had to endure every day. I usually sat near the front of the bus, the closest seat I could find to Anna, or else the kids picked on me for one reason or another

"Thanks, Anna. See you tomorrow," I announced as she slid the doors open to let me out.

"No problem, sweetie. I'll bring some of that yogurt you love in the morning."

I smiled, I loved Anna's breakfasts. They were the best way to start the day. I often didn't get breakfast from home before I had to leave for the bus. Mom was always asleep, never bothering to get up and help me get ready for my day. I was lucky if I got lunch on most days.

Stepping off the bus, I looked back at Anna one last time. She was shaking her head in disappointment, and it made my heart hurt. I didn't like it when she got sad, especially when I was the cause.

I was around enough sadness.

My mom wasn't there, again. I was not surprised. It was rare for her to pick me up from the bus stop. I made sure to always smile wider and bigger as I stared back to show Anna I wasn't fazed by my mom's absences. Trying to ease the worry I knew she felt. Anna hated that I had to walk home by myself. She said six year olds are too young to be walking by themselves. It wasn't that bad, except in the summer, I got really hot and sweaty. Anna

142

always made sure to bring me a water bottle so I wouldn't get dehydrated.

Sometimes if there were enough kids absent, she would drop me off right in front of my house. Those were my favorite days, but they were few and far between.

Anna waved one last time and I waved back. Watching some of the kids stick their tongues out at me as the bus drove by, but I didn't pay them any mind.

"Sticks and stones," I whispered. Repeating what my stepdad always said, over and over again in my head.

I never met my real dad, but my mom had shown me a few pictures of him. Including the one that's framed on my nightstand. She didn't tell me much about him, but she did tell me he wasn't a nice guy and I was better off without him. My stepdad, Phil, wasn't so bad, but he worked a lot. Which made him cranky. As much as I wished he was home more because he played with me, the house was quieter when he wasn't. He yelled at my mom all the time to get out of bed, take a shower, clean up the house, and I didn't like that very much. It scared me sometimes when he was in a really bad mood. I always made sure to give my mom extra hugs and kisses after he was done making her cry.

They fought a lot.

I thought about my mom as I was doing my ballet walks down the sidewalk. Pointing toe to heel, with my feet turned out, but putting my arms out at my sides to practice my balance like my instructor showed me. Humming a tune from Swan Lake as I danced my way home. I'd been a ballerina for as long as I could remember. It was my life, the only time I was truly happy. Not having to worry about anything around me, but the music and rhythm. My instructor said I was born to dance, picking up on new techniques without any hesitation at such a young age.

I would always rush home from class to show my mom all the new moves I learned. She would lay in her bed and watch every last one with a sparkle in her eye, telling me I looked beautiful. Then she would pull me toward her, rolling me onto her bed and we would cuddle for hours, watching movies while she played with my long hair. I slept in her bed more than I slept in my own, always scared of monsters under my bed. She understood my concern, so she let me sleep with her almost every night. My stepdad usually slept on the couch, especially over the last year or more, but I don't really remember.

"Momma!" I shouted, walking into my house, shutting the door behind me.

Silence.

"Momma! I'm home!" I made my way toward her bedroom, down the narrow hallway, off the living room. Knowing exactly where she would be. She wasn't laying in her bed, which only left one other place.

"Momma," I said again as I opened the closet door in her room, and peeked in.

She was sitting in the small space at the far end of the closet, where she tucked all her junk away. She would sit on the ledge, breaking down all alone. She didn't acknowledge me, just continued to cry, staring off into space. I grabbed the stepping stool, placing it along the edge of the ledge. Giving myself a boost, so I could crawl to her, like I always did when I found her in here.

"Hey, Momma," I whispered, wrapping my arms tight around her waist, laying my head on her tummy. "I'm home now. No more crying."

She sniffled, kissing the top of my head and rubbing my arm. "I'm so sorry, Lexi. I'll come pick you up tomorrow. I... I lost track of time."

"Okay." *She wouldn't.*

"Maybe we can go to the park? Get some ice cream? I'll make it up to you," she promised, pulling me in tighter.

"Okay." *We wouldn't.*

"I'll be better tomorrow. I promise."

I looked up at her tear-stained face and nodded, wanting to believe her. My stepdad said she lost me one time and since then, she barely left the house.

I just hugged her and kissed her like I always did, wishing tomorrow would be better.

Knowing it wouldn't.

𝕸𝖆𝖗𝖙𝖎𝖓𝖊𝖟

"What are you still doing up? You need to be sleeping," I stated in a harsher tone than I intended.

Daisy's eyes widened with fear, shying away from me, immediately reminding me of her mother. Amari used to make that exact same face when our father spoke to her with the same dominant tone.

After all these years of not wanting to be anything like him, I was my own worst nightmare, my reality.

I was my father.

We were both one and the same.

It was the price I paid for the choices I made and the life I led.

El Diablo.

Daisy, or Briggs, as she called herself now, was the spitting image of my sister, except she had Michael's fair skin. During her parents' funeral she told me she was no longer Daisy. Her new name was Briggs. I let her have it because it granted her peace, though to me, she would always be Daisy. My sister's favorite flower.

Even after two years of living with me, my eight-year-old niece was still fucking terrified of me. Not that I gave her a choice in the matter, it was easier for her to see me as a monster. I never wanted her to love me. I didn't deserve it.

She didn't deserve it.

The two women who loved me the most were both six feet under. There was no way in hell I would provoke fate again. Which was why she had a nanny, but Esteban was responsible for her. I assigned him as her permanent bodyguard. If anything happened to her, it was his life I would take, and he knew it.

"I can't sleep," she whispered so low, I could barely hear her. Tucking her tiny frame into her chest, leaning deeper into the couch as if she wished it would make her disappear.

"It's late, Briggs. You have school in the morning, and I don't have time for this. Go to bed."

145

She bowed her head with the shame I wanted her to feel. I swallowed hard, knowing all she needed was for me to take her into my arms, and tell her everything was going to be okay.

It wasn't.

I refused to lie to her, making her think it would. The nightmares she had every night were proof of that alone.

"I don't want to be by myself, Uncle," she murmured again, peering up at me with hopeful eyes. The same eyes Amari would use when she woke me up, crawling into my bed late at night.

Keeping Daisy at arm's length wasn't just for her benefit. It was also for mine.

"You need to get used to being by yourself. That's life, peladita," I called her, "*Little girl.*"

She nodded, holding back the tears that were threatening to surface. I reprimanded her anytime she cried in my presence, telling her it was a sign of weakness. It didn't take long for the crying to stop when she was around me, scared of the consequences it might evoke. She scooted off the couch, so tiny and frail, walking past me. You would think after two years I would have built up enough resistance from wanting to hold her, comfort her, tell her I loved her.

If anything, the urge became stronger.

I watched her go into her bedroom, closing the door behind her, as I made my way over to the makeshift bar.

Waiting.

Rubbing my forehead from the constant splitting goddamn headaches, which never seemed to go away. My doctor said it was from lack of sleep, and diagnosed me as an insomniac. He prescribed sleeping pills, but I never took the fucking things.

My demons wouldn't let me.

I was worth more dead than alive in this world. And the second I forget that, would be my demise.

I downed my glass of whiskey as I heard Daisy crying from a distance, slamming it onto the bar when it was empty. I grabbed the bottle instead. It was the same thing almost every night. Her room was the only one in the penthouse that wasn't soundproof.

I needed to hear her cry.

146

My feet moved of their own accord, my body being pulled by a string. Or maybe it was my heart. Drawing me closer and closer to her door like it did every night. I stood there, leaning my forehead against the cool wood. The bottle of whiskey firmly clutched in my grasp. My other hand gripping the doorknob, fighting everything inside of me to turn it. Feeling every last ounce of her pain and distress, silently praying I could take it all away.

I couldn't.

The sobs came harder and harder, twisting the dagger in my heart just a little bit more. All I could imagine was her little body shaking with her blanket pulled tight under her chin. Maybe pretending her mother was there, or worse…

That I was.

I turned around, sliding down her door like I always did. Sitting with my back pressed up against it, my elbows resting on my knees out in front of me. I took another swig from the bottle, leaning my head back and listened to her cry all night long.

It was my way of being there for her.

Even though I would never allow her to know it.

There were times when she would sleep through the night, undisturbed by the nightmares that haunted the both of us. I would slip into her room, and sit in the armchair by her bed. Watching her sleep through the darkness until the sun started rising. I'd allow myself to kiss her forehead, letting my lips linger as I made the sign of the cross like my mother had done to me, time and time again.

And then I'd leave. Vanish like I was never there to begin with.

Letting her continue to think she was alone, when in reality, she always had me.

147

Nineteen

Lexi

Three years had gone by and not much had changed. I was now nine years old, still holding onto the hope that my mom would miraculously become an attentive mother, not lost in her own world anymore. I longed for a mother like most of the kids at my school had. Overhearing kids in my class talk about how their moms would attend meetings, recitals, or even the simple gesture of making breakfast for them, always filled me with envy.

I hated that feeling.

My mom never attended any of my school functions, award ceremonies, or parent/teacher nights. Most people assumed I didn't have a mother, which was really sad. She still barely left her room, or got dressed for that matter. She struggled day-to-day to keep pushing through the haze that clouded her mind.

I wanted her. No, I *needed* her, to be a part of my life outside of our house. To take some interest in my life, since I always took so much interest in hers.

Trying to push all the sadness that lived inside of her away.

The recital of *Swan Lake* for my class was only three days away, and I was beyond excited. I auditioned for the lead role of the white swan, and to my surprise I got it. I remember that day, running into my mom's room, jumping into her bed to tell her my big news. She just smiled, pulling me in for a hug. Not saying a word.

I practiced all day and night, till all my steps were perfect. I wanted to make my mom proud of me. Maybe then she would come to more productions in the future.

She swore she would make it to this one. She wouldn't miss it for the world, she said she couldn't wait to see me on stage. This would be the very first time she would see me dance outside of our house. My stepdad on the other hand, never missed any of my shows, but it wasn't the same. I couldn't wait to have her there, sitting in the front row, watching all my hard work pay off.

I was on my way home from my rehearsal. I could hear them from the driveway before I made my way to the front steps. They were fighting again, calling each other names. Our house was small, so it didn't take much for their shouting to echo off the walls into the night. No one came to pick me up once again. It was a normal occurrence. I wasn't sure if they just forgot about me or just didn't care how I made my way home. I was lucky enough to have one of the girl's moms bring me home. It was a long walk in the dark for a girl my age.

I chose to believe the second one.

It hurt less that way, but not by much.

I went straight into my bedroom, not bothering to tell them I was home. They were too caught up in whatever argument they were having this time. I threw my bag on my bed and grabbed my ballet shoes. I scooted my dresser out of the way, transforming my room into a stage. Putting on my headphones to drown out their yelling coming through the thin walls.

I listened to Act II, XIV from *Swan Lake*, one of my solo pieces. Getting lost in the music, the intensity of the instruments vibrated through my core, translating into movements through my body. Turning each step into an extension of the music. Pirouetting in tight circles around the small space, gracefully stepping, leaping into the air effortlessly. The balls of my feet pounded into the floor in a quick pattern, getting ready for my big finish. Feeling as if I was one with the music. Sauté, step, arabesque, and pose. Repeating the steps over and over, until my bones ached and my joints were raw.

No pain, no gain.

It was the only time that happiness surrounded me.

The only time I felt free.

I was just about to go on piqué when I felt the front door slam, rattling the whole house. Breaking my concentration, and making me miss the next step. My toe slipped on the hard wood floor, causing my heel to fall awkwardly.

"Ouch!" I whimpered, catching my balance before I twisted my ankle.

I sat on the floor, removed my shoes, and stretched my ankle. I decided to call it a night, and headed straight for the shower. Hoping the warm water would loosen my sore muscles from all the rehearsing. I stayed in there until the water ran cold, changed into my nightshirt, and got ready for bed.

I still slept in my mom's room, but not because I was scared any longer. It was our time together, just her and I. Usually, it was the most time we spent together all day. I looked forward to it. She would hold me in her arms all night, hugging me close. It was the only time I felt truly loved by her.

Taken care of and safe.

"Momma," I whispered as I walked into her room. "Momma, you awake?" Tapping on her shoulder. "Momma."

She startled. Turning over to face me, her eyes hazy and confused. "Hey... baby..."

"Can I sleep with you?"

She nodded, her eyes already shutting. She was always so tired even though all she did was sleep. She scooted over, opening her arms for me. I smiled, crawling toward her, nuzzling my body into the curve of hers. She immediately wrapped her arms around me, pressing my back firmly against her front as tight as she could. Like she always did.

She was so cold, her skin felt like ice. Not like the warm, comforting heat I was used to every night.

"Mom, why are you so cold?" I asked, shivering. Snuggling deeper into the blanket that was laying on top of us.

"I don't know, baby. You'll keep me warm."

I happily nodded, smiling again, kissing the palm of her hand.

"You're such a good girl, Lexi. I don't know what I did to deserve such an amazing daughter. I love you so much," she declared, kissing my head.

I felt tears fall onto my neck, as she squeezed me harder.

"Momma, are you crying?" I tried to turn to look at her, but she wouldn't let me. As if it pained her to have me see her like that.

"I wasn't always like this, baby. I remember the day I had you. It was the happiest day of my life, Lexi. You were the most beautiful thing I had ever laid eyes on. I used to spend hours just holding you tight, staring into your bright green eyes. So proud that you were mine. I think that's why you like to snuggle so much with me now." She let out a small chuckle between the tears. "I'm so sorry, baby. I'm so sorry for everything. You deserve a better mommy than I've been to you. I wish I could change things. I wish I could be what you deserve," she cried into my hair.

"Shhh... It's okay, Momma. You can still change. I know you can. I'm here to help you get better. We can start a routine together, get you out of the house more."

"I love you, Lexi. I need you to always remember that, my sweet girl. Please remember that. You are such a strong little girl."

"I know, Momma. I love you too. You will be better after my recital. I know it will make you smile, and proud. You'll want to come to all of them. I just know it. I can't wait for you to see me up on the big stage. I wish it were tomorrow."

She cried harder. Sobs wreaked havoc on her body, shaking the entire bed.

"Momma, please don't cry. I hate it when you cry. It hurts my heart too much," I said, my voice breaking. Tears began to form in my eyes. It wasn't easy seeing and feeling her break down, unable to do anything for her. Unable to stop the pain that always took her away from me.

"I'm so sorry, Lexi. For all the pain I caused you," she sobbed.

"Momma, you know I'll forgive you for anything. I promise. For anything," I cried right along with her, unable to control the emotions soaring through me. I would do anything to take her pain away.

"I love you so much, baby. Don't ever forget that. Not for one day."

"I know, Momma, I know." I fervently nodded as she kissed all over the top of my head. Her skin was still freezing cold. "I'm going to get another blanket. I think you're getting sick." I tried to get up, but she held me firmer.

"No. Don't leave. All I need is you. Just you."

"Okay…" Something wasn't right but I stayed, giving her what she needed.

I'd wait for her to fall asleep, and then I'd go get another blanket for us. I knew my warmth wasn't enough. She cried a little longer, but eventually her breathing became shallow, I could barely hear it. Her deep sleep took me under too, and before I knew it, I had fallen asleep with her.

I woke up the next morning in the same position as the night before, except only my mom's heavy arm lay draped across my stomach.

My eyes fluttered open, the sun shining bright on my face from the window by her bed.

"Momma," I groggily said, wiping sleep from my eyes. "Maybe we should do something fun today. We could go to the park, get you some fresh air. It looks like it's a pretty day outside."

It was always hard for me to get her up in the morning. She slept like a rock. A bomb could go off in the house and she would stay asleep. I heard my stepdad yelling at her all the time, to stop taking so many pills. They weren't good for her.

I rolled over, still half asleep into the nook of her arm, gently laying my arm across her. She was even colder than she was last night, but now she felt so stiff too. My arm laid motionless, not rising and falling as she breathed in and out.

"Momma?" I peered up at the side of her face, my eyes opening wide. "Momma!" Sitting straight up, I took in her pale white complexion. Her lips slightly open with a bluish-purple hue to them. "Momma! Momma!" I got up on my knees, shaking her as hard as I could. She didn't move. "Momma!" I shook her again. "Why aren't you moving? Why aren't you waking up?" I placed my head over her heart.

Nothing.

I put my hand over her mouth. "Momma! Why aren't you breathing?"

I jumped out of bed, running as fast as I could into the living room. "Dad! Dad! Dad!" I screamed all the way through the house.

"Lexi, it's too early," he grumbled as I shook him on the couch.

"Dad! Please! It's Mom! She won't wake up! She's not breathing! I don't know what's going on!"

He bolted off the couch running toward the bedroom. "Fuck!" he shouted as soon as he got to her. "What did you do, baby? What the fuck did you do?" He shook her, taking her into his arms. Looking at all the pills on the nightstand then back to her. "Shit, what did you take? Baby, what did you take?"

I stood in the doorway and watched everything move in slow motion. Tears running down my face, as I wrapped my arms around myself. Still being able to feel her cold, lifeless skin on mine. A feeling that would never leave me. I sank down to the floor, rocking back and forth, watching my stepdad try to breathe life back into her.

Pumping on her chest…

One, two, three.

Screaming at me to call 911. I couldn't move, I couldn't talk, I could barely even breathe. My body in shock, my mind was spinning, my heart was pounding.

My life was ending…

Dad fell to his knees and broke down with his face in his hands. Sirens sounded in the distance. People talking all around me. Chaos from every corner of the house.

I just sat there.

Knowing right then and there I would have to break my promise to her.

I would have forgiven my mother for anything…

But I would never forgive her for this.

Martinez

"Read em' and weep, gentleman," I grinned to the high rollers sitting at my table.

I collected my chips, tipped the dealer, and left. I flew into Vegas that morning to handle some business and blow off some steam at the same time. Who ever said you couldn't mix business and pleasure, obviously had no clue what he was missing out on.

Briggs was back home with her nanny and Esteban, like always. I had a fucking thirteen-year-old, hormonal teen girl at home that made me want to pull out my fucking hair. Our relationship was still rocky and that was putting it mildly, but at least she stopped hoping for and seeking out a bond with me.

"Mr. Martinez, wait. Here are the documents for the quota you asked for," James, my financial manager for the casinos, announced, joining me as I made my way toward the elevator.

I swiped my keycard against the access pad for the penthouse floor. Stepping in with him by my side, letting the doors close behind us.

"These numbers are still off, James," I said, shaking my head, rubbing my fingers against my lips.

"I know... I think—"

"I don't pay you to think. I pay you to handle my fucking money." I shoved the documents into his chest, hard.

He huffed out from the unexpected blow.

I turned my attention to the chick that was in the elevator with us, watching her get down on her knees in front of me. She unzipped my slacks and pulled out my cock. Immediately deep throating me like she had something to prove.

I grinned. Our eyes connected as I watched her suck me off for a few seconds. Unraveling from the feel of her pouty lips wrapped around my cock. I looked over at James, who was looking everywhere except at the scene going down in front of him. Reaching over, I hit the button to the next floor, waiting till we came to a stop and the elevator doors opened.

"Get the fuck out," I ordered, grabbing the back of the chick's hair, leaning my head back against the wall before he even left. Once the doors closed, and the elevator started moving again, I pressed the emergency button, causing it to halt between floors.

She released my cock with a pop, gasping for air. "Don't you want to go up to your place?" she panted, batting her eyelashes at me.

"Do you want to suck my cock, or do you want a tour around my penthouse? Because only the first one sounds semi-appealing to me."

A small smile crept around her mouth. "I want the infamous El Diablo to fuck me."

I wasn't surprised that she knew who I was. There were very few people who didn't, especially women. Gossip always traveled fast, especially for the elite and corrupt. I was the most eligible bachelor who had more money than he knew what to do with. Not to mention I was hung like a fucking horse. I got used to women throwing themselves at me, falling to their knees with their mouths open wide and their legs spread even wider.

And it never got fucking old.

I chuckled. "Is that right?" Gliding my fingers toward the back of her neck, I slowly and intentionally, massaged the soft nook area. Her head subconsciously leaned back into my touch, and she closed her eyes. I roughly gripped her hair, causing a moan to escape her swollen, cock sucking lips. I pulled her up to stand in front of me, eyeing her up and down. Her tits made me immediately want to stick my dick in between them, and come all over her average face.

With my other hand, I started to unbutton the front of her dress, easing it off her shoulders, leaving her bare before me. I could already see her bare pussy was fucking glistening with wetness. My knuckles caressed the roundness of her breasts as her nipples hardened from my touch. Everywhere my fingers went, they left behind a craving for more.

The way she breathed.

The way she subtly leaned into my embrace.

The way her mouth parted and her tongue moved to wet her dry lips.

Her goddamn body trembled with every movement of my hand.

I leaned forward, lightly touching my lips against her ear. "I'm going to make you beg," I murmured, not being able to control the insatiable urge.

She drew in a breath against my lips, as soon as my fingers found her wet folds. I roughly pushed my middle finger into her pussy, causing her to gasp from the intrusion, but she quickly recovered. Melting into my hand.

"If you're a good girl, I may let you come. Is that what you want?" I taunted, knowing damn well it was.

"Yes," she moaned.

"Say it."

"I want to come."

I finger fucked her until her eyes closed, her knees buckled, and the scent of her arousal surrounded us like it was a part of the goddamn air. When I felt like she was close to coming, I pulled my fingers out of her pulsating pussy.

Her eyes instantly opened, chest heaving, anticipating my next move.

"What do you say?" I coaxed, trying to hold back my impatience from asking the fucking question again.

She enticed my lips to touch hers. "I want to come," she whispered against them.

I smacked her pussy, hard. She shuddered, whimpering.

"What. Do. You. Say?" I gritted out.

Her eyes dilated, trying to step aside, but I grabbed her around her throat and shoved her against the wall, holding her in place with my tight grasp. Her hands instantaneously went right to mine. Prying at my fingers to let go.

"Did I say you could go, yet?" I sneered, trying to hide my pleasure to her pain I was causing.

Her eyes darkened.

"You wanted El Diablo to fuck you, right? Isn't that what you said? Isn't that why you got down on your knees and sucked my cock in a goddamn elevator?"

"Fuck you!" she shouted not backing down.

My cock twitched.

"What do you say?" I repeated, pressing her harder against the wall.

She glared. "Let me go or I'll scream."

I grinned, tightening my hold around her neck. "Scream," I paused. "I fucking dare you."

Her mouth opened as I intensified my grip, lifting her off the floor a little, so she couldn't make a sound. I tilted my head and pouted, wanting to provoke her even more. Her pussy was fucking wetter, visually betraying her exaggerated stare.

"Don't knock on the devil's door, sweetheart, and expect him not to answer." I brought my fingers up to my mouth, licking them. Placing them back on her clit, rubbing her bright red nub faster and with no mercy.

If there was one pivotal lesson I learned about a woman, they loved to be stimulated, slowly. Let them ease into your hand or mouth. Too much stimulation wasn't entirely bad, it wasn't entirely good either.

Finally easing up on my torturous movements against her clit, caressing it side-to-side with the palm of my hand. It didn't take long for her eyes to glaze over and her breathing to even out.

My stare caught her dark dilated eyes. Fighting the urge to give me what I wanted, but knowing I would make her come if she did. The internal battle was evident all over her face.

Her eyes rolled to the back of her head. "Please…" she panted.

"Please, what?"

"Please… make me come…" she breathed out effortlessly.

I smiled, big and wide, my dark eyes mirroring hers. I let her go, pushing her down onto her knees. Not letting her come.

She obviously didn't know who the fuck she was dealing with, and my patience was already wearing very thin.

She peered up at me with hooded eyes, completely sedated and confused. She reached for my cock, but I shoved her off, and turned around. Tucking my dick back in my slacks, hitting the elevator button. Making it move again.

"What the fuck?" she breathed out.

"My cock deserves better, sweetheart. I'd call you a cunt, but you clearly lack the depth and warmth."

"Go to Hell," she spat, gathering her things.

"I live there."

I walked out without looking back.

Twenty

Lexi

I wish I could tell you things got easier for me.

I wish I could tell you I never felt any more sadness.

I wish I could tell you I didn't cry again.

That my story got better.

It didn't...

If anything, it got worse.

Four years had gone by since my mother accidentally committed suicide with me in her arms. The coroner concluded it was an accidental overdose. She mixed too many different pills, and it caused her to go into cardiac arrest. My stepdad never let me forget that she accidentally took her life.

I was punished daily for her sins.

Whether I was awake or asleep.

He turned into a different man after her funeral. He was barely ever home and when he was, he was half the man he used to be. He was drunk more often than not, empty whiskey bottles littered the house, replacing the empty pill bottles my mother always left lying around.

Except to the outside world, he was still the perfect, doting stepfather.

I was only twelve years old but felt way older. I guess maybe my whole life had been that way. I went through more than any kid my age was supposed to.

But I never let that define me.

Thank God for my ballet instructor Susan, I couldn't survive without my dancing. It was my escape from the Hell I had been through since that morning.

My only form of therapy.

All the parents and the kids knew what my mom did. We lived in a small town in Rhode Island, and nothing stayed behind closed doors. If I thought the kids alienating me before my mother decided to end her life, I was wrong. Now I pretty much lived in my own little world, where I lived and breathed ballet.

"You doing okay, Lexi?" Susan asked, pulling me away from my thoughts.

"Yes, Ma'am." I nodded, stretching my leg up on the top barre.

"Everything okay at home?" she pried, walking over to adjust my posture.

I shrugged, not wanting to tell her the truth. I never told anyone what happened at home. Too scared to be judged, too terrified of what would happen, too afraid of the truth itself. So, I kept my mouth shut, it was easier that way.

"You know you can always talk to me, right?" she assured me, locking eyes with me through the full-length mirror.

I nodded again, smiling. Desperately wanting to take her up on her offer, but again frightened by the repercussions.

"You want to go through that new routine again?"

"I'd love that." Breathing a sigh of relief the questioning was over.

For now, at least.

I spent the rest of the afternoon lost in the tranquil beauty of the music, running my routine till my legs were shaking. Susan dropped me off like she always did when I stayed late. Never letting me ride my bike home when it was dark, knowing it wasn't safe.

Little did she know my house wasn't either.

I walked into the pitch-black house, waving good-bye to Susan. It looked as if my stepdad hadn't been home all day, which only meant he was drinking out tonight. I went straight into the shower, letting the warm water seep into my sore muscles. Stretching again before I went to bed.

I tried to fall asleep, but I couldn't. It never mattered how hard I ran myself ragged. How much I pushed every last muscle in my body, how exhausted and drained my joints were. I wouldn't allow myself to drift off to sleep.

I would always wait.

It was better that way.

It wouldn't take long until I felt him.

It. Never. Did.

"Baby…" I heard him whisper above me, the scent of strong liquor immediately assaulting my senses. "Baby, I miss you so much…"

I pretended I wasn't there. I hummed Swan Lake in my head, getting lost in the symmetry and rhythm of the gentle lull of my movements. Reciting every last step in my mind. Picturing I'm the prima ballerina for some huge ballet company.

I didn't hear him call me my mother's name.

I didn't listen to him telling me he loved her.

I didn't pay any mind to the fact that he thought I was her.

My mother.

I just lost myself in my own thoughts, where it was safe, where I was loved, where no one could hurt me.

When he touched me. When I felt his hands all over my skin, clawing, invading, molesting. When I smelled his breath all over my face. Attacking every last fiber of my being.

I fall.

Over and over again.

I go into a dark place within myself, hiding in the black corners of my mind.

Waiting.

I could feel myself drifting, fading into nothing. Broken in two. A cold remnant of the little girl I once was. A figment of the innocence I used to have, turning into dust. I didn't exist anymore and I was nothing.

I wanted to scream.

I wanted to cry.

I wanted to fight him off.

I did none of those things. Nothing. I laid there, and took it. I let myself get used, played with as if I was nothing but his toy. Because in the end it didn't matter, the damage had already been done. Again and again for the past year. The first time he did it, he told me, promised me it would never happen again. Then, there he was, in my bed a few months later. Days became weeks, and weeks became months.

Now I'm alone with the monster almost daily.
Except I once used to call him…
My stepdad.

Martinez

"Ve por ella, Esteban," I ordered, *"Go get her, Esteban."*

The sound of my voice echoed through the large, damp, concrete basement of the building I lived in. Esteban and I stood in the dead center of the open space, with my men waiting in the surrounding corners.

His intense, heated glare went from me, to the man who was knocked the fuck out in front of us. He was showcasing all my handy work, beaten within an inch of his life. Silver duct tape sealed his mouth and eyes shut, blood dripped down his bruised, mangled face. His arms tied behind his back, and his legs strapped to the steel chair he was sitting on. A plastic visqueen lined the area beneath him. His head was draped over like he was dead, but the motherfucker was still alive.

"Are you sure you want to do this? She's sound asleep in her bed," he responded, not moving an inch.

I cocked an eyebrow. "Are you questioning my authority? Because I strongly suggest you fucking listen, and go get my niece. Unless you want to end up like this fucker." I kicked the chair, causing the man to stir.

It was Briggs' fifteenth birthday at midnight, and I had brought her a little something to celebrate. She was the guest of honor, and the show couldn't start without her.

After years, I finally got the motherfucker.

A few nights prior to today's events, I came home late from a business trip, not bothering to let Daisy know I had returned, I never did. I headed straight to my office to tie up some loose ends since I'd been away a few days. I shut the door behind me and switched on the video feed from the cameras I had all over the penthouse. Wanting to make sure things were continuing to run as smooth as always during my absence. It wasn't much of a surprise to see Esteban and Daisy on the couch, watching a movie together. He was ordered to never let her out of his sight, so he was around her all the time as her bodyguard.

Just her goddamn bodyguard.

I wasn't a fucking idiot. I knew Daisy had a crush on him, but I couldn't control that. What I could control was what Esteban did about it. My niece was gorgeous. She had long brown hair and bright blue eyes, exactly like her mother. Looking, and acting, more and more like Amari as the years went on. There were times where I couldn't even tell the difference, she had the snarky little mouth too. I found myself almost calling her by her mother's name on several occasions, but catching myself before it left my mouth. Esteban was young, but he was still older than Daisy. I knew if he touched her or gave her a thread of hope, the crush would have turned into love somewhere along the way.

Then I would have no choice but to cut off his cock and put a fucking bullet in his head.

Not thinking twice about it.

Daisy had been with me for almost nine years. I knew she had a hard time at school, and with life in general. Everyone knew who I was, what I did. Kids treated her like shit because their parents feared me and hated what I stood for, leaving me no choice but to have her move schools several times.

I owned New York City.

Everyone loathed her because of it, reminding me of my childhood. She hated it as much as I did. I saw a lot of my youth in her, it was hard not to. Except, she didn't have any friends. Parents told their kids to stay away from the Mitchell girl. I, on the other hand, had more than I ever cared for, but not for the right reasons.

Leo was the only true friend I had growing up. To this day, he is the only person I could trust.

My confidant.

So, I gave him a job as my financial manager. Responsible for making sure I stayed rich as fuck. Daisy's so called friends consisted of the characters in the books she was constantly reading. Always had her damn nose in a book, while most kids would be out playing and having fun together. I always made sure she had the books she wanted. Who was I to complain, it kept her out of my hair at least for a little while.

I may not have been involved in her life directly, but there was never anything that Briggs ever wanted, that I didn't get her.

Including revenge.

She admitted to Esteban how she felt responsible for her parent's death, but not going into much detail on why she felt that way to begin with.

He sighed. "This won't change—"

"Dime, Esteban," I demanded. *"Tell me."* Cocking my head to the side, narrowing my eyes at him. "You are aware she's a child, right? Esto puede cambiar todo," I added, *"This can change everything."*

"With violence?" he questioned, having the balls to step toward me.

"With justice," I countered, shoving him away. "Now are you going to fucking get her? Or do I have to make you?"

He reluctantly nodded, making his way over to the elevator and hitting the button.

"Esteban," I called out, causing him to look over his shoulder at me. "She's fifteen. Keep your dick in your pants, unless you want me to shoot it off."

He spun, facing me, surrendering his hands. "Señor, eso—"

"That wasn't a question." The elevator doors opened and I nodded toward them, dismissing him.

He finally fucking left, but it took longer than I expected for him to return with Daisy. As soon as the doors opened again, she came into view. Esteban retreated to the corner of the basement, wanting to hide from the scene before him. Her eyes were closed tight, she knew that tonight her life would change once again, shaking any sense of comfort.

Struck with the coppery scent of blood that lingered in the damp space, she stood there, unmoving. She slowly, cautiously opened her eyes, holding onto the courage for as long as she could. I could smell her fear from a distance, there was no mistaking it.

"Por fin," I stated, breaking the silence, *"Finally."*

Her eyes widened as she took in the scene in front of her, it was then she checked out.

163

She was there, but she wasn't. I was fine with that, the end result would grant her peace, and it was all I wanted for her.

"Venga," I ordered, "*Come*."

She looked back at Esteban who was standing in the corner of the room, the shame and remorse eating him alive.

Her.

"I bring you a gift, and this is how you react?" I voiced, bringing her attention back to me.

I leaned up against the wall behind the motherfucker in the chair. My arms folded over my chest, one leg draped over the other. The sleeves of my shirt were rolled up, the ends covered in blood.

"A gift?" she whispered loud enough for me to hear.

"Briggs, I won't tell you again. Come here."

She stepped off the elevator, the doors closed behind her, causing her to jump. She shuddered, wrapping her arms around her chest in a comforting gesture. Suddenly cold.

I grinned. "Are you scared?"

She didn't know how to reply, so she didn't say anything at all. Not realizing I noticed as she dug her nails into the palms of her hands, to keep from passing out.

I noticed everything, especially how much she reminded me of myself, that night in my father's office.

I spoke with conviction, "You're my niece. You're the daughter of my only sister, who I loved very fucking much. I would never physically hurt you. Don't you ever fucking offend me like that again, by letting that thought cross your mind. Do you understand me?"

She peered down at the fucker in the chair, taking in all the blood, ignoring my question. I let her have it just this one time. I couldn't fucking blame her, I wouldn't trust me, the devil, either.

I followed her stare. "It was a hit and run," I answered the question, which had been reeling in her mind from the minute she opened her eyes.

Her head snapped, and our gazes locked.

"And this," I nodded toward the chair, "is the man who ran," I declared, needing her to understand the point of tonight.

The peace I was giving her.

164

The both of us…

Her eyes scanned his body, confused and overwhelmed by the turn of events. She couldn't look away from the motherfucker's gruesome appearance. Especially the name "Amari" I'd carved into his chest.

She sucked in a breath.

I jerked my neck toward Esteban, who understood my silent command. He made his way to the fucker, his eyes pleading with Daisy to forgive him for what was about to happen.

It was time she saw him for what he truly was. Anyone who worked for me did the Devil's dirty work.

He roughly ripped off the tape from his eyes, followed by his mouth, before throwing a bucket of freezing cold water on his face, causing him to stir into consciousness. Gasping for air that wasn't available for the taking.

Esteban quickly retreated back to the corner of the basement, proving to me he was in love with my fucking niece.

The motherfucker strapped to the chair, immediately started screaming and thrashing around like the pussy he was. I didn't pay him any mind. He deserved everything he was about to get. Actually, he should have considered himself lucky it wasn't much worse. Trust me, it would have been, had Daisy not been in the room, witnessing.

This wasn't about me, and it took everything in me to remember that. It was for her. For the first time in her life, I could see her internal struggle between right and wrong. Wanting retribution for the lives of her parents. For the purgatory she was forced to live in daily.

With me.

"You didn't kill your parents, Briggs. He did," I reminded, fueling her battle of good versus evil.

"LIAR!" he yelled out, and I resisted the urge to knock him the fuck out again. He was scaring her. I craved to place my hands over her ears, her eyes.

To hide.

From him.

From me.

From herself.

Evil always won. I made goddamn sure of it.

"YOU'RE A FUCKING LIAR!" he screamed bloody murder, whipping around even harder, faster, almost making the chair fall over. Used to the theatrics.

No one paid him any mind as she visibly struggled with her conflicting emotions. One right after the other.

"It's midnight," I stated, ready to get this fucking show over with. I raised my gun, pointing it directly at the back of his head. He suddenly stopped moving, seizing all movement, even his breathing. He knew.

They always knew.

She screamed, shaking. "No! No! No! You don't have to do this!"

"Happy fifteenth birthday, Daisy."

And with that...

I pulled the trigger, blowing his fucking head off.

Twenty-one
Lexi

Tonight was my ballet recital. I was thirteen and one of the top girls in my ballet class. The velvet curtain opened and the spotlight beamed on me, ready to follow my every move around the stage. It was a full house that night, but I wasn't nervous. I was performing a solo to George Gershwin's "Rhapsody in Blue." A very intense, bluesy piece I'd worked months on perfecting. The music came through the speakers, and I was immediately transported to my happy place.

The instrumental jazzy rhythm assaulted my senses, taking over my body, manipulating it like a master puppeteer. Carrying me from step to step. The tempo went from fast to slow and vice versa. Sauté arabesque stage right, Piqué attitude, ballet run to center stage. Taking a deep breath for the hardest part of the performance, rond de jambe to fourth position, plié preparing for ten Fouetté turns which I was yet to nail without a stumble.

Turning and turning, the lights blurring in the distance as my leg whipped me around. Landing the combination of turns without faltering even a little bit. I smiled big as I leaped through the air, finishing my routine with a pirouette and a bow. The spotlight faded and the stage turned dark. The audience exploded in applause. This was my second favorite part of dancing, the admiration and the love, even if only for a few seconds I mattered to someone.

When I took my bow at the end of my performance, my eyes wandered over the crowd, trying to find him. The blinding lights obscured my vision though and a sense of relief washed over me. Not seeing his smug face among the patrons was a blessing. He never missed a performance, no matter what, he was always sitting somewhere usually lurking in the shadows, hiding in plain sight.

I hated him.

The mere thought of him made me sick to my stomach, and my skin crawl. I immediately hoped something bad happened to him, causing him not to be here tonight. Then I loathed him even more for making me wish bad things. I never wanted him to know he changed me in any shape or form. Thinking that he'd won, or that I was broken.

He may have owned my body, but I preserved my soul. The second I turned eighteen I would be gone and out of his grasp. He would never be able to crawl in my bed and touch me with his filthy hands. He'd never see me again. He would be dead in my eyes, along with my past, and all the shit I've been through.

I would win.

My life would be mine.

Only mine.

I stayed behind after the recital to help Susan clean up. It was late by the time we left the auditorium. I silently hoped he was passed out drunk when I walked inside. But I knew I wasn't that lucky. Even hammered as shit, he'd manage to find me.

I said goodnight to Susan, waving to her before I stepped foot inside. The entire house was pitch black, a rare occurrence. He always kept a light on, making sure he could see through the haze of his drunken stupor. I shook off the eerie feeling, going straight for the shower. Dreading the rest of the night that hadn't even started yet.

Most kids loved going to bed, ending their day. Hating that tomorrow was another school day. Me, I looked forward to it. I stayed in the shower until the water ran cold, like I always did. Rubbing all of my sore muscles, washing my hair a few times, letting my conditioner stay on longer than needed.

Prolonging the inevitable any way I could.

I threw on a hoodie and some pajama pants, even though it was hotter than Hell outside. I was still always cold, at least that's what I told myself. Sometimes if I layered my clothes, he would be too drunk to find his way in. Not being able to get under all the armor I shielded my body with. I'd thought that through the years he would start doing more than just molesting me, expecting me to do things back to him. Or worse, rape me.

He didn't.

Thank God for small miracles, except now I hated being touched, even when dancing, I couldn't stand the feel of people's hands on me. Stemming from my mom dying with her arms wrapped around me, to my piece of shit stepdad touching me, pretending I was her.

It didn't matter. I didn't need anyone. All I needed was ballet and myself.

I took one last look in the mirror, trying to see what he talked about. Looking for my mother through the reflection, staring back at me. I never saw her. The image of her dead body was engrained in my mind, too engaged in my soul, too attached in my heart.

I shook off the thoughts, turning off the light before I walked into my bedroom. It was then that I saw it. A torn out piece of paper from my notebook, placed on my pillow.

I sat down on the edge of my bed, running my fingers over my stepdads handwriting. Hesitating to read what he had to say.

Lexi,

I want you to know I'm sorry. I can't begin to tell you how sorry I am for everything I have ever done to you. I never meant to hurt you. I never meant to cause you any pain or distress. I'm sick, Lexi. I'm a very sick, fucked up man, and I can't stop hurting you. No matter how many times I tell my mind it's wrong, it doesn't listen. It's like an addiction. And because I can't stop, I have decided that I'm leaving. I can feel myself about to cross a line that even someone like me knows is sick. I don't deserve your forgiveness. I don't expect it either. I left some money on the kitchen counter that should get you by for a little while. Please have peace of mind that you won't ever see me again.

I promise.

I read the letter until I had it memorized word for word. Staring at it for, I don't know how long, thinking it was a joke. Waiting for him to walk through the front door. He would come home. He would keep hurting me. This wasn't truly over.

For some reason I started crying. Tears streamed down my face onto the paper that held his final goodbye. For the first time since my mother left me with this monster.

169

I could finally breathe again.
I was relieved.
Even though…
I was alone.

Martinez

She ran. She ran as if her life depended on it, not being able to get away fast enough. Reacting exactly how I expected her to. I let her go, giving her the space I'm sure she needed to wrap her head around what she just saw. At least now, I felt that she'd have peace in her soul. Knowing she wasn't responsible for the death of her parents. I wanted to be her savior, not the monster that haunted her dreams every night since she was six.

"Clean up this fucking mess," I ordered, leaving my men to it. My bodyguard followed close behind. "Stay," I ordered him as I stepped into the elevator.

"Boss—" I hit the button to the rooftop, letting the doors close in his face.

As soon as they were shut, I let out a long breath from deep within my soul. Leaning my head against the wall, ascending toward heaven.

The irony was not lost on me.

I made my way toward the edge of the roof, looking out over Manhattan. My hands placed in the pockets of my slacks, not giving a fuck that they were still blood covered. Enjoying how it felt to be by myself, no protection around me. Standing at the top of the building.

Vulnerable.

Exposed.

Alone.

Taking in the high-rise buildings, the night air, the dark sky, the lights illuminating the streets, and the cars driving in the distance. I took in every last detail, trying to come down from the high from killing someone always gave me. Trying to ignore my plaguing conscious, which was trying to reprimand me for what I just did in front of my niece.

Amari's daughter.

I knew she was probably rolling over in her grave right now, so disappointed in me, and my actions.

My decisions.

My choices.

My indiscretions.

I couldn't help but think how many times my sister had been disheartened since I gained custody of Daisy.

Did she regret leaving her in my care?

I could see Amari standing in front of me, shaking her head with tears streaming down her face. Staring at the monster, the spitting image of our father glaring back at her.

I didn't know the difference between good versus evil anymore. It all blended together, forming a clusterfuck of God knows what. For the first time in as long as I could remember, I struggled with my decision. Not knowing if I had done the right thing in this situation. Or if I just condemned Daisy even more. Regret started creeping in slowly.

Why didn't I just let her sleep?

Let her keep the small piece of innocence I just crudely ripped away from her. Sat her down like a normal human being, and told her the truth, giving her peace of mind that way. The questions were endless and unforgiving. There was a fine line between right and wrong. I had done so much wrong I was now excusing it for making it seem like I was doing something right for Daisy. When all I really did was contaminate the poor girl.

Making her more like me.

"I'm sorry, Amari," I whispered into the dark. I hadn't apologized to anyone since the day I was in Daisy's hospital room years ago. Nine fucking years those two words had not left my lips. "Fuck…" I breathed out, running my hands through my hair, too much bullshit weighing on my mind. "I've lost my way, sister. I don't know who I am anymore. There are days where I can't even look at myself in the mirror. Disgusted with what is staring back at me… our father. I wish you were here. I wish you were here every fucking day," I confessed. "I know I'm fucking this up.

171

Daisy, your daughter. My niece. Is the only thing that's keeping me alive. I'm tired, Amari... I'm so fucking tired." Rubbing my hands down my face.

The smell of his blood immediately assaulted my senses, every last fiber of my being.

"I see so much of you in her, it's fucking scary. And I can't... I won't allow her to know or see how much I love her. I'll give her the world, Amari. She will never want for anything. But I can't give her my love. I can't let her into my fucking hollow heart." I felt myself losing it as I looked into my sister's eyes. "Mamá must be so disappointed in me. Please tell her I am so sorry, so fucking sorry. I can't go back. I can't change the things I've done. I am who I am. It's too late, the darkness settled in. I own it now. It owns me. Please forgive me, I know I don't deserve it, but I'm asking for it anyway." I looked up at the sky, and she was gone. Vanishing into the thick air that surrounded me. "I love you, Amari."

I stayed up there for I don't know how long, repenting for my sins. Trying to find the man I once was, already knowing he died a long time ago. I took one last look at the world I created, and left. Taking the elevator back to my penthouse floor. Wanting to go straight to my office like I always did, and drown myself in work. Hoping it would mask the voices of Amari and my mother that filled my mind. Wanting to tone out the screaming.

I didn't have to go into my office to stop my conscious from spinning out of control. The moaning coming from Daisy's room put a halt to everything. The closer I got to her bedroom, the more profound her sounds of ecstasy echoed down the halls. I didn't have to wonder who the fuck she was with.

Or what the fuck I was going to do to him. His fate was decided a long time ago. Now, he gave me another reason to put a fucking bullet in his head.

His first mistake was betraying me in my own home. His second error was not locking the goddamn door. Not that it would have stopped me. Wanting to use the element of surprise, I slowly pushed down the handle, slipping into the room unnoticed. He was laying on top of her, the sheet barely covering their bodies.

Rage quickly took over every last fiber of my being. It didn't matter that I had just killed a man. I wanted to kill another.

This motherfucker.

"Ah—" I didn't falter, interrupting Daisy from her happy fucking ending.

I sprang into action with nothing but fury coursing through me. "YOU, MOTHERFUCKER!" I roared.

Daisy screamed, jolting out of her skin as I roughly ripped Esteban away from her. Throwing his body across the room, his back hit the wall with a loud, hard thud, tearing through the drywall. I was over to him in two strides, picking him up and slamming him up against the doorframe. Hearing a hasty crack in its wake.

"YOU PIECE OF FUCKING SHIT! AFTER EVERYTHING I'VE DONE FOR YOU!" I snarled, picking him up off the ground again and punching him in the face repeatedly.

His body fell lax against my strong grip. I didn't let up, punching him in the stomach, causing him to fall forward, crumbling to the ground in front of me. I immediately bent down, flipping him onto his back and straddling his waist, beating him to an inch of his life.

"NO!" Daisy screamed from where she knelt on the bed. She hadn't moved, barely making a sound, the entire time I beat the fuck out of him. "PLEASE! STOP! PLEASE I'M BEGGING YOU! I'LL DO ANYTHING! ANYTHING!"

I ignored her pathetic pleas, continuing my assault on Esteban's face and body. I hit him until my knuckles felt raw, and there was nothing left of his fucking pretty boy face. I stopped and stood over his barely conscious frame, hearing Daisy release a sigh of relief. Thinking she'd won. That she got through to me.

Not a fucking chance.

I reached into the back of my slacks, and pulled out my gun, aiming it right at Esteban's head.

"NO!" she cried out.

Jumping off the bed, lunging right in front of him, throwing her half naked body in front of the gun. It was now placed directly on her forehead. Her body shielding what was left of Esteban's sorry excuse of a fucking life.

173

"Get the fuck out of my face," I gritted through a clenched jaw.

"No! Please! Please! Please! I'm begging you. It wasn't his fault." She got down on her knees, tucking the thin white sheet under her arms, setting her hands in a prayer gesture out in front of her. "I'm begging you, pleading with you on my knees to please not do this! Please, Uncle! You don't have to do this!" she bellowed through tears.

I scoffed. "You think your pitiful performance is going to work on me? You don't know me, peladita. Get the fuck off the floor before I make you, and trust me, you don't want it to come to that."

She shook her head. "No."

I cocked my head to the side, no one had ever told me no before. I would be lying if I said I wasn't just a little fucking proud of her at that moment, she wasn't backing down from me.

"You look like a fucking whore on your knees. NOW, GET THE FUCK UP!"

She shook her head again. "No."

"What? You love him? You love that piece of shit?" I pointed to Esteban's lifeless body.

She swallowed, hard. "No, Uncle. I don't," she answered honestly.

The truth of her revelation causing me to jerk my head back, stunned.

"So, you are a whore," I viscously spewed, more pissed off at myself for allowing this to happen under my goddamn nose. "Your mother would be so proud."

She frowned not wavering. "Please. Please, don't do this. Not for me, okay? You don't have to do shit for me. Do it for my mom. The only sister you had. The one you loved so fucking much," she reminded, throwing the words I spoke hours ago back at me.

My eyes glazed over, narrowing them at her. For the first time I didn't hide the fact that the mere mention of her mother could bring me to my goddamn knees.

I slowly lowered my gun, grabbing my phone from my pocket, and walking toward the big bay window in her room, calling one of my men. "Venga a recoger a este hijo de puta antes de que yo lo

174

mate," I roared into the phone, *"Come get this son of a bitch before I kill him."* I hung up.

Her questions of who I really was, what I was feeling, what I had gone through in my life, what happened to me that made me the way I was, were burning a hole in my back. She wanted to know what I was thinking.

If only she knew…

If only *anyone* knew.

I shook away the thoughts when I heard footsteps ascending down the hall. I took one look at my men, and nodded toward the piece of shit lying in my niece's arms. Turning to face the window once again, internally battling my demons. Not being able to look at her any longer, feeling as though this changed everything.

They quickly picked him up, dragging him away from her. I heard them taking the blanket off the bed and wrapping it around him. I knew he was half-conscious when the men stood him up, probably hunched over, reeling in pain. Placing his arms around their necks for support.

If it weren't for Daisy, they'd be dragging him out in a body bag.

Even that didn't grant me satisfaction.

This was the last time I would see my niece as Daisy, this was when Briggs was born for me. This was when everything changed in our dynamic, our future relationship.

Our family.

She wanted to be a big girl, play with big boys, then I would give her exactly what she fucking wanted.

They carried Esteban toward the door, breaking me from my train of thought.

"You know what?" I said out of nowhere, bringing all of their attention back to me. I turned around, narrowing my dark, daunting, soulless eyes directly at Esteban. "I changed my mind," I simply stated.

And before it registered what I just said. I lifted my gun and shot him.

"NO!" Briggs yelled out, placing her hand over her mouth.

Hearing him groan out in pain was when she realized I shot him in the leg, inches away from his goddamn cock.

175

"The next time you fuck with what's mine, Esteban, the bullet will go in your fucking head."

With that, the men turned and left, leaving a trail of his blood on the floor.

"Briggs," I announced, lost in my thoughts again, staring at her shred of innocence that stained the sheets on the bed.

I walked over to her, every step precise and calculated with the same vicious expression on my face. There was nothing but a hatred, spewing glare in hers. I gripped her chin harshly, forcing her to look up, making her look me dead in the eyes.

Using the same words my father said to me the night my innocence was taken.

I spoke with conviction, "You're a Martinez now."

And she was.

Twenty-two
Martinez

"There he is," I nodded toward the black car pulling up alongside my strip club. "Supply him with the usual," I added, turning to go back inside. I didn't need to stick around, Rick was one of my trusted men, he dealt with the exchanges.

I needed to get back into my office, to make a phone call to Briggs. I was sending her to Miami for the next month, to handle some business that just came up. She had been working for me for the last two years, dealing drugs. She dropped out of school a few days after her fifteenth birthday. A birthday I choose to fucking forget. I made the decision to bring her into the family business that night, after I found her with that motherfucker, Esteban. He was lucky he was still alive, working some corporate job upstate.

At least this way I knew what Briggs was doing, and who she was doing. I could keep an eye on her, and by that I mean...

I could still control her.

At the end of the day it kept her safe, and I didn't give a shit if it was the right thing to do or not. It was *my* way of making things right for her.

I never sent her on dangerous deliveries. It was mostly college parties and meetings which she only attended in my presence. Meaningless shit like that. Everyone knew she was my niece. If someone fucked with her, they fucked with me. And no one wanted to fuck with me.

"How much does he owe?" Rick asked.

"Thirteen grand."

"You let him keep half?" he questioned, grabbing my arm to stop me. I looked from my arm to him, and he released his grip, stepping back. Once again peering in front of him.

177

"He pushes drugs for me at NYU. Supplying all the punk ass kids with their fix, taking Mommy and Daddy's money. You want to do it?"

He shook his head, smiling. "I would for the pussy. I mean look at that girl, she's a fucking knockout."

I spun, looking in the direction of his gaze. "What the fuck?" I breathed out, watching her step out of the backseat of the piece of shit car they pulled up in.

"Don't like them young, boss?" Rick nudged my shoulder, earning him another 'touch me again, motherfucker,' look.

"I don't like being blindsided," I gritted out through a clenched jaw, adjusting my suit jacket as I fully turned to face him. "What the fuck is she doing here?" I snapped as soon as they walked up to me.

"Oh... that's umm... shit... Lexi, I told you to stay in the fucking car," Luis, my dealer from NYU, shouted at her. Peering back and forth between us, nervous as shit. Anxiously rubbing the back of his neck. "It's fine, she's cool," he contested, shuffling his feet in the dirt below him. Looking everywhere but in my eyes.

"Who the fuck do you think you are, bringing a little girl here?" I stepped toward him, shadowing over his scrawny frame. He stumbled back, catching himself before he fell on his ass.

"I'm not a little girl," Lexi interrupted, stepping forward. Immediately bringing my attention to her.

She stood in front of Luis with her hip cocked and her hand leaning on it. Not backing down, a challenging glare in her eyes. She was definitely a feisty little one, her demeanor ready to strike back at anything I had to say to her.

No matter what.

"Luis, I would have never pegged you for a pussy. This girl has bigger balls than you do. You must have forgotten to warn her who the fuck she's dealing with. Oh, wait... she shouldn't fucking be here in the first place."

They all stood in the middle of the parking lot, as I paced back and forth, never taking my eyes off Lexi. She shifted her weight from one hip to the other, swinging her hair over her shoulder with nothing but intrigue written all over her face. Studying my

178

predatory stance, wanting to know what I was thinking, what I was feeling.

"I don't like to be disrespected, Luis. And this little stunt doesn't sit fucking well with me. Rick, what do you think we should do? A bullet to his leg? Or maybe something to this little girl over here," I taunted, stopping in front of Lexi.

She still hadn't taken her eyes off me. I cocked my head to the side, taking in the fact she didn't fear me. I couldn't remember the last time that happened.

"No, sir... Lexi, go back to the damn car. Now!" Luis ordered, roughly grabbing her arm and tugging her sideways, harder than he needed to.

"Ow! Easy, asshole," she yelped.

I didn't hesitate. I stepped toward them, pulling her away from his grasp, and shoving him hard in the chest. He lost his footing, stumbling to the ground. A few women standing in line waiting to get into the club gasped. Crouching down in front of his face, I grabbed him by the collar of his shirt.

Ignoring our audience, I gritted out, "Didn't your mother ever teach you not to put your hands on a woman? Do I need to teach you some fucking manners, boy?"

He fervently shook his head no.

I scoffed in disgust, releasing him from my grasp, and pushing him back down to the ground. I stood and turned around, narrowing my eyes at Lexi. Finally getting a good look at her. Disregarding the way she was still staring at me.

Without saying a word, I placed my hands in the pockets of my slacks, gradually eyeing her five-foot-four frame up and down with a fascinated regard. She had long, dark brown hair, cascading all around her face, and legs went on for days. She wore a white tattered t-shirt, two sizes too big, knotted at her hip, exposing her stomach, and cut off jean shorts with the pockets hanging out the bottoms.

She was young.

A child.

A goddamn little girl.

She. Was. Trouble.

179

I took her in, inch by inch, until I knew I got the effect I wanted out of her. It was easy for me to intimidate people, and she wasn't any fucking different. Except there was a sudden flush in her cheeks was subtle enough to where no one would notice, other than me.

I noticed everything.

Especially her.

I made her nervous, but not because she was scared of me as I intended…

Even at that young of age, this girl knew what she wanted.

Me.

The attraction was coming off her in waves. Her mind reeling with mixed emotions, thinking I could be her savior, or her possible demise. All little girls wanted a Prince Charming. A knight in shining fucking armor.

Little did she know, I was the villain in this story.

We locked eyes, and for a split second, I saw something familiar in her bright green stare. Something I had always seen in mine, only now, it was being reflected back at me.

Solitude.

A raw, agonizing burn in her gaze. A pain no one else could understand, or even recognize, unless they've lived through it themselves. An unspoken connection brought on by darkness.

Hell.

A group of rowdy customers exited the club, interrupting the moment we were having. She shook off the sentiment, clearing her throat. I made her uncomfortable because she knew I could see and feel it too.

She knew I could see and feel everything.

"Take a picture, old man, it will last you longer," she spewed, wanting to break the effect I was having on her.

I smiled, arching an eyebrow. "There's no need for name calling, little girl. Rick isn't that fucking old," I chuckled, pointing over to him.

She wanted to smile, but she hid it by looking over toward the busy street instead. Not wanting me to see any more than I already had. She was trying to take control of the situation we found ourselves in. Her vulnerability radiated off of her, making her feel weak and out of control. As much as she hated it, she loved it even more.

I realized right then, this girl needed to stay the fuck away from me, and she didn't strike me as anyone who followed fucking directions.

I glared at Luis who was brushing himself off. "Don't bring the little girl with you again. I won't warn you next time."

"If you have something to say, say it to me. I'm standing right here. For your information, he didn't bring me. I came with him, and if I want to come with him again, I will. You can't tell me what to do just because you're old enough to be my father, old man."

Not faltering, I turned my attention back to her. Stepping right into her personal space, my six-foot-four muscular build looming over her petite frame. She didn't cower, if anything she stood taller. I cocked my head to the side, reaching for a piece of her hair, twirling it around my finger.

"Old man, eh? Your lips are saying one thing but your body... your body is betraying you, *little girl*. It doesn't think I'm old. It likes me just fine..." Just to prove my point, I brushed my knuckles along her cheek, enjoying the soft feel of her skin.

Her breathing hitched and her eyes dilated.

"My body and my actions are none of your business and stop calling me a little girl," she replied in a sultry voice.

"You became my business as soon as you stepped foot on my property, and you being here has fucked with that. You're a child. Can't be older than what? Fifteen?"

She grimaced, embarrassed. Looking around the parking lot, avoiding me at all costs.

"I can smell it on you. You want me. Is this turning you on, *little girl*?" I scoffed, taking my hand away from her face.

The loss of my touch clearly affecting her.

"You look me in the eyes when I'm talking to you." I grabbed her chin, bringing her gaze back to mine.

Her eyes widened and her lips parted as I gripped her chin harder. "This is an adult establishment, the best one in New York City. Women take their clothes off for money, a lot of it. You want to come back? I suggest you come for an audition when you grow a pair of tits and an ass. Until then, you're no use to me. Now be a good little girl, turn around, and go sit your ass in the fucking car. If you don't listen, I won't hesitate to take you over my knee and teach you some goddamn respect like your father should have."

I was finally getting to her. She immediately jerked her face back, away from my grasp. The hurt evident all over her solemn expression.

All I wanted to do was put an end to this conversation, or any fucking illusions of who she thought I was in her head. I didn't have time for this bullshit, the last thing I needed was to fucking babysit.

I spoke with conviction, "Go play with your Barbie dolls, sweetheart. Let the men handle business." And with that I abruptly turned, walking back toward the club's back entrance.

"Take care of it, Rick," I called over my shoulder, never once looking back.

I saw him before we even pulled into the parking lot of the strip club on Twenty-third Street. It was known to be one of the most pristine establishment in New York City. At least for a strip club anyway.

It wasn't hard to miss him. The man was built like a brick house, muscular, solid and tall. Standing at least a half foot taller than the guy next to him. They were obviously having a heated conversation. I never wanted to be a fly on the wall more than I did at that moment.

I couldn't stop staring at him, the man exuded dominance. He was dressed in an expensive suit, which probably cost more than the piece of shit car I was sitting in. His black hair was slicked back away from his face. I pictured it falling at the end the day, framing his narrow cheekbones perfectly. He was devilishly handsome. Tan skin that can only be accomplished from spending hours under the sun, a masculine face and nose that highlighted his strong cheekbones and jawline. His dark facial hair only added to his appeal. He was a fine specimen. His bright blue eyes are what caught my attention though. They looked like they could reach into your soul and possess you.

He wasn't even looking at me, and I could feel him all over.

I was drawn to a man who had to be twice my age, like a magnet. Feeling his pull on me. But, I couldn't help it. I was fifteen years old, and it was the first time in my life I ever felt an attraction to someone. I hated guys. I steered clear of them at school, even my poor foster father who never did anything to me.

Yet, there I was, physically propelled toward a man I had never met before. There was something about him, and I could see that from a block away. I felt like I had seen him before, met him somewhere, but I knew it was impossible.

Where would I have met a man like this?

His presence was comforting and afflicting all at once. The way he just stood there, consumed me in ways I never thought possible. There was a predatory, yet captivating look in his eyes, like he had the answer to every question I ever thought of. I couldn't tear my gaze away from his, and I didn't want to.

I could watch this man all day, and it still wouldn't be enough.

My heart pounded out of my chest as we pulled into the crowded parking lot just after midnight. I stared out the passenger window ignoring all the rich and probably famous people, dressed to the nines. A line wrapped around the huge building with customers eager to go inside and get a taste of the erotic dancers.

Luis put the car in park, glancing over at me. "Lexi, stay in the car. I will only be a few minutes. Lock the doors, okay?"

"I know why we're here, Luis. You do remember smoking weed with me, right? You used to live in my neighborhood. Your parents still do. I know you sell drugs at NYU. I'm not stupid."

"Stay in the fucking car, Lexi. You don't know what this man is capable of. I didn't tell him I was bringing anyone."

"Then why did you bring me?"

"You know why… Your fucking foster parents are having another one of their parties. You don't need to be there."

"I've been there since you've been away at college," I whispered loud enough for him to hear.

183

Luis was always nice to me. He was almost twenty-years-old and had been looking out for me for the past two years. Ever since I moved in with my foster parents.

"Lexi, just fucking listen. Why is that so hard for you to do?"

I shrugged, nodding, annoyed as I watched him open the car door. I couldn't blame him for wanting to make money on the side. His parents didn't have any, often leaving him to fend for himself, exactly like I had to. I never realized how expensive college could be until my advisor at school told me. She said I would have to apply for all kinds of loans and grants if I ever wanted to be admitted into a good school. The only one I was interested in was Julliard, and I had no idea how I was going to make my dream come true.

After my stepdad ran off, it only took three days for the principal to call me into his office to tell me they got an anonymous phone call, informing them I was home with no parental supervision. A few hours later I was sitting in Child Protective Services, waiting to meet my caseworker. They looked for him everywhere and I secretly prayed every night they would never find him.

They didn't.

I had been thanking God ever since. It didn't take long for them to place me with a family. I was only at the boarding house a few weeks top, which was surprising because I was technically not an ideal foster candidate. Meaning, I wasn't a baby or a toddler. The only downfall was I had to move from the only place I'd ever known to Manhattan. Leaving behind Susan and my dance studio. I often wished she would have adopted me, letting me stay in my home town.

We wrote emails to each other every so often, but I never got up the nerve to ask her why she couldn't take me in. Too apprehensive about what her answer would be. The last thing I wanted was to stay in a place I wasn't welcome. My foster parents weren't so bad though. I'd been living with them in a small New York apartment near the Manhattan Bridge for the last two years. They provided me with a roof over my head and food to eat, other than that, I was pretty much on my own.

Thank God there was a ballet studio not far from their home. I'd ride my bike over there every day after school, just to watch from the windows. Wishing I could be dancing like they were. Yearning for the music that once swept me away from reality, to take me away again. One day I got caught up in the melody, dancing right outside the studio along with the girls, while they were practicing a routine inside. It never crossed my mind that I could be seen, then the bell dinged above the studio entrance, startling me. I almost jumped out of my skin.

"Honey, you have been here for weeks. What are you doing out here?"

I bowed my head, embarrassed I'd been caught. "I'm sorry, ma'am. I was a dancer back home in Rhode Island. Watching you gives me peace. I apologize for interrupting your class, I will be going now," I said, walking past her to grab my bike.

"Don't be silly. Come inside. You probably know the routine better than most of my girls," the instructor gestured to the building.

She walked me in and introduced me to the other dancers. They were all very welcoming, inviting me to dance with them for the day. I didn't have to be told twice. When the class was over, the instructor told me I had a talent like she'd never seen before, and I was allowed to come to class as long as I helped out around the studio. I'd been there ever since.

The sound of the car door shutting brought me back to the present, pulling me away from my thoughts. Rolling down my window, I watched Luis walk toward the two men in suits. I sat there like I was told, for a second, fighting the urge to open the door. I hated being told what to do. I wasn't a child, I had never been.

Especially now.

I'd seen too much.

Experienced more than anyone my age should have.

Making me feel and act older than I actually was.

The wind effortlessly made its way into the car, bringing a strong masculine scent of cologne with it, assaulting my senses and every last fiber of my being. It had to be *him*. Before I even knew what I was doing, I stepped out of the car and followed Luis across the lot. I didn't receive the warm welcome I'd expected. To be honest, I didn't expect anything of what had just happened.

All I knew was my nerves were set on fire the entire time I stood there with them.

Watching him.

Inhaling him.

Feeling him.

A hot blaze roared through my body, like nothing I had ever experienced before. He had me questioning who he was, and how he had this hold on me. I hated and loved the new found feeling he produced deep within my core.

It was overwhelming.

It was frightening.

It was all consuming.

It. Was. Everything.

I wanted to know every single thing about him, including the man beneath the ruthless bastard...

Behind the power.

Behind the suit.

Behind the dominance.

Underneath the bright blue, soulless eyes which showed no emotion whatsoever. Not one.

"Lexi," Luis announced, parking his car in front of my house.

"Hmm..." I replied, still lost in my thoughts of tonight.

"Martinez has no sanctity of value for anything or anyone. Nothing is sacred to him. He respects nothing. It's why no one shakes his goddamn hand. He's a dirty, ruthless motherfucker, Lexi. You need to stay away from that son of a bitch. He won't think twice about fucking you over or fucking you period. You won't be fifteen forever. I know what you're thinking, I can see it in your eyes. And if I can see it, I know he could too."

I would remember his exact words for the next three years. Until I would see him again.

"It's why they call him... El Diablo."

Knowing all I wanted was to meet The Devil.

Twenty-three

Martinez

Austin Fucking Taylor, the good ol' boy who was proving to be a major pain in my ass. He was damn lucky he made my niece happy. The last thing I needed or wanted was for Briggs to fall in love with a fucking southern boy from Oak Island, North Carolina. But, fucking fate slapped me in the goddamn face again. You'd think I'd be used to it by now. She'd been with him for the past three years, playing house in the apartment I provided for her.

Not him.

They met in Miami at one of the parties I sent her to supply. Things didn't become official until I watched them run into each other a year later, on one of my cameras at the dance club I owned downtown.

I ran a background check immediately, discovering he was fucking harmless. He started traveling with her behind my back, and when I called her out on it, she conned me into hiring him as her bodyguard. I wasn't a goddamn idiot. I knew they were fucking each other. Briggs seemed to have a thing for bodyguards. All those romance books she read, she wanted a hero.

It wasn't like she needed defending, up until recently, with Hector. He had been an old acquaintance of mine, who wanted to fuck my niece since she grew tits and an ass. The second he requested a meeting alone with her, was the moment I knew I could test Austin. I just didn't know he would show up to the meeting, fucked up on *my* drugs. Both of them trying to recover from the three days of non-stop partying with clients. Things went south fast. Austin was lucky I didn't put a fucking bullet in his head. Hector, on the other hand, wasn't so lucky.

Needless to say, Austin passed with flying colors, defending Briggs with his life. Exactly what I was paying him a fuck load of money to do. But, it wasn't about the cash. He loved Briggs, even a blind man could see it, the man wore it proudly.

A man like me could respect that about a man like him. He wasn't made for this life, and neither was Briggs, but that didn't stop me from bringing her into it anyway.

I heard the lock release on Briggs' apartment door. She lived there, but I owned it. The door swung open, revealing Austin and her pretty much dry fucking each other in the hallway. His hand immediately reached in her panties.

"Jesus Christ, you can't even keep your fingers off my niece's pussy long enough to walk through the goddamn door!" I roared, taking in the debauchery in front of me.

"Uncle!" Briggs shrieked, shoving Austin away to pull down her dress.

"You're lucky it was my fingers and not my tongue. Next time knock on the fucking door before you make yourself at home in our apartment," Austin spewed, pissed I was there unannounced and uninvited.

I cocked my head to the side, arching an eyebrow. "Our?"

"Did I stutter?"

"Austin…" Briggs coaxed, gently placing her hand on his chest, trying to get him to back down.

He wouldn't.

And I fucking respected that too.

"This isn't her apartment. It's mine. I pay for it. Briggs, how about the next time you ask someone to move in, they are aware of who fucking owns it first."

"There won't be a next time. I'll start paying for it. Just tell me who to make the check out to," Austin said, not backing down.

He hated me. I guess I would too if the woman I loved was related to a man like me. I'm sure Briggs told him all about her childhood, painting me to be the villain I always wanted her to think I was. The monster that didn't show her any affection when she was growing up. Showing her the cruelty and reality of the world instead.

I grinned, narrowing my eyes at him. Contemplating if I really wanted to go through with what I had been thinking, ever since Briggs fucked up the meeting with Hector. Austin may have been the one on drugs, but she allowed it to happen. When she was supposed to be in charge and in control of the situation, proving to me she was being blinded by love.

I looked back and forth between them, before my stare settled on Briggs. She eyed me warily, knowing I wasn't there for fucking chit-chat.

"I've decided to make some changes. You want him involved in every aspect of your life, peladita? I can't stop you… but I'm personally over the fact that you're spreading your legs for the goddamn help again."

Austin stepped toward me, and Briggs held him back.

I scoffed, standing. Placing my hands in the pockets of my slacks, I rounded the corner of the island unfazed. Stopping about a foot away from them. Briggs stood right in the middle, waiting to intervene if needed.

Even after all these years, she still feared me. And I would be lying if I said I didn't fucking hate it.

"Since you're so fucking involved in my business and what's mine," I paused, looking at Briggs, "including this apartment, I've decided to promote you."

"No!" Briggs yelled, stepping toward me. Knowing what I was about to do.

My niece knew me as well as I knew her. I could control Briggs. Now, since I knew Austin wasn't going anywhere, I needed to control him too. And nothing made a man think he was in control more than power did. I knew Austin would be chomping at the bit.

I was about to make him an offer he couldn't refuse.

"You can't fucking do this, Uncle! I won't let you. He's not—"

"Baby, I don't need you to answer for me," Austin sneered, pulling her aside to stand in front of me instead.

Man to fucking man.

"What you did in Colombia took some fucking balls. I can appreciate a man that protects what he thinks is his. You would have shot Hector in the fucking face had Briggs not stopped you.

189

Without even batting an eye, I know you would have pulled the fucking trigger. I was fourteen when I had my first taste of blood. I murdered a man point blank, protecting what I thought was also mine," I informed, giving Briggs a piece of my life's puzzle. A glimpse of who I was.

Even though she would never know the truth about my life. I wouldn't allow it.

"Uncle, please… don't do this," Briggs whispered, her head bowed with an expression I couldn't see.

"I don't need both of you. Austin here," I nodded toward him, "is now in charge."

"What?" he replied, confused.

"You want to be boss man? Well then, here's your fucking chance."

"You want me to take over Briggs' job? I can't do that to her," Austin stated with a sincere tone, shaking his head. "I could never take this away from her. It's—"

"She will be right there with you. Won't you, Briggs?"

She glared at me with an expression I had never seen before. She loved Austin too much to ever leave his side, especially when it came to this life. She wouldn't say no. I had her right where I wanted her.

Bottom line.

It would keep them safe. I would make sure of it.

"He doesn't know what—"

"And that's why you'll teach him. I'll have someone else take over the traveling for the time being. He will run New York with you. Look at it this way, he will have plenty of time to fuck you in your own bed," I mocked, repeating what I overheard him saying to her as they opened the door.

It was the first time in over fifteen years, after everything I had put her through, made her see, made her experience, that she wanted to tell me she fucking hated me. I could see it in her eyes.

And it took everything inside me not to tell her I loved her more than anything in this world at the same exact moment.

My phone rang, breaking through her plaguing thoughts. I grabbed it out of my suit pocket, putting a finger out in front of me before I turned to answer it.

190

"Habla," I ordered, "*Talk*," walking out onto the balcony, shutting the door behind me.

"Boss, there's this girl at the strip club. She says she needs to talk to you. She won't fucking leave. She's adamant about seeing you, and only you."

"Get rid of her."

"I tried, she—"

"I don't give a flying fuck, get rid of her, or I'll get rid of you."

"Her name is—"

I hung up, placing my vibrating phone back into my pocket. I walked back inside, ignoring the calls. Waiting not-so-patiently to hear the two words that would forever change my niece's life, in ways I never expected, and would spend the rest of my life trying to make up for.

"I'm in."

I nodded and left.

Getting into my limo, pouring myself a glass of whiskey to take the edge off what I had just done. We still had to make a few more stops on my way back to the strip club, lining everything up for the coming weeks. Needing to meet with some partners, to let them know Austin was taking over Briggs' territory.

Effective immediately.

My head was fucking pounding by the time I walked through the back entrance of the club and into my office. I sank down into my leather chair, placing my elbows on the desk, instantly resting my head in the palms of my hands. Contemplating if I was doing the right thing by putting Austin in charge. My thoughts plagued my mind day and night, one right after the other. So unforgiving and malicious, punishing me for intervening in my niece's life once again.

Power changed people, but I figured it might have been in Briggs' best interest if she saw the truth beneath the fiction. Or at least that's what I told myself.

The commotion from the hallway outside of my door broke my concentration, dissolving my conflicting thoughts. I leaned back in my chair, rubbing my fingers back and forth over my mouth. Trying to overhear the voices getting closer and closer to my door.

"I know he's here! I saw him get out of his limo and sneak in through the back! This is bullshit! I'm talking to him whether he likes it or not. I've spent all day here, and I don't have any more time to waste."

The uproar came closer and closer.

"Ma'am!" Rick shouted after her.

"I told you to stop calling me that! My name is Lexi! L-e-x-i!"

I grinned, amused. Shaking my head, the fucking girl still had brass balls. I couldn't help but wonder if she was here because she had grown a pair of tits and her ass filled out. It had been three years since I last saw the little spitfire and my cock was more than eager to see what waited behind the closed door.

My demeanor quickly changed as soon as I watched her barge into my office without a care in the world, especially for the pissed off man sitting behind the desk.

"Well, well, well, look at what we have here. Have you ever heard of a goddamn phone?" I asked, cocking my head to the side. Taking Lexi in.

Rick ran in after her, out of breath. "I'm sorry, boss. I—"

"Leave us," I ordered in a harsh, demanding tone. Waving him away with my hand.

He apprehensively nodded, taking his sweet ass time to leave. I resisted the urge to tell him to move fucking faster. Shutting the door behind him, not a moment too soon.

Lexi swallowed hard as soon as he left, stepping further into my office. Looking from me over to the chair in between us, silently requesting permission to sit down. I didn't grant her any leniency. She sure as hell didn't deserve it. She should have known better than to barge into my office like an un-caged animal. She must have forgotten who she was dealing with, and I was fully prepared to fucking remind her.

But mostly, I just wanted to fuck with her. She made it so damn easy.

I glared at her with a predatory regard, placing my feet up on my desk one by one, and leaning back further into my chair, slowly, sensually rubbing my thumb over my lips. Visually making her extremely uncomfortable, as my eyes wandered over her body. It would take an idiot not to realize that Lexi didn't like being admired, like most girls with her appearance would.

I didn't give a fuck. I wanted to look at her, so I did. She was no longer a little girl, for damn sure. Her dark brown hair was longer, cascading all the way down the sides of her face and shoulders. Soft curls dwindling at the ends, accentuating the silky allure it still had to it. She was wearing thick, black eyeliner, emphasizing her intense green eyes that were trying to stare directly into my soul.

It wouldn't take long until she realized I didn't have one. And for some reason I couldn't fucking fathom, it bothered me more than it had in years.

I never stopped rubbing my callused fingers over my mouth, as her gaze followed the movement of my hand, causing her pouty fucking lips to purse as she watched my every move. Triggering my fingers to wipe off the bright red lipstick from her mouth.

My scowl trailed down her neck toward her tits, which were on full display, just waiting to be freed from her hot pink lacy bra, right down to her narrow, tiny waist. I immediately envisioned latching onto it, guiding her down my cock.

A thought that should have never crossed my goddamn mind, but I was still a man.

And she was like the forbidden fruit I wanted to fuck.

Her revealing cutoff top showed off her tan stomach and her pierced fucking bellybutton. Narrowing my eyes, I continued my visual assault down to her slender thighs, wanting to nestle my face between them. My cock twitched at the thought of her riding my face. She still had legs that went on for miles, barely covered by a small skirt, more like a piece of fabric that hid what I knew was her perfect fucking pussy.

Topping it all off, she wore fuck-me heels. This girl was just asking to be fucked twelve ways to Sunday, barging in here dressed the way she was.

"What are you looking at?" she asked, needing to break the silence between us.

"Whatever the fuck I want. Or did you forget this is my office you so rudely intruded in on?" Arching an eyebrow, I cocked my head to the side. Adding, "So tell me… did you dress like a whore for me, little girl?"

I jerked back like he had hit me, stunned. "I didn't—"

"That wasn't a question, sweetheart. Allow me to let you in on a little tip. I'm surrounded by fucking whores twenty-four-seven. If I wanted one, all I would have to do is walk outside that door." He pointed directly behind me. "They're a dime a dozen, dropping to their knees, itching to get a taste of my cock. Is that what you want?"

I sat down in the chair in front of his desk, slowly crossing my legs. Leaning over on the bureau, giving him an ample view of my cleavage. I knew he liked what he saw, his eyes seemed to keep settling there.

I had spent the last few months, debating if I was really going to do this. Every time I looked at my acceptance letter to Julliard, I knew this was my only hope in being able to attend the school. He was my last resort. Believe me, I didn't want to have to sell my soul to the Devil.

But what other choice did I have?

It took me forever to apply the pound of makeup I had on my face, not to mention trying to find the sluttiest clothes at the local thrift stores. I started helping out a lot more at the dance studio these last few years, and Mary, my instructor, was adamant on paying me, now that I was older. She didn't give me much, but it was something. I'd been saving almost all of it, and I had enough for my first and last month's rent at a shitty apartment, miles away from school. I would have to find a loop-hole in Julliard's strict policy for first years students. There was no way I could afford living on or near campus.

Although none of that mattered to me. All my hard work had finally paid off, and I got accepted to the school of my dreams.

Julliard.

This job could set me up for life. As much as I didn't want to be sitting here in his office, whored out, it was my only choice. I realized after our first short encounter that nobody stood up to Martinez. As much as he seemed to get off on my appearance, he also enjoyed my snarky tongue. It's not like I could help it, I wouldn't show fear to anyone.

Especially him.

"Well, here's a little tip for you," I retorted, bringing his attention back up to my face. "Maybe you should take one of those whores up on their offers, it might help get rid of your shitty attitude. Or they could just help remove the stick that seems to be permanently shoved up your ass," I proudly stated, smiling.

His eyes glazed over. It was quick, but I saw it. He didn't falter, not that I expected him to. "I'd agree with you, but then we'd both be wrong."

I smiled, big and wide at him. I couldn't help it. I liked his asshole demeanor. I had him right where I wanted him. Before I lost the courage, I blurted out, "I need a job, Martinez."

He didn't waver. His expression was unaffected. Blank. I couldn't tell what he was thinking, or if he was thinking at all. I couldn't read him, and it made me nervous more than anything. He retracted his legs from his desk, pushing back his chair. The sudden movement caused me to jump.

He never took his cold stare off of me. Slowly standing, he buttoned his suit jacket and loosened his tie. I'd never met anyone who didn't seem to have any emotions or feelings, any reactions to anything. As if he was just callous and detached from the world.

Or maybe he just knew how to pretend like he was. I knew all about pretending and for some reason, it made me feel better. Feeling as though there might be someone out there like me, but not just someone…

Him.

I cleared my throat. "Isn't this usually where you answer? Do you give all your whores the silent treatment?" I nervously laughed.

Nothing.

I pulled out the acceptance letter from my purse, laying it on the desk in front of him. His eyes went from me toward the paper

195

for just a second, as if he already knew what I was going to show him.

"See here is the thing. I'm a ballerina. I've been a ballerina my entire life. I don't ever remember not dancing. It's who I am, it's in my blood. To make a really long story short, my mom is... I mean she's..." I stammered, not wanting to share my pain with anyone. Let alone a complete stranger. Breaking our connection, I looked around the room as if the walls held what I was trying to say. "I don't have anyone. Okay?" I simply stated, rubbing the back of my neck, seeking comfort.

"Why is this my problem?"

My head jerked up to look at him once again. I frowned, my disappointment evident from his response. "I got accepted into Julliard. I don't have any money. I mean definitely not enough for tuition, housing, food, and everything else that I'll need. I just need a job. I came to you today because your place is the best strip club in the city. Fuck... probably the state. Jesus, maybe even the world."

"Kissing my ass isn't going to get you a job." He eyed me up and down. His eyes brazen and dilated. "You want to be a stripper, sweetheart?" he challenged, making his way over to the leather couch on the other end of the room. He sat down, leaned forward, and placed his elbows on his knees. His eyes bored into mine like he was calling my bluff without having to say a word.

There was something animalistic about the way he stared at me. Almost like a lion before it attacked its prey, luring me with his eyes and his captivating demeanor. Making me more nervous.

And wet.

"You think you got it in you? Huh? Then take off your fucking clothes."

I shook my head. "What?"

"Did I fucking stutter? Take off your fucking clothes, Lexi. Let's see if you got what it takes to be my whore. Bring those perky little tits out, let me see what I'm working with."

"I... I... I'm... I..."

"What's wrong? Not so cocky now, are you? That's what I thought, nothing but a fucking pussy with a nice rack." He narrowed his eyes at me with a sexy, arrogant expression that I

196

wanted to smack off his face. "You know where the door is. Don't let it hit you in the ass on the way out."

"I know what you're doing." I didn't move an inch. I wasn't done with him, yet.

He slowly, purposefully nodded. "Is that right?" he drawled out.

"You're trying to intimidate me. You don't scare me, Martinez," I stated, trying to hold my composure as best as I could.

I knew he was testing my limits. Provoking me on purpose, but this was a power struggle I wasn't willing to lose. There was too much at stake.

My future.

He slid back onto the sofa. His legs were wide open, filling up the expanded space that now seemed smaller with him sitting in it. He extended his arms, resting them on the backrest of the couch, angling his head to the side.

Watching.

"The floor is all yours." He motioned for me to come closer. "By all means, call my bluff. Strip for me, Lexi."

He watched me for a few seconds or maybe it was minutes, time just seemed to stand still. My heart was in my throat, and my pulse quickened with every breath. Martinez didn't bat an eye. He was calm, cool, and collected, displaying no emotion at all. So in control of his surroundings, of his demeanor.

Of me.

Manipulating me to do what he wanted without even trying very hard. I wanted to please him. I wanted to make him eat his words. I wanted him to like me.

This man really was the Devil.

The more severe and intense the situation, the better he was at remaining in control. He thrived on it, and there I was willingly feeding it to him. I had only just met the man, and I would do anything for him to keep looking at me with those sinful, blue eyes.

He looked right through me.

I swallowed hard as I stood, hanging on to the back of the chair for support. The cool air caused my already heightened skin to rouse. Our eyes stayed connected the entire time as he watched my

197

every move, like he was trying to ingrain it into his memory. Grabbing my ballet CD from my purse, I steadily walked toward his receiver, even though my legs were shaking. With my back now turned to him, I shut my eyes for a few seconds, needing to steady my emotions that were yearning to get the best of me. Before I could give it another thought, I placed the CD into the player and pressed the arrow button.

The soft melody of the piano vibrated through the speakers, filling the space between us.

"This should be interesting," he sarcastically stated.

I ignored his jab, letting the music calm my body like it always did. I would never be able to listen to this song again and not think of him. A part of me thought he wanted that.

Me thinking of him.

"I don't have all fucking day. Tick tock, sweetheart."

I took one last deep breath and turned to face him. Nothing had changed about him, and I didn't understand why I expected him to. I shook away the thoughts. I was a performer, goddamn it. I had been doing this my entire life. This wasn't any different. Just less clothes, but not by much.

Slowly, I inched my leg out to the side, stretching, pointing the toe of my sky-high heel. Accentuating my toned muscles from years of ballet training. I gradually leaned forward, sensually rubbing my hands down my thigh, to my knee, then down to my calf, grabbing onto my ankle. I aligned my torso along my leg, leisurely making my way back up. Never taking my lustful eyes off of him. My hand continued its assault up the side of my body as I spun to face away from his daunting eyes.

Glancing over my shoulder, I slowly worked my hips as my hands went for my shirt. Easing it up my torso, taking it over my head effortlessly. Bringing the small piece of fabric across my chest, and out to the side, dropping it at my feet.

I teasingly grinned as my leg développéd to the side, almost reaching my ear. Showing him just how flexible I was. My skirt inched up, bunching at my hips, revealing my barely-there panties. Keeping my leg up, I pivoted my body to face him once again. Slowly, I brought my leg down, hooking my thumbs into the waist

198

of my skirt, gracefully working it off my hips down to my feet. Pointing my toe, I flicked the discarded clothing toward him.

He narrowed his dark, dilated eyes at me. Recognition with an intensity I had never seen before. A gleam in his eyes that needed to break through all the sadness and despair, all the things that ate away at him. His serious expression captivated me in a way I had never experienced before. Which only added to the plaguing emotions that were placed in between us.

I stood there exposed to the devil, in nothing but my bra and panties. He sat on the couch more bared to me, and he was fully clothed.

The irony was not lost on me.

I shut my eyes, needing to get lost in the music. Hoping like hell I would make it out of here alive, and I wasn't talking physically. I listened to "Any Other Name," the intensity of the instruments vibrated through my core, translating into the sexual movements I incorporated in my ballet. I couldn't open my eyes, too scared of what I'd see.

The man I would find staring back at me.

I didn't have to wonder for very long. I felt him before he even touched me, his dominating presence attacking my senses. The smell of him all around, overwhelming me in ways I couldn't begin to describe. I felt his strong, callused fingers caressing all along my spine as if he was trying to make sure I was real. I hated to be touched. Even after all these years, I despised it.

Though in that precise moment.

In that second.

With him...

I wanted him to touch me everywhere.

My chest rose and fell with each brush of his fingers against my skin. He was standing behind me, moving my hair to the side. Lightly skimming his lips across my exposed flesh, igniting tingles all over my body. From the side of my neck, to my shoulders, awakening a craving deep within my core for the first time in my life.

"Do you have any idea what I can do to you, Lexi? How I could make you feel? How much I could make you come," he groaned into my ear, his raspy voice letting me know I was having an effect on him.

As much as he was on me.

I sucked in air as his fingers caressed the sides of my torso, and again along my back.

"Tell me," he urged, never stopping the torment of his fingers. "Have you ever been touched?"

I moaned in response, my cheeks turning a bright shade of red. I felt him move in front of me, he never stopped caressing my skin. His thumb skimmed across my lips, wiping off my lipstick as if he'd wanted to do it since I walked in.

"Where, Lexi? Where do you want me to touch you?" He slid his fingers up my stomach, slipping them into the edge of my bra. I just about came undone, and he had barely touched me, yet. Not the way I wanted him to touch me. This is agonizing, pure torture. Another moan escaped my lips just from the anticipation of what he was going to do next.

"Here?" he taunted, grazing my cleavage with the tips of his fingers.

I didn't say a word. I could barely breathe. He pulled down the straps of my bra, and in one quick but sudden movement, it was off. My nipples hardened from the cold air, but my body was burning for him. I could feel his stare all over me. Yearning to touch me as much as I desired him to feel every last inch of my body.

My soul.

"Jesus Christ," he breathed out.

I immediately opened my eyes. Never imagining the man glaring back at me would look so torn. So conflicted, so sad. I was more blown away by the fact I got to witness some sort of emotion, and sentiment from him.

"Alej—"

"You're so fucking beautiful, cariño." He froze, his eyes widened, completely caught off guard with what he just called me.

Cariño.

He didn't even try to hide the shock. It was plain as day, consuming his face. His body betrayed him. The pain and shame swallowed him alive in front of my very own eyes.

"What does that mean? What did you—"

He scowled, his demeanor rapidly changing into the man he'd always been. "Get the fuck out of my office," he roared out of nowhere. "Now!" Grabbing my clothes off the floor and throwing them at me.

I shuddered. "Wait… what? Why?" I asked, confused by the turn of events. "What just happened?"

"Get fucking dressed! You look like a goddamn whore!"

I couldn't put my clothes on fast enough for him, barely having my tank over my head before he was over to me in two strides, grabbing my acceptance letter and taking ahold of my arm. Pulling me toward the door.

"Let go! You're hurting me. What the fuck, Martinez?"

"If I wanted lip from you, I would unzip my fucking slacks," he gritted through a clenched jaw, shoving me out of his office. Throwing my letter at my feet.

"Why? We weren't done talking. Please! What just happened? I don't understand. I thought… I thought there was something here. You felt that, right? I know you felt that!"

"I don't hire little girls pretending to be women. I don't fuck them either. Don't waste my fucking time again. Do you understand me?"

I jerked back, the blow of his words almost as effective as his fist would have been. I could feel the tears pooling in my eyes. Threatening to surface. I bent over grabbing my papers. They were the most valuable thing I owned and he was shitting all over them.

"I need your help! Why are you being such a dick to me? Why are you being so cruel? What happened to you?"

He took one last look at me with his once again dark, cold, soulless eyes, and rasped, "The Devil happened."

And with that, he slammed the door in my face.

Twenty-four

Lexi

I stepped out onto the dark stage, taking a deep breath like I did before every performance. This show was different, it was personal, it was me.

The Dance of the Dying Swan is a high point for any ballerina's career but to me it held a different sentiment. Six years ago, I was supposed to be the white swan, but I never got my chance. This time around, I was both. The black and the white. I was finally in a place in my life where I was dancing…

For me.

This moment, I wasn't yearning to dance for my mother, wanting to make her proud. Make her see there was more light in her life than darkness. None of it mattered anymore.

This was my closure.

I was the prima ballerina in *Swan Lake* at The American Ballet Theatre in New York. People from all over the world paid money to come see me perform. I was twenty-four years old and living my dream.

What I had worked so hard for had finally come to fulfillment.

The stage lights came up, and the sad, melodramatic music started. Instantly taking me away to a deep, dark and depressing place. A place I needed to be to pull off this routine.

The performance of a lifetime was what they called it, and they were right. Not too many ballerinas got this chance, and for that, I was eternally grateful.

I'd been rehearsing day and night for the last six months, barely stopping to eat or sleep. And even then, I was still going over the routines in my mind. This act was the closing scene. If I did it right, there wouldn't be a dry eye in the sold-out

202

Metropolitan Opera House. Almost four thousand people would feel the emotions I projected through my movements.

I started to move, floating across the abundant stage with my back to the audience. My arms like swan wings, gliding up and down as I made my way to center stage. Turning ever so slightly to face the orchestra. Arching my back, my pointe shoes continued their assault on the Marley floor beneath me. The melody of the stringed instruments pulled at my heart, mimicking my own sadness, carrying me effortlessly from step to step.

Piqué, arabesque into a beautiful bourrée. My torso leaned forward as my arms floated behind my back. Repeating the movements over and over again, each becoming more and more intense as the music heightened. Turning in tight circles, flapping my wings, letting the lights blur before me. The natural movements of my body instinctively taking me away to the only place I had ever felt comfort.

Music and dance were my peace.

They made me feel whole.

I danced like it was my last show, as if my life, my happiness, my world depended on it. Gliding fluently around the stage from one corner to the other. Turning and twisting, leaping through the air as if I had been a swan in captivity all my life.

Finally, free.

The routine was over too soon. For the big finish, and the demise of the beautiful swan, I positioned myself into a pirouette turn with a dramatic landing. Easing down to my knee. Sitting back on my heel with my left leg stretched out in front of me. I lowered my upper body to my knee, bringing my wings above my head.

Slowly falling.

The music started to fade as my body rolled up one last time before gracefully dying.

The stage went dark. Everything around me was black. Everything went quiet.

Silence all over.

The curtain dropped, separating me from the crowd. I stood up, taking a deep breath, preparing for my grande reverence. Standing in fifth position with my arms in demi-seconde.

Waiting.

The curtain lifted. The lights came on. A domino effect erupted from the rows of people, everyone stood. Applauding, whistling, cheering. I looked out at the audience, imagining all the beautiful tear-stained faces almost knocked the wind out of me.

For the first time in my life.

I felt at home.

After a few minutes, I walked forward to center stage, and did a rond de jambe into a curtsey. Placing my hand over my heart, and bowing my head as the curtain came down again. The rest of the performers took the stage behind me. The curtain lifted one last time. The crowd once again went wild, and I loved every second of it. Even though there would be more performances, nothing would ever compare to my first. I didn't want the night to end.

We exited the stage, and I was bombarded by the staff of our company and the choreographers. It would be a matter of minutes before the happy patrons would make their way to my dressing room wanting pictures, signatures, everything under the sun, and I happily gave it to them. I was exhausted but I wouldn't change a thing. My body ached, my feet throbbing in pain. I couldn't wait to slip my pointe shoes off. I placed all the bouquets of roses on the table, shutting the door behind me, needing some privacy. A moment to myself to breathe.

I sat down in my director-style chair, and unlaced my shoes. Kicking them off one by one, my toes relished the freedom. Flexing and rolling my stiff ankles. Standing, I slipped off my tutu, and placed it on the counter. Only leaving on my leotard and dance tights to go home in. I gazed in the mirror, getting ready to remove my caked on make-up.

"Nikolai," I shrieked, alarmed. Placing my hand over my chest. Looking at the man that appeared in the mirror. "Jesus, you scared the shit out of me."

He smiled, pushing off the wall. "Is that anyway for a prima ballerina to talk?" He pecked my lips, handing me another huge bouquet of red roses.

I laughed.

I had been seeing Nikolai on and off for the last year or so. I didn't really keep track, too consumed with work in the theatre.

Not that it mattered anyway, the relationship wasn't going anywhere, and we weren't serious. He was always traveling, something to do with his work or what not. At least that's what he told me. I wouldn't see him for weeks, and then out of nowhere he would just show up. Tonight, being the perfect example. He was a gentleman, sweet, attentive, caring. Buying me things I never asked for, taking me into fancy places I wouldn't step foot in without him.

He was like my very own Prince Charming.

"How about we go back to your apartment? And you let me rub your sore muscles." He kissed along my neck, down to the top of my exposed shoulders. Peering at me through the mirror.

I smirked. "Oh yeah?"

We hadn't done anything more than kiss. He was very patient with me. I still hated to be touched. Kissing was even too much for me, sometimes. The only man I'd ever...

It didn't matter.

I hadn't seen Martinez since he kicked me out of his office all those years ago. I wish I could tell you I stopped thinking about him. I wish I could tell you I hated him. I wish I could tell you a lot of things. It was like he put a spell on me. Etching himself into my mind, making me think about him more often than not. Especially when I was alone. It was hard not to let my mind wander, but it always wandered to him. When a man had an effect on you like he did on me, you couldn't help but ask yourself...

Why?

Nikolai always respected my boundaries. I knew he wanted more, of course he did, but I wasn't ready. To be honest, I didn't know if I ever would be. I thought about going to see a therapist a few times, though just the thought of talking to a complete stranger made me uncomfortable. Maybe it was because I hadn't met another man like Martinez, another man that set me on fire like he did. Maybe I had daddy issues or abandonment problems... whatever it was, I guess I just didn't care. I wasn't looking for answers, because deep down I knew another man like him didn't exist.

"Come on, baby doll, let me take you home." He grabbed my bag and hand before I could answer, leading the way out the door.

He spent most of the limo ride back to my place, on the phone. Speaking Russian to someone on the other end, completely ignoring me. I didn't mind though, I just gazed out the tinted window as the lights of Manhattan went by in a blur. Sitting in his limo always reminded me of Martinez. I almost expected to see him if I turned my head.

Growing up, I didn't think having a driver or a limo would be as common as it seemed to be. I had never been in a limo until Nikolai came along. I met him at the coffee shop by my apartment. I didn't have enough cash for my espresso, and he swooped in and paid the barista.

We'd been talking ever since.

I continued to watch the city lights pass by, waiting for Nikolai to wrap up his conversation as we were a few blocks from my apartment. It was near NYU, at one of the most expensive and posh buildings in all of Manhattan. I moved in after I accepted the offer to attend Juilliard the fall semester. The school administration never brought up the fact that I was violating the housing policy by living off campus. Which I thought was odd, but I wasn't about to question it. I'd been living there since. Looking back, I still remember how I panicked, dashing through the city that week, trying to get any strip club to hire me after Martinez pretty much told me to go fuck myself. Not one of them gave me a chance. I started to get paranoid, thinking they knew who I was before I even walked through the door.

Smiling at the thought.

I recalled walking out of the last establishment after being rejected again. I sat on the curb of the sidewalk and fell apart, not having a clue what I was going to do. After a few seconds of humiliating myself in public, and enduring awkward stares, I got up, brushed off the back of my legs and started walking toward the nearest ATM machine to pull money out of my account. I needed to take the six o'clock bus back to my foster parents' house. That morning, they informed me I needed to find my own place since I turned eighteen and I had graduated from high school.

Meaning they didn't get assistance from the state any longer to take care of me so they wanted me out. I was no good to them anymore. I shook my head as I typed in my code, checking my balance before making a withdrawal. The balance flashed on the screen, almost knocking me on my ass by what I saw. I swear I was about to pass the fuck out.

"This can't be right," I said to myself, looking at the quarter of a million dollars on the screen. I immediately peered around me, thinking someone was playing a practical joke. "This isn't mine. There's got to be some mistake."

I canceled the transaction, grabbed my card, and slid it into my back pocket as I made my way inside the bank. I sat, waiting on the white leather sofa for the older lady sitting behind the desk to finish up what she was doing. My legs bounced a mile a minute, anticipating what they were going to tell me.

"What can I help you with, Miss…"

"Lexi."

She nodded. "Lexi, what can I help you with?"

"I think… no, I know there's been some sort of mistake. I went to pull money out of my account, and there's too much savings in there."

"I'm not following."

I nervously laughed. "I had like a couple grand in my account yesterday. I just looked, and there's way more than that."

"Hmmm… let's check it out." Placing her glasses on her face, she looked down at the paper I filled out to be seen. She began typing a bunch of numbers on her keyboard in front of her. "The money was deposited this morning, dear. Looks like it came from an overseas account."

"An overseas account? I don't know anyone overseas. Listen, there's got to be some sort of mistake here. I don't want this karma, I already have a black cloud following me around today, ma'am. I'm sure someone is panicking right now, wondering where the hell their money is."

"The account can't be traced, Lexi. But it's definitely your money. I have all the proof sitting right here." She turned the screen so I could see what she was talking about.

"Oh my God," I breathed out, realizing she was right.

She chuckled, "Looks like you have a guardian angel, sweetheart." I made a withdrawal, thanked her for her help and left.

I hailed a cab and went straight to my school. I walked into the financial support office and immediately paid off all my tuition. Within the next couple of days I paid off all my loans too. The search for an apartment when you have money is so much more fun and easy. A realtor scheduled a few showings and I found one of the most luxurious, fully furnished apartments that money could buy. The move was a breeze, I only had a suitcase of clothes and a few more things. I hadn't spoken to my foster parents since the day I left. I could finally breathe, and I didn't even know who to thank for the fortune. They say money doesn't buy happiness but it sure as fuck buys comfort.

"What are you thinking about over there?" Nikolai questioned as he shut my apartment door behind him and leaned up against it.

"Huh?" I questioned as I placed my keys and phone on the foyer table.

"You've seemed lost in thought all night." He took off his suit jacket, tossing it over the back of the couch. Pulling off his tie, he strutted over to me with a predatory regard. A look I had never seen from him.

"Oh," I whispered, not knowing what else to say.

He roughly grabbed my chin, angling my face to where he wanted it. "Do you have any idea what you do to me? How much I think about you?"

I shyly smiled, looking up into his eyes.

"This skintight leotard, accentuating all your subtle curves." His other hand pushed aside the flaps of my coat, skimming his fingers up the front of my body.

My stomach instantly dropped, instead of fluttering. An unsettling feeling coursed throughout my core, but I let him keep going. Needing to push myself through the discomfort. I just wanted to be normal with a man, who had been nothing but kind to me.

He released my chin. Walking around me, eyeing my body with the same predatory regard. Only stopping when he was behind me. He pulled off my coat, throwing it beside his on the couch. His lustful eyes peered up and down, tilting his head to get a better view.

208

Bringing his lips to my ear, he whispered, "Your body is sinful. That's all I kept thinking about while I watched you perform tonight, Lexi. It took all of my willpower not to reach into my slacks and stroke my cock right then and there."

My eyes widened, my breathing hitched. He never spoke to me this way before. Everything about him in this moment was so foreign to me. It was like I was with another man, not the same one I'd spent time with this last year.

"I couldn't take my eyes off you. No one could. My dick is hard right now just looking at you."

"Nikolai, I—"

"Shhh… let me take care of you," he murmured against my lips. Easing me down onto the couch, readily laying his muscular body on top of mine. Kissing me.

At first it was soft, like he was testing my boundaries, taking my slightly parted lips as an open invitation to slowly slip his tongue into my mouth. He tasted of scotch and something else I couldn't quite put my finger on. I was so confused and overwhelmed all at once, but I didn't tell him to stop. He deepened our kiss, tightly gripping the back of my neck. Tangling his tongue with mine in an urgency I'd never experienced before. Showing me he'd been waiting for this moment for a long time.

When he parted my legs with his, placing his hard cock right on top of my heat. I shuddered. His hand skimmed down from my neck to the side of my breast, leaving a trail of disgust in its wake. He groaned, loud and hard from deep within his chest, taking my trembling for something that it wasn't. I shut my eyes tight, desperately trying to block out the memories of my stepdad.

His touch.

His scent.

His sounds.

I placed my hands on his chest, but again didn't stop him. Thinking that maybe if I felt him, I would realize it wasn't my stepdad, I was with him. The man I was supposed to be interested in, the one I should want to do these things with. Intimacy had always been hard for me. It was why I never dated.

I couldn't.

Pulling down the front of my leotard, he kneaded my breast. I went with it, even though my mind was screaming for him to stop. Yelling for him to get the fuck off of me.

"Jesus, Lexi, you feel fucking amazing," he rasped near my ear, making my stomach recoil. Fighting the bile that began to rise up the back of my throat.

I let him think this was going to happen.

I let him touch me like he never had before.

I let him feel like I was his.

When in reality, I was suffocating to shove him off me. Another little piece of me dying inside. It seemed like the more time went on, the longer I let him have his way with me not, saying a damn thing about it.

I tried.

He became more aggressive, more demanding, more consuming. Grinding his hard cock up against me. When his hand moved toward my pussy, and his mouth retreated toward my nipple, I couldn't do it anymore.

It was too much.

Memories flooded my mind, one right after the other. Playing like an old movie projector above me. I couldn't stop them from appearing, one scene and then the next. They were ruthless and unforgiving.

"Fuck," I whimpered, leaning my face away from his. Forcefully shoving him off of me to stand. I couldn't get away from him fast enough.

He stumbled back, catching himself on the coffee table.

"I'm sorry, Nikolai. I'm really sorry, but I can't do this." I lifted my leotard back up, tucking my breasts safely behind the slim cotton material.

He glared up at me, his chest heaving, his nostrils flaring. "Do you want to fuck him? Is that what this is about? Or are you already fucking him? Because, you sure as hell don't want to fuck me," he viscously spewed.

"What are you talking about? Who... what..." I asked, shocked. Not being able to connect my thoughts.

"I see the way he looks at you. I see the way you look at him, too. You don't hide it very well."

210

I shook my head, confused. "Who the hell are you talking about?"

"Your dance partner. The goddamn pussy who touches you like you're his." He paced back and forth in front of me, roughly pulling at his hair.

"Are you for real? We're acting. We perform together, it's part of our job."

"You're MINE!" he roared, the veins pulsating in his neck. Making me cower away from him.

"You think I'm a fucking idiot, don't you? After everything I've done for you. Waiting around like a lost fucking puppy. You're nothing but a fucking cock tease, Lexi."

"I'm no one's, especially not yours. Now get the fuck out of my apartment!" I screamed, pointing toward the door. Tears began to surface, and my body began to shake. My adrenaline kicked in to high gear.

"Oh no, baby doll. I'm not going anywhere and neither are you." He lunged at me, catching me completely off guard. Pushing me up against the adjacent wall, my back and head hit with a hard thud as he caged me in with his arms. My vision instantly clouded, seeing nothing but spots.

For a split second, I thought this was a joke. God couldn't be this cruel. He would never make me go through this again. My heart immediately dropped, and I instinctively screamed, trying to fight him off. Pounding my fists against his hard chest. He chuckled against my face, pressing his body and cock closer to mine.

"Fucking scream. You're just making me harder."

"Somebody help me! Somebody fucking help me!" I shouted bloody murder, putting up more of a struggle.

"The walls are fucking soundproof, Lexi," he rasped in a menacing tone that made my body shudder.

"What?" I scoffed, pathetically thrashing around my entire body, trying to push him off and away from me.

He held me closer. Close enough to where I could knee him in the balls. My leg came up in between his, and connected with his dick. He hunched over and I thought I could run, but it backfired on me. He was able to enclose me even more.

He laughed.

The motherfucker laughed.

He rose up, clearing his throat. Staring me dead in the eyes. "You're going to pay for that, bitch." Before I even saw it coming, he raised his hand and backhanded me across the face so hard, I instantly tasted blood.

He didn't let up, hitting me in the face a few more times. I could barely hold my own weight. The room went out of focus as he punched me in the stomach repeatedly, until I fell over onto the ground. Hyperventilating for air that wasn't available for the taking. He kicked me in the ribs, causing me to fall on my back. Cringing, trying to curl into the fetal position to protect myself. All I could see was red seeping into my eyes.

He dropped to his knees in front of me, and grabbed me by my hair. Forcefully making me look up at him. Excruciating pain radiated through my entire body.

"This is how it's going to go down." He pulled out a knife from his pocket. I didn't have time to contemplate what had just happened before he dragged me by my hair over to the couch. "I'm going to rip off your clothes," he sneered, gliding the knife effortlessly down the front of my leotard and the elastic band of my dance tights. Ripping away my clothes, leaving me in just my sports bra and panties. Releasing my hair, he shoved me back down onto the ground as if I weighed nothing.

"And then... I'm going to pull out my cock." He unbuckled his belt, jerking out his sorry excuse for a fucking dick. "Now, I'm going to fuck you with it. With or without your fucking consent, you no good fucking cock tease."

He tackled me to the floor, gripping my hair from the top of my head this time, slamming it into the hardwood floor. Pain radiated throughout my body as I choked from the sudden loss of breath, the wind knocked out of me with his entire weight resting on my beaten body. My vision turned black again, forcing me to blink away the white spots.

"Don't pass out. It won't be as much fun if you pass out. But trust me, it won't stop me if you do."

I felt him scoot over my panties, exposing me. Breathing into the side of my neck. "I've never been with a virgin. Thanks for that." His dick nudged into my entrance.

Before I could scream, or put up a fight, the door to my apartment slammed open. Breaking the drywall behind it.

"What the fuck?" Nikolai roared, immediately turning and blocking my view.

I shut my eyes, slipping into the darkness. A loud popping sound ricocheted off the walls, causing me to startle. A sudden warmth sprayed my face, my neck, my chest, and Nikolai's body came crashing down on me. All two hundred pounds of him fell lax on my petite frame. If I thought I couldn't breathe before, this was proving me wrong.

The sudden weight of his body was thrown off me as if he weighed nothing.

"Stop fucking screaming," someone snarled close to my ear. I could barely hear them.

Was I screaming?

They wiped at my face, cleaning off the blood from my eyes so I could see.

"Stop fucking fighting me," the mystery man sneered again.

Was I fighting?

They roughly gripped my arm, pulling me up to stand on my wobbly legs. I instantly fell over into a solid muscular chest. His arms wrapped around me, holding me close, making sure I wouldn't fall. His scent immediately assaulted my senses.

I would know that smell anywhere.

Forever engrained in my mind.

"If you know what's good for you, stop fucking screaming and stop fighting me."

What?

My eyes fluttered open, still barely able to see through the haze of blood and God knows what else. I peered up through my lashes, locking gazes with dark, cold, soulless blue eyes.

For some reason, I heard myself scream bloody fucking murder that time. It all happened so fast I didn't have time to register what occurred next. All I saw was his gun raised above his head.

"I warned you, cariño."

213

With sheer blunt force, the gun came crashing down. Hitting me on the back of the neck.

And then everything went black.

Part 3

Twenty-five
Lexi

I felt the soft, warm sheets beneath me before I even opened my eyes. My body felt like it was one with the mattress. A floating sensation coursed through me. My mind was as light as a feather, even though my body felt as heavy as a brick, sinking further and further into the linen sheets. My eyes fluttered open, or maybe they were still closed, the room I was apparently passed out in, was pitch black. I couldn't see an inch in front of me.

It actually brought me comfort.

I was used to the darkness. I'd lived in it my whole life.

"You're up," a deep masculine voice startled me.

How long had he been there?

I didn't say a word or make a sound, I hadn't even moved. I couldn't fathom how he knew I was awake. I barely realized I was awake. My eyes fluttered shut again.

Why was I so damn tired?

Before I could finish that thought, the night's disturbing events came crashing down on me. What was supposed to be one of the most memorable nights of my life, turned into one of the most traumatic encounters. Adding to the endless pile of bullshit gone wrong in my life.

I tried to sit up, but my body refused to cooperate. I sank back down, whimpering in pain, unable to move from the place I laid. Before I could even blink, I felt a strong, solid grip grab my arm, helping me sit up. I hadn't even heard him move, it was like he floated through air or something. His unexpected touch made me flinch. I always dreaded the feel of people touching me, but at this moment it seemed even worse.

216

He didn't call me out on it, but he also didn't remove his hands. Instead, he propped me up against the headboard. The mixture of his masculine scent and musky cologne surrounded me, penetrating my pores. Consuming me as he hovered above my battered frame. Resting my head back, I took a deep, painful breath, inhaling the smell that haunted me for years. Martinez. It made me feel dizzy, but content simultaneously. I eased into his embrace, ignoring the sharp pain that accompanied my movement. His presence brought a sense of calm and security over me. No one has ever had that effect on me before. My body in sync with my emotions melted into his touch even more.

He suddenly tensed for a split second, surprised by the unexpected change in my composure.

"Close your eyes," he ordered in a tone I didn't recognize, making me think I had an effect on him too.

I was about to ask why, when his hands vanished. All I heard was the sound of a light switch, clicking over on the nightstand. The light immediately blinded me, illuminating the bedroom. Emitting a sharp pain in my head that radiated in the back of my eyes. I suddenly understood why he told me to shut my eyes. I blinked away the haze and discomfort, finding him sitting in the armchair a few feet away. He just sat there like he never moved at all.

Did I just imagine him so close to me?

I watched him looking at me the same way he always had. It was like no time had passed between us. He was sitting back in the armchair with one leg placed over his knee, and his fingers brushing across his lips. He looked exactly the same, as if he hadn't aged a day in the last five years. Except now he looked tired, exhausted even. Looking like he hadn't slept in days. I couldn't help but wonder if it was from staying with me, watching over me, guarding me…

Or if it was just because of the life he led.

I chose to believe the first one.

His black hair had fallen around his face, framing it perfectly like I once imagined it would. I instantly pictured him running his hands through it all night, restless, worried, waiting for me to wake up. He was as handsome as fucking ever. Better than I remembered him even.

He was sporting more facial hair than the last time I saw him, making him appear more distinguished, rugged, and dangerous. Not that he needed any help accomplishing the last one. His bright blue eyes looked serene, but still void of any emotion. They were empty, no feeling pouring out of them whatsoever. His expression was vacant, and unforgiving. I never wanted to know what he was thinking more than I did in that second. The man was a blank canvas as always, so calm and collected, so naturally in tune with his surroundings.

So. Fucking. Him.

He wore black slacks with a black button down shirt. The first few buttons unfastened, showing off his big, muscular chest and what appeared to be a silver chain hanging around his neck. It looked like he was trying to hide it under his collared shirt, making it nearly impossible to see what it was. I found myself desperately wanting to know. My eyes instinctively wandered down to his arm, admiring how tan his skin was. His sleeves were rolled up, exposing a black beaded bracelet around his right wrist.

Another piece to this man's puzzle.

My heart pounded against my chest, my mind reeling with thoughts of why I was there, and what he was going to do with me.

He was one of the good guys, right?

I wanted to look around the room, but I couldn't will myself to look away from him. Our gazes locked, emotions running wild. Neither one of us wanting to break the intense connection we shared. Every last fiber of my being screamed for me to ask him what I wanted to know. I knew I wouldn't get any answers, but it didn't stop me from wanting to ask.

I opened my mouth to say something, anything, when he intercepted. Reading my mind, stating, "You want answers."

I hesitantly nodded, not being able to find my voice. The emotions stirring through me were crippling me in ways I never thought possible. The anguish consuming my body and mind, an ache resonating in my soul. Only producing a possible fabricated illusion of what I still felt occurring between us. It still felt so fucking real to me.

Like he wanted me there.

Like he had wanted me there for a long time.

"How did you know what was happening in my apartment?" I blurted, pushing through the sentiments that were taking control of me. Needing to understand what he was about to divulge. Hoping he actually would.

He narrowed his eyes, once again looking at me with a familiar desire. The desire I had been dreaming about since the last time he touched me. I dreamt about him almost every night for the last five years. Sitting in the armchair by my bed, watching me sleep. There were times when I woke up in the middle of the night and I swear I just felt him there with me. Guarding me, like a dark angel trying to keep the nightmares at bay.

"Please, Martinez…" I begged, going against everything I ever believed in.

He cleared his throat, and sat forward in his chair searching my face for I don't know what. Eyeing me up and down, contemplating if he was going to tell me the truth or not. Never in my wildest dreams did I expect what he was going to reply.

Rasping through his fingers, "You live in my building. My men have always kept an eye on you."

𝔐𝔞𝔯𝔱𝔦𝔫𝔢𝔷

Lexi wasn't scared of my presence, and that bothered me in ways I couldn't begin to describe. It was such a foreign feeling, I refused to get used to.

She jerked back. Shocked with the truth I just revealed, having been watched unknowingly for four years. "Why?" she blurted, before she lost the courage to question me further.

I continued to rub my thumb along my lips, taking her in without her realizing I was doing so. Her dark brown hair was still long, flowing all around her face and down the sides of her body. She was thinner than the last time I saw her, which displeased me. Making me think she wasn't taking care of herself properly. Her

219

complexion pale, her pouty lips dry from dehydration. Her usually bright green eyes, solemn. Wanting to know the truth.

Wanting to know everything.

Especially about me.

Even with a marred up face, she still looked fucking beautiful. Her appearance was breathtaking under the dim lights of the room. I'd spent the last twenty-four hours, sitting in this goddamn chair, waiting for her to wake up. Resisting the urge to lay with her, pull her into my arms, and keep her safe. I hated fucking cuddling. But with her it would be different.

I knew everything would be different.

I also wished I could revive the motherfucker Nikolai just to fucking kill him again. Slowly torture the piece of shit this time around, until he begged me for mercy.

The thought alone calmed me.

I carried her broken body back to my limo, immediately calling the doctor I had on my payroll. Making sure he was waiting for us the second we walked through my penthouse door. I laid her head in my lap in the limo, ordering my driver to buy wet wipes from the gas station near my building. Impatiently fucking waiting for him to bring them back. I fucking hated seeing Nikolai's blood and brain remnants on her creamy skin. Tainting her perfect fucking flesh.

I closed the partition to give us some privacy, no one was allowed to see her naked but me and the doctor. Gently wiping off the dried blood from her face and her body, checking the bruises and wounds on her beautiful face. I carefully cut off her sports bra with my knife, exposing her breasts, needing to see the damage the motherfucker had caused to her ribs. Softly, feeling down the sides of her stomach to the top of her waist. I cleaned her off the best I could, given the shitty circumstances we were in.

I never wanted to physically hurt her. It pained me to have to knock her out, but I had no choice in the matter. She wouldn't stop screaming and fighting me, we were seconds away from Nikolai's men coming boss's. Her hysterics could be heard through the entire building, easily giving away our location. We wouldn't have made it out alive, so I did what I had to do, saving both our asses.

220

Without thinking twice about it, I removed my suit jacket, unbuttoned my shirt, taking it off to put it on her. She drowned in it. I took my suit jacket, and laid it over her, to provide extra warmth. Ignoring the fact I liked seeing her in my clothes.

Dark thoughts loomed in the back of my mind.

Thirty minutes later we were back at my penthouse. I carried her in the elevator, and she didn't stir once. I tried not to let my worry for her take over, telling myself she would be fine. She was just exhausted and overwhelmed from the night's traumatic events. Dr. Valdez checked her thoroughly, making sure she didn't have any broken bones or any severe internal injuries.

She didn't.

She would be sore as fuck for the next few days, but everything would fade with time and rest.

Except, her memories. Those were now a part of her forever.

Dr. Valdez injected her with a strong painkiller and a sedative to keep her comfortable. Leaving a bottle of pain medicine on the nightstand for her to take as needed. He informed me she would sleep for the next few hours or so, and wake up when she was ready. I didn't leave her side for one fucking second.

Once he was gone, I bathed her in the bathtub, making sure to hold her head up the entire time. Running the warm water and soap over every inch of her battered body. Trying to pull the remnants of the motherfucker's skull out of her hair. When I was finished, I lifted her up into my arms, gently drying her off, and laying her back in bed. Dressing her in some clothes that I ordered one of my men to go collect from her apartment. Along with other essentials she might want or need while she recovered.

"Are you just going to sit there, and be all you?" She gestured her hand toward me, working it up and down.

She still hadn't even realized she was freshly clean and in her own clothing. Too consumed by the man sitting before her.

Me.

"I asked you a question, Alejandro, I expect an answer," she ordered, pulling me away from my thoughts. Enjoying the way my name rolled off her tongue.

She had never called me that before.

I grinned behind my hand, not allowing her to see how amused I really was by her snarky little mouth.

"How did I not know that was your apartment building? And why were your men watching me?" she repeated, elaborating the same question. Jerking her head, waiting to hear my explanation. She was a feisty little thing when she wasn't getting her way, that's for damn sure.

"You need to get some rest," I simply stated, trying like hell to stifle my laugh.

She sighed, annoyed. "This is bullshit. You break into my apartment, and proceed to knock me fucking unconscious. Now, I'm in a room with you, in..." Her arms rose to her sides as she looked down at her body, realizing the blood was gone, she was clean. She cocked her head to the side, looking up at me. Feeling her head, running her fingers through her washed hair. "You undressed me? How did you do that? Where did my clothes come from? Oh my God, you saw me naked, didn't you?" She couldn't get the questions to come out fast enough. "What the Hell?" she gritted, frustrated.

I didn't falter. "Yes. Very carefully. My men collected some of your belongings from your apartment, along with other things you might need." I leaned back into my chair, moving my hand so she could see my expression. "And it's nothing I haven't seen before, sweetheart." I grinned.

Her eyes widened in disbelief, her mind spinning out of control. Not knowing what she wanted to ask me first. I wasn't surprised when she blurted, "Are you going to hurt me?" The girl had no fucking filter.

I shook my head, trying to hide the amusement she always provided me.

"How long were you there? Did you let Nikolai hurt me?"

"You," I declared in a husky tone, "let that piece of shit hurt you. I shot him in the fucking head... for you."

The realization of my statement caused more turmoil, than ease. She peered around the room, avoiding my eyes. Her emotions getting the best of her, and for the second time in I don't know how long, I resisted the urge to hold and comfort someone.

Her.

222

"I want to go home," she whispered so low, I knew she didn't want to say it.

"You're not safe there anymore. You need to be here."

She frowned, tears pooling in her eyes. I couldn't remember the last time I saw a woman cry. It had been that goddamn long too. I was never around a woman long enough to give a fuck.

She bowed her head, defeated. And I hated seeing her so overcome. It wasn't in her nature. Which only proved to me she needed to be here.

With me.

"You promise you won't hurt me?"

"Look me in the eyes when I'm talking to you," I instinctively ordered.

She peered up at me through her long, dark lashes. A few tears streamed down her face. She instantly wiped them away with the back of her hand not wanting me to see her looking so weak.

"You're safe here for the time being," I answered her question the best I could. "Nikolai wasn't who you thought he was. You can't go home because his men will kill you. They're already out there looking for you, as we speak. Your fucking screaming didn't help the situation. I barely got us out of there fast enough and unharmed."

"What about you?" She gave me a questioning stare.

"What about me?"

"Are you in danger, too?"

"Cariño, I'm always in fucking danger. Everyone wants me dead."

"Because of me?"

"Because of everything."

She grimaced. It hurt her to hear the truth coming out of my mouth. Not granting her the peace she so urgently yearned for. She felt bad for me, and I would be lying if I said it didn't faze me. Someone caring about my well-being. It had been an even longer time since anyone gave a shit if I was dead or alive.

"Did you know Nikolai?" she flat out asked.

"I suggest the next time you get a boyfriend—"

"He wasn't my boyfriend," she interrupted. "I barely knew him. I've never… I've never had a boyfriend."

223

I blew off her reply, refusing to let it sink in. Knowing exactly why she felt the need to share that with me. I stood abruptly instead, not paying her any mind. Walking toward the bed, shocking the shit out of her. With wide eyes and parted lips, her chest rose and fell with every step I took, bringing me closer to her. Anxiously waiting for what I was going to do next.

I nodded toward the bottle of pills on the nightstand, breaking her train of thought before hovering above her. Her eyes followed my lead, quickly making their way back up to me.

I couldn't help but notice how tiny and vulnerable she looked. How exposed she was to me in that second. Making my cock twitch at the sight of her.

She slowly licked her lips, trying to govern her unsteady breathing. Hoping I didn't realize how much she wanted me to touch her, hold her, comfort her.

"So... I'm safe here. With you?" she coaxed the same goddamn question in a different way.

I stepped back, and she immediately hated the loss of my dominance over her. I nodded toward the pills again, rasping, "Don't take more than two of those, unless you want to be in a fucking coma. If you need anything, pick up the house phone and dial zero, the maid will bring you whatever you need."

Her breathing hitched as I reached for the switch on the lamp, thinking I was going for her. I shut off the light, instantly feeling her disappointment that our time was over.

"Get some rest, Lexi. You're going to need it." I turned, making my way out of her room.

"You don't have to answer my question," she whispered loud enough for me to hear, stopping me dead in my tracks. "You saved my life. That's enough proof for me to know it."

Her response rendered me useless. My feet glued to the goddamn floor beneath me, my mind yelling to go back to her while struggling with my own demons until finally I said, "De más formas de las que tu nunca sabras, cariño," murmuring, "In more ways than you'll ever know, cariño."

And I left.

Twenty-six

Martinez

Motherfucker.

This was not supposed to happen. She was not supposed to be in my home, in one of my guestrooms. Laying in one of my goddamn beds, like we were playing fucking roommates. I couldn't get away from the clusterfuck of a room fast enough.

This was bad.

The blaze in her eyes.

The feel of her skin.

The smell of her scent all around me.

I. Was. Fucked.

But it didn't matter. I was already going straight to fucking Hell. I just didn't want to drag her into the inferno with me.

I hauled ass into my limo, telling the driver to take me to the nearest bar. Tugging my hair away from my face, wanting to rip it the fuck out the entire ride to the shitty hole. The drive seemed to last fucking forever.

"Stay," I ordered to my bodyguard like a fucking dog, stepping out of the limo.

"Boss—" I shut the door in his face.

I wasn't my fucking father. I never rolled with more than one bodyguard, unless I had to. Often, I would go places by myself, not giving a fuck if I was protected or not. Leo always said I was asking for a bullet in my head. I had a death wish that would become my reality one day.

Maybe I did.

So fucking tired of being the goddamn Grim Reaper.

"Bourbon," I ordered from the bartender with her tits on full display. Taking a seat on the stool farthest from the other customers. "Keep 'em coming."

"That's what she said," she giggled, thinking she was so fucking clever.

Bringing my attention to her, I glared up.

"My name's Julie." She extended out her hand.

"I asked for a drink, not your fucking name."

Her eyes dilated. See, here was the fucked up thing about women. They loved men like me. No matter how much of an asshole I was to them, they still wanted to get down on their knees, and deep throat my fucking cock.

The shittier I was, the better I'd fuck them.

Lexi proved to be no different.

I've fucked up so many times already when it came to her, I was surprised I could still fucking see straight. I lost all reason with her. I'd been protecting her for years. I couldn't help myself. Soon enough she'd realize just how dangerous of a thing my protection was. I needed to get her out of my head, which was fucking funny considering she was in my penthouse.

She wanted me, maybe as much as I wanted her. There was no way in hell I would ever allow it to happen. I had to prove to her this illusion she had in her mind about me, about *us*...

Was just that.

A fucking fantasy.

A creation of a fairy tale in her mind.

I didn't do happily ever afters, and the sooner she realized who I really was, the better.

My phone rang, pulling me away from my thoughts. "Habla," I answered, "*Talk*." Waving off the chick to fetch my drink. She rolled her eyes, strutting away. Purposely swaying her ass with every step.

"Boss, the girl is fucking crying."

"She has a name, asshole. It's Lexi. Learn it."

"Got it, Boss. Lexi's crying."

"What do you expect me to do about it? Read her a fucking bedtime story?"

226

"I just thought you'd like to know. You told us to keep you informed."

I spoke through gritted teeth. "About her safety, not hormonal bullshit. I want you to make sure she's safe. That's what I'm fucking paying you for. Not to call me and waste my fucking time because the girl is having a fucking meltdown."

"Should I... go in there? Maybe try to calm her—"

"You touch her, I'll rip your fucking cock off, and make you sit on it, mierda," I spewed, "*Fuck*" and hung up. Throwing my phone on the bar. "Whose balls do I have to bust to get a goddamn drink around here?" I roared, looking all around me. Leaning my elbow on the hard surface, pulling at my hair again. Making a mental note to fire the son of a bitch.

"Everything okay?" the same familiar voice shyly asked, setting my drink down in front of me. "I wasn't trying to eavesdrop. I just heard... I mean... it sounded... really bad," she breathed out.

I took a swig of my bourbon. "My, my, whatever the fuck your name is, what big ears you have."

I could feel her anxiety searing off of her onto the makeshift bar between us. "I'm sorry," she added, wiping down the surface with a wet rag.

"What exactly are you sorry for?" I asked, finally looking up from my drink. "The fact that you can't mind your own goddamn business, or the fact that you're throwing yourself at me when you know damn well you shouldn't be," I paused to let my words sink in. "I'm the wolf, the one your momma warned you to stay away from." Downing the rest of my liquor, I slid the empty glass toward her. Signaling for another.

"I just... I wanted to make sure everything was alright. Friendly conversation. Remember, I'm Julie. That phone call seemed intense, that's all," she flirted, making her way around the bar, standing beside me. Placing my drink in front of me.

I looked down at the glass, ignoring her advances as I brought the bourbon up to my mouth. "Ah." I smacked my lips together, savoring the fiery liquid moving down my throat. I looked up, grinning, taking in her curvy body as she leaned against the bar. I watched her swallow hard. Taking in my penetrating stare, licking her perfect dick-sucking lips.

Baiting me.

"Let's cut the bullshit."

"Excuse me?" she replied, surprised.

"Say it."

She raised her eyebrows. "Say what?"

"You want me to fuck you."

She gasped. "How dare you?

I grinned again, cocking my head to the side. "How dare I what? Speak the truth? Come on, sweetheart, aren't we a little old to be playing games?"

She blushed, and it looked so revealing on her light complexion.

"Don't play shy… *Julie*," I said, accentuating her name. Grazing her name badge that was placed on her left tit, with my finger. "It only turns me on more. I love the chase. It's the wolf in me." I pushed off the stool, placing my glass beside me.

She took three steps back as I came at her, the wall stopping her momentum. I smiled, caging her in with my arms. She sucked in another breath, her minty flavor scent hitting my senses.

I leaned in near her hair and inhaled her smell of vanilla and honey. "You smell edible," I groaned, running the tip of my nose against her cheek and smiling.

Her eyes dilated with lust, like no one had ever talked to her that way before. The realization made my cock hard. "I want to fuck you," I breathed out against her ear, continuing my assault down the side of her neck. "So the question really is… can you leave with me now?"

She pressed her delicate hand on my chest, not pushing me back, but not pulling me in either. I didn't give a fuck that we were in public or that this was her place of employment. They wouldn't fire her. I'd make sure of it.

"I don't like waiting." I glanced up into her eyes, removing my mouth from her neck. Sheer disappointment passed through her eyes.

"Yes," she practically, fucking moaned.

228

I ran the tip of my finger along her cleavage, and her chest suddenly rose, making her tits look bigger. She would have let me fuck her up against the wall, but I had other ulterior motives. Ones that involved taking her back to my penthouse.

I didn't give a shit about her. She was a means to an end. Lexi's room was the closest to mine. All I had to do was leave my door open. I never brought women back to my penthouse, no one knew where I lived. I made an exception, having no other choice in the matter.

This would prove once and for all I wasn't the man she thought I was. I'd make her believe I was savoring every thrust. The slapping sounds of my balls against her ass. Every push and every pull.

Her screaming my name, begging me to let her come.

It was what it was.

End of story.

"You're not staying the night. I don't cuddle. I don't whisper sweet nothings in your ear. I don't make love. I take. And then I take some more," I stated, emphasizing the words. "I fuck, Julie. I'll fuck you until you can't come anymore."

She took in every word as if I recited poetry.

"After I'm done, I'll tell you to get the fuck out of my bed," I crudely added.

Her eyebrows lowered, causing her face to frown. At least I wasn't a liar.

"Love me or hate me, sweetheart, but lead the fucking way."

She hesitated for a second, and then pushed off the wall. She hollered to her boss that she was leaving for the day, and walked out. I followed her, nodding toward my limo that was parked on the side. Watching her closely, her demeanor read of a woman who had never done this before. Almost like she was breaking all her rules, knowing that she was putting her job in jeopardy. Shitting on her morals and giving into the desire I promised her.

For a second I felt bad.

I almost wanted to tell her to stay. That it wasn't a good idea.

Almost...

"Coming or staying?" I asked, walking in front of her. "Trust me... I plan on making you come, a lot."

She bit her bottom lip, and I silently laughed.

I took her back to my penthouse, knowing Lexi heard everything like I wanted her to. I fucked her exactly how I promised and then some. It was late into the night by the time I was done with her and kicked her the fuck out the same way.

Not even saying goodbye.

I jumped in the shower, needing to wash away my sins. The fact that I caused Lexi pain, when in reality all I wanted to do was to provide her with comfort.

I waited until I knew she would be passed out, probably from the pain medication she took for more than one reason tonight. Her door was now closed, knowing it was open when I came back earlier with my fuck buddy. She had slammed it, shutting out the noise. Really yearning to shut me out.

Or at least trying to.

I slowly opened her door, careful not to wake her. Walking into her room, I hovered over her petite frame, which seemed smaller since I last left her and that was only a few hours ago. She was curled into her pillow, the blanket almost covering her head as if she was trying to drown out the noises coming from my bedroom or possibly her own mind. Even in the dim lighting from the hallway, I could tell she had been crying. Her face flushed, her lips swollen.

I gently brushed the hair away from her face, wanting to feel her soft skin against my callused fingers. She softly moaned in contentment, even in a deep sleep she liked my touch. Although, she probably fucking hated me now that I made her listen to me fuck another woman.

Exactly like I needed her to.

I moved away from her, even though it was the last thing I wanted to do, taking a seat in the armchair by her bed.

She needed to stay away from me. I wanted her to stay away from me. I should've made her leave, but it didn't matter because *I* couldn't stay away from her any longer.

And in the end…

I didn't fucking want to.

So instead, I watched her sleep. Protecting her the only way I knew how. Except there was no protecting her…

230

From. Me.

"God, you're fucking huge," I thought I heard a woman loudly moan.

I groaned, moving my head side-to-side on my pillow, nestling my sore body into the mattress. Not comprehending if I was awake or asleep at that point. Thinking I was just hearing things in my dream. It took me forever to fall asleep after Martinez abruptly left me, without a care in the fucking world. Leaving me all by myself. The tears just wouldn't stop flowing, one right after the other soaked into my pillow, until I had no more to shed. They were taxing and ruthless, just like him. If I was asleep, I didn't want to wake up, I was emotionally, physically, and mentally drained.

"Yes, right there! Fuck me right there! Just like that… please… please make me come!" I overheard. This time it was loud and clear.

Startling me awake. I immediately sat up, forgetting I had been beaten the night before. I grabbed onto my ribs, trying to ease the pain as I peered around the empty room.

"What the fuck?" I whispered to myself, taking a few calming breathes. Wiping the dead sleep from eyes, I blinked a few times, trying to adjust to the darkness around me.

That's when I heard, "Ride my cock, sweetheart. Fuck me!" Recognizing the dominant tone immediately. The sounds of their bodies slapping together echoed through the hallway into my room.

My stomach dropped, my hand went to my chest, trying to hold my heart from shattering into a million pieces. It was too late, piece-by-piece, moan-by-moan, it broke, bleeding all over his white, linen sheets. I couldn't help but continue to overhear the filthy shit coming out of Martinez's mouth from afar. Along with the screams of bliss from the random whore he was intimately sharing his bed with. I knew that much for sure, the way they were talking to each other proved they didn't know one another.

They were relishing in the pleasure their tangled, insatiable bodies were bringing to one another while I was fighting the bile that rose in the back of my throat. After everything I had been through in the past twenty-four hours, I was forced to sit there and listen to Martinez fuck another woman. I couldn't catch a fucking break. Fate was such a bitch. Before I knew what I was doing, my feet hit the cold marble tile, running to the en suite bathroom. Falling to my knees in front of the toilet, I ignored the sharp pain that radiated through my body as I emptied the contents of my stomach while I continued to hear raw, sexual sounds beating into my head.

He didn't give a flying fuck that I could hear what they were doing, what he was saying to her, how much he was making her come. The ecstasy he was pounding into her pussy over and over again.

"Just like that… take my cock," he growled.

She gagged.

I scoffed in disgust. My eyes filled with tears again, my lips trembled, and whatever little piece of his soul I thought I saw when he looked at me, crumbled beneath me on the cold tile floor. I fucking hated him.

Every last part of him.

He left me here by myself in his home, knowing I would be scared, anxious, overwhelmed by all the shit that happened to me. I didn't even know how much time went by while I laid, curled up in the fetal position there on the bathroom floor, listening. Making sure I took in every moan, every thrust, every plea, until I couldn't take it anymore. Engrained so deep into my heart, where all my thoughts and feelings would now be shoved too.

He wasn't who I thought he was.

Not even fucking close.

It seemed as though they went at it for hours. I had enough, I reached my limit, I pushed off the bathroom floor, ignoring my body's pleas to take it easy. I reached my door contemplating my next move.

"I hope you choke on it!" I yelled and I slammed it shut. Not caring if he heard me or not. I immediately opened my pills, taking two down without any water, wanting to knock myself the fuck out from the pain running through my body, especially my heart.

I laid back on the bed, staring at the ceiling, willing the medication to take effect. Thinking about how I got into this situation in the first place.

How did any of this happen?

I didn't understand why he had me here if he didn't care for me.

Why was he protecting me?

Nothing made sense.

Not one damn thing.

My eyes started to flutter, sleep finally taking reign again. My body sank into the mattress beneath me, heaviness coursed through me, and the room went black. Even in my sleep, I couldn't escape him. I felt him, his distinctive scent all around me, touching me, watching over me. At one point during the night, I could have sworn I saw him sitting in the armchair beside my bed. But I couldn't be sure, the drug-induced haze kept taking me under. Probably producing false illusions, the same ones I created over the years.

When I woke up the next morning I was by myself, hating the fact that I dreamt about him, again. I was in a foul mood, hating life, hating him, and hating that I was still fucking there, and I couldn't go home.

I was homeless yet again.

And I hated that more than anything.

The fucking dark cloud I carried around for years was back with a vengeance. Just as my life was starting to look up, one bad decision took it all away from me. Ripping away the life I'd work so hard for, finally loving where I was after all that hardship right out of my grasp. I didn't know what God had up his sleeve for me, all I knew was I wanted to get the fuck out of there. I wanted to go back to living my life in my little bubble.

Most of all I wanted to be able to dance again.

I showered as best as I could, my body hurting even more than it did the night before. Allowing the hot water to soak my sore

233

muscles like I had been doing ever since I was little. But this time, it wouldn't grant me any peace like it had for years. When the water turned cold, I got out and dried off in the bathroom. Wiping the steam from my hot shower off the mirror with my hand, staring down at the sink not ready to face the woman that would be staring back at me. I needed to inspect the damage Nikolai had inflicted upon my face and body. Taking a deep breath, I opened my eyes and almost gasped when I saw my reflection.

"Oh my God," I breathed out not recognizing the woman through the glass.

My eyes were bloodshot, hollow, and swollen from spending most of the night crying. Dark, purplish and green bruises circled my left eye, descending to my cheekbone, disappearing into my hairline. Another bruise ascended from my right cheek over to the bridge of my nose. Turning my head side to side, I examined Nikolai's handy work. Bringing my hand up, gently caressing my fingers over my once flawless skin. Hissing in pain as soon as they made contact. My dry lips were cracking, a sharp cut on my bottom lip making it more painful. My eyes followed my hand as I glided it down toward my chest, ribs, and stomach. Purple, blue, and black bruises covering the entire area.

My gaze never left the mirror as I took in every last inch of my broken body. Scoffing out in disappointment for how I could let this happen to me. Tears threatened in my eyes. I grew up with a predator, I should have seen the signs I should have known better than to let anyone in my life. I ended up dating a man that just waited for the right moment to strike. Leaving me more damaged now than I had ever been before. I quickly wiped away the tears that had escaped from my puffy eyes, wincing from my own touch, again. I grabbed another towel off the warming rack, and wrapped it tightly around my body, unable to look at myself any longer. Taking in my appearance was making me sick.

I opened the door, closing my eyes, welcoming the cool air on my face. Shrieking as soon as I opened my eyes to find him sitting on the corner of my bed. Placing my hand over my ribs, I bowed my head, promptly whimpering in pain.

"Fuck," I muttered through gritted teeth.

I heard the bed creak, and immediately peered up at him, but I was too late. He was over to me in three strides, getting right in my personal space without me asking him to do so.

"Don't touch me," I snapped, expecting him to back away.

He didn't. Not even deterred by my outburst. He just bent down, diligently picked me up off the ground as if I weighed nothing, carrying me over toward the bed, setting me down on the soft mattress. I instantly turned my rigid face away from him, not wanting to look into his tantalizing eyes. Pretending with everything I had left in me, that his touch, his kindness, his scent didn't faze me.

He finally stepped back, but I could still feel his warm breath on my neck. I struggled to release the nervous breath I'd been holding since I opened the bathroom door.

"Don't you know how to knock?" I asked, breathing through the anxiety threatening to attack me at any second. Hoping he wouldn't notice, but knowing he noticed everything.

"I refuse to knock on a door I own," he simply stated, talking to the back of my head.

I rolled my eyes still not looking at him. I fucking refused to give him that satisfaction. "Well, I'm staying here now. Without my consent, and against my will," I added for good measure. "So knock on the damn door if you want to come in, and I'll think about letting you in," I stated, all proud of myself.

He leaned over, grabbing my chin, turning my face to look up at him. I glared into his once again serene, bright blue eyes.

"That's the second time you've looked away from me, instead of looking me in the fucking eyes when I'm talking to you, sweetheart. There won't be a third."

I jerked my face away from his grasp, and he let me go. "I could have been naked. But that doesn't matter, does it? Little girls don't make you hard anyway, but the woman last night sure as hell did," I spewed, not being able to hold it in any longer. Mentally chastising myself for letting him know it hurt me.

He hurt me.

His face was impassive, neutral. I couldn't read one damn thing and it further fueled my pissed off mood. I abruptly stood, walking away from him. Not giving him the chance to answer. I

235

didn't want to hear his bullshit response I knew he was going to give me. I closed my eyes, biting my lip from the sudden harsh pain the swift movement caused.

"You need to rest. You're never going to heal if you don't listen to me."

"No!" I called out, turning around to face him. My temper, taking over. "Stop telling me what to do! Just because you're used to bossing everyone else around, doesn't mean shit to me. Now, leave! Don't let the door hit *your* ass on the way out!" Throwing his exact words back at him from the day he kicked me out of his office, all those years ago.

"Get in bed," he calmly ordered in a monotone voice. Pointing his long index finger toward the mattress.

"No," I snarled, stepping toward him.

His eyes glazed over, and I secretly loved finally getting some sort of emotion from him.

"Get in the fucking bed, Lexi..." His hands, working into fists by his side.

I stepped toward him again, getting right in his face this time. Looking him dead in the eyes, I clenched out, "No."

"Motherfucker!" he seethed from deep within his chest, cocking his head to the side with an eerie composure.

It all happened so fast. I didn't even see him coming. The next thing I knew he picked me up again, carrying me over to the bed in three steady strides, setting me down in the middle of the mattress.

Holding me in place, he got close to my face, our mouths inches apart. He didn't falter, speaking with execution, "I do not have time for your bullshit temper tantrums that you think I give a fuck about! When I tell you to do something, you fucking do it! I don't like to repeat myself. And I won't. Test me again, *little girl*. And watch what fucking happens to you. I'll make you scream, and trust me, it won't be from pleasure like it was for the *woman* I fucked last night."

My chest heaved as I took in his threats. Pushing me back into the pillows, he let me go. Turning and leaving me without so much as a second glance. I spent the rest of the day, stewing in bed.

Exactly how he ordered me to.

Twenty-seven

Martinez

I rode in the limo, heading to the strip club, in silence. Needing to gather all my thoughts. So much had happened in a matter of forty-eight hours. Including her.

Fucking Lexi.

That woman was going to be the end of me, and the sad part about it was, she didn't even realize it. My head was pounding, and it was barely eight in the fucking morning. I couldn't remember the last time I slept for more than an hour or two. Always sleeping with one eye open, waiting for whatever may come my way. The days wound into nights, like the spindle of a fucking thread.

I walked into my office, steering clear of all the bullshit my men were trying to bring to my attention. I sat in my leather office chair, setting my elbows on my desk, placing my throbbing head in between my hands. Allowing the silence to swallow me whole, relishing in the foreign feeling, even if it was just for a few minutes. I let it take over mind, body, and dark soul. Going from feeling so much over the last few days, to feeling nothing. My mind wasn't used to it, and it had no fucking problem letting me know it didn't appreciate the sentiment.

"Martinez," Leo interrupted, opening my office door, and shutting it behind him.

"Fuck off," I greeted, not bothering to look up.

"Well aren't you just a delightful bag of shit this morning," he chuckled, sitting in one of the chairs, facing my desk.

If it were anyone else, I would have no problem putting a goddamn bullet in their balls if they ever talked to me that way. Leo was different.

"The girl?" he asked, with no hesitation.

"A pain in my fucking ass," I simply stated.

"You're playing with fire," he declared out of nowhere, bringing my attention up to him.

I sat back in my chair, narrowing my eyes at my friend. "She's a kid, a fucking child. I need a woman, Leo. She could be my fucking kid for Christ's sake."

"So be it. But she's a—"

"Little girl," I chimed in, annoyed. Knowing where he was going with this.

"Legal. And in my book that's fucking fair game."

I shook my head. "You don't know what you're talking about."

"I don't? You haven't made me watch over Lexi for years?"

Leo was the only man I trusted with her. The only man I knew would do the job right.

"Hmm... she isn't sleeping in your penthouse right now?" He leaned forward, placing his arms on my desk. "You didn't murder one of your trusted, longtime associates for her either, right? Nikolai thought you were his friend."

"Friend is a term I use loosely. He was going to rape her. I had no choice. The motherfucker had it coming."

"Since when has another man's sexual deviance bothered you? You've dealt with men far worse than him every day of your life, and you'll continue to do so."

"What's your point, Leo? I don't have all fucking day to sit here and chit-chat like some schoolgirls in heat."

"I thought I was making it, maybe I should just draw a picture for your dumb ass."

I stood, needing to get the hell away from him as well. "Your wife makes you wear a condom, doesn't she?"

"Throw your insults at me all you want, buddy. I'm not the one that sleeps alone every night. Oh wait... I forgot, El Diablo doesn't sleep, right? Now why do you think that is?"

I glared at him.

He laughed, throwing his head back. "Oh man, Martinez. You have got it bad. So fucking badly my friend. I never thought I'd see this day happen again. You better get your skates out because your fucking world has just frozen over."

"Get the fuck out," I gritted, not wanting to hear the shit he was brewing.

"What are you going to do about Nikolai's men?" he asked, ignoring my demand, staying put in his chair. "You know they're not happy. They are fucking furious. They want the girl. You know that as much as I do. You may have pulled the trigger, but it was for her. She's your weakness, and you made that loud and fucking clear. It's only a matter of time until they figure it out."

"Why don't you let me worry about Nikolai's men."

"What about Lexi?"

"What about her? She's not anyone's concern, but mine. Are we clear? No one is to lay a fucking finger on her."

He stood, rounding my desk. "That's what I'm afraid of." Patting me on the back and walking out.

As soon as he left, I pulled my cellphone out of my suit jacket, hitting send as I sat back down in my chair.

"Boss," Rick answered after one ring.

"We good?" I questioned, rapidly tapping my pen on my desk.

"Everything's taken care of. The girl—" I hung up, cutting him off.

Spending most of the day thinking about Lexi.

It was late by the time I made it back home. Going straight into my office, needing to finish up a few odds and ends, before making my way toward Lexi's room. Thinking she would be asleep, I carefully opened her door like I had the night before. Ready to take my usual place in the armchair by her bed. I sat, watching her for a few seconds.

"I'm not sleeping," her voice rang out in the darkness.

"I know." I did the moment I walked into the room. I could feel her anywhere, especially when she was around me. The pull, the hold, the lock which only she possessed over me.

"Of course you did. You know everything, oh wise one. You know what? You're like a modern day fucking Yoda. Which seems kind of unfair if you think about it. You seem to know everything about me. Yet, I don't know a damn thing about you, other than you walk around here with a stick up your ass. You expect me to stay here, in your home, with you. And all you seem to want is for me to listen to your every command, like I'm your damn dog."

"If I had a dog, it would obey me. You, on the other hand, do not."

She wanted to laugh, but turned her head to smile instead. Thinking I couldn't see her. Taking a deep breath, she asked, "When can I leave?"

"When I tell you, you can."

"What about my job? I worked so—"

"I took care of it."

"What?" she asked, sitting up. Hissing from the immediate pain to her ribs.

I didn't hesitate. Walking over to the nightstand, opening the bottle, handing her two pills with her glass of water.

She glanced up at me, even though she couldn't see anything but my faint shadow looking down at her. "I don't like them. They make me sleep."

"No shit. You need to rest."

She reluctantly nodded, taking them, fighting an internal struggle not to argue with me. I sat back in the armchair, sinking into it. Rubbing my fingers over my mouth as I watched her contemplate what else she wanted to say to me.

"Have you been doing this every night? Sitting there? Watching me?" she finally asked what had been plaguing her since the minute she woke up in this room.

"It doesn't matter."

"It does to me."

"I'm not who you think I am, Lexi. And the sooner you realize that, the better."

"Maybe you're not who you think you are. Have you ever considered that?"

Her words resonated somewhere deep inside of me.

"What do you think is going to happen here, cariño? Do you want to be my whore?" I crudely asked, wanting to make her uncomfortable. Knowing all I had to do was push that hard limit for her.

Sex.

240

My stomach fluttered, seizing my body completely. I inadvertently writhed around in the sheets. Basking in the cool feeling against my heated skin.

"No," I replied in a voice I didn't recognize. "You have plenty of those. How about we just start off as friends? I don't have many. And for some reason I couldn't possibly begin to understand," I sarcastically stated, "I don't think you do either."

"Friends?" he drawled out, like the word seemed foreign coming from his lips.

"Yeah... I mean. We kind of sort of are, I guess. Friends help each other. You saved me so—"

"And what are you going to do for me?"

"Oh... Well, what do you want?"

"Something I shouldn't."

"Which is?"

"You. In my bed. Now."

I didn't know what to say, so I didn't say anything at all. My heart sped up, beating a mile a minute. I swear he could hear it. Sweat started pooling at my temples. "Stop trying to make me feel uncomfortable, I know what you're trying to do," I voiced in a steady tone even though my body was anything but that.

"Is that right?"

"Yes. That's right. You want to pretend like you don't feel what is happening between us. You want to make it all about sex. Your words may say that, but your actions contradict everything that comes out of your filthy mouth. You've been watching me for years, keeping me safe. Then you saved me. Now I'm here where I'm safe again. You want me to rest, you're concerned about me. You're protecting me. You—"

"Did I fuck that woman last night for you, too?"

That was like taking a bullet to the fucking heart. It would have shattered if it hadn't already the night before.

"Don't get it twisted, Lexi. This is how it's going to be. You're going to stay here until I tell you it's safe for you to go. Then you're going to leave. There's nothing here for you, especially *me*. Because trust me, sweetheart. I will make you leave."

"But I'm here now," I whispered, fidgeting with my fingers under the sheets. "Because you want me here. I don't need to be here. I've been protecting myself my entire life. You don't know what I've been through, so people who in live in glass houses shouldn't throw stones. I made a mistake, and I trusted someone I shouldn't have. It's why I don't let people get close to me. I should have known better. And even though I shouldn't trust you, I do," I paused, letting my words sink in. "I know somewhere deep inside you, lies a man who had a good heart once. Or I wouldn't be laying here. I think you lost your way, and now you're just trying to find your feet on the ground."

Silence.

Each second of stillness that passed between us made me realize I was right, and he knew it.

"You leave me by myself because you don't want to get close to me. But it's backfired on you, because all I have time to do is to think. You don't trust anyone, including yourself. Why would you bring a random woman back here? It didn't make any sense, until I got to thinking today. You fucked her last night to hurt me, to prove to me that you don't care about me. Well, you succeeded, I spent the entire night hurting, exactly the way you wanted me to. You wanted me to hate you. It makes it easier on you. Am I getting warmer, Alejandro?"

I turned, stepping out of the bed carefully, before I lost the nerve. Walking over to him in the darkness, crouching down in front of him, placing my arms on his thighs for support.

He didn't move.

He didn't tense.

He didn't make one sound.

Knowing he could see me, even if I couldn't see him. I peered up to the faint shadow of his handsome face and sinful blue eyes, knowing in my heart there was more emotion evident on his expression than there had been in years.

Taking him by surprise.

"Well, guess what? I'm not going to make it easy for you."

He instantly stood, pushing back the armchair from the impact of his abrupt stance. It skidded across the floor. I would have fallen on my ass had I not expected his reaction.

"Go to fucking sleep," he snapped, walking out of the room. Slamming the door behind him.

I smiled.

For the first time since I had been there, I fucking smiled. Lying back down in my bed, I snuggled into my pillow and comforter, feeling happy and content with myself. I took a deep, liberating breath. Allowing the pills to take me under, and I would succumb to a good night's sleep. Finally. Dreaming of the blue-eyed man who had captured my heart.

Knowing as I soon as I passed out, he would come back in. Pull up his chair next to my bed.

To watch over me.
My dark angel.

Twenty-eight
Lexi

Three months went by at a slow and steady pace. I felt every second, every minute, every hour, counting down the days until he said I could leave. I wanted to be able to step outside and soak up the sun without having to worry about getting killed. Most of all, I couldn't wait to dance again. This was the longest I had gone without dancing.

Living in this penthouse was starting to take a toll on me. I may have been physically healed, but mentally and emotionally, I was far more messed up than I ever was before. I never realized how much I truly hated being by myself. Maybe I was too distracted with ballet to notice the absence of people around me, before but I found myself craving conversation and human interaction. Dance was my entire life, my escape from reality, my happy place. Where there was no negativity, no violence, no memories…but it was also a lonely place.

My whole life.

After I fully recovered, I started leaving my room. Venturing out into the penthouse, since I wasn't permitted to go outside. Martinez said it wasn't safe yet. He was handling it as fast as he could, but it was going to take time. The only problem was he didn't know how much time, and I was slowly losing myself.

At times, I wandered around aimlessly through his penthouse in hopes that maybe I would find him. That maybe we could talk again, even though all we seemed to do was fight. I was lonely, and could have really used some company.

I barely ever saw him, though. He was there less and less as the days went on, never telling me where he was going, or when he would be back. We never talked about had happened that night,

244

both in denial, both pretending. We barely exchanged more than a few words when our paths crossed and that was mostly him telling me I still couldn't leave, it still wasn't safe, and the men looking for me hadn't given up yet. I hadn't seen or heard any more sexcapades either since the second night I was there, thank God for small miracles.

A woman did show up late one night, knocking on his door as I walked toward the kitchen to get some water. I opened it without thinking, much to his disapproval. She looked young, maybe a few years older than me. I didn't have to question if she was one of his random whores, she had his eyes. At first I thought it might be his daughter, but he dismissed me before I could ask her who she was. My curiosity got the best of me though and decided since he wouldn't give me any answers I should get them on my own. Instead of heading back to my room, I lingered around the hallway. Their conversation seemed tense and made me slightly uncomfortable but my instinct was right, they were related. She was his niece, Briggs. They didn't seem to have a loving relationship, which didn't surprise me in the least. She stayed at his penthouse for a few days, never leaving her room. I didn't see her again, and he never mentioned her after that.

Anything I needed or wanted was delivered right to my room at any point in time. Even though he made sure I was well cared for, he never fulfilled my one desire that would cost him nothing.

Companionship.

All I really wanted or needed was for him to keep me company, even if words weren't spoken. I still felt him at night, watching me sleep. Every time I opened my eyes to catch him sitting there.

He wasn't.

I guess loneliness could make you imagine what you truly wanted, and I still wanted him. So fucking much. The sad part was, for the first time in my life, I felt safe. With him. Which confused me more than anything.

That morning I decided to venture further into his penthouse. So far I'd found a library and a movie theater, I spent a few days in both, but neither had been a good distraction. Today, I hit the jackpot. A huge gym was hidden in the never-ending corridors. As soon as I walked in, it became the only room that provided me with some type of comfort. His potent scent lingered in every crevice of the open space. I secretly hoped that one day I would walk in, and he would be there, working out his frustrations, preferably shirtless, sweat dripping down his chest and abs. I had to shake off the image.

There was every possible piece of exercise equipment known to man in the abundant space. Mirrors lined all the walls, expanding from the floor to the ceiling. The space was lined with dark, hardwood floors and some exercise mats throughout it. An expensive stereo system had been set up in the corner of the room, with speakers spread evenly in the space. It also housed a sauna and private restroom, equipped with showers and everything under the sun.

I don't know what came over me, but I just started dancing, the music playing in my head. I spent the entire day in that room, getting lost in the movements and rhythm that were deeply embedded in my soul. By the end of the day, I was exhausted, pushing my body more than I should have after so many weeks of not dancing. I took a shower, letting the hot water soak my sore limbs. Shortly after that, I headed straight to bed. I was out before my head even hit the pillow. Dreaming of him like I did every night for the last three months. For the first time, I was eager to wake up the next day. Knowing I could dance. My eyes fluttered open, taking in the bright light shining through the curtains. Stretching my sore limbs, my body physically spent from the day before. I sat up and looked at the clock beside my bed, it was already eleven in the morning. I had slept in late for the first time since I could remember.

Throwing on a tank top with some cotton shorts, I tossed my hair up in a high bun on the top of my head, and brushed my teeth, going about my normal morning routine. His maid, Maria was nice enough to make me food whenever I was hungry. She would stick around and keep me company as I ate every morning. Sometimes during lunch and dinner too. If it weren't for her, I would have no one to talk to, except maybe to myself. Excitement couldn't begin to describe what I felt as I made my way toward his gym after I finished my breakfast.

I rounded the corner in the long, narrow hallway. Seconds away from walking into what recently became my heaven. Smiling from ear-to-ear as I opened the large, wood door to the gym. Nothing could have prepared me for what laid in front of me.

All of his gym equipment had vanished, as if it was never there to begin with. Not one piece of gear was left in the wide-open space. All of it replaced with every piece of ballet equipment I could ever need, and then some. It had been turned into my own personal ballet studio.

Just for me.

I sucked in a breath, placing my hand over my heart as I walked around the room with nothing but astonishment and wonder. Tears threatened my eyes as they took in every last detail of the special place he'd made for me.

A beautiful, black leather sofa sat against the center of the back wall, accented with comfortable, grey pillows. A ballet barre extended the full length of the mirrored walls, parallel to the couch. A square, wood box of rosin placed beside it. I softly ran my fingers along the barre, gripping onto it for support. This was all just so damn overwhelming. The massive, black armoire in the back corner caught my attention next. I practically leaped over to it, excited to see what it held. I opened each drawer, one by one, taking in all the contents. Different kinds of leotards, bright, neutral, patterned colors, showcased in one drawer. Several pairs of ballet tights lined the second one. Skirts in all different styles, colors, and patterns took over the next. Topping it all off with an endless supply of sports bras in the bottom drawer.

The choices were endless.

My pointe shoes and ballet flats were laid out on the dark hardwood floor, and sitting right next to them was a black dance bag full of brand new pairs of both. I wiped away the tears that started streaming down my cheeks. I was in this room less than twenty-four hours ago. I couldn't believe the transformation from the masculine gym to this beautiful, feminine space. The surprises were never-ending. I walked over to the sound system, finding an abundant amount of ballet CD's, everything from Mozart to Gershwin. Including the soundtrack to *Swan Lake*.

My feet moved of their own accord, ripping off price tags from the designer apparel. Ignoring how much they cost. Standing behind the portable room divider in the corner, I changed into the most beautiful, elegant, soft attire I'd ever worn. Grabbing my tattered, worn-in, pointe shoes, and lacing them up my ankles. I went right to work, not wasting another minute. Dancing around the room like I never had before. Thriving in the emotions of finally feeling like I was home. Every turn, every step, every pose was an extension of the only happiness I'd ever known. I danced until I couldn't dance anymore.

It was late into the night by the time I was so exhausted I couldn't push through any longer. Sweat glistened over every inch of me, and I could barely stand on my own two feet. But it didn't matter because I knew when I woke up the next morning, I could do it again. That alone gave me some peace of mind. I slipped off my pointe shoes, taking in the damage I had inflicted upon my poor toes. Welcoming the pain and blisters. Placing the shoes exactly where I found them. I stretched my limbs on the barre one last time, loving the way my sore muscles ached from a job well done.

I took one last look at the room, before turning off the lights and closing the door behind me. Leaning my back against the solid mahogany surface, smiling, thinking about Martinez, and what he had done to his space. How much I appreciated him at that moment, for absolutely everything he had done for me in the last few months. Behind his dark, cold demeanor, I could tell the man had a heart. Even though he would deny it. I got the sudden urge to talk to him, hug him, and tell him thank you a million times over.

I pushed off the door, walking back to my bedroom, when I heard the front door slam shut. Rattling, echoing down the expansive hall. I didn't give it a second thought, I dashed through the penthouse to see if he was home. I felt him before I saw him, his masculine scent lingering all around me.

"Hey," I rasped, out of breath as soon as I got to him, hunching over. Placing my hands on my knees for support. My body shaking from the excitement that he was there, in front of me.

We could finally talk.

I could express how much the room transformation meant to me. How much *he* meant to me.

He stopped dead in his tracks, surprised by my behavior. Instantly eyeing me cautiously. Not saying a word. Something about the way he was looking at me revealed pain in his usual dark, cold, soulless eyes. I had never seen him appear so internally conflicted, nor did I understand why. He was fighting some sort of internal battle when it came to me. Avoiding me at all costs, not wanting to admit I had an affect on him too. He stood there with his hands in his slacks, just staring with no expression. I wanted to stay lost in his eyes at that moment, savoring the way he was looking at me. The way he pulled every sentiment from my body as if it belonged to him. Especially the way I was making him feel.

I never wanted it to end.

It was as if we were the only two people in the world.

"Alejandro," I coaxed still out of breath, overwhelmed by my emotions. "I can't believe—"

"Don't," he interrupted in a frayed tone.

I stood upright, stepping toward him. "I just want—" He put his hand out, gesturing for me to stop.

"Don't," he repeated in a stern voice. Forcefully accentuating the word.

I reached out, placing my shaking hand on his chest and he let me.

"All I want is—" He shoved away, causing me to stumble back. Catching myself before I fell, as he brushed past, walking away from me. Not allowing me to finish what I so desperately wanted to say to him. I grimaced, hurt. "What the hell?" I whispered to myself. Wavering for a few minutes as I watched him stride toward his office, like he did every time he came home.

Dismissing me. Again.

I took a deep, calming breath, before following after him. The man was like Jekyll and Hyde, doing something so meaningful and loving for me, then shoving me away, when all I wanted to do was thank him. His office door slammed shut before I could catch up to him. I stood in front of the wooden space for a few seconds, flexing my fists at my sides, fuming. He needed to step down off his damn high horse and treat me with some respect. I knew in the back of my mind this wasn't going to end well. But I didn't give a shit. Nothing was going to stop me from barging into his office, a replay of a failed attempt all those years ago.

I swung open the door, smacking it into the wall with a loud thud. He was sitting in his chair, his elbows placed on the desk with his head resting in between his strong hands. He didn't even startle, as if he was expecting me to trail in after him. He peered up with a menacing glare, I knew stepping foot in his office without being told to enter would piss him off even more. I was treading over the imaginary line of his boundaries, and I didn't care.

Not for one second.

"What is your fucking problem?" I hissed, frustrated he was being this way with me, yet again. He was ruining everything he had done for me that day which pissed me off more than anything. "You're giving me the worst case of whiplash known to man, Martinez."

"Lexi, don't," he growled in a cold and detached tone.

"Don't what? Huh? Don't talk to you? Don't look at you? Don't touch you? What can't I fucking do, now? All you do is bark orders at me! I'm sick of it! I'm not your dog! I just wanted to thank—"

His chair slid back as his fists connected with his desk beneath him. "Don't fuck with me! I am not in the mood for your bullshit! This is your last warning, sweetheart. Get off my cock. Don't fucking provoke me! Mind your own damn business. Turn around and go put on one of your tutus I bought you, and twirl your ass out of my fucking office. Now!" he roared, the veins in his neck protruding.

I jerked back like he had hit me. "You're a fucking asshole!" I screamed, grabbing the door behind me and slamming it. Locking myself in his personal space. Letting him know I wasn't going anywhere. "You leave me here by myself, all fucking day, for days at a time with no one to talk to except your damn maid! Yet, here I am. Trusting you, thinking about you, and wanting you to fucking acknowledge the connection we have! I know you feel it too! Try to deny it all you want, but you wouldn't have ever done what you did for me today, if you didn't care!"

250

He just sat there with his body hunched over his desk. Anger rolling off his back as his chest heaved. I roughly ran my hands through my hair, trying to compose myself but it was no fucking use. I was too pissed, too hurt, too over all the bullshit he kept putting me through.

"I just wanted to say thank you! What you did for me today... that room... my own space..." I fervently shook my head, my emotions getting the best of me. I could feel them taking over. I shoved them all the away not wanting him to see me cry. "No one has ever done anything like that for me before. No one has ever cared! Today was one of the best days of my life, and you're shitting all over it! You're fucking ruining it, you bastard! You're hot! You're cold! I can't keep up anymore! I want to leave, but then again I don't... because I'm scared that I'll never see you again. I hate that! Relying on you. Do you understand how hard that is for me?!" I yelled through my emotions, stomping my foot on the ground, needing to get my point across. Needing him to understand.

He didn't move.

He didn't say one word.

He didn't even blink.

Nothing.

That was all I needed to lose my shit.

"Oh my God!" I was over to his desk in three strides, shoving off everything with as much force as I could muster up. The piles of paperwork, documents, and folders were thrown to the floor in an instant. Leaving nothing in my wake. Knowing he spent hours upon hours organizing and dealing with whatever the fuck was important to him.

He never once wavered, glaring at me as if I was nothing but a piece of shit standing in front of him.

"What is it going to take? Huh? To get some sort of reaction out of you!" Slamming my fists down on the desk, gritting through the pain it caused. "What do I have to do for you to show me the man behind the expensive, goddamn suits?!"

He stood ferociously, taking the desk with him. Flipping it over, causing me to jump back before it landed on me. His chair slammed into the bookshelves behind him, rattling the columns, sending some books crashing to the floor. Chaos erupted all around me. I turned to run, to get the hell away from him, but it was too late. He was already ahead of me, getting in my face, and invading my personal space. Before I knew what was happening as my back connected with the adjacent wall, near his flipped over desk. The force of my own momentum, knocked the wind out of me. My eyes widened as I gasped for air that was available for the taking. Stunned by the drastic turn of events with his dominant, demanding, arrogant presence looming over me like I was nothing but a scared little kitten.

I never expected what happened next.

Not. One. Damn. Thing.

Martinez

"Didn't I tell you not to fuck with me?" I seethed, inches away from her mouth.

"I-I-I—"

Lexi sputtered, her demeanor quickly changing from a lioness to a scared mouse.

"Didn't I warn you I wasn't in the mood for your fucking bullshit tonight?"

"I'm sor—"

"Didn't I tell you not to fucking provoke me? You mess with The Devil, sweetheart, you get the fucking horns."

I hated that she was fucking apologizing to me. I hated that she never listened to a goddamn word that came out of my mouth. But most of all I hated that I didn't give a flying fuck I was scaring the shit out of her. I would never physically hurt her, but she didn't have to fucking know that.

Maybe next time she would fucking listen to me.

She shook her head, back and forth with her lip quivering. Making my cock twitch at the sight of her. Images of me grabbing her by her sinful hips and fucking her up against the wall skated through my mind. I stepped back before I did something I was going to fucking regret. I'd spent most of the previous night, watching her on the security camera I had installed in the gym. I couldn't take my eyes off the recording. Following the way she flawlessly moved for hours across the hardwood floor with nothing but the music in her head.

The smile on her face alone was enough for me to make the call to have the equipment cleared out. Replacing it with everything she would need for her own studio.

A ballet studio in my fucking penthouse.

I shook away the images, the effect she had on me, the cord I couldn't fucking cut for the life of me. Unhooking my cufflinks, I rolled up the sleeves of my collared shirt. Unbuckling my belt next, pulling it out of the loops of my slacks with a snap.

"You want to meet the man behind the expensive, fucking suits?" I mocked in a threatening tone. Tilting my head to the side.

"What are you—"

Not allowing her to finish her goddamn question. I raised my hand and swung the belt down on the corner of the desk, right by her leg. She gasped as it hissed through the air. Her eyes widened with fear, instantly cowering back and away from me. I just wanted her to shut the fuck up, and do as she was told. I just wanted to get her out of my mind. She didn't belong there, no one did.

I didn't falter.

"Don't you dare. You can't—"

Gripping my belt tighter, I slapped it again on the wooden floor in front of me. It echoed off the walls. She immediately shuddered, panting profusely. Her tits rising and falling with each stride that brought me closer to her. My grasp white-knuckled the belt the whole time, not letting up on my assault. I leaned forward not being able to control myself any longer. Her vulnerability was becoming too much for me to bear. I dropped the belt to the floor, closing the distance between us.

Catching her off guard, my body engulfed her tiny frame, I kissed along her neck and then down her collarbone, as I gritted out, "What, cariño? What can't I fucking do?"

She didn't say anything, but she didn't have to. Her body was already betraying her mind, her breathing was pitched, her face flushed, her lips parted. The desire in her eyes was screaming at me to take her in my arms. Give her what she yearned for.

She wanted me to kiss her.

She wanted me to touch her.

She wanted me on top of her.

Instead I lifted her legs around my waist and I pushed into her, brushing my hard cock against her awaiting pussy so she could feel my need for her. Running my hand up her thigh to her waist, gripping onto her fuckable hips. Imaging how wet I was making her, how much I could make her come and scream out my goddamn name. My lips hovered over hers, on the verge of connecting as she panted profusely.

I wanted to give into her.

But, I let her go, causing her to hiss at the sudden loss of my lips against her heated skin. I couldn't do it. Everything about us was wrong, so instead I said, "That's what I fucking thought." And walked away.

Leaving her with nothing but the insatiable need for my cock.

Twenty-nine
Lexi

I couldn't believe I'd been with him for a half of a year now. One minute I was furious with him, the next I was terrified of him, and then I wanted him more than I had wanted anything in my entire life. I couldn't fathom how my emotions could go from one extreme to the next, within seconds.

Especially when it came to him.

The night in his office three months ago was a tipping point in our relationship. Some things changed, while others remained the same. He was still cold, and distant, trying to ignore me as the days went on. Little did he know, I could see the subtle looks he gave me more often now than before, the indecision in his eyes. Then one night, he came home earlier than usual from whatever the hell he did during his days.

When I walked into the dining room to eat my dinner, I stopped dead in my tracks. He was already in there, sitting at the head of the table, waiting for me. For a second, I contemplated turning back around and walking out on his ass. But I stayed, giving him the benefit of the doubt. I would be lying if I said I wasn't torn with how I felt about seeing him, especially under less extreme circumstances. His eyes were serene, full of stillness again, while a smile played on his lips, a smile I couldn't overlook.

He wasn't dressed any different, still hiding behind the expensive suit. Except this time his suit jacket was missing, his tie had been loosened, hanging low from his neck. The first few buttons of his colored shirt undone, displaying that silver chain necklace I saw the first night he brought me here. And exactly like that night, I was anxious to know what it was.

255

He nodded for me to take a seat next to him, breaking my train of thought, but I didn't obey. I sat on the other end of the long, narrow table, defying him once again. A grin appeared on his face as I took my seat and grabbed my napkin. Strategically placing it in my lap. I ignored him and his stupid handsome face, pretending as if I didn't care he was there with me.

When in reality, I did.

He cleared his throat. "How was your day, Lexi?" he asked, breaking the uncomfortable silence between us.

My head perked up. I just about fell out of my chair, shocked by his trivial question. He never took any interest in anything I did during the days. I was left alone. I shrugged as an answer, not ready to give him the time of day. I thought I saw him grin again, but didn't pay him any mind. He spent most of dinner asking me random questions, and I casually answered them with one word or a nod.

Who was this man, and what did he do with Martinez?

I was just happy to see he pulled the stick out of his pompous ass, for a little while, at least. Once I was done with my meal, I threw my napkin on the table and abruptly stood, leaving without even so much as a goodbye. I went to my room, trying to brush off our encounter. Forcing myself to believe it was a one-time thing. I didn't allow room for hope, I couldn't take any more disappointments.

But the next day, there he was again.

Waiting for me.

In the following months, it was the same exact routine. Eating together almost every night, sometimes he'd even stick around for dessert. Little by little, I started talking to him more, forgiving him for being who he was.

The Devil.

He never answered any of my questions, brushing them off, or changing the subject. Always turning the tables on me. I had no choice but to answer him. They were never personal, just random conversation you would have with a friend. We weren't friends though.

To be honest, I didn't know what we were.

One night, a few weeks after, he said he wanted to discuss something with me. He was going to allow me to go back to work. But, I had to keep an arsenal of bodyguards with me at all times, since it still wasn't safe for me to be on my own yet. With one of his limos and drivers taking me to and from work. At that point in time, I would have agreed to anything just to get out of the house. I had no idea how he managed to keep my job open, considering how many ballerinas were trying out for The American Ballet daily. I'm sure it cost him a great deal of money, or some threats.

Either way, I appreciated it nonetheless.

I fell back into work like I had never been away. It was so liberating being back in the real world, and not being in the penthouse all day and night. I felt like a new person, and I had Martinez to thank for that. On most days I'd be home from work by five in the afternoon, I always tried to put in a few more hours of dance in my studio and then head down to the dining room in time for dinner.

With him.

"I'll be right back," I announced, peeking my head into the dining room after work on evening. "I'm going to go change out of my dance clothes real quick." I went to turn and leave, but a strong, masculine voice stopped me.

"Don't," Martinez ordered.

I started to notice when I came back to the penthouse after work, he liked seeing me in my ballet attire. He would eye me up and down with a wicked look in his eyes. The same exact one he was staring at me at that moment.

"It will only take a few minutes. I'm a mess."

"I like you a mess," he simply replied.

Apparently, I was a glutton for punishment as I stayed in my uniform, even though I was sweaty and wanted nothing more than to shower and change. Just to see the look on his face as I walked over to my usual seat and while we talked over dinner. Sometimes on the weekends, I would catch him leaning against my studio door, watching me with a greedy regard. It was then I realized why he had a couch put in the room. It wasn't for me. It was for him. Even though he still hadn't used it, yet. Maybe afraid of what would happen if he actually sat down and watched me rehearse.

Like with everything in my life, it didn't take long for me to get ballsy. Once dinner was over, I hated seeing our time come to an end. So, over the past few weeks, I started knocking on his office door after I showered. At first he seemed shocked by my forwardness, but as time passed, I felt as if he eagerly waited and expected it. Leaving the door ajar for me when he never did before.

The fact I was relying more and more on Martinez wasn't something I ever overlooked, if anything…

I welcomed it.

I knocked on his office door, waiting for him to say I could come in. It wasn't uncomfortable to sit in there with him, given the circumstance of what happened months ago. It was as if it never occurred, his office was as immaculate as it was before we both flipped our shit. The piles of documents, paperwork, and folders he seemed to always have on his desk were now organized on his shelves and in cabinets.

I laughed when I realized he had moved them.

"Come in," I heard him call out through the wooden door.

I pushed the door open, peaking my head in, smiling when I saw him. He narrowed his eyes, nodding to the seat in front of his desk. I stepped in, shutting the door behind me. Taking a seat in my usual spot, tucking my legs underneath me. Looking over the new stack of documents, which weren't there the night before.

"So… Mr. Martinez, how much work do you have to do tonight?" I teased, much to his amusement. Twirling a strand of my hair around my finger as I bit my bottom lip.

"Mr. Martinez? I could get used to you calling me that, cariño," he said, not looking up from his work.

I rolled my eyes, grinning. Making a mental note to call him that again. "What do you do in here all night anyway?" I asked, reaching for one of his folders. The warning glare he shot me was enough for me to retract my hand back into my lap.

"I work, Lexi. How do you think I pay for your comfortable lifestyle?"

It was my turn to narrow my eyes at him. He scoffed, throwing his pen down on the desk, and leaning back in his chair, looking more relaxed.

"But what do you do?" I added. "You know, besides all the illegal shit."

He cocked his head to the side. "There's more than that?" A smile played on his lips.

Smartass.

"Hmmm…" I brought my index finger up to my pursed lips.

"I can see the wheels spinning in that pretty head of yours. Just say it," he ordered, reading my mind like he always did. The man had a fucking gift, reading people.

"Are you aware that they call you 'El Diablo'?"

He grinned, resting his chin on his steeple hands. He just sat there and flashed me his devilish grin. His tantalizing eyes quickly changed into the predatory stare, I'd grown to yearn for.

"You like that, don't you? Being known as 'The Devil'?" I questioned, licking my suddenly dry lips.

His silence was deafening. His intense glare, like an array of tiny razor blades on my skin. Penetrating deep within my core. Making me feel hot and nervous all at once. I couldn't fathom how he always had this effect on me with just a simple look.

"Do you even know why they call you that?" I blurted, needing to make conversation, and break the trance he had on me.

Desperately wanting him to answer my questions. He leaned forward, resting his elbows on his desk. His thumb running back and forth over his lower lip, undressing me with his dilated, mysterious eyes. My heart sped up, heat raced through my veins from his not so subtle regard. When he caught me staring at the movement of his mouth, he leaned back and grinned again.

Growling, "If I fucked you, cariño. You'd know why too."

Martinez

Her eyes intensified, waiting for my next move. "My name isn't cariño."

I peered deep into her eyes, and without thinking, I rasped. "When you own something, cariño, you can call it whatever you want."

259

She beamed with a gleam in her eyes. Staring back at me with a starry gaze that was new and unfamiliar. "Only problem is, you don't own me, Mr. Martinez," she murmured so low I could barely hear her.

I chuckled, "I'm not sure if you've noticed, but I own everything." Once again leaning back into my chair, giving her the space she didn't want.

"What does cariño mean?" she asked, changing the subject. Needing to control the effect I had on her. Unfolding her legs from beneath her, squirming a little in her chair.

"It's a term of endearment in Spanish, like saying honey or baby."

"Oh..." she purred.

"Don't read too much into it, it's a term I use loosely," I lied.

"Oh..."

"I really like the way you say that," I paused. "Cariño."

She blushed, bowing her head so I wouldn't notice. I was about to tell her to look me in the eyes when I was talking to her, but my phone rang, breaking our connection and ruining the moment. It was starting to take its toll on me. My willpower to stay away from her, fading more and more as the days went on. I actually looked forward to coming home to her. Wanting to make her laugh, to see her smile, to talk to her, to watch her fucking dance.

To have her in my bed every night... and every morning. I was falling for her, and I hadn't even touched her, yet. Fuck, I had already fallen for her.

Which was a deadly combination for a man like me.

"Habla," I answered, "*Talk*" on my phone.

"Boss, we have some trouble at the dance club."

"Why is this my problem?"

"Trust me, boss. I wouldn't have called if I didn't think you would want to make it your problem."

I hung up, throwing my phone on the desk. Taking a deep breath, pulling the hair back away from my face. The last thing I wanted to do was go back out at this time of the night. I was fucking exhausted, or at least that was what I told myself, knowing it had to do with the beautiful ballerina sitting in front of me.

"Is everything okay?" she asked, out of concern.

"I have to go." I stood, grabbing my suit jacket from behind my chair.

"Can I come with you?" she warily questioned, bringing my attention back to her. Batting her fucking eyes at me.

"Lexi, I—"

"I promise I'll listen to you," she coaxed in the sweetest fucking voice, making it nearly impossible for me to say no to her.

"Your nose is actually growing right now. You are aware of that right?"

She bowed her head, disappointed.

"You have five minutes to meet me at the front door."

She immediately peered back up at me with wide eyes. A smile spread across her face.

"If you're not there. I'm leaving."

She enthusiastically nodded. Bolting off the seat, hauling ass out of the room. Stumbling over her own two feet, catching herself at the last second. I laughed, not letting it deter her.

I shook my head, berating myself. "What the fuck are you doing, Alejandro?" I murmured, rubbing the back of my neck. Trying to ease the sudden splitting headache I felt looming.

I holstered my guns, put extra magazines, in my suit jacket. Grabbing my phone on my way out. Lexi was already waiting by the door when I walked up. Her long, dark hair flowed loosely around her gorgeous face. She was wearing a pair of low cut, tight fucking jeans that accentuated her luscious ass, and a belly shirt, which left very little to the imagination. A studded bellybutton ring hung temptingly on display. A pair of fuck-me heels, finished off her barely their getup.

"I wasn't trying to eavesdrop, but I heard your man say they needed you at your dance club. I've never been to a club, so I didn't know what to wear. I hope this—" I wiped off the red lipstick from her pouty goddamn lips.

"Your nose is growing again, cariño. Not trying to eavesdrop my ass."

She threw her head back, laughing, and I resisted the urge to laugh with her. Instead, I grabbed her hand and led her out the door. "You don't leave my side unless I tell you to. Do you understand me?"

261

She nodded, following me out to the limo with four bodyguards I had escorting us. Usually I would only take one, but since Lexi was with me, I chose to be overly cautious. I spent most of the ride on the phone, while Lexi sat beside me, fidgeting with her fingers. Her leg bouncing up and down, anticipating what the night would bring. At one point, I subconsciously reached over, placing my hand on her thigh to calm her. She tensed from the unexpected gesture, but I squeezed her thigh in reassurance. She relaxed, easing into my touch. I spent the rest of our ride trying like hell not to move my hand further up her thigh.

When we arrived at the club, I had the bodyguards do a sweep before letting Lexi out. The dance club was packed to the brim like it was every Friday night. Everyone dressed to the nines, my drugs and booze flowing like fucking water. It happened to be Latin night, the salsa rhythm pounded through the speakers. We walked in through the back entrance, avoiding the crowds I fucking hated. Drunken strangers, grinding up against you as you tried to make your way inside, was not my kind of night. I'd already done my share of partying. I was too old for this fucking shit. I left Lexi with the bodyguards at my VIP table, ordering them not to let anyone near her. I needed to make nice with some of the regular high rollers, who all spent a fuck load of money on everything I had to offer.

When I was done, I turned to find Lexi dancing, provocatively swaying her hips to the music without missing a beat. Not paying any mind to the sets of male eyes that were solely focused on her. I saw it happen before it actually went down, one of the men eye fucking the shit out of her, slid past the guards. The motherfucker caged Lexi in with his arms, pinning her against the wall. The fear in her eyes was enough for me to push through the fucking crowd, yelling at my men to turn the fuck around. I got to her just as they were about to intervene.

Roughly grabbing the random motherfucker by the back of his collared shirt, dragging him away from her. Throwing him up against the adjacent wall. It was my turn to cage him in.

"You don't touch what fucking belongs to me," I growled, knocking the fucker to his knees. Stepping back and nodding to my men to get this piece of shit out of my club. They would have to deal with my wrath later for not doing their fucking jobs.

I turned my attention back to Lexi, who was shaking in the corner from the motherfucker who scared her. As soon as she felt my touch against her cheek, my fingers caressing the side of her face, she relaxed.

"You okay?" I asked, pulling her into my body.

She nodded unable to form words yet. I hated seeing her weak. It physically pained me to watch her shut down. I acted on pure impulse, without thinking twice about it. I grabbed her hands, placing them around the back of my neck. Bringing her as close to my body as possible. Wrapping my arms around the small of her back, I savored the feel of her exposed skin, clinging to my back. I slowly spun us around in slow circles. Taking my time until she smiled, getting comfortable, and content again.

I rested my forehead on hers, staring deep into her bright, green eyes as I swayed around with her. Moving us effortlessly around our private space. Blocking out the people near us.

The moves.

The music.

All bringing back painful memories from my past. Seeing flashes of my mother and Sophia dancing and laughing in our living room. I hadn't danced since then, another lifetime, another world, another man. I shook off the memories as fast as they came. Pushing Lexi away from my body, turning her in a circle, ending with a dip. She laughed, and I swear it was the most contagious sound. I looked down at her, both of us losing ourselves to the undeniable connection we always shared.

She stood up on the tips of her toes to whisper in my ear, "Thank you, Alejandro. For everything."

The feel of her in my arms.

The smell of her against me.

The look in her eyes.

I didn't fight it any longer. I smiled. Laughing with her, enjoying the fact that for the first time in a long time. I was happy. *With her.*

The upbeat rhythm transitioned into a slower Latin melody. Lexi looked up at me through her lashes with lust filled eyes,

263

begging for me to lean down and kiss her pouty lips. My smile faded, reality kicked back in.

What the fuck was I allowing to happen?

I completely let my guard down. "Fuck," I breathed out, stepping back and away from her.

She stepped toward me, placing her hands on my chest. "What just happened? Why did you push me away?"

"Because you got me to smile and laugh with you in a span five minutes? Because I've changed? Because you've changed me? I'll break it down for you, little girl. You make me lose sight of who I am, I'll admit that. I find myself thinking of you in moments that I shouldn't. I can't have that, and..." I gestured in between us, "we can't happen," I snapped, turning back into the cold, callused man I needed to be.

She grimaced, her eyes instantly shutting. The hurt was plain as day on her face. She didn't try to hide it. Her hands slid down my chest to her sides, defeated. It took everything inside me not to place them back on me again.

"Watch her. See what happens to you if you don't this time," I ordered my men, then turned and left not looking back. I couldn't handle seeing the disappointment on her face.

I sifted through the crowd, making my way toward my office, to find out what the fuck was so important that I needed to be here. I honestly didn't think the night could get any fucking worse.

"Fucking-A," I spewed as soon as I saw a drugged out Austin Taylor, sitting in the seat in my office.

Briggs had left him a few months ago for reasons I didn't want to get into. She just showed up on my goddamn door, late one night saying she needed a place to crash for a few days. Lexi was actually the one who answered the door and I almost bit her fucking head off for being so careless. I'm sure she was dying to get to know Briggs but I made sure that didn't happen.

I spent the next fucking hour dealing with Austin, when all I wanted to do was be with Lexi. I actually wanted to fucking apologize, and tell her I didn't mean it. Tell her whatever I needed to, to make things right again. I couldn't get out of there soon enough. Finally, after what seemed like forever I was able to go back and find her. Leaving Austin in my office to sleep off his drug-induced haze, wanting to know where the fuck Briggs was.

I couldn't help but feel responsible for him, thinking how much I had to do with his addiction. I shook that off like I did everything else that night.

"Boss, we didn't—" I shoved him out of the way as I took in a drunk-ass fucking Lexi.

"Who the fuck gave it to her?" I seethed, trying to remain calm, but my limits were being pushed to the max.

"Well, you said to make sure she was taken care of," he explained, gesturing to her dancing on the fucking table.

"I meant for you to make sure she was protected not let her become two sheets in the wind! Now get the fuck out of my face," I yelled, shaking my head, ready to put some goddamn bullets in these worthless sons of bitches' heads. I was over to her in two strides, reaching for her hands, pulling her down and over my shoulder. Carrying her off the table.

"Heeeeeyyyyyy... I was dancing... I don't even likes yous anymores..." she slurred, reeking of whiskey, vodka, and God knows what the fuck else. Protesting by slapping my back and kicking her legs.

I sat us down on the leather couch, placing her swaying body next to me, her head spinning with a glazed over look in her eyes. She could barely hold her head up. Just one more thing to add to the clusterfuck of a night I was having.

"Boss, she's fine. She's just a little drunk," Rick assured, trying to save his sorry ass.

As if on cue, Lexi leaned over toward me, and threw up in my lap. I held her hair back, scooting her face toward the floor as she continued to heave liquid, until she couldn't anymore.

I shot him a menacing glare. "Obviously, she's fucking not."

"I'm sooooo sorry..." Lexi drunkenly giggled. "I feels betters though..."

I leaned her back up against the couch, wiping her mouth with a napkin. Ripping the glass of water from one of my men's hands.

"Lexi, drink this." I placed the glass near her lips.

"No... no... more... no more... drinkies." She shook her head from the glass. Pushing it away, causing me to drop it. It shattered upon impact with the floor, near our feet.

"Fuck me," I murmured, frustrated.

She peered up at me through her lashes, grinning. "You... don't's let's me..."

I shook my head, trying hard as fuck not to laugh. Even drunk as shit, she was still fucking adorable. I cleaned my slacks up as best as I could, before standing and picking her up into my arms, cradling her like a baby. She leaned in, nestling into my chest, sighing in contentment as her body went lax, almost immediately passing out. She stayed just like that the entire ride back to my penthouse. Snuggled in my arms, softly snoring. I took her straight into her room, and stripped the clothes that smelt like puke off her body.

She inhaled my scent and half moaned, "Alejandro," as I gently laid her on the bed. She spread out like a cat, stretching then curling up into a ball. I quickly walked to my bedroom, and changed out of my soiled pants, went into the bathroom, and grabbed three Ibuprofen from my medicine cabinet. Making my way back into her room. Padding down the hallway, needing to get back to her. She hadn't moved.

I reached for her and sat her up. "Cariño, you have to take these."

She half-opened her beautiful eyes and smiled at me. "I really love it... when yoooouuu... call me that... it sounds sooooo sexy... it makessss me all hot and wet... you're the only man that'sss ever been able to do that..." her head bobbed, struggling to remain upright.

"Lexi—"

"I know... you're going to be alls... yoooouuu... but you're not a bad man... mmm hmm... I know yous..." She nodded. "More than you... know you. One day you're going to... loovvveee me... because... I already think... I'm falling with you... In yous. In love." Her head stopped moving, and she looked me dead in the eyes for a split second.

I swallowed hard.

266

She sluggishly smiled. "Night... night... Mr. Martinez." She laid back, shutting her eyes, and was out within seconds.

I stayed with her for a few minutes, brushing her hair away from her face. Caressing her cheek, taking in all her dainty features. She was so breathtakingly beautiful.

I was fucked.

I sat back in the armchair and rubbed my temples in an effort to calm my migraine to no avail. I watched her sleep like I had every night for the past six months, taking in each and every word she drunkenly just shared with me. Knowing in the back of my mind.

She. Was. Right.

Thirty
Lexi

"Oh God," I groaned in pain, immediately grabbing the pillow, wrapping it around my pounding head. Trying to remember what the hell happened last night.

"Splitting headache? You really shouldn't be so careless with alcohol," Martinez chimed in, sitting in his usual spot in the armchair near my bed.

"Mmmm…" I moaned as I rolled over to face him, blinking away the hangover haze. "Maybe you shouldn't have been an asshole to your guest. Driving me to drink in the first place."

"Oh, so it's my fault you decided to drink double your weight in booze?" He stood, walking over to the window.

"I didn't think I was drinking that much at the time. I don't usually drink, and now I know why," I retorted. Squeezing my eyes shut, praying to God to take it easy on me.

"You need to get dressed," he simply stated, roughly pulling the curtains back. The bright sunlight beamed through the window, causing me to flinch in pain.

"What the hell, Martinez! A little warning please," I roared, flipping over so I was face down on the bed.

He chuckled, "Close your eyes."

"Asshole," I whispered under my breath. "I'd ask you to leave the room, but you've already seen me naked," I replied, feeling the sheets on my unclothed skin.

"And both times you were unconscious. Though, I will give you some credit. You didn't throw up on me the first time. Lucky me. Don't worry, sweetheart, I looked but I didn't touch."

I sank into the mattress, mortified. Ignoring his statement about looking. "I threw up on you?" Shaking my head, the embarrassment settling in. Making me flush all over.

268

"And yourself," he added for good measure.

I couldn't even look at him, all I wanted was to disappear. Fade into the comforter and pretend like I didn't make an absolute ass of myself in front of him. In front of his men and thousands of club goers. I fucked up. All I wanted to do was forget about how he snapped last night. One minute he's throwing a man off of me, then we're dancing and laughing, and the next he's pushing me away again. Acting like a complete fucking dick. I shouldn't have been surprised but it had been months since he treated me that way.

A little part of me thought I had finally broken through his icy demeanor, only realizing it was just another illusion in my delusional head. I had no intention to get wasted, and make a fool out of myself. Which was exactly what I accomplished. I only downed like three, maybe four…or was it five? I lost count.

They went down like water, one right after the other. I didn't realize how strong the shots would be. I couldn't remember anything after the last one went down. The rest of the night I spent blacked out.

I hope I didn't say anything stupid…

I opened my mouth to say something, quickly shutting it, not knowing what to say. I heard him shuffling across the room, I peeked open one eye, thinking he had left so I could pass back out. Forget this ever happened.

I wasn't so lucky.

"Here," he coaxed from above me.

"Go away, Martinez. Let me bask in my humiliation for a little while longer." I slowly flipped back over, peeling my eyes open one at a time. Barely able to make out his form, the light was so bright behind him. Rapidly blinking, cursing myself once again for being so careless, as he called it. He was holding a glass of ice water and some buttered toast. I sluggishly sat up, pulling the sheet with me as I leaned my bare back against the cold headboard, shuddering. Grabbing the water, I gulped it down. Welcoming the cool sensation it left in its wake.

"Oh my God, life changing," I practically moaned, taking a bite of my toast.

"You need to get dressed," he repeated with an agitated tone, causing me to peer up at him.

His eyes bared something I couldn't quite place, too shocked he was showing me any emotion, when he had been so reserved all this time. Sharing what he wanted, never what he didn't.

"Are we going somewhere?" I asked, needing to know.

"Yes," he simply stated. Our eyes never wavered from one another, completely captivated in each other's stares.

"Is everything alright?"

"Nothing is ever alright."

"Are we—"

"I'm in the business of making things wrong. I'm not your Prince Charming, and once you realize that, it would make things a lot easier."

"On you?"

"No. You. I know who I am. It's you that doesn't," he paused to let his words sink in. "Now get dressed. I'll be in my office." He turned and left.

I stayed there for I don't know how long, rationalizing what he had just said. Trying to figure out what happened last night, racking my brain for memories if I had said something to him. I shouldn't have.

Once I took a shower and brushed my teeth, I felt so much better. Almost like a whole new person. I dressed casually in a maxi skirt and tank top with sandals, leaving my hair down with just some mascara, blush and lip gloss. Foregoing my usual make-up. I knew I took longer than he probably expected, but he didn't say anything when I walked into his office ready to go. We rode in the back of the limo in an awkward silence, listening to the rain pelt off the roof. Craving for him to put his hand on my thigh like he had the night before. Yearning for him to comfort me with a simple touch of his hand.

He didn't.

He was staring out the dark, tinted window, leaning against the armrest on the door. Rubbing his fingers across his lips, lost in his own thoughts, in his own demons. In his own world like I had never witnessed before.

The car ride could have lasted a minute, an hour, or a few hours. Time just seemed to stand still. It felt as though every

270

second that passed between us was another moment in time for him. Another place he revisited often, or even worse, he never left.

He was there…

But he wasn't.

Without thinking, I reached over and placed my hand on top of his. Lacing our fingers, giving him a reassuring hold. Wanting to provide him with some sort of comfort if I could. His eyes quickly darted down at my kind gesture as if he was waiting for something I didn't quite understand. His hand remained lax, and he didn't return my sentiment. After a few seconds he looked back out the window, not giving my affection any more consideration. Too consumed by his own plaguing thoughts.

We drove through a set of huge cast iron gates, up a long narrow road surrounded by trees, for what I assumed would be for privacy. My heart sped up a little more, the closer we got to our final destination, not knowing where the hell he was taking me. Tree after tree whipped by the tinted windows, casting shadows in our path. Blurring into the background. Fading into the distance. The trees suddenly cleared, and we were faced with fields of what looked to be daisies. A massive house appeared out of nowhere with acres of breathtaking greenery surrounding the property. It was then that I realized…

We were at a cemetery.

Martinez

As soon as the driver hit the brakes, I opened the door and exited the car. I needed to get out before she had the chance to speak. I knew she had tons of questions that'd been attacking her mind, since I told her to get dressed that morning. Last night proved one thing, and one thing only. I was letting my guard down, allowing weakness to seep in through the cracks. I was letting her in. I couldn't fucking help myself. She was turning me into a goddamn pussy. I was always the man who exuded nothing but control and power. I thrived on it.

It was the only reason I was still walking.

Still breathing.

Still fucking alive.

I couldn't trust myself with her. I had proven that too many times over the years. She was falling in love with 'The Devil,' now I needed her to run away from my hell.

"Stay," I ordered the bodyguards. Stepping out of the limo, pulling Lexi out with me. Our hands still entwined from her gesture during the ride. The driver handed me the oversized, black umbrella, giving me the excuse to let go of her hand.

Ignoring the hurt look that passed over her face. She peered up at me, searching my eyes for the answers she desperately wanted. Opening her mouth to confront me again, but quickly closing it when she caught a glimpse of my ominous glare. I didn't want to provide her with any ease or reassurance. That's not what this was about, it was the exact opposite, and she needed to comprehend what the reality of living in my life would bring.

"Come on." I nodded, holding the umbrella over the both of us. Leading the way for her to finally meet the man behind the expensive fucking suit.

The closer we got to my reality, the more I realized I was doing the right thing. Until there were no more steps to take, no more thoughts to doubt, no more emotions to pull. Until there was nothing but the truth, staring back at us. Handing Lexi the umbrella, I stepped out into the pouring rain, not caring that every inch of my body was being covered with the downpour, which fell from the sky. Looking up as Heaven's tears streamed down my face, and fell to my feet. I vaguely watched the lightening before me, subconsciously counting the seconds until thunder would strike.

The storm was getting closer…

I wanted it to cleanse me, save me from my impulses, my decisions, my choices. The pain, the misery, the hurt, were as real as the women buried in front of us. As much as I wanted it to go away, it never would. It was a daily reminder of what I lost.

Of who I am.

I watched Lexi from the corner of my eyes, holding the umbrella in one hand, the other rose to her mouth as she read the two gravestones. Taking in the fresh daisies I had delivered every morning, catching her attention.

"Alejandro is this—"

I didn't falter, putting an end to the fantasy in her head. I spoke with conviction, "This is what happens to the women who love me."

Our eyes locked.

"Welcome to my Hell."

A loud crash of thunder struck above us. She shuddered, sucking in a breath, her eyes widening. Wrapping her arms around her tiny frame for warmth and comfort, taking in my words.

"This is my life, Lexi. People die around me daily, from my bare hands and from others. I've killed people just to prove a point, slaughtered men without thinking twice about it. I am a ruthless motherfucker who prefers torture as a form of vengeance. My hands are still covered in my mother's blood. And my sister's..."

"Did you—"

"Yes. I may not have pulled the trigger, but that didn't save them from dying either." I stepped away, turning my back on her. I needed some space. I had never admitted those words to anyone.

"I know what you do is dangerous. I know that there's a reason why you're like this. Oh my God... this explains so much. But I know you... I see through you. Under the expensive suits there is a man with a huge heart. I'm living proof of that. You're not evil. You just think you are."

She stepped forward, dropping the umbrella to the ground. I could hear her come up behind me. Reaching her arms out. "It's okay, Alejandro, I'm so sorry, I know what it's like to lose a parent."

I turned to face her, the rain pouring all over us now.

"I know what it feels like to be alone, to feel like you have no one on your side. But you have me. I'm here for you, no matter what," she wept, her voice giving out on her. Reaching for me.

I couldn't take this much longer. I didn't want her sympathy, her concern, or her fucking love.

"Don't touch me, Lexi, you need to stay away from me," I cautioned, moving her hands away from my body.

273

"Alejandro, please... please... just let me..." she pleaded in a voice of pure desperation and sorrow.

"Don't fucking touch me. I'm warning you. What is it going to take for you realize I'm no good for you?!" I shouted, raking my hands through my wet hair.

She didn't fucking listen, continuing her assault, trying to touch my face, my arms, and my chest. Her hands burned as if she was touching me with holy water. Sinking further into Hell, right along with me. It seared everywhere she placed them, everywhere she touched me, leaving behind deeper scars than the ones I already carried.

"Why won't you just let me in? I can help...we can help each other. Why do you insist on fighting this?" she implored, gesturing between us. "I understand you don't want me to end up like the other women who have loved you, but that is not your choice to make. It's mine," she stubbornly declared, not letting up with her hands on me.

"You have no fucking clue what you're signing up for." I roughly jabbed my finger toward their graves.

"My life isn't made for you, it's made for no one but me, it's the price I pay for taking lives that don't belong to me," I gritted through a clinched jaw. Hoping she would back the fuck away from me.

"I'm so sorry, Alejandro, but I'm not going anywhere," she mourned, leaning in to engulf me in her arms.

I roughly grabbed her wrists tighter than I intended to, holding her in place. I seethed close to her face, "Then I might as well start digging your grave right next to my mother and sister. You can finally fucking hate me when I lay you to rest."

I let go with a shove, leaving her standing there. Trying like hell to figure out what it was going to take to get rid of this girl.

Before I killed her too.

Thirty-one
Lexi

I sat up startled, looking around my dark room, searching for the man that usually lurked in the shadows. Sadly, only getting glimpses of the empty armchair every time lightning struck, illuminating the whole room. Light and darkness took turns, over and over again, but no Martinez. The storm hadn't let up all day, the rain was steady, and the thunder was loud. Memories of my childhood came flooding back. Snuggling up to my mom when the storms were bad. I wished I had that comfort now.

I couldn't sleep.

I'd been tossing and turning for the last few hours unable to forget about what happened that morning. Closing my eyes, only to see two gravestones behind my lids. I never expected what he shared with me, not for one second. As much as I was relieved he was finally giving me a piece of his puzzle, I was also devastated he was using it to push me away. As if he thought he wasn't worthy of having anyone care for him, or wanting to stick with him through the good and the bad.

It hurt my heart just thinking about him.

Reminding me that we had more in common than I could have ever imagined. When I got back to the limo, he wasn't there waiting for me. It was only the bodyguards standing, watching my every move. All four men were still there.

He left by himself.

He shouldn't have left on his own. Unprotected in a world where he was worth more dead than alive. The whole drive home I couldn't shake the feeling that something bad would happen. Anxiety had taken over and the minutes felt like hours.

He never came back to the penthouse that night. We didn't have dinner together. I hadn't seen him since he left me standing in the cemetery with the reality of his harsh truths. I spent the whole day curled up on the couch closest to the front door. Afraid I would miss him if he unexpectedly showed up.

Waiting for him to come home.

To me.

It was around midnight by the time I picked myself up, and went to bed, hoping that maybe, just maybe he would end up in my room.

He didn't.

I rolled over, looking at the clock on my nightstand. It read three-thirty A.M. I groaned, crossing my arms over my face. There was no way I was going to get any sleep, not until I knew he was home. I sprawled out, stretching, not realizing I had been curled up in a ball most of the night. Sheltering myself from the storm. The sheets were sticking to my anxious, overheated skin, making me burn up, even though I was just wearing a tank top and panties. Taking a deep, exaggerated breath, I untangled my body from the confining linens. I swung my legs over the edge of the bed, and placed my feet on the cold hardwood floor, stifling a yawn.

Before I knew it, I was at my door, turning the handle. I stepped out of my room, peering down the black hallway toward his room. The silence was deafening all around me, eerie flashes of thunder had my heart beating a mile a minute. My feet padded against the marble floor, a force pulling me to him by a chain.

A chain that only he ever held.

I was a few steps away from his bedroom when I noticed his door was ajar. He never left it open. I'd never even seen what was lying beyond the door, it was the only room in his penthouse I'd never been in. My stomach fluttered and my heart pounded with each step that brought me closer to his room, silently praying he would be in there.

Safe.

I slowly, quietly pushed the heavy wood open, gingerly stepping inside. Being careful not to make any noises in case he was in there. The room was dead silent, not even a sound of a clock to break the monotony. I knew one thing for sure, the man

277

never slept. The events of the day must have taken a toll on him if he was sound asleep. His body physically giving up on him, when his mind was probably still reeling in his slumber. For some selfish reason the thought provided me with some comfort, that maybe he had as shitty of a day as I did. Worried about me, as much as I was worried about him.

I felt his presence before I actually saw him, his scent immediately assaulting my senses as soon as I was in the room. I stopped dead in my tracks when the full moon illuminated his latent body. He was asleep on the left side of the big king sized mattress, a massive, black wooden four-poster bed, centered on the far wall. Each post had intricately carved designs, towering up toward the ceiling. Four vast beams connected into a square up above, draped with black, sheer curtains that fell to the floor near the head of the bed. The carvings continued on the headboard that extended the height of the posts, and onto the low footboard. It reminded me of a king's bed in medieval times.

He was lying shirtless under the dark canopy, on his back with one defined, toned arm underneath the pillow behind his head. Accentuating his chiseled abs and bare chest. The other arm, placed at his side, pulling the sheet that was resting on his lower abdomen, taut. Leaving very little to the imagination.

I stood there for a few minutes, just admiring him, taking in every last inch of this man's muscular body. He was a work of art. Being this handsome had to be a sin. As his chest moved, my eyes caught a glimpse of something shiny on his torso. Stepping closer, I noticed a silver cross hanging from the chain he always wore. The bulky, huge, silver expensive watch he normally wore too was gone, but the black, beaded bracelet remained secure around his right wrist. My eyes continued down his length.

Even in his sleep, he exuded dominance.

I couldn't take my mesmerized gaze off of him.

Now that I knew he was home, sleeping safely in his bed, I could go back to my room and get some sleep. I should have never intruded in the first place. But I didn't want to go. The empty space beside him called my name, my desires were winning the battle over sensibility.

I wanted to lay next to him, I wanted him to take me in his arms and protect me from all the ugliness of our world. I knew his decision to take me to the cemetery and give me a peek into his past, a glimpse of the life he led was meant to scare me away but the truth was it only made me want to get closer to him, I wanted to be with him now more than ever. It was as if his dark side was luring me in, the pull he had on me was palpable, I could no longer resist. The closer I got to the mattress, the more I realized this is where I belonged. In his bed, falling asleep next to him every night, and waking up to him every morning…

With him.

I didn't want to be alone anymore.

My fingers glided along the silk sheets, feeling the soft fabric under my touch. Gently sitting down on the bed, careful not to wake him. Scooting my body up to lay next to him. Peering at the side of his devilishly handsome face, watching him sleep, exactly the way I imagined he watched me for months. Never understanding why, until that very moment.

Peace.

My transfixed gaze went back to the cross, hanging low on his chest. His lull breathing causing it to rise and fall, calling for me to reach out and touch it.

It all happened so fast, exactly the way everything had since the first moment I saw him.

One minute my hand was in the air, reaching to touch him. Next, my fingers grazed his cross as I was roughly flipped onto my back, shuddering, gasping for breath as he sadistically gripped me around my throat. Suffocating in pain from the brutal grasp around my windpipe.

I couldn't breathe.

My legs kicked, my feet sliding on the silk sheet as I fought for my life. My fingers tearing into his, clawing and ripping at his hands. Opening my mouth, gasping, silently pleading with him to release me. I continued to struggle, becoming weak and losing my fight. He straddled my waist, his heavy weight lying directly on top of my small frame, hovering above me. One hand wrapped around my throat the other pointing a gun directly at the center of my forehead. His face inches away from mine, he opened his dark, dilated eyes, they were vacant of any life. Black pools stared down at me as I finally realized, I just met...

El Diablo.

𝕸𝖆𝖗𝖙𝖎𝖓𝖊𝖟

I watched her from the mausoleum, up on the hill. The worried expression on her face was as transparent as the emotions pouring out of me. Which was why I had to walk away, leaving her alone with her fate. Standing next to the gravestones of the only family I'd ever have. I thought bringing her here, showing her there was no life for us together and the reasons behind it, would have made her run away from me. Leaving the darkness behind, never looking back. I thought this would be the end of us, coming full circle with nowhere else to turn. Seeing my past and present colliding with such a force, brought on only by me. Nothing of what I thought would happen, did.

Not one fucking thing.

If anything it backfired on my ass, I gave her exactly what she wanted. The truth that laid beneath the fiction she created in her mind. The pieces of my fucked up puzzle that held so many unanswered questions, still loomed in the distance between us. I watched her walk back to the limo with her head bowed low, her arms wrapped around her. Rick ran over to her with an umbrella, guiding her to the car. She peered around one last time, as if she knew I wouldn't be sitting in the limo waiting for her. Not feeling my presence. I saw her staring unknowingly up the hill as the limo faded in the distance.

With her heart breaking for me.

I watched the limo leave, taking what I desperately wanted to be mine with it. Standing there with my hands in the pockets of my slacks, for I don't know how long. Watching the rain pour down from the sky, flooding upon me for my behavior. Silhouettes of my mother and sister appeared through the storm clouds, with no remorse. As fast as they appeared, they were gone. I spent the entire evening there, waiting for a sign that I was doing the right thing, an epiphany to get us out of this fucked up situation. Nothing happened. I let the rain wash away my sorrow, Lexi's face haunting my thoughts.

Burning inside.

A feeling I was accustomed to.

Except this time, I felt like I couldn't take it anymore. My demons pulling me under, dragging me further and further into the ground. Burning me alive, when I'd already been dead all this time. That was the problem with the whole situation, Lexi revived me.

She was trying to save me when all I would do was destroy her.

Darkness fell over the cemetery by the time I said goodbye to my mother and sister. Apologizing for not coming to see them sooner, I couldn't remember the last time I was here. It pained me to think about it. It was late by the time the limo came back and got me, and it was even later by the time I got back to my penthouse. Walking in a daze, fighting an internal battle to rectify the situation. Resisting the urge to go into Lexi's room, knowing she'd be wide awake.

Waiting for me.

I took a shower, leaning my forehead against the ceramic tile. Letting the scolding hot water run down my back, welcoming the burn. My body physically aching for some rest, some sleep, something, anything that would make my mind stop running wild like a hamster spinning on a fucking wheel. I stayed in there till the water ran cold, getting out, throwing on some boxer briefs, and instantly fell back on my bed. Instinctively, taking my gun with me. Placing it under my pillow with my strong grasp around it. I was just going to close my eyes for few seconds, let the rain soothe my splitting headache.

Instead, I passed the fuck out.

I couldn't remember the last time I slept so solid, so sound. I was used to every little noise waking me up. Never being able to relax enough to allow my REM cycle to lull me away. There was no rest for the wicked, the demons that haunted me never slept. No matter how exhausted I was, they were right there waiting.

I didn't have to open my eyes to viciously attack my prey. I had been waiting for someone to kill me all my life. It was only a matter of time until they found me in a moment of weakness. Without thinking, I acted on pure impulse, savagely gripping the shadow's throat beside me, coming in contact with the motherfucker in my bed. Before I even fully opened my eyes, I immediately flipped them over, straddling their body, locking them in place by their throat.

My first initial thought wasn't my safety.

It was hers.

No one ever came into my bedroom, not even Lexi. I silently prayed for the first time since cursing God that they came into my room first, having no idea she was in the penthouse with me. My grasp tightened harder at the mere thought that something could have happened to her. Needing to kill the motherfucker in my grasp with my bare hands as they struggled against me. Putting up a fight as I suffocated the life out of the bastard. It wasn't until I hovered above them, pointing my gun directly to their fucking forehead, that I opened my dark, dilated eyes.

Ready to fucking kill.

Realizing very fucking quickly it was Lexi beneath my hold, fighting for her life. Her tiny frame struggling with everything she had in her, fear and panic like I'd never seen before.

Of me.

My eyes widened, crudely jerking back in horror from the scene unfolding under me. Still straddling the woman choking under my grasp, I instantly eased up on my ruthless hold around her throat. Sliding my hand down to her collarbone, pinning her to the bed. Easing up on my weight, still looming above her. She immediately gasped for air, clutching onto her neck, coughing every few seconds. Her eyes watering, her body shaking, desperately trying to breathe in the air I so violently ripped away from her.

The terror on her face was enough to bring me to my knees and beg for forgiveness. Exactly the way she had just begged for her life, moments ago. She withered beneath me, slightly arching her back, fixing her eyes on the barrel of my gun. Her mouth opened wide, panting profusely. Her wide, brazen eyes shined with fear,

282

tears threatening to spill over. A heated glare I was more than familiar with, stared back at me at the same time. Her thoughts running wild as she tried to recover, bunching the silk sheets in her trembling hands. Her coughing subsided when the air finally ran through her lungs, panting profusely. She wanted to say something, opening her mouth and closing it several times not knowing what to say

Where to start.

Where we stood.

Her lips were swollen, pursed, and a bright shade of red. Her face flushed, sweat glistened down the sides of her temples. Shaking to her core with terror. The fear that I was going to hurt her more than I already had. Her hair was fanned out all around her. The left strap of her tank top ripped and torn, exposing the top of her breast. Her hard nipple slightly peeking through the slim, cotton fabric.

I'd never seen her look so fucking beautiful before.

I took my hand off her collarbone, strategically placing it beside her on the bed. Shifting my weight forward. She sucked in a breath the closer my face and body got to hers. Never breaking our intense stare, I slowly moved the gun from her forehead, sliding it down her body. The cool metal leaving a trail of desire in its wake.

I softly pecked the corner of her lips, murmuring, "Do you have a death wish, cariño?"

Her breathing hitched against my lips.

"What did you think would happen if you came into my room uninvited?"

Her mouth shut, swallowing hard. Licking her lips.

"After everything I showed you today. Why would you think I'd be the man you could take by surprise? Do you want me to hurt you?" I asked, pecking her lips. Running my nose lightly up the side of her face, causing her to shiver.

"You're always hurting me," she said just above a whisper. "This is just the first time you've done it physically. I've been hurt so much worse, Martinez. You're not the only villain I've ever crossed paths with."

I scoffed out, "What do you want from me?"

"Everything."

Nothing about her confession surprised me. Nothing about the feelings I had for her did either. I never wanted her more than I did at that moment, finally holding her in my arms, feeling her skin against mine, loving the way she was looking at me. Wanting me to make everything right. My mind had been spiraling out of control all day, shouting at me to let her go, to push her away.

I wanted her more than reason, more than what was right or what was wrong. I wanted her more than anything. And I had known that since day one. There was no turning back, only going forward. Pulling her into my Hell with me.

"Te gusta estar a mi merced?" I questioned, "*Do you like being at my mercy?*" Grinding my hard cock right against her pussy. Never letting up, hitting all the right places that would drive her fucking crazy.

She shuddered beneath me, moaning with every thrust of my hips. Resisting the urge to shut her eyes. Her wetness seeping through the silk of her panties. I guided my gun down her trembling thighs, laying it aside. Brushing my fingers along the same path, up where she wanted me the most.

"Quiero hacerte mía," I groaned, "*I want to make you mine.*" Skimming along the edge of the top band then slipping the tips of my fingers in through the side of her panties. "Your body is throbbing for me, begging me to touch it."

She moaned in response as I scooted them aside. Quivering when the cold air came in contact with her bare folds.

"Tell me what you want," I ordered against her lips, kissing them ever so lightly. Needing her to tell me this was okay, already knowing her body was craving my touch. But I needed her mind, desperately yearning to hear the words I knew would destroy us both. Everything about this situation was new for both of us.

I hadn't kissed a woman in years. Never caring for it, all I ever wanted was to fuck. But with Lexi, I wanted it all. Especially, to claim her goddamn mouth, nipping, sucking and licking. Reveling in the feel of her pouty lips against mine. Imagining them wrapped around my cock. Everything about her was addicting, exactly like the drugs I fucking sold.

"You..." she breathed out.

Once I heard the word leave her lips, everything else became fucking fair game. "What do you say?" I taunted, sliding my tongue along her bottom lip.

"Please…"

"Please what?"

"Please touch me."

I grinned, failing miserably to hide the pleasure only she could cause. Grazing her cheek with the tips of my fingers, I placed a fallen piece of her hair behind her ear. The simple gesture made her lips part as her eyes glazed over, lightly brushing my fingertips against her soft bare folds.

Our eyes stayed connected and for a moment I saw a certain innocence pass through hers, knowing she was a fucking virgin. She didn't have to tell me, her lust filled gaze showed me everything I needed to know. They spoke volumes. She bit her bottom lip, enticing me, using her sexuality without even knowing what she was doing.

I cocked my head to the side, pulling her closer to me by the nook of her neck. Caressing in between her folds, circling her clit, rubbing the nub side to side, and back and forth. Spreading her open. Smoothing her moisture. Getting her ready. I guided her hands above her head, pinning them to the bed. She couldn't hold still, arching her back, her perfect tits rising near my face.

"You're so fucking wet."

She purred, rotating her hips against my hand. Baiting me to give her what only I could ever do to her body.

"I want to feel you come on my fingers, cariño, I want to see your face get flushed, your breathing hitch. I want to feel your pussy pulsate so fucking hard it pushes my fingers out of your sweet little hole." Biting her bottom lip, kissing her softly. "I want to know what you taste like, here." I slid my tongue into her mouth. "And here." Pushing my finger into her tight opening. I kept up with my soft torture for a few seconds, loving the feel of her slickness against my callused fingers.

She tilted her head back, tempting me once again. "Please…" Luring me in to kiss her.

I didn't have to be told twice. I kissed her with everything I had to offer, I fucking ravished her. Pushing my middle and ring fingers into her wet opening, she moaned into my mouth, shoving her tongue in at the exact same time. I savored both the taste and feel of her, how her body angled perfectly beneath mine, how she was melting against me. Taking everything I was giving her and wanting more. I released her hands and they instantly tangled in my hair.

"Fuck," I groaned in between kissing. Wanting the same thing she did. "You feel that?" I uttered, hitting her g-spot harder and more demanding. Making it almost impossible for her to answer. I never once stopped kissing her, assaulting her lips.

I couldn't, even if I had wanted to.

"Oh, God..." she panted, her pussy clamping down onto my fingers so fucking tightly, making it difficult to move in and out.

I reluctantly let go of her lips, removing my soaked fingers from her pussy, causing her to whimper at the loss. Her tank top and panties were ripped off within seconds, kissing my way down her neck, to her breasts, sucking a nipple into my mouth, biting just a little. Enough to make her squirm and rotate her hips against my hard cock. I wanted to admire her body, taste every last inch of her skin.

But first, I wanted to fuck her with my tongue.

I went right for it, not allowing her to ease into me, already overstimulated from my touch. I sucked on her clit, moving my face side-to-side, feasting on her until her legs started to shake. Her body trembled, her hands ripping at my hair, clawing to escape, trying to move further away from my face.

I growled from deep within my chest, locking my arms around her legs, anchoring her hips firmly against my mouth, not letting her move away from my skilled tongue and lips. I gripped her harder and rotated her hips in the opposite direction, changing the motion of my tongue.

The sensations intensified for both of us as I made her fuck my face.

She screamed out, "Alejandro!" Climaxing so fucking hard. I'd never seen or felt something so intense before. I didn't falter, pushing my tongue into her opening as far as it would go, wanting to taste every last drip of her come. Licking her clean, like a starved man.

I crawled up her sexually exhausted body, making my way toward her face. Her frame melted into the mattress, so heavy, so satiated. Her eyes were serene, as I leaned forward, claiming her lips again. Soft at first, letting her savor the salty sweetness, tasting herself for the first time. Until I couldn't take it anymore, and I devoured her mouth exactly the way I did her pussy moments ago. Her small, delicate fingers started traveling down my chest, roaming to the elastic of my boxer briefs, wanting to reciprocate. As much as I wanted her hand and lips wrapped around my hard cock, this wasn't about me. I swiftly grabbed her wrists, pinning them to her sides.

"No, cariño," I huskily stated, peering deep into her eyes.

She narrowed her eyebrows, confused.

A sign of hurt flashed over her face. Releasing my grip, I cupped her cheeks, easing the blow, and I spoke with sincerity, "I would never physically hurt you. No matter what the circumstances, I need you to know I'm not capable of causing you physical pain. I didn't know it was you before... Do you understand me?"

She nodded with a genuine expression, knowing it was my way of apologizing to her. Saying sorry was a sign of weakness, and I couldn't bring myself to say the two words. To show her that I had a weak side, buried under all the bullshit. I really wanted to beg for her forgiveness, over and over again for what I'd done. Not just for tonight, but for all the other times she mentioned. But in the end, I was who I was, not even Lexi could change that.

I just wasn't made that way.

"You look so fucking beautiful right now. You're fucking beautiful all the time. I don't say it because it makes me want to be with you," I added, needing to speak some truth. To show her I wasn't a complete bastard when it came to her.

I kissed her one last time, memorizing everything about her at that moment. Her eyes, her flushed cheeks, her pouty lips, and messy hair. I laid down, swiftly bringing her along. She curled into me, nuzzling into my torso. An arm draped across my chest.

"Go to sleep," I whispered, kissing the top of her head. Inhaling her vanilla scent, trying not to remember the last time a girl laid in my arms.

I shook off the memories, pulling Lexi closer. Feeling her plaguing emotions stirring all around us. Consuming me. I lazily rubbed her back not wanting to stop touching her soft, silky skin. It didn't take long for her breathing to even out. I shut my eyes, loving the fact that she was there with me.

"I love you, Alejandro," she sighed in her sleep. Her body fell heavy into my embrace.

I wish I could say I didn't expect it. That I wasn't prepared, or didn't fucking know she would say it.

I did.

If it had been anyone else, I wouldn't have hesitated to tell them to get the fuck out. She was different. She was mine. I laid there with my arms wrapped around her, never wanting to let her go. Kissing the top of her head, letting my lips linger. I knew what I had to do now, even though it would kill me. Without a second thought, I moved her gently off my body.

Murmuring, "I'm so fucking sorry."

And left.

Thirty-two

Lexi

I smiled, sinking deeper into the silk sheets of his bed. Envisioning everything that happened last night. His masculine scent engulfing me, surrounding me, I couldn't have been more blissfully content. I was happy in his bed. For the first time in my life, something gave me hope and happiness, other than ballet.

Him.

It was late into the morning by the time I stirred, the sun shining through the curtains, yesterday's storm long gone. The irony wasn't lost on me. The grim day turned into a beautiful night, filled with pleasure and love. Filled with everything I ever wanted. I immediately reached for him. His side of the bed was cold and empty as if he hadn't been there for hours. I sat up, taking the sheet with me. Searching the vast space for any sign of him. Looking for him.

I was alone.

"Alejandro!" I shouted, thinking maybe he was nearby, showering or watching me sleep.

Silence.

My eyes went to the bedside table, hoping to find a note. He didn't leave one. I took a deep breath, laying back into the mattress, craving to feel him in any way I could. Needing his touch. I didn't want the feel of his hands all over me, and everything that happened between us the night before, to go away. Finally, being able to lay in his arms. I instinctively reached for my neck, softly touching the tender flesh lying beneath my fingers.

Letting my mind wander to the erotic images of last night. Each and every touch, every moan was engrained into my soul. I never let anyone close to me, not like I did with him. Nothing

289

Alejandro did to me in bed brought back the memories of the monster I'd lived with all those years.

I smiled.

My stomach fluttering, my pussy throbbing just at the mere thought of his hands and mouth on me. I reached for my lips, softly brushing my fingers over them, remembering the way he claimed my mouth. Making me taste my sweet arousal. It was the most surreal, erotic, experience of all my life. I couldn't wait to do it again.

With him.

I knew he probably needed some space with all of the conflicting emotions tearing into him. This was all new for him as well. I didn't care that he had left me here alone, I had made my way into his cold heart, and dark soul. I was embedded in there, whether he wanted me to be or not.

Only his.

As much as I didn't want to leave the comfort of his bed, his room, his space, I knew I had no choice. The Head Master of ABT wanted to talk to me. I'd been in such a hurry to get home to him on Friday that I promised I would come in Sunday for a meeting. I reluctantly got up, going straight into my room to get ready. It was no longer a space I felt comfortable in, already wanting to go back to his room where I felt his energy all around me. It didn't take long to get ready, throwing on some clothes, foregoing a shower.

I didn't want to wash off his scent, just yet.

The limo drove me to the academy with my usual brigade of bodyguards surrounding me. I didn't mind, it was another way of Martinez showing feelings, keeping me safe at all costs. I spent the entire ride looking out the tinted windows, thinking about him.

What he was doing? What he was thinking? How he felt after last night? What would change between us now? I had more questions than I ever did before with less answers.

This didn't change just one thing.

It changed everything.

Exactly how I hoped it would.

"Come in," I heard the Head Master call out from her office, breaking me away from my thoughts.

Her assistant led me in, shutting the door behind me.

"Lexi, I was wondering when you would make it in," Michelle greeted, nodding for me to take a seat in front of her desk.

"I'm sorry, I got held up this morning," I apologized, trying like hell to control the flush of my skin. Thinking of the reason why I was late. Martinez's tongue working its magic, the kissing, the nipping... I shook my head, clearing my throat. Willing the visions to stop playing in my head. Now was not the time to be fantasizing about him.

"No worries. You're here now."

I smiled, taking a seat, crossing one leg over the other.

"So, I'm just going to get right to the point."

"Okay."

"There's a job opening at The Royal Ballet in England. And it's pretty much yours, if you want it."

I lowered my eyebrows, stunned. "What?" I nervously laughed. "How?"

"Lexi, I've never seen talent like yours. You were born to dance. It's in your blood. It's who you are. I don't want to hold you back, you need to soar, honey. This is a once in a lifetime opportunity. One that I think you would regret not accepting."

I didn't say anything. I honestly didn't know what to say. Or even where to start. I just sat there staring at her dumbfounded, in awe of the news. I never expected this, not in a million years. I never thought studying or working abroad would be an option for me.

"You've told me yourself, you don't have anyone. You have no reason to stay here, nothing to hold you back from this extraordinary opportunity. Can you imagine what it would be like to live in England, Lexi? Dancing? Living the dream that other ballerinas would kill for. Out of every dancer in the U.S...they want you, Lexi."

"Right..." my voice cracked. I was in shock, unable to form a coherent thought.

She frowned, cocking her head to the side. "I was expecting a much more elated response. I mean—"

"No, I'm just... it's just... wow..." I stuttered, unable to find the words. "I guess I'm just taken by surprise. They want me?"

291

"Honey, you work your ass off. There have been nights I don't think you even went home and slept. You live and breathe ballet. That is the dedication these places look for. You're in your prime, sweetheart. This shouldn't be a surprise. It should be an honor."

"Oh no! I know. I am. I can't even begin to thank you. It's just been an overwhelming weekend. That's all."

"With Mr. Tall, Dark and Handsome?" she questioned, wiggling her eyebrows. I smiled and let out a little laugh.

I never asked Michelle why I was permitted to take so much time off. What the academy was told. Letting it slide, just in case they changed their minds if I brought it up.

"He's definitely easy on the eyes," she added.

"You have no idea," I scoffed, bowing my head, finding the heat spreading across my cheeks.

"When he came to see me about your job—"

"Wait, he came and saw you? Personally, talked to you?" I interrupted.

"Yes, I assumed you knew. The morning after your big performance, I got a phone call from Mr. Martinez, wanting a meeting in regards to you. It sounded urgent, so I met with him that evening. He let me know you'd been hurt, and needed some time off to recover. He was very concerned for you, Lexi. I didn't think twice about it, I told him you could take as much time as you needed. I've never seen you with him, I assume whatever you had is over?"

My hand instinctively went to my throat. "Yeah... I mean it's complicated," I stated. My mind trying to wrap around what Michelle had just informed.

"Is it going somewhere? Your relationship with him?"

"I am not sure, as I said it's complicated." I shrugged in response.

She leaned over her desk with her hands out in front of her. "Well, then, honey. I would make damn sure because an opportunity like this," she paused, eyeing me, "won't come again."

"Thank you so much for everything, Michelle. Can you give me a few days?"

"I can give you until the end of the week. They need someone over there effective immediately."

"Okay." I stood, opening the door to leave.

"And, Lexi?"

I turned.

"Sometimes your heart can be wrong."

I nodded, leaving. Whispering to myself, "I hope not."

It was like one thing after another. I went from having nothing, to possibly having everything I had ever wanted, in the matter of a few days. If she would have asked me this months ago, before Martinez... I wouldn't have thought twice about accepting the offer, I would have jumped on the next plane. It was what I'd been working so hard for all my life. Pushing my body to the limits, sacrificing so much.

"I wanted this, right?" I whispered to myself. My thoughts raged a war with my heart. In less than twenty-four hours this man had me questioning everything.

My thoughts didn't let up on the way back home.

Home...

I actually thought of it as *my* home.

He was home to me.

I waited for him all day on the couch, anxious to see his handsome face. To breathe him in, to feel his arms wrapped around me. He never showed up. I woke up in the middle of the night still on the couch, jolting awake, feeling his presence watching over me. When my eyes fluttered open, I was alone. Nothing but the darkness of the penthouse surrounded me. My inner turmoil made me believe in an illusion, a figment of my imagination. What wasn't there and maybe had never been.

I refused to think that.

I stayed on the couch, waiting. Falling in and out of sleep, secretly praying he would walk in, scoop me up into his strong arms and take me to bed. His bed. No such luck. Sleep finally took me under, rewarding me with dreams of his skilled hands and tongue. Of his body all over me. The next morning there was still no sign of him. No traces he'd ever come home. I got dressed and went to work, once again distracted by thoughts of him all day. It went on like this for four days.

Four days I didn't see him.

I didn't talk to him.

293

I didn't feel him.

It was as if he had disappeared.

No one told me where he was when I asked, I tried calling his cell several times to no avail. By the fifth day I was beyond restless, thinking maybe I'd never see him again. Feeling devastated that he took the choice away from me, vanishing from my life as if he was never there to begin with. Racking my brain, I tried to think back to that night.

Had I done or said something wrong?

I was going stir crazy, sitting on that couch every night just to wake up disappointed in the morning. That evening, after eating dinner alone again, I went into his room. My body and mind yearned for a part of him. A fix, like he was my favorite kind of drug I couldn't live without. Walking around the massive space, I took a real good look around for the first time. His room oozed masculinity and dominance, adding to its intimidating feel. A huge, black armoire was positioned on the left wall, almost taking up the entire space. The vast sliding glass doors on my right led out to the balcony, overlooking the city lights of Manhattan.

An array of colors blurred in the distance.

His bedroom suite was four times larger than mine, and mine was quite large. The walls were painted a dark shade of gray with expensive black and white art spread evenly around the walls. Two black end tables on each side of his bed, embedded with detailed woodcarvings along the edges, which matched his canopy bed frame. My toes immediately curled into the soft, shag, black accent rug that laid directly underneath his bed, as I ran my fingertips along the polished wood. Everything about his room was dark, and immense.

Just like him.

I couldn't help but wander toward his walk-in closet. It was immaculate. Hundreds of collared shirts lining multiple racks on one side, dress pants and suit jackets on another. Ties of all colors and patterns hung on the far wall. Dress shoes of every kind lined the floor. The man didn't own one piece of casual attire. Not one t-shirt, pair of jeans, sneakers or even sandals.

My fingers skimmed over the collared shirts, running the tips along the soft fabrics. I don't know what got into me, but I found myself pulling off one of his white collared shirts from the hanger. Bringing it up to my nose, clutching it tight against my chest. Inhaling deep. Before I knew it, I was taking off my clothes. Only leaving on my panties, sliding the cool dress shirt on. I was drowning in it, but I didn't care. It made me feel close to him, and at that moment, that was all that mattered to me.

I made my way over to his bed, running my hand up and down the post, remembering our night together. Which now seemed like years ago. I couldn't help myself, I pulled back the covers, sinking deeply into his sheets. Lying in the exact spot he did, nights before. Aching to feel him any way I could. Sighing in contentment when my skin hit the silky linens, the aroma of our ravenous bodies still lingered in the space. I hatefully kicked off the covers, cursing at myself for being so fucking weak.

He left me.

And there I was still waiting for him.

More so now than ever before.

I sat up, bringing my knees to my chest, debating if I should leave. Go back to my room, and drown my sorrows. But the mirror on the wall across from his bed caught my attention. It was parallel to the mirror behind me that I just noticed, too. I peered around the room, realizing they were the only mirrors, both angled toward the bed.

I saw my reflection staring back at me, feeling as though it had changed in the last few days. Like I looked older or something I couldn't place my finger on. It could have been his shirt, but I felt...

Sexy.

Enticing.

Beautiful.

Is this who he saw when he looked at me?

My fingers moved on their own accord, unbuttoning his white collared shirt, desperately wanting to see what he did. My nipples were hard, calling out for me to touch them. Roll them between my fingers, like he had. Flicking and pinching the small pebble just enough to set my body on fire. I had played with myself before, but the sensation was nothing like I'd felt at that moment. The desire to feel the way he made me feel was so overwhelming, so consuming, and so fucking real…

My fingers hooked the lace band of my panties, sliding them down my freshly shaved legs. Throwing them beside me on the floor, and leaving his unbuttoned shirt on. Taking in the image of my body through the glass, trying to imagine what he saw when he looked at me with his hypnotic eyes.

The eyes I couldn't get enough of.

I stared at my naked body, pulling my hair away from my face. My fingers started to trace the outline of my pouty lips, remembering the way he looked at my mouth when I talked, with such hunger. The tip of my tongue glided against my fingertips, tracing from my neck to my collarbones, leaving a trail of my saliva in its wake. I repeated the same process with my other hand, except this time I touched my hard nipple, lightly at first. Then, I pulled on it, remembering the way his teeth felt when he lightly bit me. I rubbed my breast, while my other hand slowly treaded toward my belly button. Using the tips of my fingers, I circled it. Tugging at the diamond stud dangling, remembering how captivated he was with my belly button ring the first time he saw it. My hand moved toward the top of my pussy, caressing the lining of my soft, bare folds.

I was wet.

For him.

"You're so fucking wet." His voice rang through my head.

I touched my clit, circling it, just like he had. Manipulating the bundle of nerves, harder, faster with more urgency. I moaned, leaning back, supporting my weight with one hand, still sitting up. My head fell back, and I closed my eyes imagining he was the one touching me. I moved my fingers from my clit to the opening of my pussy, and pushed my middle finger in, adding my index finger. Easing in and out of my tight hole, beginning to breathe heavier the closer I got to my climax. I glided my fingers back to my clit, riding my hand with the sway of my hips. Imagining I was riding his cock.

"Oh, God," I panted, picturing his face in between my legs. "Alejandro…" I clenched, about to come undone. I opened my eyes, wanting to see myself in the mirror.

Coming face to face with Martinez.
Through the reflection in the glass.

Thirty-three
Lexi

I gasped, jumping out of my skin. Grabbing for the blankets, trying to cover myself.

"Don't," he ordered in an authoritative tone. The same one he used the night I came running to him, after he surprised me with my dance studio.

"I'm sorr—"

"Don't," he repeated in the same dominant voice, leaning into the doorframe, his hands in the pockets of his slacks. Fully dressed in a suit. Not one hair out of place.

How long had he been there? Watching me?

I slid from the bed, wanting to close the distance between us. "You haven't been here. I… just… I don't know… I'm so—"

"Don't," he snapped one last time, pushing off the doorframe. His dark, cold, soulless eyes never wavered from my face. I retreated back to the bed. I couldn't remember the last time he looked at me like that.

My stomach fluttered.

My heart dropped.

The closer he got to me.

He stood at the foot of the bed, directly in front of me. Cocking his head to the side, he narrowed his eyes at me. "By all means, keep going, Lexi," he spoke with conviction.

"I—"

He leaned forward, placing his tight grip onto the footboard. "That wasn't a suggestion. Fuck your tight little cunt for me." Slowly eyeing me up and down with a look I'd never seen before. "Spread your legs. Now!" he roared, in a primal tone.

298

I jumped, overwhelmed by the turn of events. Seeing this side of him emerge, once again was unsettling. I looked into his vacant eyes, silently pleading for the man I was with days ago to come back to me.

"Why can't you listen for once in your fucking life? You came into my room, rummaged through my closet, and started fucking yourself. Now finish." He glanced down at my heat before quickly moving his calculated gaze back to my eyes. "Touch your pretty, little pussy. I want to watch you come, carino."

"Can you—"

"No." He didn't waver. Bright blue, tantalizing eyes eagerly waiting for the show.

I swallowed hard and took a deep, steady breath. Wanting to please him, I leaned back onto my hand. Spreading my legs slowly, hoping he would let his guard down with me again. Moving my jittery hand where he ordered me to touch, I hissed upon contact on my clit. The nub was still sensitive from my assault, before he interrupted.

He arched a demanding eyebrow, waiting. "I'm not a patient man," he growled. White knuckling the bed.

I reluctantly went right back to what I was doing. Except this time, I didn't have to fantasize about him. He was standing right in front of me, watching me with an expression I couldn't read, once again a blank canvas, a mystery.

"That's right, Lexi. Just like that." His sultry voice setting my nerves on fire. It didn't take long for my body to respond, working my clit harder and more demanding.

My eyes half closed, my legs trembling the closer I got to giving him what he wanted. I couldn't hold back any longer. As much as I wanted to stare into his eyes, my body betrayed me. My back fell against the mattress, my lips moaning his name, "Alejandro..." as I shattered from the orgasm.

I panted profusely, trying to catch my bearings from what had just occurred between us. Anxiously waiting for his next move. I felt him before I saw him. His face buried in between my legs. Not giving me a chance to recover from my own high. His tongue was relentless, licking from my opening to my clit, working me over with his skilled lips. The lips I'd been dreaming about since the last time I saw him. I let him have his way with me, every last part of me belonged to him.

"Ah..." I moaned, my back arched off the bed as he slid his fingers into my pussy while sucking hard on my clit.

His body took on a whole different demeanor. The cold, calloused bastard was gone, and the warm, passionate man from nights ago was back. He was being gentle with me, like he was afraid I would break. His mouth and fingers taking their time making love to me, building me up, and letting me enjoy the sweet torture of his tongue. My body began to tremble, a feeling only he could generate from me. There was something different about him in that second. He was living in the moment, feasting on me as if he needed to prove he owned my body, mind, and soul. He wanted me to feel worshiped, my body burning for him in every way possible.

My heart rapidly beat in my chest, making it difficult to breathe. My breath became erratic, urgent, and heady. Falling over the edge.

"Oh, God," I screamed out in a voice I didn't recognize, climaxing so fucking hard I saw stars.

I withered around, coming down from the pleasure, feeling loved and adored. I hadn't realized he released the hold he had on my thighs, and was on top of me within seconds. His large muscular frame made me feel so tiny, so safe. I couldn't wait to stare into his serene eyes, to feel as though he was mine, once again. Savoring the feel of his secure arms and his hard cock against me. Breathing in his scent.

I felt his breath along my lips. "You think I'm yours to tease?" he murmured in a condescending tone.

My hooded eyes shot open, never imagining I would see the man glaring back at me. Jerking back, confused. "What? No, I—"

"Did I say you could fucking speak?" he sneered.

My eyes widened, no longer tranquil and at peace. Immediately wanting off his roller coaster of emotions, starting to walk a thin line between love and hate.

"Little girl, I'm not the man to do that with. I'm not yours to fuck with, not now... not fucking ever," he roared, getting closer to my face. "Do you want to be my whore? Is that what you want?"

He was trying to scare me, push me away, wanting me to think he didn't care about me. I wasn't going to let him get away with the bullshit he was trying to portray.

Mirroring his menacing glare, I stated, "Yes." Challenging him with my eyes.

He didn't falter, sitting up between my legs, sliding the zipper of his slacks down with a devious grin on his face. He roughly tugged my thighs toward him, effortlessly sliding my heated body down the silk sheets. Placing me where he wanted me, a few inches away from his dick.

"You want me to fuck you like a whore, *cariño*," he mocked, pulling out his hard cock, fisting it in the palm of his hand. Jerking himself off.

My eyes dilated as I took in his length, my chest rising and falling. Watching the tormented man in front of me, making me want him even more. He reached for a condom in his wallet, not even bothering to get undressed. I knew what he was about to do.

Actions speak louder than words.

Shutting my eyes immediately, I fisted my hands in the sheets, pressing my fingernails hard into my skin. Bracing myself for the ton of fucking bricks that were about to crumble down on me.

"You look me in the fucking eyes when I'm talking to you," he ordered, crudely grabbing hold of my chin, tilting my face toward him.

With glazed, watery eyes, I opened them. Tears spilling out of the corners as I watched him roll on a condom. His glare hadn't wavered from mine.

I replied, "Yes." Not wanting him to feel the pleasure of my pain.

I wasn't going to back down. I knew what I was getting myself into by provoking him. I had witnessed both sides of this beautiful man.

The good and the bad.

Heaven and Hell.

The love...

Now, he was going to show me his hate.

The Devil wasn't sedated anymore. He leaned over, his lips getting close to my face, his cock at my opening.

In a sick, twisted way I wanted this. His dominance had always been an aphrodisiac for me. I knew if I uttered the words he would stop. There was no trepidation, only a power struggle that I refused to lose.

He scoffed out, "Wearing my fucking shirt, trying to pretend like you belong to me. Well, I'm about to show you that you don't." Gently, thrusting his way through my virtue. Not wanting to hurt me... yet. Letting me adjust to the size of his cock, the harshness of his actions he was about to prove. His words a hurricane of emotions, harsh then soft and mesmerizing all at once. His touch didn't feel intrusive, didn't inflict fear, but I didn't feel loved either.

Which was what he really wanted.

I gripped the sheets tighter, biting my lower lip until I tasted blood. Preparing my self for the pain I knew was coming. It wouldn't be his movements that were causing me pain, that were breaking my heart, that were killing me inside.

It was the fact that he wouldn't even look at me. Proving once and for all that he didn't care about me, that he didn't want this, didn't want us. He was just taking the easy way out.

Fucking me into understanding.

Knowing, I wouldn't be able to forgive him after this.
Knowing, a part of me would always hate him. Taking away the one thing I held so sacred away from me.

My heart.

After everything I'd been through, it was always mine. I never let any of the shitty things that happened break me down, make me weak. Ever. I wouldn't have been able to survive if I did.

This was our ending, when it should have been our beginning.

Softly thrusting in and out. Subsiding the discomfort to pleasure instead. He stopped for a few moments when he was deep inside me. As if his actions were killing him, too. A pained look crossed his face, but it was gone as fast as it came. My hands instinctively reached for him for comfort, for support, for something other than what he was giving me. He roughly pinned them over my head, not allowing me to touch him, even for one second, to feel his warmth, his turmoil, or his fucking love. Knowing that's all it would take for him to stop what he was about to do. His tempo changed, gone was any tenderness he showed thus far. He started to thrust in and out of me, making me feel like I was nothing but his toy.

His whore.

Not showing me any connection, any love, anything of the man I knew that still lived inside of him. Making me feel as if I was nothing, as if what we shared was nothing. Tears rolled down my face, and I couldn't hold back the heave that escaped from my chest. He immediately stopped, hovering above me, his eyes finally staring down into mine. Another sob escaped my lips, shuddering beneath him. Willing him to come back to me.

He angled his forehead on top of mine for one split second, for a moment in time. I saw what he so desperately tried to hide.

His love.

"Alejan—"

He roughly flipped me over, placing me on my hands and knees. Taking me from behind, unable to control his desire to look into my eyes. To take me how he really wanted, to make me feel like I was his. Thrusting in and out of me with such urgency, such yearning, fighting a battle of right and wrong, for the first time in his life. I caught his tormented reflection in the mirror. Tears slid down my face as my lips quivered from the pain all around me. Not physically, but emotionally. I was grieving for what I lost, for what he was taking away from me. I gave him my body willingly, but all he wanted was to destroy my heart, leaving it shattered on his bed, finally achieving his goal.

Our eyes locked in the mirror and he showed me everything I so desperately wanted to see. A growl escaped from deep within his chest, allowing his demons to prevail. His body collapsed over mine, shoving my head down to the bed. Not allowing me to see the truth beneath the fiction.

He fucked me harder, more demanding, until finally I heard him groan and felt him shudder, shaking my body from his own orgasm. This was supposed to be his way of freeing me from his Hell, except it was the opposite. He had just dragged me deeper along with him, burning me alive.

303

I hissed when he pulled out, feeling the loss of his touch, my body almost collapsing on the silk sheets. He immediately got off the bed, leaving me in a pool of the pieces of my broken heart. Not saying anything as he shuffled around the room and disappeared into the bathroom. I closed my eyes, letting more tears stream down my face and onto his bed where a part of me would always remain. I would remember the sound of him pulling back up his zipper as he hovered over me.

"I warned you. I told you I don't know how to love. I ordered you to stay away from me, time and time again. I'm not the man you think I am. I never was... You wanted a piece of me, a piece of El Diablo. I gave you what you wanted, now get the fuck out of my room."

I placed my hand over the hollow space where my heart used to lay, trying to breathe through the pain of his words. Shutting my eyes as tight as I could. Not strong enough to look up into his eyes, too weak to handle what I would see, or what I wouldn't. I slowly eased my way off his bed as far away from him as possible. My body screaming for me not to move, I was so hurt, so broken, in every way possible.

Walking toward the door, I stopped. Whispering, "The man behind the expensive fucking suit," my voice breaking, my body shaking, "is nothing but a fucking coward."

And I left.

Martinez

I was a bad man, but I never claimed to be anything else. I did what I had to do to save her fucking life, even if it meant destroying mine in the process. It took everything inside me not to reach for my gun and put a bullet in my fucking head, ending my misery.

My sorry excuse of a fucking life.

Death would be too easy, though. I didn't deserve to rest in peace. Living was the price I paid for the lives I'd ended. Playing fucking God when I was really The Devil. I contemplated if I was really going to do this, for days, for nights, the entire time I was away from her. Praying I would find the courage I needed to pull it off.

I watched her on the security cameras from the other condo I owned in the building. Battling the life I wanted and the one I deserved. My mind was made up as soon as she laid in my bed. Wearing the same white collared shirt that brought back memories of the girl I spent years trying to forget. Realizing very, fucking quickly, what I had to do. My feet moved of their own accord as I made my way to the penthouse, taking the fucking stairs two at a time, not wanting to waste a minute waiting for the elevator. My shoes pounded into the steps, echoing through the stairwell. A fucking rope tugging me to her. Reassuring myself over and over again that I was doing the right thing.

I needed to be the hero for once.

Fucking exhausted of being the villain.

Lexi didn't deserve a life full of violence, always looking over her shoulder, waiting for her time to come. I wanted her to live a life of happiness, a life I'd never be able to provide her.

Safe.

Easing the door open, I walked in on Lexi finger fucking herself in my bed. I stepped further into the room unannounced, and enjoyed the show for a minute. My cock pushed against my slacks from the sight of her perfect, pink pussy, glistening from her own arousal. Soft moans filled the room, making me think twice about my plan. I would never forget the look on her face when she came eye to eye with my reflection.

Even though I shouldn't have, I gave her pleasure before giving her pain. I couldn't fucking help myself, I needed to give her something, knowing I was just about to break her goddamn heart. I couldn't have possibly hated myself more than I did at that moment. Knowing what I was about to do. Fucking her over, making her think she was just another whore in my bed.

When she was everything, except that.

My dark soul screamed at me to make it right, make love to her how I deeply yearned to. Every time my eyes found hers, I thought I would break down and not be able to continue. Deep down I knew she felt and saw each and every moment of weakness. That's how profound our connection was, which was all the more reason to let her go. To push her away. To make her fucking hate me. I would die before I ever let anything happen to her.

Every Devil needs an Angel.

And she was mine.

I laid in bed for hours after I brutally kicked her the fuck out of my room, thinking about my life. Coming to terms with the fact that Lexi was the first woman I ever truly, wholeheartedly loved. I was a boy trying to be a man in the past, trying to save a relationship with a woman who wasn't right for me. Who'd never fought for me. Who didn't believe in us. Who'd left me broken for years.

Lexi was made for me, and that realization alone nearly brought me to my knees.

I fucking loved her.

I loved her with every breath in my body, every piece of my fucked up heart, every last part of me belonged to her.

"What the fuck did I just do?" I scoffed to myself. Sitting up on the edge of the bed, roughly pulling back the hair away from my face.

I didn't think twice about it, I ran. I fucking ran for my life that was in the room next door. Not giving a flying fuck what was right and what was wrong anymore. Ready to get down on my knees and beg for forgiveness if I needed to. Whatever it took to make her look at me again, the way she always did.

Always seeing the man I no longer thought existed.

"Lexi!" I called out in pure desperation as I ran down the hall, needing her to know I was finally fucking coming.

For her.

"Cariño! I'm so fucking sorry," I apologized as soon as I rushed into her room. She wasn't there. "Lexi!" I shouted, making my way into her en suite bathroom. Nothing. Panic started to take hold as I ran to her ballet studio next. "Lexi!" She wasn't in there either. The room was dark and untouched.

I ran around the penthouse cursing it was so fucking immense. Searching every corner just to come up empty.

Memories from when I was fourteen came flooding back, trying to find Amari and Sophia. Fear set in, the room started to spin, my stomach fell to the fucking floor. Crouching down, unable to stand any longer, I buried my head in my hands, heaving for air.

My whole fucking world was crashing down on me.

"What the fuck," I roared, standing abruptly, getting on the phone.

"Hey, bos—"

"Where is she?" I spewed, not giving Rick a chance to finish.

"Lexi's in the penthouse."

"No, motherfucker, she's not. Now where the fuck is she?"

"Boss, I... I... don't... she—"

"You have five minutes to fucking find her or you won't live to see another day." I hung up, quickly dialing another number.

"Hey, man—"

"Lexi's gone, Leo. I can't find her."

"What do you mean you can't find her?"

"Exactly what I just fucking said!"

"Jesus, calm down. I'm on my way over."

I hung up, pacing the living room for what felt like years. Waiting for someone to give me something to go on. Calling every last resource in my phone. Leo showed up, and we spent the next forty-eight fucking hours, threatening, harassing, making sure everyone knew we meant fucking business.

I sat in my office chair, my elbows on my knees, with my head in between my hands. Feeling like a fucking failure. If something happened to her because of me. It would be my demise.

I'd put that bullet in my fucking head.

Leo walked back into the office, sighing, throwing his phone on my desk. "I found her."

I shot up off the chair. "Where?"

"She's in England, man. I just got off the phone with Michelle, the Head Master over at Lexi's dance theatre. She accepted a job at some hoity toity academy or some shit."

"What? Since when?" I asked, fuming. Pacing my office again. "How did I not know about this?" I stopped dead in my tracks, the realization hitting me. I'd left her alone for five fucking days. She wouldn't have gone if I hadn't pushed her away.

307

"I guess since she left here. What the fuck happened? What did you do now?" Leo questioned, pulling me back to reality.

I grabbed my gun, heading toward the door. Immediately making another call. "Make sure my plane's ready. I'll be there in thirty minutes." I hung up.

"Goddamn it, man. Wait up, I'm coming with you," Leo said, running up behind me.

The flight to London was seven hours. Seven damn hours of me cursing, punishing myself for letting the one light in my life walk out my door. We couldn't get there fast enough. I had a driver waiting by the time we landed that morning. I didn't have to wonder where she would be, she lived and breathed dance, using it as her only escape. We headed straight toward the theatre, finally walking through the doors an hour later, feeling some sort of peace as soon as I felt her presence near me.

I found her.

The sweet melody of the song she played to dance for me in my office all those years ago, blared through the speakers. Filling the huge space, shattering my fucking heart a little more. She was dancing on stage by herself, people, which I assumed were other performers and instructors, filled the first few rows.

I stayed by the door unable to move, hiding in the shadows as I had for years, without her knowing. I couldn't take my eyes off of her, mesmerized by her gracefulness, the way she poured her heart and soul out when she danced. I'd never seen her look so breathtakingly beautiful before, her body so in tune with her flawless movements.

As if she was dancing just for me.

Like we were the only two people in the world. I felt every movement she was effortlessly trying to portray. A painting that came to life. I'd seen her dance before, but nothing like this. She was so full of life, so happy in her element, so content in her surroundings. The dark cloud I shadowed over her had been lifted, breaking free from the hold I had on her all these years. I leaned back against the door, needing the support. Defeated, as I watched her dance as if her life depended on it.

She was saying goodbye to me.

I hung my head, my heart and mind raging war on each other. I wanted to storm up on that stage and grab her. Take her back home with me and cherish her, show her how fucking sorry I was, and never let her go again. The song faded, I looked at her one last time. Memorizing every last thing about her. Everything I loved.

Nodding to Leo, I turned and left.

"Martinez!" Leo yelled, grabbing my arm. Stopping me when we were outside of the building. "What the fuck are you doing, man? Go get her."

"No," I simply stated, facing him. She was no longer mine to get.

"What do you mean? She's in danger, that's why we're here. You still haven't—" I peered back toward the theatre, my solemn expression causing Leo to abruptly stop talking.

Never taking my eyes off the building, I asked, "What do you know about me, Leo? No one fucks with me. I've spent my whole life making sure of it," pausing to let my words sink in.

I revealed, "She was never in any fucking danger. I took care of it the next day."

And left...

Part 4

Thirty-four
Lexi

During the holidays, The Royale Ballet theatre in England performed Tchaikovsky's The Nutcracker Suite. It was our final show of the season, and I couldn't wait for the break. My partner, Matthew, and I were performing the Pas de Deux. The music soon became my favorite, so romantic, so powerful, so all-consuming. Dancing to it was the most intense feeling I had ever felt in my career. Matthew's strong hands wrapped around my waist, lifting me into a grande pas de chat.

Floating through the air as if I weighed nothing. The music became more intense the closer we got to the finish. I turned and faced him for our last lift of the night. Développé, passé, pirouette, plié. Using every last bit of energy, he picked me up, placing me on his shoulder. The music faded, and the applause rang out. Setting me down, he presented his arm to me as I curtsied. Rapidly following and bowing his head.

"Great performance tonight, Lexi!" Sabrina, the Head Master praised in my dressing room after the show.

"Thank you." I smiled, kissing both of her cheeks and pulling her into a tight hug.

"My beautiful girl," she lovingly stated, cupping my face in the palms of her hands. "I can't believe it's been ten years of you performing here with us. A decade of lovely memories made of dancing. I couldn't be more proud of you if you were my very own."

Sabrina was like the mother I never had. From the moment I stepped off the plane, she was waiting for me at the luggage claim, welcoming me with open arms. Puzzled when I didn't grab a suitcase, not knowing that everything I took with me was already

311

in my dance bag, hanging over my shoulder. She whisked me off to the theatre to meet my new dance family and begin to practice. It was a hardcore schedule, which left little time to think about who and what I ran from. The first few days... hell, the first few months, were exactly that.

Hell.

The days and nights blended together, the word sleep was no longer a part of my vocabulary. All I was trying to do was survive this new life. My fresh start. I hadn't seen or heard from Martinez since I left him that night.

Trying to mend the pieces of my broken heart.

Failing miserably to do so.

Sabrina had been nothing but good to me. I had my own place to live, fully furnished with everything I could possibly need when I arrived. I hated it. I didn't want to be alone anymore. She noticed it immediately, I didn't have to tell her. Taking me into her home instead, giving me a bed to sleep on and food to eat. Housing a complete stranger out of the goodness of her heart. Making me feel like I was wanted for the first time in my life. She loved me instantly, and the feeling was very mutual. For the first few years, I drowned myself in work again, dancing all hours of the day and night. It was the only life I'd ever lived where I was happy and content, except something had changed inside of me. Something I didn't ever get back.

To this day, I couldn't tell you what it was, but I changed into someone I didn't recognize anymore. My outside emotions started matching how I felt on the inside. Like a piece of my soul was taken. The darkness and reality of my life started to take me under. Even after everything he had done to me, put me through, made me see... I still loved him.

For years I loved him very fucking much. I still do.

I never shook off the feeling that I was being watched. Sometimes I felt as though if I looked close enough, I would see him. Possibly even find him staring back at me.

I couldn't do it anymore.

It hurt too fucking much.

A year became three and three became six, and before I knew it, I was a few months away from being in England for seven years. That's when I met him. His name was Will. He was charming and handsome in a boyish way. An American, like myself, from Colorado working there on a visa. He had the sweetest smile, and the most contagious laugh. It was so good to laugh again, to smile, to feel like I wasn't dead inside. I met him at a café, drinking espresso, reading an American newspaper. He was a relentless flirt, asking me out only after a few hours of us talking over nothing.

We casually started dating not too long after meeting. Life was so simple with him, so positive and pure. He was patient, caring, and attentive, every girl's living dream. It took me a while to let him get close, especially in an intimate way. He didn't have the effect Martinez had on me, and, in the back of my mind, I knew no one ever would. Sabrina was the only person I ever told about my life, about *him*. She told me if I ever truly wanted to be happy, I needed to try. Let go of my past and walk—not run—into my future.

So I did.

One night we were drinking heavily. Laughing turned into kissing, kissing turned into touching, and touching turned into being intimate with someone who didn't consume my body, mind, or soul.

I cried, I cried so fucking hard after we were done. He didn't ask any questions, he just held me in his arms. The way I yearned for Martinez to do, for God knows how long, even at that moment in another man's arms, I thought of him. Still craving his presence, his scent, his love.

Will and I never talked about what happened, we just went on. Little by little, things got easier, I started to live life again. Letting myself find the girl that I left in Martinez's bed.

With him.

It had been three years of us being together. We were out at a fancy restaurant celebrating our anniversary, when Will confessed his undying love and devotion to me.

"Lexi, I love you. I want you to be my wife," he simply stated, like he was telling me how his day was.

I looked at him wide-eyed, never in a million years thinking that I would be someone's wife. "I...I don't..." I stuttered.

313

"You don't have to answer right now. I plan to take you ring shopping, and formally propose. I just wanted you to know where I stand." bringing his wine glass up to his lips.

Something caught my eye in the glass window behind him. *Martinez.* I swear I thought I saw his dark, cold, soulless eyes staring at me from outside. I blinked and he was gone, the moment ruined by the man I shouldn't be thinking about.

I walked outside the theatre after my performance, smiling as soon as I saw Will on his motorcycle, parked out by the curb. He hardly ever attended any of my performances, he said I had amazing talent but the ballet bored him to no end. I couldn't complain too much, he always picked me up when my shows were over, trying to make up for not being seated in the crowds.

"Hey, gorgeous," he greeted, taking off his helmet. Reaching it out, wanting to hand it to me.

"Will, what have I told you about picking me up on that thing? And not bringing a helmet for yourself."

"You live right around the corner, baby. As much as I wish you lived with me, you refuse. For reasons I don't understand, you still live with Sabrina."

"Choose your battles wisely tonight, Will," I brushed him off, securing my bag on my back.

It was true. I was thirty-four years old, living with my mother type figure. After ten years of living in England, I never found a reason to leave Sabrina's after she took me in. Or maybe I just never wanted to plant roots in a city that never felt like home to me. It was easier that way, hiding behind my rigid dance schedule as an excuse to not have time to look for a place. I was getting older, and my dancing years would soon be behind me, which scared me more than anything. I couldn't imagine a life without the one thing that had been constant throughout it.

"I stay with you more often than I stay with her," I replied, smirking, not wanting to cause another fight. I was exhausted and just wanted to get home, crawl into my bed and pass out.

"Come, prima ballerina, your chariot awaits."

I grabbed the helmet out of his hands, kissing his lips before placing it over my head. Straddling the bike behind him, hugging him close. We merged onto the highway, heavy traffic coming in all directions, he hit the throttle, jerking me back. I must have startled him because he turned around, eyeing me to see if I was okay.

The second I realized it, I was too late.

"Will!" I screamed.

He sharply turned back around, the truck in front of us stopped out of nowhere. Will immediately reacted, down shifting the bike, brakes squealing, swerving, skidding across the road. My arms tightened around his waist like a vice, hiding my face, bracing for the impact as his bike plowed into the back of the truck, head on. Metal crunching, arms suddenly empty, glass and my body flying through the air, screams echoing in my ears.

Darkness.

They say right before you die, you see your whole life flash before your eyes.

All I saw were bright blue tantalizing eyes.

By the man who still haunted my dreams.

𝔐artinez

I sat in the hospital chair by her bed, just like I did ten years ago in the armchair in her room. Leaning over with my hands out in front of me in prayer gesture, waiting. I hadn't fucking moved for the last five days. Fighting with the goddamn hospital to get the best doctors money could buy. No matter what they fucking cost, I'd pay for it in cash, right fucking then, if it would bring her back to me. They said it was only a matter of time until she woke up.

Day after day I heard the same thing, to be patient, to talk to her, to hold her hand. They kept her in a medically induced coma to stop the swelling in her brain. Two days ago, they started to pull her out of it since all her vitals, blood work, and scans were coming back normal. But here I sat, still fucking waiting. She had yet to open her eyes. My patience was being stretched to the limit, my prayers going unheard, no matter how many times a day I pleaded. I even removed the cross from around my neck and placed it on hers, having faith it would bring her back to me.

315

It was late into the night when I thought I heard her stirring. The steady beeps of the machines had lulled me to sleep. I was so fucking exhausted, I couldn't see straight. Fluttering my eyes open, I found her staring at me wide-eyed as if she was seeing a ghost. She blinked a few times, trying to focus. Narrowing her brows, thinking her mind was playing tricks on her.

"I'm here, cariño," I whispered in a soft tone, reaching for her hand.

She winced at my term of endearment, closing her eyes tight. Moving her hand away from me. I abruptly stood, causing her to jerk back. I wanted to go to her, I wanted to caress her cheeks and show her it was me.

Her Alejandro.

"Fuck..." I breathed out, walking out of her hospital room, leaving to get the doctors. They needed to know she was awake.

I stood back in the corner while they checked her for what seemed like hours, making sure she was okay. Shining lights in her eyes, taking vitals, asking her question, after question. What she remembered? What she didn't? How she felt? It was fucking endless.

By the time all the specialists were done, she had fallen back asleep, tired. I sat back in the chair, waiting for her to wake up again. Refusing to leave her side, even for a minute.

The next time she woke up, I was wide awake. Her eyes hazily found me sitting in the same exact same spot she had before. Even with all the bruises and cuts on her face, she was still fucking beautiful. I wanted to reach up and place a strand of hair behind her ear, kiss each and every imperfection that marred her flawless skin. But I couldn't. I had to sit back and admire her from afar. She looked older, her eyes no longer full of life. Staring at me like she didn't know who I was, when she was the only one who ever knew.

It was me that didn't.

Her hand instinctively went to the cross hanging from my necklace, bringing it up to her face to see what it was. Peering back and forth between the cross and me, silently asking me if it's what she thought it was.

316

"It was my mother's. Her protection," I divulged, breaking the silence between us. "She never took it off. At least, not until I took it off of her. The day she was murdered, taking her last breath in my arms."

She narrowed her eyes at me, taking in what I had never shared with anyone. Another piece to my puzzle.

"I've never taken it off until a few days ago. You needed it more than I did, Lexi."

She started to pull it off.

"It's yours now, cariño."

She reluctantly stopped, placing it back down on her chest. Her blank gaze roamed the private room, avoiding me. Taking in her surroundings, the vases of flowers on her bedside table from the Royale Ballet, including the daisies I had delivered every day to brighten her stay.

"Will," she simply stated, just above a whisper.

Hearing her speak another man's name was like taking a bullet to the fucking heart, but what could I expect. I deserved that and much more.

"I'm so sorry, Lexi," I sympathized. Bowing my head, not wanting to see her despair. I knew firsthand what it felt like to lose someone you loved several times in my life.

She instantly shut her eyes again, understanding my subtle response. The pain wreaked havoc on her mind. Tears slid down her face, and her small, frail frame shook uncontrollably. I resisted the urge to wipe them all away. Instead, I leaned forward in the chair, my elbows placed on my legs with my hands clasped out in front of me.

Waiting.

"How did you know I was here?" she asked, wiping away her tears that wouldn't cease. The question had been plaguing her since she woke up the first time, finding me unexpectedly sitting beside her.

I took a deep breath, stating, "Cariño—"

"Stop, fucking calling me that," she said through a clenched jaw. Her eyes still shut.

I surrendered my hands even though she couldn't see me. "Lexi, stop pretending like you don't know who I am. You know

317

the answer to that question. But if you need me to say the words, then I'll tell you. I've always kept tabs on you. It's who I am. I needed to make sure you were safe at all times."

"Why are you here, Martinez? You're not needed nor wanted," she responded, ignoring my reply.

"Look me in the eyes, Lexi."

She instantly opened hers, rage quickly taking over. Bringing back memories of the time in her life she wanted to forget. "Leave. Now!"

"No."

She scoffed, shaking her head. "You have some brass balls, buddy. You think you can come in here, say some sweet bullshit, and I'm just supposed to forget everything you did to me. Everything you put me through. Well, I'll make this visit really short for you, since you're such a busy man and all. It will be a cold day in Hell, before I'd forget. I won't."

"I don't expect you to forget, Lexi. But I'm praying you can forgive."

"I never took you for a religious man, Martinez. How has praying worked out for you in the past?" she viciously spewed, catching me off guard. "Is that what it will take for you to leave? Okay. I forgive you. Your conscience, or whatever the hell you have, is clear. You can go now."

"I'm not leaving without you. You're hurt."

"No shit," she gritted.

"No, cariño. The doctors..." I sighed, dreading to break the news I knew would only cause her more pain. Killing her a little more inside. She already hated me, I might as well be the one that broke it to her. "You can't dance professionally anymore. The doctors did everything they could do, Lexi. I sent for the best surgeon. You have multiple fractures and breaks to your left tibia. The impact from your landing shattered that ankle. Along with several torn tendons in that knee."

"You don't know what you're talking about, I want to speak to a fucking doctor. You're wrong! Get out! Just go, I don't need you! You're wrong!" she repeated, in hysterics. Furiously shaking her head. Fists clenched at her sides. "Why are you trying to hurt me? You're wrong," she continued to whisper over and over again.

"You flew through the air, Lexi! Your body was in the back of the guy's truck. If you hadn't been wearing a helmet you would have died, too. Half your ribs are broken, your arm fractured. Your hip dislocated. You're lucky to even be alive with the injuries you sustained to your spine. Even luckier that you'll be able to walk again. You have a long road to recovery that you can't make on your own. You will need more surgeries in the months ahead, not to mention the physical therapy."

I didn't falter. I stood up and whipped the blankets off her broken body, making her see the truth in my words. All she did was stare down at her leg like it was the only thing that was important to her. Reaching for the cast that ran the length of her entire leg. The high dosage of pain medication didn't allow her to feel any of the agony she would be in, if she weren't on it.

"What the fuck?" she bellowed, sucking in air. Her chest heaving as she brought her hands up to her mouth. "My dominant leg. This happens to my dominant leg?!"

"Cariño—"

"Stop fucking calling me that!" she seethed, pounding her fists into the bed. "I'm not your anything! My name is fucking Lexi!"

There was only so much I could take. Cocking my head to the side, I glared at her, willing my temper to stay at bay. "There is no reason for you stay here any longer. You don't even have your own place to live. Sabrina works all the time, you know that more than I do. There is no one here for you, no one to take care of you. Let me be the man to do that. I can get you the best doctors. Anything you need. Come back home with me until you're better. If you want to leave once you are healed, I will let you go freely."

She turned her face away from me, knowing I was right. I gently grabbed her chin, looking deep into her eyes. I coaxed, "I promise, but please give me a chance to help you, Lexi."

She hesitated, weighing her options for a few seconds. Jerking her chin out of my grasp, she snapped, "I'm not going because you want me to, I'm going because I need to. Nothing more, nothing less."

It was far from what I wanted to hear.

But it was a start.

Thirty-five
Lexi

I was devastated when Martinez told me I couldn't attend the funeral, still stuck in the hospital, not well enough to travel. Although, he did fly me to Will's gravesite, allowing me to say goodbye before we flew back to New York. He sat there, letting me cry, taking a few blows to the chest, as I took all my frustration and sadness out on him. Will wasn't close to his family, which was why he was working in England in the first place. I never met them, so I couldn't expect his family to postpone the funeral for me. They didn't owe me anything.

Martinez didn't give me any grief for breaking down in front of him when I was sitting in the wheelchair in front of his tombstone, knowing it was for another man. I thanked Will over and over again. The only reason I was still alive was because he gave me his helmet, and it cost him his life. Martinez actually tried to give me his shoulder to cry on, attempting to comfort me. I pushed him away, proving to him I didn't need him anymore. Ignoring the hurt look on his handsome face.

Sabrina was devastated when she found out the extent of my injuries, but more so with my decision to return home. One night while she was visiting me in the hospital, yet again, trying to make me change my mind. She told me she understood my choices. She could see I was still very much in love with Martinez. She wanted me to be happy, to find my peace. This was my chance at it. The motorcycle accident ended one chapter of my life, to allow another to begin. With him. It didn't matter how many times I told her I was leaving England because I didn't want to be a burden to her. She never believed me.

It didn't matter.

Nothing did anymore.

I was so depressed, struggling on a daily basis to keep going. Losing my desire for it all. I lost my career, my boyfriend, and my whole entire life, in a matter of seconds. Everything I held so dear to my heart had been ripped away from me. Dancing was all I ever had, and now that was gone, too. I had no reason to go on, not one.

Every surgery I had undergone in the last six months, felt like just another setback to moving on with the rest of my life. Or whatever the hell was left of it. At least I could finally walk, somewhat. The crutches hurt my arms, but I didn't need Martinez's help as much when I used them. Which gave me the space to be by myself, without him always hovering over me. I had a wheelchair to get around in, but it required me to ask him for help getting in and out of it from wherever I was laying or sitting. Despite how many times I told him just to help me and leave, he would just ignore me. Carrying me all around his penthouse, foregoing the chair. I had to try like hell to disregard how his masculine scent still had an effect on me.

The son of a bitch was handsome as fucking ever. Often catching myself staring up at his strong jaw as he carried me from room to room. I couldn't believe how he just got better looking with age. As if he was a fine wine. One day I managed to get myself in the chair to stroll along the penthouse, needing to get out of my room. Never going toward my ballet studio, scared it wasn't there anymore, but even more terrified if it was.

I passed by the room Martinez turned into his gym. He was working out all his frustrations without a shirt on. His gym shorts hanging low around his slim waist, showing off the fuck-me muscles, proudly on display. He was even broader, more muscular and well-built than I remembered. Sweat dripping off his chest, accentuating all the toned muscles of his defined, sculpted body. I watched for a few minutes then moved right along, needing to head back to my bedroom. Clutching the cross hanging from his necklace that I had yet to take off. The last thing I wanted was to be caught ogling him.

As I made my way past his bedroom, I couldn't help but laugh at the memory from when we flew back home, a few weeks after I was medically released from the hospital. Remembering how he actually tried to take me into his room, saying it would be easier if I slept in there. How he could hear me and get to me faster if I needed anything. I laughed sardonically and simply reminded him I didn't need to be his whore anymore. I'm sure he still had plenty of those in his life. He didn't say one word after that, swiftly taking me to my old room instead.

"Lexi, get the fuck out of bed. Get dressed," he ordered, walking into my room. Uninvited, like always. Forcefully opening my curtains, burning me with the light.

Oh… and I had Martinez on my ass twenty-four seven. Trying to breathe life back into me. Trust me, I'd already laughed plenty at the thought.

"I'm tired," I simply stated. "And open your eyes old man, I'm already dressed." I took my pillow and placed it over my face, welcoming the darkness once again.

"It's noon. You did this yesterday and the day before and the day before that. Should I keep going, princess?"

"No, but I know you will," I murmured through the pillow.

"Really cute. You've been doing this for the last six fucking months," he reminded.

"And there it is." I threw the blanket over my head. "Who cares?! What do I have to get up for? Nothing! I can't dance, I can't fend for myself, I can barely fucking walk!"

"You have crutches. You need to—"

"Don't tell me what I need! I'll tell you. I need you to get the fuck out of my room! Get off my ass! You're not my savior, Martinez! I don't even fucking like you! Now leave because you won't like me when I'm really angry!"

Yanking the blanket and pillow off of me, he scoffed, "Don't worry, sweetheart, I don't really like you right now."

"Good! Then the feeling is mutual!"

He leaned over, abruptly picking me up. He wasn't fazed by my weak attempt to fight him off. "Stop manhandling me!"

He threw me over his shoulder as if I weighed nothing. "Stop pretending like you don't want me to," he mocked, walking through the hallway, smacking my ass.

"You arrogant bastard!" I pounded on his back as he carried me out of the penthouse, getting into the elevator.

"This arrogant bastard is going to take you somewhere, whether you like it or not. I can't take this woe is me bullshit anymore," he stated, hitting the down button.

"Where are you taking me?" I demanded, giving up on my struggle, it was no use, he was a fucking brick house.

He gently set me down in the limo minutes later, carefully swinging my legs in and finally answered, "To your past."

When the limo pulled up to his private hangar, I would be lying if I said I wasn't intrigued as to where he was taking me. His private plane was ready to go, waiting on our arrival. He pulled me from the limo, taking me into his strong arms, onto the plane. Setting me down in the beige, leather chair, taking his seat next to me. I refused to show him any interest, watching a movie through the entire flight. Feeling his eyes on the side of my face the whole time. An hour later we landed, a driver already waiting for us. He once again carried me off the plane, grabbing my crutches on the way out. His bodyguards close behind us. As soon as we started driving toward our destination, I realized where we were.

I snapped my head in his direction, glaring at him. Asking, "Why the hell are we in Rhode Island?" Panicking as I waited for his answer.

"It's time for you to face your fucking demons. So here we are, sweetheart... Welcome to Rhode Island."

I opened my mouth, quickly shutting it, unable to form the words. My mind spun with questions I knew he'd never answer. I turned my face toward the tinted window, trying to calm my unsteady nerves. Trying to think of anything other than the demons that still lived in my hometown. Fidgeting with my fingers that were placed in my lap, battling the memories of the house I'd only known as Hell. He placed his hand on my thigh in a comforting gesture, assuming it would provide the reassurance it once had.

It did.

My heartbeat steadied, my stomach eased, my memories subsided. Only concentrating on the feeling of his callused fingers as he softly rubbed along my thigh. He continued to peer out his window, not paying any mind to the way his simple touch still made me feel. We drove in silence for what felt like forever, passing by my old elementary school, the ice cream shop I used to bike to. The sick feeling creeping back, but Martinez never stopped caressing my thigh.

The limo pulled onto the old, dirt road, driving toward my past. I shut my eyes, taking a few deep breaths, willing the memories to stay locked in the back of my mind. The bus driver leaving me on the side of the road, having to walk home by myself every damn day. The image of the helpless little girl always eager to get home, foolishly thinking she would find her momma waiting there for her with open arms. Asking her how her day went, telling her she loved her, walking out of the goddamn house to make sure she made it safely. My lips began to tremble, my chest started to heave, tears rolled down the sides of my face. Remembering every disappointment, every broken promise, every last lie that spewed out of her mouth.

Instantly shaking off the image of her dead body lying next to me. So cold, so blue, still feeling her arms around me. Shuttering from the feeling. I suddenly jolted when I felt Martinez's fingers wipe away my tears. The morbid memory sinking back down in the deep, dark corners of my conscious. It was no use, my pain wouldn't stop.

The ambulance.

The funeral.

My stepdad coming into my room every fucking night.

The first time he touched me.

The second…

The third…

And every time after that.

His smell.

His touch.

Telling me he loved me, thinking I was my mother.

I sucked in a breath, holding it in when the car came to a complete stop. I didn't have to open my eyes to know where we were. I could feel all the negative energy. Leaning my head back against the headrest, I licked my lips. Tasting my memories that wept out of my eyes.

"Why are you trying to hurt me?" I bellowed just above a whisper.

He wiped away another tear, caressing the side of my face. "Cariño, I'm trying to help you."

And with that he opened the door.

𝕸artinez

I scooped her up, carrying her out of the limo. Meeting Rick, who was waiting for us with her crutches on the other side. Her eyes were still tightly shut as I walked us up the empty driveway of the vacant, run down, shitty house. It looked like no one had lived there in years. There were no other houses for miles away. As soon as I got close to the front door, out of nowhere she started fighting me. Punching, clawing, screaming to let her go. I did. Trying to gently place her on the ground before she caused herself more pain.

"Lexi, stop, you're going to hurt yourself," I voiced, struggling against her.

Standing on her good leg, she opened her tormented eyes, grabbing the crutches immediately out of my grasp. "All you do is hurt me! Why would you bring me here! You have no right to do this to me! Who the fuck do you think you are?" she screamed, her body shaking.

"Cariño, let me explain. I'm not—" She cold clocked me, making my head sway from the unexpected blow to the face. I grabbed my jaw, moving it around as she shook out her hand from the throbbing.

I couldn't remember the last time someone hit me.

"I hate you. Do you hear me? I fucking hate you," she gritted out. Pounding on my chest, shoving me as hard as she could, pissing her off more because I didn't waver.

"You are evil! I fucking hate you, Martinez! What sick fuck would do this to someone! You're not trying to help me, you're hurting me. Just like you always have!"

I caught her wrists in the air. Looking her deep in the eyes, showing her this wasn't malicious, it was me genuinely trying to execute what haunted her to this day. Blow after blow, the woman

325

I knew was gone. A stranger stood before me. She abruptly turned, roughly jerking her wrists out of my hands. Looking at the house in front of her. Her chest heaving, panting profusely. I could see each and every memory that tortured her course through her mind, wreaking chaos all around her.

She didn't falter, throwing the crutches on the pavement. Crudely limping toward the side of the driveway, ignoring the throbbing pain in her leg. Each step more determined than the last. Stumbling, almost falling to her knees. It took everything in me not to run to her, not to pull her into my arms and take her away. But she needed to face her fears, her darkness, her past. She leaned forward grabbing as many stones that lined the driveway and stood back up, teetering, the rocks overpowering her.

"Cariño—"

She fiercely started hurling the stones at the house. One right after another, losing her balance with each forceful throw that erupted from her frail frame. Endless sobs escaping her mouth, her body shaking with fury. The windows shattered causing shards of glass to splatter everywhere. Deep, hard dents mangled the front door, and the siding came loose, falling off the sides of the house. Leaning forward again, she grabbed more stones, throwing, aiming, and chucking handfuls in all directions toward the dump. Frantically trying to bring down the house that caused her so much pain.

"You were never there for me!" Another stone ricocheted. "You left me with a monster! A fucking predator!" Another. "You were supposed to be my mother! You didn't do shit for me!" Three more stones. "I have no one in this world! I'm by myself! I've always been by myself!" Stone after stone after stone recoiled off the fallen house as she bawled her eyes out. "I fucking hate you! You sorry excuse for a fucking mother!"

I'd never seen anyone breakdown like that before. Yet, I stood there watching her in silence, not even my touch would ease her pain now. Her mind was running wild, she couldn't get it to stop, the memories and images playing out in front of her, with no end in sight. Remembering the last time she was let down. Hurt and rejected.

"I hope he's burning in fucking Hell! I hope someone murdered him, making him feel nothing but the pain! The pain he put me through for years!" She threw every last rock she could at the house. Frustrated her handy work wouldn't tear it down.

Losing her footing, she fell to the ground. Screaming out in pain. Instantly placing her hands over her ears, trying to tune out the voices that surrounded her everywhere. Desperately trying to shut out the past. I lunged into action unable to hold back any longer, falling to my knees right beside her. Pulling her convulsing body into my arms. She didn't fight me. The strong, fearless woman was gone. Replaced by a scared, lost little girl who still remained inside of her. I rocked her back and forth, trying to soothe her, whispering reassuring things in her ear.

She clutched onto me for dear life, letting me hold her, letting me take the burden off of her. Kissing the top of her head as she physically crumbled in my arms,

"Why would you bring me here? Why would you do this to me? How do you even know?" She shook uncontrollably, her voice breaking with each word that escaped her mouth.

I grabbed her face in between my hands, making her look at me. I spoke with conviction, "You. Have. Me."

She frowned, sucking in air as she took in my words. Staring me deep in the eyes. Relaxing into my touch, calming down a little.

"You're not alone, Lexi. Not anymore."

"I don't know anything about you. How do—"

"I wasn't brought into this life. I was born into it. The man you see, the man I am. It's always who I was supposed to be. I don't have anyone left in this life either. But you're mine, Lexi. You've always been mine," I paused to let my words sink in. "I went for you. After…" Shaking my head, deeply shamed by my actions. "I had never been so fucking scared in my life, like I was those two days you were gone without a trace. Needing to find you, to make sure you were okay. When you left, you took me with you, cariño. I have spent the last ten years of my life, just moving along, doing what was expected of me. Every dark day was the same thing. I'm so fucking exhausted of this Hell, there are days I've contemplated on ending it all."

Her eyes showed so many emotions, crippling me in ways I never thought possible.

"I need you to remember all of that when you look at me. Do you understand?"

She fervently nodded, unable to form words. Tears streamed down her face as I allowed her into my truths. I wiped them all away as fast as they came.

"When Leo called me the morning of your accident, and told me you were badly hurt, hanging on by a thread, I thought I'd lost you for good. The last memory I've held onto these last ten years was the night I left you sleeping in my bed. Your hair spread out, your tiny frame beneath my sheets, so at peace. I have yet to see that woman in the last six months. The one I think about day and night. I brought you here to help you find your peace again, Lexi," I murmured, softly pecking her lips, tasting her salty tears.

Surprised she didn't push me away. Barely controlling the urge to devour her fucking mouth, but it wasn't the right time, or the right place. I had to kiss her, though. To feel her lips against mine.

I couldn't not fucking kiss her.

Pulling back, nodding toward Rick. He popped open the trunk of the limo, bringing me what I needed, to end this once and for all. I stood, bringing her with me, grabbing her crutches, securing them under her arms. I kissed her one last time, looking deep into her eyes. Finally, seeing a glimpse of the man she always knew lived inside of me.

Rick handed me what I needed, and I released her. Walking back toward the beaten house. She stood there with wide eyes, her mouth dropped open with the realization of what I was about to do. She watched as I laced the entire house with gasoline. Throwing the red can at it before peering back over at her. I flipped open the lighter.

"I can chase away your demons, but they'll never stop chasing you. Do you want to do this?"

She swallowed hard, taking a deep breath before walking toward me on her crutches. She consciously peered from the house back to the lighter I held in my grasp. Contemplating the dark ghosts of her past and the brightness of her future. With a shaking hand, she reached out, taking the lighter, stating, "Thank you."

328

I nodded, as she flicked the lighter, igniting the stream of gasoline that lead to her porch. Watching the flames engulf the rundown shithole of her childhood.

Sending her past to burn in Hell.

Thirty-six
Lexi

The night we flew back from Rhode Island six months ago, he carried me into his bedroom, and I went willingly. He set me down on his cool, silk sheets, propped my feet up, handing me my medication. Knowing I needed to dull my pain in more ways than one. He was so gentle, so caring and compassionate.

I spent the rest of the night in his arms content, at peace, happy for the first time since I could remember.

"Get some rest, cariño. You're safe, I'm here," he whispered into my hair.

I shook my head, nuzzling deeper into his chest. Unable to be close enough. Emotionally, mentally, and physically exhausted, I fell asleep sometime before dawn. His soft touch skimming my back pulled me under, soothing me. I startled awake, searching for him, finding myself alone. For some reason I didn't panic, I didn't have to. I felt him there with me even though I was alone in his room. His side of the bed was still warm, causing a smile to tug at my lips. He came in minutes after I woke up with a tray full of every kind of food known to man.

"Why are you smiling, cariño?" A grin spread across his handsome face. Knowing damn well why.

"Wouldn't you like to know?" I smiled again, sitting up.

He chuckled. "I see you haven't lost that saucy little mouth."

We ate breakfast in his bed together, not bringing up the events of the previous day. Spending the entire Sunday there, talking about nothing important but it still seemed like everything. We ended up spending every Sunday this way. Sometimes we would watch a movie. Sometimes he would let me watch reality TV, while he worked on his laptop in bed. It didn't matter what we

330

were doing as long as it was together. Falling asleep in his arms every night, only to wake alone every morning. I was convinced the man never slept.

I headed to my room to get dressed like I did every morning, ready to start my day a few weeks after we got back. I opened my closet only to find empty hangers, walking over to my armoire next, opening each drawer, nothing. My bathroom was even empty. I stormed down the hall to his office, barging in without knocking.

He wasn't fazed, like he was expecting me.

"What the hell, Martinez? Where did all my stuff go?" I asked, cocking my hip to the side, hands placed on my waist.

"Good morning to you to, Lexi." He grinned.

"That smile is not going to work on me, buddy. Answer my question."

"They are where they belong, cariño. Where you belong, in my bedroom. In my life."

I hadn't left his room since.

It had been over a year since he brought me back to live with him, seeing a different side to the man I still loved with all my heart. He'd bring me breakfast in bed almost every morning, and was home to eat dinner with me every night. Spending more and more of our time together, making up for our time apart. He took me all over New York City, shopping, visiting art galleries, and going to fancy restaurants I'd never frequented before. We did almost everything together.

He kissed me, touched me, and held me without reservations. Out in public and behind closed doors, whenever the mood struck him, he would just act on it.

We behaved as a couple.

Him and I.

The cold, dark, soulless eyes replaced with a serene, calm, tantalizing gaze. I found myself thinking about him all the time. I wholeheartedly believed him when he said there were days he thought about ending it all. Sometimes I would watch him from afar, and I could see his struggle. His decisions were not without regard any more. See, my demons were laid to rest in the fire. His... were alive and thriving all around him every day. But at the

331

same time, it was a new beginning for us. Starting a new chapter of our lives, together. I often wondered if they would ever truly go away. Quickly realizing that El Diablo would always be a part of him, it's who he was. Call me crazy, but I loved that man just as much. Every side of him consumed me. Every part of him engulfed me.

He was mine.

No matter what.

Life was finally looking up after years and years of heartbreak and disappointment. He had been there for everything, taking care of me, supporting me, making me feel wanted for the first time ever, with him. He held my hand through the countless surgeries for my leg, and attended my physical therapy sessions with me. Motivating me to keep going, when my body wanted to give up. I just teased him saying he liked the view when I stretched. I always made sure I wore tight leggings that hugged my ass just right.

Martinez even recruited one of the top orthopedic surgeons on the East Coast to take my case. I could finally walk on my own without any pain. Even had been given the okay to begin dancing again. All my injuries had subsided but I had yet to put on my ballet flats since the accident. After months of avoiding the corridor that housed my dance studio, I finally got up the nerve to go see if it was still there one morning. Closing my eyes, I slowly walked in, only opening them to find the room just like I'd left it. I hurried into his office, tackling him in his chair.

"Thank you, thank you, thank you!" Kissing him all over his face. Able to finally say thank you. Just like I wanted to the first time I found it.

"To what do I owe this pleasure, cariño?" He stroked my cheek, a grin playing on his lips.

"You kept it. After all these years, you kept my studio, my sanitary. Why?"

"I wanted to keep apart of you here, hoping you'd find your way home again. And here you are." He kissed my forehead, wiping away the tears I didn't realize were falling.

"Thank you. I can't even begin to tell you what this means to me."

"Show me," he groaned.

332

"Look who's decided to wake up," he taunted, pulling me away from my thoughts as he walked into our room.

I rolled over, sitting up. Bringing the silk sheet with me, covering my bare breasts. Martinez made up an elaborate story why my pajamas never made it to his room. Saying he had no idea why they weren't transferred, and he would take care of the man in charge. I wasn't stupid, I knew he'd thrown them out. I had yet to replace them, becoming comfortable enough to be naked around him.

Even though we were closer than ever, we hadn't been intimate. I mean, he gave me mind-blowing orgasms all the time, but he never allowed me to touch him. Knowing that was all it would take for him to lose control. I think a part of him was still closed off when it came to us having sex. Scared he wouldn't be able to take me how I yearned for. Having a repeat of what happened years ago. I knew he would never do that to me again. He barely survived it the first time.

I didn't push it.

I didn't have to.

For once, his words spoke louder than his actions.

"You need to get dressed," he ordered, tugging my foot toward him at the side of the bed.

I squealed, laughing. "You want clothes on me? That's new."

He leaned forward, hovering above me. Caging me in with his strong, defined arms. "You just like being at my mercy." He breathed against my lips, causing shivers down my body. "Now, get dressed." He snapped down his teeth, backing away, much to my disappointment.

"Where are we going?" I asked, not getting up, watching how he moved around his room.

The way his back flexed, the way his black slacks hugged all the right places, how tall he fucking was. His whole backside was delicious. I shook off the image before it got me in trouble, and we'd never leave the penthouse.

"If I wanted you to know, I would have told you. I'm not going to tell you again. Get dressed."

See... still an asshole.

333

The limo was waiting for us, along with the usual bodyguards. It didn't take long to get where he was taking me. We pulled up to a brick building not far from his penthouse in the center of Manhattan. His men got out first and did a sweep around the property before I was permitted to get out. Some things never changed. He took my hand, helping me out of the limo, leading me up a set of stairs toward the back entrance. He unlocked the frosted, glass door, leaving the light off as I entered behind him.

"Alejandro, why are we—" He flicked on the light, rendering me silent.

𝕸𝖆𝖗𝖙𝖎𝖓𝖊𝖟

I watched as she made her way around the immense, open space. I stood off to the side with my hands in the pockets of my slacks, giving her a moment to take in all the things around her. Grinning as I watched how her eyes danced around the room. Not knowing where to look first. The glazed look in her eyes was all the thank you I needed.

"Is this—"

"It's yours," I simply stated, snapping her attention to me.

My voice echoed from where I stood. A smile spread across her face as she tried to keep her tears at bay. I grabbed the documents off the front counter, stepping from the tile onto the hardwood floors, toward her. Without saying another word, I handed her the deed to the building. She took the papers in her shaking hands, looking at what it was. Blinking rapidly, trying to focus on the big letters that read her name on the front.

"Oh my God," she rasped, placing her hand over her mouth as she went through the document.

"Just because you can't dance professionally anymore, Lexi. Doesn't mean you can't teach it and continue to do what you love, sweetheart."

She peered up at me, wide eyed, her mouth opening and shutting. Shaking her head in disbelief.

334

"This is too much—" I placed my index finger against her lips, silencing her.

"I bought this studio for you. You have everything you need, as you can see, to start your own company. The building is yours, Lexi. My name isn't attached to it in any way. Free and clear. No matter what happens… it's yours."

Her eyes blurred with more tears, stunned and overwhelmed by my gift to her. I caressed the side of her cheek with the back of my fingers, trying to soothe her emotions. She leaned into my touch, closing her eyes for a second. Telling me what her words couldn't.

"How am I ever going to thank you for everything you have done for me?"

"Dance for me."

She jerked back, opening her eyes. "What?"

"You heard me."

"I can't—"

"You can. And you will." I pulled away, taking her hand and walking toward the back of the studio. Stopping in front of the door that read, "Cariño," in elegant handwriting on a silver plaque. She beamed up at me as I opened the door, revealing a private dressing room stocked with everything a ballerina could ever want. She stepped in slowly, turning in a full circle, in awe of the space. Running her hands along the armoire that held every piece of designer dancewear, nothing but the best for her. Grabbing her dance bag I'd replaced from the accident, I handed it to her.

"It has everything you need." I kissed her soft, supple lips. "Go." Spanking her ass. "Now."

I walked away, getting the controller to the sound system. She still hadn't fucking moved as if her feet were stuck to the floor beneath her.

"I don't like to be kept waiting, cariño."

She took a deep, reassuring breath, placing one foot in front of the other as if she was telling herself to do so. Making my way out to the studio, I pulled up a chair. I sat down, leaning forward, placing my elbows on my legs with my hands clasped in front of me. Waiting for her to emerge minutes later.

She took my goddamn breath away. She was dressed in a light pink, low cut leotard that accentuated her breasts. Her hard nipples poking through the skintight fabric while her luscious ass peeked out the bottom. Foregoing the bra and tights, wearing leg warmers instead.

My cock fucking twitched at the sight of her.

She stretched for a while on the barre as I watched the way her body bent, curved, and twisted in all directions like she hadn't been away at all. Her leotard riding up, exposing more of her bare skin. I didn't give her time to contemplate her next thought, hitting play on the controller. She laughed to herself, peering at me through the mirror when the melody registered in her head.

Our eyes locked.

The song she played in my office the first time she came to see me, the very same song she danced to the day I went looking for her in Europe, blared through the speakers. In a way, we'd come full circle. No words needed to be spoken between us, to have the same exact thought.

She walked over to the barre, flawlessly extending her right leg out to the side, gently placing her ankle on the polished wood. Reaching her left arm up in the air and bringing her torso down to her knee, holding the stretch. Repeating the same movement with her left leg. Never breaking eye contact with me through the mirror. She held onto the barre with her left hand, grabbing her ankle with her right, effortlessly pulling it toward her chest as her leg extended forward. Perfectly standing on one leg. She had the longest, goddamn legs I'd ever seen.

After stretching, she started to dance for me. Her body twirled, her arms soared, and her feet glided in all directions of the room within seconds. From one end to the other, there wasn't a spot on the wooden floor her ballet flats didn't touch. She was so in sync with the music, the dancing, the heart and soul of her entire life. Forgetting I was watching her, getting lost in her element, pushing herself further and further. If you hadn't known about her accident, you'd think she never stopped dancing.

The song was nearly over when she stumbled, but faultlessly recovered, taking ahold of her ankle behind her, stretching her knee and thigh muscles. Working out the kinks that built up over the last year. I could see the sheer disappointment passing through

336

her eyes, as much as she tried to hide it by continuing her steps. Frustrated that her leg had already given out on her.

I paused the song that I had on repeat.

"Go stretch again, cariño," I ordered in a dominant tone. Nodding to the barre.

"I'm fine," she stubbornly replied. Shaking her legs and arms out. Getting back into position, looking at me through the mirror.

I cocked my head to the side, arching an eyebrow. She narrowed her eyes at me, but begrudgingly listened. I pressed play, allowing the melody to once again take over. She placed her leg on the lowest barre, making her ass stick out in my direction.

Tempting me.

She closed her eyes, needing to get lost in the music, wanting to push away all the negative thoughts, already feeling discouraged. I stood, taking off my suit jacket. Rolling up the sleeves of my collared shirt as I stepped onto the hardwood floor. I slowly came up behind her, catching her off guard.

She froze, turning around, opening her eyes. Peering up at me through her lashes. "What are you doing?"

I leaned forward against her ear, grinning. "I'm helping you stretch." Getting down on my knees in front of her.

Her eyes dilated. The feeling of disappointment replaced with nothing but lust. She placed her arms out to the side, resting up against the barre, supporting her weight. I grabbed her ankle, lifting it up in the air, rubbing along her leg as it was fully stretched, before setting it on the lowest barre. Running my other hand up her side, easing her over toward the extended leg. She understood what I was doing, reaching for her ankle, stretching. Standing back up, bringing her arms above her head, I caressed along her leg again, casually turning her torso so her leg was still placed on the barre behind her. Making sure I rubbed along her pussy as I pressed against her back. Leaning her forward, stretching down to her standing ankle.

Her breathing hitched as I touched her all over her lower body. Her ass, her legs, but especially her pussy. She came back upright, holding the barre for support again, her leg still behind her. My lips softly kissing the inside of her thigh to where she wanted my mouth the most. Sliding over her leotard, I licked from her opening

337

to her clit. Sucking her nub into my mouth, one hand holding her in place, the other pushing into her warm, wet fucking heat.

"Oh God," she panted, lust-filled eyes staring down at me while I stared up at her.

I was finger-fucking her pussy while she was riding my goddamn face. She sucked in her lower lip, her head wanted to fall back, but I wouldn't allow it. I pulled the front of her leotard, holding her firmly in place so I could watch her face come apart. She climaxed within minutes, shaking, trembling, and screaming out my name. It never took her very long to come when I was on my knees in front of her.

Lexi loved to watch.

I stood, bringing her leg down, devouring her mouth. Loving how her body responded from every single touch of my hands. Melting into me, rising up on the tips of her toes, moaning when she tasted her salty, sweetness off my lips and tongue. I pulled away first, and she whimpered at the loss, thinking this was the end of our intimate time together.

Unaware that it was only the beginning. I was far from fucking done.

I grasped her wrists, placing them high above her head. Stepping back, I made her twirl in circles for me like the ballerina in a jewelry music box. Wanting to hear her laugh. See her smile. Ease her worry that she wasn't as great of a dancer as she used to be. Tugging her back toward me, our chests collided. My hands went to her cheeks, pulling her in for another kiss. Stripping off her leotard, only leaving her in her leg warmers and her ballet flats.

"The windows are tinted. The door is locked. My men are guarding the building. It's just me and you, baby," I breathed against her mouth, answering the questions in her mind.

Wanting her to stay right there at the moment with me.

I twirled her one last time to face the barre, pressing the front of her body against it, locking eyes with her reflection again. Her eyebrows lowered, confused by what was going to happen next. With a primal regard, I glared at her naked, flawless body in the mirror. Seeing how tiny she looked in comparison to me. Leaning forward, I brushed my nose up the side of her neck, never breaking the contact of our stares.

I whispered close to her ear, "When we get home, Lexi. I will take my time with you in my bed. Feeling your naked skin against mine. I will kiss, touch, and lick every last part of your sinful fucking body. Making you come until you can't anymore. But right now," I paused. "I'm going to take you on this barre. Fuck you in this studio. Combining the two things you love, ballet and me."

Her eyes widened when she heard my zipper, pulling out my hard cock. Jerking it in the palm of my hand. Rubbing it up and down her ass cheeks.

"Yes," she purred, pushing her ass out onto my cock. Putting to rest any hesitation I may have had.

I didn't need a condom. I knew she was on the pill, even if she wasn't, I would have fucked her without one regardless. I wanted to feel her in every way possible. Placing her leg back on the lowest barre. I eased into her opening from behind, stretching her slowly, gently, letting her adjust to my size. Rubbing her breasts, stimulating her clit at the same time. Playing her body like it was made just for me.

"Alejandro," she panted when I was balls deep inside of her.

"Fuck, you feel good," I growled, thrusting in and out of her pussy. There was something animalistic in my voice I'd never heard before.

Grabbing her cheek, I turned her face to claim her goddamn fucking mouth again. My fingers never let up on her clit. I couldn't get enough of her. It started off slow, but my movements became urgent and more demanding. Her mouth parted, her chest heaved, feeling her wetness slipping out of her onto my balls. I alternated between my palm and fingers to manipulate her nub, her hips moving in the opposite direction that I stimulated. Her clit overly exposed from the angle.

"I'm going to... God... I'm gonna..." she moaned in between kisses.

"Come on my cock, baby. Let me feel your sweet tight fucking pussy."

Her eyes widened in pleasure. Her pussy tightened, squeezing the fuck out of my shaft. Feeling her come drip down my balls. I didn't falter, not allowing her any time to recover. I pulled out,

339

picking her up and laying her sideways, parallel along the freestanding barre. I straddled it. She whimpered in yearning as my nails raked down her torso. Clutching onto her hips to steady her as she gripped the wood she was laying on above her head. In one thrust I was deep inside her, sliding her soaking wet pussy up and down on my cock. Her back rubbed along the barre as I slammed into her, thrust after thrust. Moan after moan. Her mouth parted, her breathing escalated, and when her eyes started to roll to the back of her head, I yanked her neck forward so that they would stay open.

It was the most intense feeling in my entire life. Nothing compared to having sex with Lexi.

Not one damn thing.

No one did.

She went fucking crazy. Moaning. Screaming. Climaxing over and over again, her body trembling. I gripped her hips harder, knowing there would be markings when I was done having my way with her. Her noises grew louder the closer I got to coming.

"I'll never get tired of your fucking pussy. It belongs to me. You're fucking mine," I growled from within my chest. Thrusting in one last time, releasing my seed deep inside of her.

Right where it fucking belonged.

I shook with my release and kissed her passionately, both of us panting profusely. Helping her off the barre, she threw on her clothes.

I took her home.

To my bed.

Where I continued to have my way with her for the rest of the goddamn night.

Thirty-seven
Lexi

"Where are we going?" I whined again, sitting beside him on his private airplane.

Failing miserably at watching the movie playing in front of us. Yesterday during dinner he casually mentioned we were taking a vacation. I'd never taken a vacation in my entire life, and when he told me, I pretty much jumped in his lap. Kissing him all over his face, expressing my joy. Which of course led to him taking me on the dining room table, swiping our plates filled with food onto the floor. I don't think there was a place in his penthouse we hadn't had sex in or on, since we started being intimate a year ago.

It was as if he wanted to make up for all the years he could have been inside me. The man was insatiable, waking me up in the middle of the night with his cock inside me, coming up behind me in the shower, and especially in my ballet studio. My place of business, and the one in the penthouse. Finally using the black leather couch, in the room more often than not. Watching me dance just for him.

He said I had always been dancing for him. It didn't matter if he was in the room or not. The way I moved was his. Everything about me was his.

He owned my body, heart and soul.

"Cariño, you asking every ten minutes is going to make this five-and-a-half hour flight seem longer than it already is," he sarcastically stated not looking up from his laptop in front of him.

Earning him a glare from me. "I thought we were on vacation. Why are you still working, old man?"

It was his turn to glare at me. "Old man? You weren't screaming that last night or again this morning."

341

I scowled. "This." Wiggling my finger at him. "Will not get you back in here again." I pointed to my pussy.

He cocked his head to the side with a mischievous grin, setting his computer on the beige, leather chair beside him. He picked me up around my waist, wrapping my legs around him, placing me on his lap instead.

"Cariño, you and I both know that if I want in... I'm getting in." He pecked my lips, tugging my bottom lip between his teeth.

"I'll let you in right now. If you tell me where we're going," I countered, grinding my pussy on his cock for good measure.

"Is that right?"

I nodded, smiling all proud of myself.

Our relationship changed even more in the last year. He was a different man when it came to me. He started working less, spending more time with me. Taking me out on dates like a real couple, spoiling me every chance he got. But none of that really mattered to me, I was happy just lying in his arms at night, feeling loved, even though he never said it to me. He didn't have to, though. I felt it. I didn't work full time, I just taught few a classes during the week, all age ranges. He scheduled whatever the hell he did with his days, when I was teaching, coming to pick me up in the limo more often than not. I cooked dinner for us almost every night, unless he was taking me somewhere to eat.

I even had several recipe books for Colombian food shipped to the penthouse, wanting to learn his favorites. The first time I cooked for him, I surprised him with Bandeja Paisa, a traditional Colombian dish. The tormented expression on his face when he saw the food was one I had yet to forget. I thought he would have been happy, but it was the exact opposite, he disappeared into his office after we were done eating without saying a word. I gave him his space wondering what put him in such a foul mood. Silently praying he would tell me what was wrong when he came to lay with me.

He didn't.

I still woke up alone every morning, usually finding him in his office. I knew his demons were still there. Alive and present. They hadn't gone away, but they didn't matter to me anyway. When I was with him they subsided, his dark, soulless eyes replaced with the serene gaze I'd grown to expect.

And that was good enough for me.

"As tempting as your offer sounds…it's called a surprise, Lexi. You will know when we get there. Now sit down and be a good little girl while I finish up some work."

I kissed him, rubbing my fingers along his solid, muscular chest through his gray collared shirt. Leaning forward, making sure to put my breasts right in his face as I whispered in his ear, "Are you sure you know how to use that laptop? I know it's before your time and stuff. You know… you old men have a hard time with technology and such. I don't want you to hurt yourself before we even get there."

I sucked in air when one of his hands gripped my hair from the nook of my neck, crudely tugging my head back. Nudging my torso, making me sway my hips on his cock.

"Why do you provoke me?" he rasped, clutching my hair harder.

"Because I can," I sassed. He jerked my head back further by my hair.

Not in pain. In submission.

"Little girls who are bad, Lexi, don't get to come. Now you don't want that, do you?"

"Wait, what?" I tried sitting up straight, but he held me in place.

"And we both know how much you love to fucking come." He grabbed my mouth with his free hand. "I want nothing more than to stick my cock in that saucy fucking mouth of yours. The one that never seems to know when to shut the fuck up. But I have work to do."

He swiftly let go, setting me on the seat beside him. Grabbing his computer and going right back to work. That was Martinez, hot one minute and cold the next. I knew what battles to choose, this wasn't one of them. There was a reason he was trying to occupy his mind. He'd been like this all morning. Lost in his own thoughts, no matter what I did or said there was no pulling him out of it. So I let him be for the rest of the flight, trying to keep my eyes on the movie and not what he was doing. Hoping that maybe he would tell me when he got there.

I must have fallen asleep sometime during the movie. When I woke up, we had landed. Martinez was on the phone, speaking Spanish to someone on the other end. His tone was neutral, but his demeanor screamed with tension. Ending his call, he grabbed my hand, leading me out of the airplane and down the stairs. As always, he had a limo waiting for us. The first thing I noticed was an arsenal of bodyguards, more than what we usually had when we went anywhere. I didn't recognize any of their faces, other than Rick's who was barking out orders. I tried to ignore the uneasy feeling settling in my stomach, paying attention to my surroundings instead. Holding onto Martinez's hand so tight.

I sat in the seat next to him in the limo. He immediately lifted my legs to rest on his lap, with his hands set on my thighs as if he knew I needed his touch. When in reality, he seemed like he needed mine more than I did his. The silence was deafening all around us, no one spoke a word the entire drive. He just peered out the tinted window, letting his plaguing thoughts take him under. This was supposed to be a vacation, but so far it didn't feel like that at all.

We passed what appeared to be slums with their colorful bright stack homes, buildings upon buildings, and natives walking in every direction. Staring at the limo and security cars that formed a line in front of and behind us, like we didn't belong there. The unmanaged, dirt roads made for an uncomfortable ride. We turned down a secluded path with palm trees on either side and drove for about ten minutes. I started to see an infinite amount of water all around us before we took a sharp left down a surprisingly nice paved road. Up until that point they had been uneven, jagged, and coarse.

An endless amount of beautiful tropical trees mixed with lush greenery took up the sides of the road. Definitely something that had been planted there for a purpose, they weren't natural. You couldn't see anything behind the landscaped wall as we sped closer to our destination. Wherever we were going, they wanted undisclosed privacy and spent a small fortune to provide it.

My eyes widened when we pulled up to the massive iron gates. Lined with a dozen or more men, holding assault rifles tightly in their grasps. They were dressed like soldiers, carrying more weapons on their bodies. The gates opened immediately, letting us pass through, obviously expecting our arrival. Martinez glanced over at me, feeling my fear, reassuringly squeezing my thigh for comfort. The driveway was about a hundred yards and it led to a roundabout where the driver parked the limo.

He grabbed my hand before opening the door to step out onto the limestone pavers that led all around the enormous property. Still not saying a word. My eyes widened when I looked up. This wasn't a house. This was a mansion. I'd never seen anything like this before. A tan waterfront estate with a terracotta tiled roof, resembling a villa. There was a stoned path in between the ten cathedral archways, five on each side, which held one vehicle in each port. The live-in part of the estate was settled further back on the property.

I could smell the salty breeze coming off the water as he led us up to the home. The courtyard doors opened for us, revealing four older women dressed in maid uniforms standing there, greeting us as we walked in. Of course Martinez instantly dismissed them with a wave of his hand. Grand, angled stairs led up to a set of ten-feet-high, custom made iron doors with intricate latticework covering all the windows. Opening to a wide foyer with shiny marble floors. Walls as far as I could see. He let go of my hand, knowing I wanted to look around and wander.

My jaw dropped as I turned in a full circle, taking in my surroundings. Stopping to look at him. He nodded with a small smile playing on his lips, giving me the okay to go explore. First, I made my way into the elegant main sitting area. The sun was shining through every window in the wide-open space, illuminating the huge family portrait over the mantle.

I heard his footsteps coming in my direction, abruptly stopping when they were close. I turned around, looking at him as he leaned against the wooden post. His strong arms crossed over his chest. He was glaring at the portrait with cold, soulless, dark eyes.

"Alejandro," I murmured, my voice echoing through the mansion. His intense gaze reluctantly wavered to mine. "This is your family's vacation home, isn't it?"

He narrowed his eyes at me. Each second that passed between us felt like minutes, hours, days. My heart beat rapidly in my chest, waiting for his answer. He peered back up to the portrait, unable to resist the urge any longer.

"This used to be one of my favorite places to come to, growing up. My mother would bring my sister, Amari and me here every summer."

My mouth parted, I never expected what would come out of his mouth next.

Looking back down at me, he stated, "I haven't been back here since she was murdered under my father's orders."

Martinez

Everything looked exactly the same. I spent a small fortune making sure it was well taken care of on a daily basis. Out of every home my father owned, this was always my mother's favorite. I couldn't part with it. This house was the only memory I kept alive from my past, selling off every other possession that was in his name. I couldn't bring myself to come here, too many good memories now mixed with the bad.

I pushed off the post, needing a moment to myself. Walking out onto the veranda, resting my elbows on the ledge. Taking a deep breath as I looked out at the sun reflecting off the water. Remembering all the happy times with the two women that were taken away from me too soon. Memories cut short by unnecessary violence. My eyes went to the Olympic-sized pool where I first learned how to swim. I could still see Amari teasing me because I couldn't hold my breath as long as she could. My mother watching adoringly as her two prized possessions enjoyed what it was really like to be kids. Laughing, running around, playing tag, and whatever else we used to come up with.

We were all peaceful without my father around barking orders. Thank God he hardly ever came with us. It was the only time I ever felt free from the Martinez name.

I bowed my head, shaking off the images playing in my head like a goddamn movie reel, missing them even more now. I felt Lexi come up behind me, wanting to comfort the broken man in front of her, but knowing better than to do so.

"Why did you bring me here if this house brings you so much pain?" she asked, walking up beside me.

"I wanted you to see the good part of my life growing up, Lexi," I simply stated the truth, looking back out at the water.

"This place is gorgeous. I've never seen such a breathtakingly beautiful estate in all my life." She gently placed her hand over mine on the ledge. I let her, relaxing under her touch.

"My mother spent years making sure it was a little piece of heaven. A safe place for my sister and I to be kids."

"Where are we?"

"Colombia."

"Oh..." I could feel her fidgeting next to me, her anxiety burning a hole in my side.

"I'm not going to sugarcoat it for you. I'm wanted more dead here than I am in the States. I run Colombia, which is all the more reason they want me gone. For your safety, I can't take you out of this house. I wish I could, but I won't risk your life. I'm sorry, cariño."

"Are you serious?" she questioned, turning me to face her. "I don't care about any of that. All I want to be is with you." I turned my head away. "Look at me." I did, taking in her sincere expression. "We could be in a shack right now and I'd be happy. None of that matters to me. I come from nothing, and I can appreciate the beauty in all of this, but it doesn't matter to me." Placing her hands on my chest, looking deep into my eyes. "You matter to me. I love you, Alejandro."

"Lexi—"

"I know. You don't have to say it back. I know you love me, because I know you. In here." She set her hand over my heart. "Let's make some new, amazing, happy memories here. Your mom would want that."

"Yeah..." I nodded. "She would."

For the next two weeks, we did just that. Spending our days relaxing, talking, and swimming in the pool. Seeing her in a tiny piece of cloth she claimed was a swimsuit, instantly made me fucking hard. Let's just say not much swimming was done, and I owed her some new suits. Our nights were spent lying together out on the lounger, on the patio, after dinner. Lexi wrapped in my arms, both of us staring up at the sky, watching the sun dip into the water. Sometimes we would talk, but often we didn't. There was no need for words.

We just enjoyed one another's company. Then I'd take her to bed and spend hours consumed with her body. There wasn't an inch of her skin that I didn't touch, lick, or kiss. When I was done having my way with her, she'd lay in my arms, passing out as I rubbed her back. I stayed with her for a few hours, watching her sleep, the way her chest would rise and fall with each breath, how her pouty lips would part, her hair cascading all around her face. She was so content and happy. It brought me great joy knowing I was the cause.

Late into the night I would slip out of the room leaving her to rest. I'd sit in front of the family portrait over the mantle, rubbing my fingers over my lips, staring at it for I don't know how long. Contemplating over and over if I was the same man as my father. The one I hated so fucking much. Watching the ghosts of my mother and sister dancing around me, wondering when my time would come, too. Praying their souls were resting in peace. Every morning the sun would come up, and Lexi would wake, knowing where I was. She'd sit with me, laying her head on my lap, as I ran my fingers through her soft brown hair.

The only angel in the room.

It was our last night in Colombia and Lexi had already been teary-eyed twice that day, saying she didn't want to go back to our lives in New York. She wanted to stay in her little piece of heaven with me, forever. I promised I would bring her again soon. We laid out on the lounger for the last time, both of us lost in our own thoughts. Her head rested on my chest as I caressed the side of her arm.

"Do you want children?" I found myself asking out of nowhere.

She scoffed, "I don't know." Nervously laughing. "I've never really given it much thought."

"Yes, you have."

She shrugged, knowing I was right. "I don't think I'd be a good mom to be honest. I'm probably not maternal. There's no need to bring a kid into my mess. I didn't exactly have the best upbringing, no example to lead by."

I caressed her cheek. "You'd be an amazing mother. Any kid would be lucky to have you as their parent."

She smirked, her mind running wild. I didn't have to ask what she was thinking. It was blatantly obvious. So I wasn't surprised when she asked, "What about you?"

I peered back up at the sky. "If you could live anywhere in the world, where would it be?" I questioned, ignoring her.

She sighed, disappointed. "That's easy. Italy. Off the Amalfi Coast. Live in one of those houses on a cliff. The people are supposed to be very welcoming. It would be a nice change of pace from New York."

"I'll take you there one day," I simply stated, smiling down at her.

"I look forward to it." She nuzzled her body closer to mine. "How about you? Where would you live?"

"Cariño, I've been everywhere. There's very little I haven't seen. I'm an old man, remember?" I chuckled.

"That you are." She nodded.

"Ask." I could feel her mind stirring, wanting to ask me more, but afraid to.

"Do you ever regret the things you've seen? The things you've done?"

"No."

She nodded again, looking back up at the stars. Not knowing what else to say.

"It wouldn't have brought me to you."

She immediately peered back at me, stunned by my response.

"I'm fucking exhausted, Lexi. You're the only thing keeping me going. I'm getting older as you like to remind me. There's only so much more I can take."

She sat up, straddling my lap. Laying against my chest, listening to my heartbeat. "Are you ever scared of dying?" she said just above a whisper. Fumbling with my mother's cross that still hung around her neck.

She never took it off.

"No, cariño. I'm not. When it's your time, it's your time. But no one fucks with me. I've spent my whole life making sure of it."

My response gave her the peace she needed. For now.

"The things I regret, haven't happened yet."

She sat up, looking me dead in the eyes. "Wha—"

"If something ever does happen to me. Just remember I'll always be with you. No matter what. In here." I placed my hand over her heart.

"Alejan—"

"Look! A shooting star. Make a wish, baby."

She peered up at the sky as I looked at the side of her beautiful face. Making my wish and praying to God, it would come true.

Thirty-eight
Lexi

We sat in the back of the limo on our way to the church for the christening of his niece's son. I hadn't met Briggs yet, at least not officially. I didn't count our brief run in at the penthouse. She lived with her husband Austin and their two kids in Oak Island, North Carolina. Amari, who was almost three years old, and Michael, who just turned four months. Both named after Briggs' parents, her mom being Martinez's sister.

"Stop fidgeting, Lexi," he ordered in a demanding tone. A strong hand came down on my bouncing legs, holding them still. Not looking up from his damn laptop. I swear he was on that thing more and more every day. Ignoring me in the process.

"I can't help it. I'm nervous!" I expressed, trying to free my legs from his grasp.

"Cariño, she's my niece, not my fucking mother. I don't need her approval for anything. Especially who I fuck. I'm a grown ass man. Now relax."

I scowled. "It matters to me! And I'm not just someone you fuck." Trying to shift my body away from his.

He took a deep breath, shutting his laptop, placing it beside him. Grabbing my hand, tugging me over to his lap. I wrapped my legs around him.

He pulled my hair back, away from my face, rubbing his thumb along my pouty lip. "What do you need from me? Huh?"

"I thought I've been telling you."

"No…. you've been whining. I don't like playing childish games."

I tried to get off his lap, but he held me firmer in place.

351

"Briggs and I don't have a close relationship. Not by traditional family standards, at least. She will be more shocked that I'm there than meeting you."

"But I still want her to like me," I whispered.

"I like you. A lot." He grinned, lifting up my chin.

I smiled, blushing from the simple sentiment. Making up for the fucking remark before. It was the first time he'd ever said anything like that to me. It wasn't the three words I wanted, but I still cherished it.

"Cariño, you've sucked my cock too many goddamn times to still blush like that."

I gasped, slapping him on the chest. "You ruined it." Trying to slap him again, but he caught my wrist in the air. Jerking my face inches away from his mouth.

"Well, now we are even. You've ruined me. This," he skimmed his thumb against my heat. "And these," he pecked my mouth, biting my bottom lip. "Have all ruined me. I'd like to ruin that pussy in the nicest possible way right now, right here. But I'm not going to lie, cariño, that slap kind of hurt," he lied. "So, how about I let you make it up to me?"

"We're on our way to a church and you're talking about sex, Martinez. That can't be right."

"It got you to stop whining. Didn't it?"

I smiled. I couldn't help it. He could be an insensitive bastard, but at least he always made me feel better after.

"I don't even like you right now. You should at least pretend to be sorry, or at least try to get on my good side again," I argued, smirking.

He cocked his head to the side, narrowing his eyes at me for what felt like forever, but was truly just seconds. He didn't falter. With a mischievous grin he reached over and cupped my pussy, moving his rough, callused fingers ever so slightly over my silk panties.

I gasped.

"Hmm..." he groaned, immediately making me remember the feeling of him everywhere and all at once. "Your pussy fucking likes me," he rasped, leaning in close to my ear, never stopping the light brush of his fingers against my heat. "And that's all that fucking matters to me."

We sat in the back of the church. I was thankful it didn't come crashing down on him when we stepped foot through the doors. Watching Michael get baptized was such a beautiful sight. I loved every second of it. Briggs was gorgeous. I've never seen anyone pull off vibrant purple hair the way she did. She also had bright, intricate sleeve tattoos running down her arms. More scattered throughout her body. I would have never guessed she was a mom of two, her figure was flawless. She looked like such a tender person, totally opposite of her uncle. Her husband Austin, looked at her lovingly as she held their baby in her arms. He was covered in tattoos too. Definitely had that whole bad boy thing going for him.

From what I gathered they had a rough relationship from the start, but love prevailed, and here they were a happy family. What completely caught me off guard was that Martinez knew every bible verse, every step to follow, as if he'd been going to church every day of his life.

The man was a walking paradox of contradictions.

"Unkey!" a little girl with bright blue eyes and pigtails came running up to him outside after the christening. Her chubby little legs moving faster than they should.

"Mi niña bonita," he replied in Spanish, immediately picking her up.

I jerked back, surprised. *Who was this man, and what did he do with Alejandro?*

She wrapped her tiny little arms around his neck, laying her head on his chest. Hugging him tight with her eyes closed. He kissed the top of her head. And I swear I almost fell over, stunned by what was going on in front of me.

"I miss you, Unkey. Why don't you come see me no more? Mama says you busy. I not busy. I come see you, okie?" she spoke sincerely in the cutest baby voice I'd ever heard. She held his face in between her hands, looking adoringly into his eyes.

And... my ovaries just exploded at the sight.

"We Skyped last week, silly girl."

They did? How did I not know this?

353

"That's not the same, Unkey," she giggled.

"Amari! What have I told you about running off like that," Briggs reprimanded, coming up behind her.

"Uh oh..." Amari turned around, laying her head on his shoulder. "I sorry, Mama. But my Unkey here."

She smiled, rolling her eyes. "Hi, Uncle," Briggs greeted, such a different reception to him than her daughter. She glanced over at me with questioning eyes.

"Briggs this is Lexi," he gestured toward me. "Lexi this is my niece, Briggs," he simply stated, flipping Amari over, tickling her to death.

Briggs cocked her head to the side. "I know you from somewhere. Right? You look so familiar."

"Yeah. We met briefly, a long time ago. You came to your uncle's penthouse one night. But we weren't properly introduced." I looked over at Martinez who was still entertaining his great-niece.

Her eyes searched all around her, until realization hit her face. "Oh..."

"Is she your girl, Unkey?" Amari chimed in, hanging off of him like a monkey.

"You're my girl."

She nodded, ecstatic with his response. "I good sharer. I share him," she reassured me.

We all laughed.

"Come, baby girl. Let's head back to the house. People are probably already there." Briggs looked at her uncle. "Austin left with Michael already, he needed to go down for a nap. You're coming back to the house, right?"

"Please, Unkey. We can have a tea party in my room." She clapped, excited.

"Of course. This little monkey and I have some catching up to do, and apparently some tea to drink."

Briggs nodded, reaching for Amari who leaned further into his chest.

"No. I stay with Unkey."

"Amari—"

"It's fine," he interrupted.

Briggs bit her lip, skeptically. Looking from him to the limo, knowing there were bodyguards in there. Knowing she could possibly be putting her daughter's life in danger. She didn't feel comfortable leaving Amari with him, and I couldn't blame her. A hurt look flew by Martinez's face, it was quick but I saw it. My heart immediately hurt for both of them. I knew there was so much he wanted to say, but for some reason.

He couldn't.

"I'll be in there with them," I blurted, needing to say something. Hoping it would help.

Briggs looked over at me and then back at her uncle, sighing. Finally smiling lovingly at her daughter, who was so happy and content in his arms. Not paying any mind to the uncomfortable scene playing out in front of her.

"Okay," Briggs agreed. "I'll follow you back to my house. Do you remember where I live?"

He nodded.

Amari sat next to Martinez in the limo, hugging his arm as she told him all about her baby brother. I sat across from them, admiring the bond they shared. She showed him that she knew how to count to ten and recited all her colors. Letting him know all the things that were important to her. He paid close attention to each and every word that came out of her mouth. And for the first time since I met him, I thought about having a family one day.

With him.

I peered out the window, trying to shake off the thoughts. Feeling his intense gaze on the side of my face as if he knew what I was thinking, without me having to say anything. He turned his attention back to the enthusiastic little girl, grabbing at his chin. Needing his undivided attention.

Briggs and Austin's home was beautiful. It sat right on the water, and had a dock that extended out toward the lake. Countless pictures lined their walls. Their kids were the center of attention, but they also had a number of them alone, as well as plenty with their friends and family. All of their memories hung proudly on display. Their home was so inviting. You could feel so much love everywhere.

I couldn't help but think of our future. *Would we ever have what they did, one day?* Wondering if it was in the cards for us, if he wanted more with me. *He wouldn't have brought me back with him if he didn't, right?*

I didn't have too much time to dwell on my suddenly, plaguing thoughts. Briggs pulled me away, introducing me to all her friends, who were more like family, she said. She called them the good ol' boys, which included Austin. Lucas was married to Alex, Bo and Half-pint was what they called them. I guess Alex was a tomboy who was a part of the group growing up. None of the boys wanted to see them together and made sure to put them through hell. Jacob was married to Lily, who was Lucas's baby sister. And that relationship was pretty much self-explanatory on why they had to keep it a secret from everyone. Especially Lucas, who never imagined they'd get together. Dylan was a narcotics detective who was married to Aubrey, a girl from California. I guess they had spent years apart before finding one another again.

All of them had kids, most of them teenagers already. From what I gathered they all had tumultuous relationships from the start but love prevailed in the end, and I would be lying if I said it didn't give me hope.

"So, tell us Lexi, what's it like being with Mr. Tall Dark and Handsome?" Lily asked, wiggling her eyebrows.

We were all sitting outside on the patio while the younger kids ran around playing in the yard. The men were off bullshitting somewhere. The only teenager that was at the party was Mia, which was Lucas and Alex's fifteen-year-old daughter. I couldn't help but keep an eye on her. She seemed to be lost in her own head.

"Eww, Lily," Briggs replied, pulling my attention away from Mia.

"Oh, come on, Briggs. Have you seen your uncle? The man is gorgeous. I think he's better looking now than he was when I first met him. I mean, look at Lexi. She's what? Twenty years younger than him?" Aubrey added, making Alex laugh. "Obviously the man has some pull."

I laughed. I couldn't help it. It wasn't just a pull, it was a tight lock. "He's umm... intense," I replied, clearing my throat. "Amari doesn't seem to think so. She adores him," I added.

"Yeah... She's loved him since day one. Austin and I were dumbfounded when he showed up in my hospital room right after I'd given birth. We hadn't even told him I was in labor yet, but of course, he would know. He was the first person to hold her after Austin and I. It was actually his idea to name her Amari. He said she looked just like my mom." She reminiscently smiled. "He's been here for every important event ever since. He sends the kids gifts all the time, they Skype at least once a week. No one else matters when Unkey is around. He is definitely not the same man that raised me. Not even a little. I mean, hell... my bodyguard Esteban took care of me more than he did."

He raised her? I started to feel like I didn't know this man at all. *What else has he kept from me?*

Taking in my surprised expression, Briggs asked, "You didn't know?"

"I just assumed it was work-related stuff when he would go out of town, or get back later than usual," I candidly spoke.

"With my uncle, never assume anything. That's the best advice I can give you. But he's taken with you. I can see it when he looks at you. I've never seen him look at anyone like that before. My uncle is hard to live with and hard to love but you have to understand when he loves, he loves hard. It is the only way he knows how to."

I didn't know what to say, so I didn't say anything. I sat there and fidgeted with my napkin instead.

"Do you love him?" Aubrey asked, taking me by surprise.

I simply nodded, unable to form the words.

"Then that's all that matters. The rest will fall into place," Alex chimed in.

"I'm going to get something to drink. I'll be right back." I excused myself, needing a minute.

All of this was a little overwhelming, I never had girlfriends to sit around and talk with. And the last thing I wanted was to answer questions I didn't even have answers to. I spent the rest of the afternoon taking in what it truly felt like to have friends and to be a part of a family. They were all so close with one another, the love these men had for their women was indescribable. I'd never seen anything like it before. I loved them all instantly. The girls welcomed me with open arms, including his niece. I even caught Martinez having what appeared to be a serious conversation with Briggs at one point.

Were they talking about me? Maybe all of this was getting to him too?

I made my way toward the bathroom, looking at myself in the mirror for a few minutes, trying to control the overpowering emotions reeling in my core. I took a deep breath, making my way back outside, looking for Martinez. I hadn't seen him for a while. Come to think about it, I hadn't seen Austin or Dylan either.

"I just don't think I can do it," I heard Martinez say down the hallway out of nowhere.

My feet moved of their own accord, standing outside the adjacent door.

"It's your only choice," Dylan remarked.

"It is what it is, Martinez," Austin asserted. "She will—"

The front door slammed open.

"Where is she? Mia, where the fuck are you?! I know you're here!" a man with a deep southern accent barged in the house, hollering.

I ran past the office door where Martinez and the boys were discussing something that didn't sound right, toward the commotion in the living room. A broad, muscular, tall man covered in tattoos, wearing a leather vest, was striding toward Mia. It all happened so quickly. No one had time to intervene. My eyes couldn't move fast enough as the man barreled through the guests, trying to get right up into Mia's face. Her dark brown eyes were wide and anxious.

"Creed!" Mia screeched, trying to back away.

The man didn't falter, grabbing her arm, holding her in place. We all stood there in shock, watching in horror as the scene played out. Creed got right up in Mia's face, hovering above her with a menacing glare. She cowered back.

"I found this in the trash," he gritted through a clenched jaw and threw something at her.

358

My mouth dropped open. It was a pregnancy test.

"You did this on purpose, didn't you?! You wanted this!" he roared, pulling her closer to him by her arm.

"I... no... I didn't! I swear!" Mia stuttered, fervently shaking her head.

I gasped.

"Look me in the goddamn eyes and tell me you didn't plan this."

"No! Of cour—"

Lucas, her dad, was over to them in three strides, hearing the commotion from outside. Austin, Dylan, Jacob, and Martinez not far behind him. My heart pounded in my chest, I swear I stopped breathing.

Lucas got right up in between them without giving it a second thought. "Back the fuck up if you know what's good for you. And get the fuck out of this house," Lucas snarled, eyeing him up and down with a threatening regard.

Creed scoffed, matching his stare. "Fuck you! Now you want to be all protective? You're too late. Your fifteen-year-old daughter went and got herself knocked up. Congratu-fucking-lations, Grandpa." He pushed him. Lucas barely wavered, ready to strike back.

"Creed! Enough!" All eyes flew to Martinez who was casually walking over to them. Creed's eyes narrowed in recognition, jerking back stunned he was there.

They knew each other?

"This isn't the time or the place. There are women and children present."

Creed scowled. "Since when the fuck do you care about any of that?"

"Since this is my niece's home. And her kids are my blood. Me and your club have never had any problems, if you want to keep it this way, I suggest you take your ass outside and walk away."

Creed took a look around, finally realizing Martinez was right. Seemingly pissed that his temper outweighed anything else. Creed stepped back, looking over at Mia again.

"This ain't over." He nodded at her.

He turned and walked out the door. The roar of a motorcycle rumbled around the living room moments later.

"Mia," her mom Alex coaxed, standing in front of her. Oh my God! Is it true? You're pregnant?" Mia stood there frozen in place. "I didn't even know you had a boyfriend? And now this? What were you thinking? You got yourself wrapped with an MC? How old is that guy? He has to be in his late twenties. Alex's eyes filled with tears as she brought her shaking hand up to her mouth. Lucas stood there with rage in his eyes, hands in fists at his side. His friends ready to hold him back.

Mia's glossy eyes wandered around the room, mortified, overwhelmed not knowing what to say. "It's not his. It's his younger brother's. I'm so sorry, Mama," she whispered, running out the backdoor.

I stood there speechless, my heart breaking for all of them. Knowing this wasn't the end of their problems.

It was only the beginning.

Thirty-nine
Lexi

There was a shift in our relationship after the christening, and not in a good way. In the last three months, Martinez started working more and more, coming home less. Sometimes he'd stay gone for days at a time, not telling me where he was going, or when he'd be back. Leaving me alone in the penthouse, worried if he was dead or alive. He'd always check in with me, but it still wasn't the same. The loving man I'd spent the last three years with slowly faded away. Leaving behind the man I ran away from all those years ago. He didn't touch me as often, barely touching me at all. I missed the way his hands felt all over my body. The way only he could ever make me feel.

I missed him.

Most of all I missed his arms around me when I slept. He never held me anymore, saying he was too busy and needed to work. We didn't laugh together. I couldn't remember the last time he smiled. His eyes were once again cold, dark, and soulless. The exact same haunting glare he wore in my nightmares. I didn't know what was happening, every day it was something different. I couldn't keep up with the rollercoaster of emotions anymore. It was as if he was trying to push me away again, deliberately shutting me out of his life. I thought all of that was behind us, not having the strength to relive it again.

Was it too much introducing me to his family?

Did it become too real for him?

Was he having second thoughts now? About me? About us?

As the days went on, more insecurities came forward, making themselves known. Creeping out at all hours of the day and night. Not allowing me to rest for one goddamn second. Dancing didn't even calm me the way it used to, no longer my escape. I didn't even recognize the woman staring back at me in the mirror anymore. I was losing myself to self-doubt and uncertainties.

Did he not love me anymore? Was there someone else?

Question after question sent me on a downward spiral. I refused to believe any of it was true, trying to ease my overly active mind the only way I could. Making up reasons and excuses for his distant behavior, sometimes it worked, but most of the time it didn't.

I woke up in the middle of the night, feeling his presence, his scent all around me. I slid my hand along the sheet, searching for him. Assuming he was lying next to me. His side of the bed was cold, like it had been for months. Rolling over I opened my eyes, coming face to face with him, sitting in the armchair in our room. A bottle of whiskey in his hand.

I sat up, taking the silk sheet with me. Covering my bare breasts. "Hey, what are doing over there?" I asked, I hadn't seen him in two days.

"Watching over you," he simply stated in a cold and detached tone. Not looking me in the eyes.

I lovingly smiled, trying to break through his icy demeanor. "Alejandro, come to bed," I coaxed, patting the spot next to me.

"No." He took a swig of the bottle. I couldn't help but notice it was already half empty.

I frowned. "What's going on? You're scaring me."

"I should have never gone back for you. You were happy. I was in the past, forgotten. I should have stayed away."

"What?" His statement slapping me in the face. "I wasn't happy. I've never been happy without you. Look at me, why are you saying that?"

"You were safe."

"I'm—"

"From me," he added.

I stepped off the bed. "Alej—"

"Don't."

Stopping me dead in my tracks, I shuddered. "I love you," I stated, needing him to hear it. "My life belongs to you."

"Did it belong to me when you were spreading your legs for Will? It didn't belong to me when you were fucking him. Getting down on your knees like a fucking whore. Did you ever think about me when he was devouring your pussy? Wishing a real man was giving you what you craved?"

I gasped, jerking back.

"Sometimes the truth hurts, baby," he snidely remarked, taking another swig from the bottle.

"You're drunk."

"Not yet. But getting there." Two more swigs. "What's wrong, *cariño*? I'm here, aren't I? Don't you want me to touch you? Kiss you? Fuck you like my little whore? That's all you wanted since you met me, I wasn't fucking stupid. You were desperate to feel loved, because Mommy wasn't there. So, here I am... What can my cock make you forget tonight?"

Tears began to stream down my face, hurt by his verbal abuse.

"Aww, here comes the water works. Did I hurt your feelings, baby?" he mocked.

"Why are you being so cruel? What the hell is going on?"

"I was never your savior, little girl. I'm your fucking demise. Have been since day one."

"You're trying to push me away again! I'm not going to let you! This is bullshit! Enough! Just tell me what the fuck is going on! I can help—"

He furiously stood, knocking the chair over. Chucking the bottle of whiskey across the room. "When are you going to fucking realize I'm not good for you!?" he screamed.

I jolted out of my skin when it shattered against the wall. "Leave! Now! Go drown your fucking demons in another bottle! I'm not scared of you, Martinez!" I shouted right back.

He was over to me in two strides, backing me onto the bed. His face inches away from mine, his body looming over me. The smell of whiskey and cigars assaulted my senses.

"I would shut you the fuck up. But my goddamn zipper's stuck."

"You fucking bastard!" I went to push him away, but he grabbed both my wrists. Pinning them above my head.

"Is this what you want?" he viciously chuckled, breathing against my lips. "I bet if I touched your pussy right now, you'd be fucking wet. For me. That's what's fucked up about us, Lexi. I've made you crave every side of me. You love the heartless El Diablo as much as you love your precious Alejandro," he crudely ridiculed, roughly letting me go. Freeing me in more ways than one.

He backed away, taking one last look at me laying there. And left.

I tossed and turned all night, restless and dazed. The hurricane of emotions lingered in the room, in the air, in my fucking soul.

Long after he left, his words still pounded in my head, over and over again. Not letting up until sleep finally took over. When I woke up the next morning the shattered bottle had been cleaned up as if it never existed. Another figment of my imagination, an illusion I knew I didn't create. My tear-soaked pillow was my evidence. I got up, going about my normal routine. Eating breakfast by myself, like I had the last few months. Anxiously waiting for the other shoe to drop, knowing last night was just the start of whatever he was planning.

But why?

It didn't matter how many times I racked my brain for answers. Nothing made sense. Nothing was right. For the next few days I went on with my life in a blur, just going through the motions. The hours and days blended together. Still no word from him. No apology, no remorse.

Nothing but silence.

I went to bed alone again, contemplating sleeping in my old room so I wouldn't have to smell him. Feel him all around me. But I didn't, knowing it was no use. The man was already engrained in my heart. His scent helped me sleep in his absence. I dreamt of the way his strong arms felt around me. Engulfing me in nothing but his warm body, the weight of him on top of me. The reassuring words he always spoke in my ear.

"Cariño," I heard him whisper. I swear it felt so real, so true, so consuming, like he was right there with me. I didn't want to wake up. I felt his lips on my neck, softly kissing, making his way up to my mouth. "Mi amor, lo siento, perdóname por todo. Eres mi vida.

Siempre recuerdalo. No importa lo qué pase. Eres mía, cariño," he rasped against my ear in Spanish.

When did I learn Spanish?

"Wake up, Lexi. Open those beautiful eyes for me."

I stirred, fluttering my eyes open. Blinking away the sleepy haze, trying to focus. My eyes adjusting to the light cascading off the moon from the sliding glass doors.

"Alejandro?" I sleepily asked.

"You're so beautiful. Do you have any idea how fucking beautiful you are?" He gazed down at me with a look I couldn't quite read.

"I was just dreaming about you."

"That wasn't a dream. I'm here. I've been here."

His eyes held so much emotion. His sincere expression was almost hard to follow. I had always been so in tune with what his eyes shared with me, and at that moment, all I could see was pain. My heart ached seeing him broken. I missed his smile, his laugh, his love. It was as if he was torn with what he was feeling, his mind wreaking havoc in a way I'd never seen before. I could physically feel his pained glare on my face as he was laying on top of me. Feeling it so much more than I could have ever imagined. Almost like I could touch it.

"Cariño, stop thinking. Just feel me." He placed my hand over his heart. "Be here with me, just me and you," he whispered, sensing my apprehension.

He watched as I started tracing the outline of his heart that was beating a mile a minute, just for me. Caressing the side of my cheeks with the back of his fingers as we stared into each other's souls, seeing our truth, our love. He softly pecked my lips, kissing me for the first time in what seemed like forever. Teasing me with the tip of his tongue, outlining my mouth. My tongue sought out his, and our kiss quickly turned passionate, moving on its own accord, taking what the other needed. There was something agonizing about the way we devoured each other's mouths.

It was urgent.

Demanding.

Burning with fire.

We couldn't get enough of one another, wanting more. Wanting everything. Trying to become one person, kissing as if our lives depended on it. His fingers glided down to my breasts, caressing them lightly, grazing around my nipples, cupping and kneading them in the palm his hand.

"Alejandro," I moaned, in a voice I didn't recognize.

Our bodies moved like they were made for each other. He tenderly kissed all over my face, along my jawline, my forehead, and on the tip of my nose. Placing his cock at my entrance, staring me in the eyes, waiting for me to tell him it was all right.

They did.

He rested his elbows on the sides of my face with my whole body lying beneath him. Slowly easing inside of me, grabbing me by the chin to once again claim my mouth. It started off slow, but his movements became urgent and more demanding. My eyes widened in pleasure, my back arching off the bed, letting him lap at my neck and breasts, nipping, sucking, licking. Leaving tiny marks in his wake. I didn't want to move, I wanted to enjoy the sensation of his cock inside me.

"You feel me inside you?" he groaned, reading my mind. Making his way back up to my mouth.

"Yes..." I breathed out.

My arms reached around, pressing him tight against my body, wanting to feel his entire weight on top of me. His warmth consumed me as he took his time hitting all the right spots. His back muscles flexed with every thrust. Every push and pull. I couldn't get enough of him.

I needed him.

I wanted him.

I loved him.

He leaned his forehead on mine, looking deep into my core. Our mouths were parted, still touching, both of us panting profusely, trying to feel each and every sensation of our skin on skin contact. His one hand snaked around to cup my ass, guiding my hips, angling them, making me take every last inch of his cock. He thrust in and out of me, going slow, cherishing me, making me feel safe, secured, and loved. Everything I ever wanted from him, he was willingly giving to me.

366

He wasn't fucking me.

He was making love to me. Taking his time to feel every last inch of me. Memorizing my body. My need. My love. His heady movements were almost as pained as the glare in his eyes. I wanted to fight him off. I wanted to yell at him and tell him to stop. I wanted anything but this.

I couldn't.

All I felt was his heart over mine. His kisses deep within the depths of my soul, his strong hands and muscular body consuming me in ways I've never experienced before. I never thought possible. His once cold and icy demeanor were replaced with nothing but heat. It radiated off of him, absorbing into my skin. I felt him everywhere and all at once. For the first time...

He was mine.

I felt it in every last breath from his lips, every last beat of his heart, every single fiber of his being. The good and bad. Heaven and Hell. Every part of him. I took what I could get. Every last ounce of him. Even though I knew in my heart.

He was only saying goodbye.

My body betrayed my emotions. I started to come apart, clawing, gripping, moaning, panting, "Please, please, please," begging for I don't know what. Climaxing all around his cock.

Lifting my leg, he put all his weight on his right knee, using the other for more momentum to thrust in and out of me. Faster, harder, deeper. I didn't want him to stop, terrified of what would happen when he did. There would be a price to pay, knowing my pleasure would only lead to his pain in the end. He was right about one thing. He wasn't my savior. Tonight would lead to the demise of my heart when this was over, when he was done showing me his love. His torment. His demons.

"Lexi," he growled from within his chest, releasing his come deep inside of me. Shaking, kissing me passionately. Until I felt him become hard again, making love to me all night long.

I let him take me. Have his way with me. Making love to me. Knowing he was trying to fuck me out of his heart, but it had the opposite effect.

He let me fall asleep in his arms.

But I woke up alone in the morning.

I laid there wide awake for hours, listening to the soothing lull of the rain coming down outside. Drawing circles on the silk sheet, concentrating on how the satin fabric felt on my skin. My mind couldn't think anymore, there was nothing else I could contemplate, rationalize, understand, or even try to explain.

I was numb.

Exactly how he wanted me to be.

I threw on my silk robe, walking down the hallway as if I was walking toward my execution. And in a way, I was. I took a deep, reassuring breath, before opening the door to his office. Martinez wasn't in his usual place, sitting in his leather chair behind his desk. Busying himself with paperwork. He was standing by the bay window, looking out at the rain just like I had been doing for hours. He stood with his back to me, his hands in the pockets of his slacks.

Waiting.

Without turning around, he declared war, "I don't love you."

I scoffed, shaking my head, "Say that to my face. Look me in the eyes, and tell me you don't love me."

He casually turned around, eyeing me up and down. His face was void of any emotion.

"I know you love me!" I shouted, fighting for him. For us.

"No, cariño. I don't."

"Liar! You fucking liar! Stop lying to me! Please! Stop hurting me with nothing but lies! Be a fucking man, not a coward," I bellowed, gripping onto the door handle. Hoping like hell it would hold me up when all I wanted was to crumble. My body shook uncontrollably. Bowing my head, not having any more fight left in me. I was exhausted from years of fighting a losing battle. A means to an end.

He stepped toward me, coming right in front of my face. My tears fell onto the floor between us. I shuddered when I felt his knuckles caress the side of my cheek, his skin burning against mine. I jerked my head away, I could take his hate, but his kindness was almost too much to bear. He wanted to remember me just like that. Falling apart in front of him. Punishing himself for taking away another life that didn't belong to him.

Mine.

He was right about one thing. All the women who loved him, died loving him. Emotionally killing me, driving a dagger straight into my heart.

He spoke with conviction, "I'm a lot of things, Lexi, but a liar I'm not. Last night was my goodbye to you. Nothing more, nothing less." He pulled his hand away, and I immediately missed his touch.

"Why are you shutting me out? I know you love me. Your eyes hold your truths. Every time I look in them I see the man you are, not the man you claim to be," I whispered, trying to be strong when I was nothing but weak.

He ignored me, reaching into the pocket of his suit jacket, pulling something out. Handing me a manila envelope with "Lexi" written on the front, in his handwriting.

"I own a condo on 4th Street. You can stay there as long as you need. It's fully furnished. The keys are in there." He nodded toward the envelope. "There's money in there, too. If you need anymore, call Leo. He will get you whatever you want or need, no matter what."

"Wow…" I breathed out, still not looking up at him. "I really am like one of your whores now, huh?"

"One day, this will all make sense to you. I promise." He leaned forward and kissed the top of my head before walking out the door.

Never looking back.

The second I heard the front door slam shut, I tore the envelope in half. Throwing it on his floor, I didn't need his fucking charity. My back slid down the wooden door, I sat there rocking back and forth, hugging my knees tight, sobbing uncontrollably. I couldn't believe he was doing this to me again. I peered around the room through glazed eyes, seeing all the memories we'd shared through the years.

"What the fuck is going on?" I asked myself, knowing I would never get an answer.

Forty
Lexi

I moved out that day, I was gone before he came back that evening. I couldn't spend one more goddamn minute in that penthouse. He was everywhere, gripping me, his scent that used to comfort me, made me nauseous now. The sight of his bed where he made love to me the night before made me sick. All I took were my clothes. Nothing else belonged to me. I left behind everything he ever bought me, the jewelry, the clothes, the ballet shit, all the fucking cookbooks. As much as it killed me to do it, I took off his mother's cross necklace for the first time since I woke up with it hanging around my neck in my hospital room. I left it on his pillow. I considered it my parting gift. I grabbed my shit and left.

I left his money and the key to his condo on his office floor. I didn't need it. I had plenty to live off. I made a good living in England, and with Sabrina refusing to accept money from me, I was able to invest in some rewarding stocks. Martinez never allowed me to pay for anything, he was adamant about that. I refused to stay in the condo he offered, opting to stay in a hotel downtown for a few days until I found a place to live. I ended up renting a small apartment on the other side of town, wanting to be as far away from him as possible. It wasn't anything special, but it was only me. I didn't need much. I bought a couch, a bed, and the essentials to make it livable. Nothing too fancy, just something I could sit and sleep on.

I knew now more than ever that maybe I wasn't meant to have a happy ending, a happily ever after. Maybe there were just some people in the world that were born alone and died alone. It was called shitty luck. I was exhausted. I'd never been more worn out in all my life. I think I slept for the first few weeks, barely leaving my bed for more than takeout food I had delivered and to use the restroom. Going right back to sleep. I was in an emotional coma. I couldn't pull myself out of the despair, nothing could help me feel better, not even dance provided me any kind of relief. I cancelled all my private ballet classes till further notice, I handed over the reigns to the other instructors indefinitely. I couldn't step foot in that studio.

All it did was remind me of him.

Ruining me.

I found my escape in sleep. It was the only time I stopped thinking, stopped caring, stopped living. I wanted to hate him, but I couldn't. In a sick, twisted way, he saved me. I no longer had my past, just my future, haunting me, and I owed that to him. On both accounts.

I finally dragged myself out of bed one morning, knowing I couldn't go on like this. I needed to return back to the land of the living. It'd been a month since I stepped foot out of my apartment, five weeks since I'd left him. I'd been counting down the days as if it would bring him back to me. I decided to shower and actually do something with myself. It was life changing, feeling almost human again. My hair styled, make-up on, and normal clothes that didn't consist of sweatpants and a tank.

I took a cab downtown, wanting to get lost, wandering around Manhattan for the day. Breathing in some much needed fresh air. I even stopped by my studio to pick up the mail that was piling up. Mostly junk mail and letters from students, wanting to know if I was alright and when I'd be back. I also had a postcard from the Royale Ballet theatre. I immediately turned it over thinking Sabrina had written me. But it was blank. I stared at it, feeling his presence all around me.

Martinez.

Even after everything I went through with him, I still felt him. A strong sense he was watching me. More now than ever. I shook off the emotion, going on with my day. The cab dropped me off in front of a newsstand by Central Park. Getting out, I paid him, but blue tantalizing eyes caught my immediate attention from the corners of my eyes. I couldn't get away from him even if I tried. Martinez was on the front page of every paper, tabloid, and

371

magazine. It wasn't just him. A gorgeous woman was on his arm in all the different pictures.

"What the fuck?" I asked myself, stunned and not able to move away from all the articles in front of me. He'd always been so private about his life. Everyone knew who he was, but he never publicized it. He refused. I grabbed all of them, opening them up one by one.

"Most eligible bachelor Alejandro Martinez off the market."

"Crime Boss Martinez taking the plunge with secret woman."

"Martinez spotted with mystery woman leaving club Saturday night."

"Are things getting hot and heavy for this new couple? Could she be the one?"

The last one I flipped to brought tears to my eyes.

"Martinez donates three million dollars to the performing arts in honor of ballet with mystery woman on his arm."

I bought a copy of all the papers, hailing a cab back to my apartment.

Is this why he left me? Did he fall in love with this woman? When did this happen?

I flew up the stairs, not wanting to waste time waiting for the elevator, taking two of them at a time. Rage overpowering all my senses, blinding me. I could barely fucking see, let alone think straight. Trying to rationalize what was going on. Hyperventilating as I hauled ass into my apartment, slamming the door shut behind me. Throwing all the papers on the living room floor, dropping to my knees, looking for answers, explanations, anything in the fine fucking print. Fuming with every sentence I read. Nothing but media gossip and speculations.

I sat up, pulling the hair away from my face, securing it on top of my head. My eyes darting around the room. My mind spinning with no end in sight. I got up, running into my bedroom, grabbing my laptop. Googling his name. I sat there on my bed watching article upon article blasted in my face. Dates going back as far as the day I fucking left.

More pictures.

More lies.

More truths.

Them dancing, holding her close in his arms. Whispering in her ear. Smiling. Laughing. Calm, serene eyes staring back at her. Holding her hand, kissing it.

Fact or fiction.

Them walking together into his penthouse. Him leading her out of his limo. All the restaurants he ever took me to. All the places we'd been to together. Different suit. Different day. Still the same woman. The pictures were endless.

Them walking out of the Met after a performance of *Swan Lake*, ABT put on. Pictures on his private jet.

"Oh my God... is that?" My hand flew to my mouth when I saw something shiny hanging off her neck.

He wouldn't...

Zooming in, it was clear as day. Like a ticking time bomb going off in my heart. It was loud. It was disastrous. It was chaotic. His mother's silver cross, the one he never took off until he gave it to me, the same exact one I wore for three fucking years was proudly hanging off her neck.

Fact.

Truth.

I was suffocating in it. My heart, my mind, my sanity couldn't take it anymore. I instantly stood, roughly slamming my laptop shut. Pushing it away before I had the chance to chuck it against the wall. My hands were shaking so badly, I had to place them under my arms. Holding myself from crumbling into pieces. My whole body felt like it was giving out on me. There were too many emotions happening all at the same time. I couldn't control any of it.

"One day, this will all make sense to you. I promise," his voice resonated in my head.

I lunged into action, grabbing my keys. Sprinting down the stairs, out to the street, hailing another cab.

"Pull over right here," I ordered once we arrived. He slammed on the brakes, and I threw money at him before the car even came to a complete stop, skidding to the curb. I ran into Martinez's building, jumping into the elevator, punching in the code to the penthouse. My heart racing as the seconds ticked by, watching the red numbers count up to the letter P. It dinged open, the mania now replaced with doubt.

What the hell was I doing? What was I going to say?

I took a deep breath, steadying myself. Slowly walking over to his place. My hand in the air, about to knock on the wooden door, but something came over me and it went to the knob instead.

It was open.

It was never open.

I stepped inside and softly shut it behind me. Immediately being comforted by the life I still wanted with all my heart. His scent was all around me again. My home. It calmed my nerves, but the anxiety for what was to come still lived and breathed in my blood. It pumped in my veins, releasing a piercing vibration at my temples. I ignored the looming feeling that I felt in the depths of my core.

The penthouse was eerie and silent. The only light came from the sun, shining in from the floor-to-ceiling windows in the living room. I turned around to leave, suddenly feeling nauseous. Something was just not right. My hand was on the handle when I heard a noise coming from down the main hall. As if being pulled by a string, I made my way toward the sound.

One step.

Four steps.

Eight steps.

Ten.

"Just like that, baby. Take my cock," I heard him groan from his bedroom. It echoed off the walls. I gasped, placing my hand over my mouth. Not wanting to be heard.

I should have stopped.

I should have turned around and left.

The truth blatantly, slapping me in the fucking face again. He'd moved on. With someone who wasn't me.

I couldn't stop my feet from moving.

Fifteen steps.

Twenty-six steps.

Forty.

To his open bedroom door.

Nothing could have prepared me for what I was about to see, about to feel. It was like taking a bullet to the fucking heart. I just never imagined Martinez would be holding the loaded gun. He was leaned up against the headboard on my side of the bed, gripping onto long blonde hair that was positioned in his lap. Jerking her head up and down as she sucked on his cock. She was completely nude lying on her stomach. Leaning on his thigh as her other hand stroked his shaft. I held my breath as my eyes rolled up their bodies.

Locking eyes with him.

I was there, but I wasn't.

Cold, dark, soulless eyes stared back at me with a sinister look I couldn't begin to explain. Sucking all the air from my lungs, taking my heart, the heart that he owned, shattering it into a million fucking pieces. Pain like that should never be experienced. It was raw, excruciating torture. As much as I urged myself not to watch, to look away, to run, it willed me to stay in place. My feet glued to the goddamn floor beneath me, about to endure, and witness the truth beneath the goddamn fiction.

I was led there for a reason. I needed to see this, as much as it pained me. Nearly killing me…

I needed to remain strong. Act unfazed. Show no weakness.

His eyes never wavered from mine as he took what she was giving him. Guiding her up and down with one hand, rubbing her arms, her back, her breasts with the other. Just like he always did with me. Attentive, caring, it wasn't just a meaningless act. A quickie. They were familiar with each other, their movements and their bodies. His hips started moving against her hand and mouth, thrusting his cock deeper down her throat. She wanted him to manhandle her, to feel his dominance as she had his cock in her mouth. She sucked him harder, stroked him faster.

His mouth parted, groaning out loud.

She moaned, pleased with herself. His movements became more aggressive the closer he got to coming. Grabbing her by the hair, pulling her head back slightly. Shoving her back down to deep throat him with each suck of her lips.

He grinned. "Is this making you wet? I know you want to join us, Lexi." Devious eyes, deliberately peering down, he locked eyes with her. Caressing the side of her face. She never let up on sucking his cock. He rasped to her, "You'd like that? Wouldn't you, *cariño?*"

The string that led me to him, snapped. "You piece of fucking shit!" I charged him.

She shrieked, jumping off the bed. Taking the sheets with her, trying to cover her naked body. Martinez didn't even move or bat an eye. He didn't even bother to cover himself.

He grabbed my wrists, lifting me over his body, throwing me on my back onto the bed in one swift move. Placing my body where he wanted, straddling my waist, hovering above me. I had to turn my head away from him. His scent I once loved was replaced with her perfume and sex.

"Let me go!" I yelled, trying to fight him off. Failing miserably at doing so.

"Get the fuck out of here! Now!" he ordered in a strong, dominant tone.

I looked back up at him, realizing he wasn't talking to me. He was ordering her, the blonde I recognized from the magazines. His mystery woman.

"You don't get to treat me like this! The Mad —"

"NOW, Clarissa!"

I jolted, his voice vibrating my entire body. She scampered around the room, gathering her things. Slamming the door when she left.

"Let. Go. Of. Me," I gritted out.

He peered back down at me. "I thought I already did. This is my penthouse. You're the one that came in like a thief in the fucking night, rudely interrupting my happy fucking ending. My dick isn't going to suck itself. So, why the fuck are you here, Lexi?"

"You fucking son of a bitch! Did you not think I'd see the papers?" Ignoring his statement. Struggling against his hold on me.

"No, you haven't left your shitty fucking apartment for a month."

"Who's fucking fault is that?" I seethed. Not fazed by the fact he had been watching me.

He cocked his head to the side, coming close to my mouth. He breathed out, "Yours. Now stop fucking fighting me, or I will make you finish what she started."

I screamed out in frustration. Frantically thrashing around, but it was no use. I wasn't going anywhere unless he wanted me to. My chest heaved, panting for air. His face still inches away from mine.

Glaring into his eyes, I replied, "Mine? What the fuck did I ever do to you to deserve this?"

"You were born."

"What? That makes no fucking sense! So is she the reason? The reason you left me? You love her?" I couldn't get my questions out fast enough.

"Would you shut up for five fucking minutes," he spewed. "You just barged in on her making love to me with her mouth. You tell me, Lexi… Do I ever let women in my home? In my bed? You have your answers. I don't need to say it for you to know. You're a smart woman, I think you can figure it out, if you just opened your goddamn eyes. You would see the truth, the one I have been so desperately trying to hide."

I shook my head, defeated. "All I did was love you. After everything you put me through. All I did was fucking love you… How could you do that to me? Flaunt your relationship in front of my face like that? Like I meant nothing to you. Jesus Christ, I guess you treat all women like shit. They just keep coming back for more. Damn you! You really are the Devil, aren't you?" I bellowed, trying to keep my voice from breaking.

"I never claimed to be anything else."

"Did you cheat on me? Were you seeing her the entire time? Were you fucking her and coming home to me?"

"No, you have to be in a relationship for it to count as cheating. We were never together, Lexi. We couldn't be. We were damned from the fucking start. Everything about us is fucking wrong. I tried to stay away from you. For years, I tried. Watching you from afar, protecting you the only way I knew how. You were never supposed to be in my life. I was never supposed to be in yours. But fate brought us together and it was only a matter of time before

377

destiny destroyed us. You want to know the truth. I'll finally show you the goddamn proof."

He leaned back, releasing me from his grasp. Getting out of bed, throwing on the black slacks that were on his floor. Not bothering with a shirt. He swiftly walked out of the room, leading me to his office. I followed close behind, never in a million years expecting what I was about to learn.

Forty-one
Lexi

As soon as I walked in, he nodded toward the files that were placed by his gun. The same files that never left his desk.

"The truth has been hiding in plain sight all along," he stated, looking from me to the files. "Go, cariño. You want the pieces to my puzzle? Well I just laid them all out for you. Solve the mystery. It's time for you to find out who the fuck I really am."

I walked around the desk, pulling back his chair, taking a seat. My stomach fluttered and my heart pounded, making it hard for me to breathe.

"What is this going to change?" I found myself asking, looking up at him. Stalling, terrified to find out the truth.

"Everything, cariño," he simply stated, closing the door, sitting in the chair in front of his desk. Leaning back to set his ankle over his knee. Our roles reversed. He nodded to the folders again.

I swallowed hard, slowly opening the first file. Gasping at the first photo. I looked at him, shocked, and back down to the photo, picking it up. "This..." I paused, choking back tears. "I haven't seen this picture since I was a kid. Why do you have a picture of my mother?" I ran my shaking fingers over her beautiful face.

"Keep going," he replied in a neutral tone.

I did, looking at each and every one of them, stacked on top of each other. One by one, laying them all out on his desk. Her face consuming me, she was alive in these photos, smiling, happy. Nothing like the woman who raised me.

"How do you have these? My dance recitals, me at my bus stop, my first day of school... What the hell is going on? How did you get these? Are these how you knew where I grew up? Did I know you? When I was a kid, did I meet you?"

379

He narrowed his eyes at me, rubbing his fingers over his lips. Contemplating how to approach the subject.

"Answer me! Where did you fucking get these?" I slammed my fist down on his desk. Welcoming the sting. Trying like hell to keep my emotions in check.

"I've known you since the day you were born, Lexi. Since your first breath, I knew who you were."

My eyes widened. "How? I don't understand."

"Open the next folder."

"Not until you answer my questions."

"A picture is worth a thousand words, little girl. Now. Open. The. Next fucking folder," he ordered, speaking through his fingers.

I pulled out the file from under the scattered pictures, opening it. "Oh my God," I whimpered, letting the folder fall to the desk like it had burned me.

The truth was too much for me to take, pictures flew everywhere on his desk. My eyes glued to every last photo, I couldn't decide which one to focus on more. Seeing all the pictures of them together, kissing, smiling, laughing together. Seeing the man I always knew still lived inside of Martinez. Realizing that the man behind the expensive fucking suit...

Once belonged to my mother.

"She was your girlfriend," I stated as a question. Letting a few tears escape, but quickly wiping them away.

"No," he said, bringing my attention to him.

We locked eyes. He leaned forward, placing his elbows on his knees. Looking me dead in the eyes, adding, "She was my fiancée."

"No..." I fervently shook my head. "No... you're lying. You're a fucking liar. Is this some kind of sick joke? You think this is funny? No..." I wallowed, my voice breaking. Unable to form coherent thoughts. Stumbling on all the words coming out of my mouth.

"Sophia wasn't always the depressed woman that raised you, Lexi. I did that to her. I turned her into someone who couldn't get out of bed, who hated her fucking life," he sadistically spewed, not caring I was physically breaking down in front of him. "I guess it's the price she paid for loving me." He smirked. "I took her virtue, just like I took yours. I guess the two of you have more in common than you thought."

I jerked back, his truths stabbing, slicing me all over. I would be nothing after he was finished. "Why are you doing this to me? I don't believe you! You're lying!" I screamed, loud enough to break glass.

He callously chuckled. "Do you know how many times over the years I had to catch myself from calling you Sophia? Stop myself from groaning out her name, instead of yours when we were fucking. All those years you've been asking me what cariño means. It was always your mother, Lexi. She was my cariño."

Tears streamed down my face. The dam was broken. I didn't care if he saw them anymore. I didn't care about anything. I was dying inside. Words could cut you deeper than knives, and his were mutilating me. "Please... please stop... Alejandro I can't..." I couldn't catch my breath, the room started to spin. Around, and around, and around.

"Oh, come on, cariño," he mocked, standing up.

Causing me to take a step back, coming in contact with his bookshelf behind me. I welcomed the sting, needing something, anything to take away the pain from the salt he kept pouring on my open wounds.

"I thought you wanted to know who I was, Lexi?" He cocked his head to the side, arching an eyebrow. "Isn't that what you've been begging for? Wanting me to let you in on my life? For you to know everything about me? My demons..."

More tears slid down my face, placing my hand over my heart. Trying to hold it together. "Did you break her too?" I wept.

He scoffed, shaking his head. "No, she broke me. She left me. Not the other way around. And she spent the rest of her miserable fucking life regretting it. But don't worry, sweetheart, your father made sure to stick the final nail in her fucking coffin."

"My father? You knew my father?" I tried taking a deep breath, but there was no air for me to take. It had all been knocked out of me.

By him.

"Oh, I more than knew him. I fucking hated him. Your daddy always had a thing for your mom. My girl. Even when we were together, he watched her from afar. He's part of the reason she fucking left me. But I didn't hate him for any of that."

I shook my head back and forth. "No, no, no, no, no," I repeated, placing my hands over my ears like a child, not wanting to hear anymore. I had enough, I'd reached my breaking point.

Why was he doing this to me? What did he want?

"Michael, the piece of shit, cheated on my sister, after they were fucking married. Your daddy fucked your mom behind my sisters back."

The truth hit me like a bucket of freezing cold water. "Please... please... stop..." I begged not being able to hear anymore, the room closing in on me, coming in and out of focus. My body shaking profusely, feeling myself drifting away. His voice echoed in the distance. I slid down the bookshelf, my legs giving out on me.

I couldn't breathe.

I couldn't fucking breathe.

"Sophia and Amari were best friends. Your father saw a moment of weakness, of loneliness, and it produced you. Michael cheated on Amari when Briggs was barely fucking walking."

"Shut up! Shut the fuck up!" I yelled out, uncontrollably. My hands going to my hair, wanting to rip it from my fucking head. "Please! Stop it!" I panted. "I don't want to hear..." heaving, "Another... fucking... Oh, my God..." gasping, "Word!" I managed to scream. Barely being able to see his silhouette through the rage.

"Is it making sense now, cariño? Are the pieces fitting together? Why your mother hated herself? Why she became so fucking depressed? Why she couldn't leave your goddamn house? She hated herself for the shitty decisions she made. Her choices ruined your fucking life."

"Please... Alejandro... Please... I can't... I can't listen anymore..." I pleaded, looking at him through blurred eyes.

He leaned over the desk. Shoving all the pictures in my direction. They flew everywhere, falling all around me. I was finally surrounded by nothing but the truth, exactly how he wanted.

"I was there the day he met you. Hiding in the shadows, in the dark. Where I've been living all my fucking life. Watching him hold you for the first time. Seeing Sophia's broken face when he told her he wouldn't be a part of your life. That you were a mistake, an accident. Your daddy never wanted you. And your mother spent the rest of her life battling her demons every time she looked in your eyes."

I shut my eyes, I had to. The pain taking me under.

"You look me in the fucking eyes when I'm talking to you," he sneered.

I slowly opened them back up, realizing that I was truly coming face to face with El Diablo for the first time.

"It was bad enough that he cheated on my sister, but the motherfucker didn't even have the balls to stick around and help raise his bastard child, nor admit his mistakes and come clean. I gave him time, I was hoping he would own up to his shit, but he never did. Still pretending to be everything my sister ever wanted," he rasped. "So I made the decision, I gave the order... to have Michael. Your father... murdered."

My mouth dropped open, sucking in air.

He snidely grinned. "I killed him, Lexi. No one else, but me."

"What? But Briggs said they were in a car accident. You killed your sister, too? No... NO!"

His eyes glazed over, the pain breaking through his glare only for a second. He shook it off, blinking it away. He stated, "Why not, I killed my own father... Now, allow me to introduce myself, here's the man behind the expensive fucking suits. Is he everything you thought he would be?"

They say crimes of passion can happen in an instant. If you blinked, you'd miss it. A person can be pushed to the brink of insanity. Teetering on the edge. I just wanted him to stop talking. I didn't want to hear any more of the vile he was so viciously spewing. I begged him, pleaded with him to stop. I never intended to hurt him.

Or maybe...

I did.

Before I knew what I was doing, I dove for the gun on his desk. Aiming it directly at him. Trying to still my trembling hands.

He didn't move.

He wasn't surprised.

It was as if he expected me to do it, like this was what he wanted in the end.

He leaned back, nonchalantly placing his hands in his pockets. Standing taller, prouder, ready for anything. Eyeing me up and down with a menacing regard. "You ever held a gun before?"

"Please... Martinez... please... just stop..." I coaxed, hanging on by a thread.

"Your hands are shaking. First rule of holding a gun. Never let your enemies see your fear. It just makes you a fucking pussy. So, what's your next move? I'm right here." He spread his arms out at his sides. "This is your chance to get rid of me. To avenge your mother's death. Do it! Pull the fucking trigger, do it!" he baited.

"Stop! Please! Fucking stop!" I screamed, sobs raging through my body.

"I'm a bad man! I've done unforgivable things. Here's your chance! Fucking take it! Send me straight to fucking Hell! Now!"

I jerked back, almost falling to the ground not realizing what I had just done. My eyes widened, my heart dropped. A loud popping sound ricocheted off the walls followed by his body falling to the ground with a thud.

"Oh my God," I breathed out.

I didn't have time to go to him, to help him. The door to his office slammed open. His niece, my half-sister, Briggs coming face to face with her uncle, lying in a pool of his own blood.

"NO!" She lunged into action, falling to her knees. "NO! NO! NO! PLEASE NO!" she screamed, placing her hands over his wound. Blood gushed through her fingers as she applied pressure.

"Briggs!" Austin yelled, barreling into the room after her. Stopping dead in his tracks, peering from her, to him, to me.

The rest proceeded in slow motion.

She looked up never expecting to see me behind the smoking gun.

"Lexi?" she said with a horrified look on her face.

I immediately released the gun. It dropped to the floor with a bang. "I... oh my God... what happened... oh my God, oh my God, what did I do?" I was in shock, my eyes never leaving him. There was so much blood.

"Fuck!" Austin shouted, instantly grabbing the gun. Placing it in the back of his jeans. "Go!" he ordered, looking at me. "NOW!"

"What?" I replied, confused.

"Austin, what are you doing?" Briggs asked, bringing my attention to her.

"It wasn't supposed to go down like this. Fuck! Go, Lexi! Now! This place will be swarming with cops in a few minutes! GO!"

I shook my head. "What—"

"Daisy," Martinez sputtered, coughing up blood. She peered down at him with nothing but love in her eyes. "Let her go. I deserved it. Let her go..." he added, his eyes fluttering. Going in and out of consciousness.

"Get out of here! NOW!" Austin shouted.

I looked around the room one last time. Overwhelmed, confused, regretful, and fucking terrified.

Why are they letting me go?

I didn't give it a second thought.

I ran.

Trying like hell not to look back.

Forty-two
Lexi

Six days, six hours, six minutes, since I pulled the trigger. The devil's numbers, the irony wasn't lost on me. I walked into my apartment, kicking the door shut behind me. Placing all the newspapers, magazines, and picture on the living room floor. Turning on the television in front of me.

"Alejandro Martinez, notorious crime boss of New York City is being laid to rest today, after he was gunned down in his downtown Manhattan penthouse a week ago. The investigation is still open, and there are no leads at this time on who is responsible for taking the life of the man, most commonly known as El Diablo. We will be going live from his funeral site in a few minutes. People are gathering from all over the world for this significant moment in time. Where justice has been served. Proving that the good guys can win, in the end. I'm Maria Castello, reporting live. Please stand by."

I grabbed my stomach immediately feeling nauseous again. This whole thing made me sick, on the brink of throwing up. My conscience. My heart. My soul. Eating away at me. I don't think I slept the entire week, barely leaving my apartment until today. I did, only because I had to. I'd been struggling with turning myself in, walking to my door, reaching for the handle, telling myself today was the day I'd confess. But I couldn't. I needed to pay for taking a life that didn't belong to me. I was no better than him.

Why did they let me go?

Even Martinez let his demise go.

Me.

Why were Austin and Briggs even there?

They never came to visit. It didn't make any sense. Nothing did. I was more confused now than I had ever been before. I didn't

386

know how that was even possible. I kept expecting the cops to start pounding on my door at any point in time. Constantly watching over my shoulder, still feeling his strong presence all around me.

His ghost.

Would he ever go away? Is this what it felt like for him? All those years of feeling the lives he took around him? Is that why he never slept? Their souls haunted him? How can I still love him? Grieve for him after everything he told me? He was with my mom. He was her demise. How do I move on from that?

I looked down at the newspapers. All the headlines were the same.

"FBI raid, Jimmy 'The Boss' Sanchez's mansion. Arrested by FBI."

"Notorious drug lords from around the world brought to justice."

"Biggest organized crime bust in world history in wake of Alejandro Martinez's death."

"Crime Bosses across the U.S. being questioned. Amongst the names, 'Benjamin 'Boss Man' Robinson was taken into custody."

"Colombia's Most wanted, Franco 'Frankie Smalls' Vasquez shot by the FBI."

Since Martinez's death, organized crime families were going down all over the world. And it was the only peace of mind I got out of the whole ordeal. At least he wasn't going to be rotting in prison.

Maybe I did the right thing?

Then why did it feel so fucking wrong?

I honestly didn't know how I felt. I would go from bawling, to numb, back to sobbing again. I was on an emotional rollercoaster going up and down, twisting all around to the point of making myself sick. I couldn't keep up anymore. I knew one thing for sure. I couldn't stay in New York anymore. Too many haunting memories lurked in the shadows.

"We are back, reporting live from Alejandro Martinez's funeral," the newscaster's voice brought my attention back to the television. "They have just pulled the casket out of the hearse—" I got up, running to the bathroom, hurling all the contents of my

387

stomach into the toilet. Unable to keep it down. Heaving it down the porcelain basin.

"Ugh!" I let out, throwing up some more. I spit, wiping my mouth with the back of my hand as I flushed the toilet.

I sat there for a few minutes, resisting the urge to do it again. Rubbing my stomach, breathing through the nausea, the emotions, the feelings, the tsunami my life had turned into. I stood, going to the sink. Splashing water in my mouth, spitting it back out. Looking at myself in the mirror.

"What did you do, Lexi? What did you fucking do?"

I went to the kitchen, grabbing a bottle of water. Trying not to throw up again. As much as I didn't want to see the broadcast, my eyes were glued to the screen. Briggs appeared on camera, breaking down, Austin holding her up. Mourning the loss of the man who raised her. The only family she thought she had left. Followed by the good ol' boys and their wives, walking right behind them. I found myself wondering if they told their little girl, Amari, her "unkey" would no longer be there to hold her, play with her or Skype ever again. The tears started to fall.

My half-sister…

And she would never even know it.

"I'm so sorry, Briggs," I wept, shutting off the television. Knowing I would never be able to shake off the image of her falling apart.

I turned on the shower, setting it on the hottest temperature possible, stepping inside, welcoming the heat. Letting the hot water burn my skin, hoping it would wash away my sins. I didn't know anything anymore. I was a black hole of nothing. All I could feel were his strong, callused fingers all over my flesh, his body on top of mine, his reassuring words. The lock he placed on my heart, I knew would never go away. No matter how much I tried, how much I wanted it to. He would always be a part of me.

My mind ran wild. I couldn't get it to stop, image after image from the day in his office, played out in front of me. I pressed my hands against the shower wall, leaning my forehead on the cool rustic tile. Closing my eyes, still hearing his cruel words.

This is your chance to get rid of me. To avenge your mother's death. Do it! Pull the fucking trigger, do it!" His words were on repeat as much as the images. Scene after scene, the sound of the gun blasting, and everything that happened after.

"I killed him, Lexi. No one else, but me."

"It was always your mother, Lexi. She was my cariño."

"I killed my own father."

I got down on my knees in the shower, instantly placing my hands over my ears, tuning out his voice, shutting out my own. I shook my head back and forth. Sobbing, pleading with God, with him, with myself to please forgive me. I never meant to hurt anybody. Needing to find some peace, some silence. The guilt was too much.

How could I go on like this?

I stayed in the shower until the water ran cold over my body, crying until I had no more tears left. I got out throwing on a cami and some panties, wrapping my hair in a towel. I grabbed the picture I left on the living room floor. It was the only thing I had left of him.

Of us.

I spent the rest of day in bed, mourning the loss of the man I killed. Crying myself to sleep. Exhausted. Alone.

"The things I regret haven't happened yet. If something ever does happen to me, just remember I'll always be with you. No matter what. In here." My hand subconsciously laid over my heart.

Feeling him.

My eyes shot open. Gasping for air. Darkness all around me, the only light was cascading off the full moon from my window. His presence, his scent, his hold was all around me. I took a few deep breaths, settling back into my sheets. Shutting my eyes again, letting sleep take over once more. Slipping right back into the same dreams.

I stirred, hearing a familiar, faint voice in my sleep.

"You're so fucking beautiful." Serene, blue, tantalizing eyes staring back at me in my dream. He was so close. So real.

"Hmmm..." I rolled over to the other side of my bed. "I'm so sorry," I found myself saying in my sleep.

"I got what I deserved, cariño. You did what I wanted you to do all along."

"I'm so alone…" I hazily spoke.

"No you're not. You have me… open your eyes, Lexi."

"You're not real… I killed you. Please…"

"Open your eyes, baby. I'm here."

I steadied my breathing, my mind willing me to open my eyes, to wake-up. Feeling with every ounce of my being that when I did.

I would actually find him sitting there.

Watching over me.

My dark angel.

Martinez

Her lips were swollen, her face puffy, her eyes bloodshot red from spending countless minutes, hours, days, crying. Mourning the loss of a man who didn't deserve her tears.

Me.

She still took my goddamn breath away. I'd been sitting here in the armchair by her bed for hours, watching her sleep. Even in her dreams she couldn't run from me. Whimpering my name, apologizing for a crime she didn't commit. As much as I didn't want to wake her, I couldn't bear to see her feeling any more turmoil, any more pain, especially on my behalf. Again. Her eyes widened seeing me for the first time.

Breathing.

Alive.

She flew up on the bed, away from me. The square picture she was holding in her sleep, floated to the floor between the bed and nightstand. Her mouth opened wide, gasping for air, her hand over her heart. Looking at me like she was staring at a fucking ghost.

"What the fuck, Martinez!?" she screamed, her back slamming against the headboard. Hitting it with a thud. She winced.

"Shhh… Stop screaming." I reached for her, but she backed further away from me. Putting my hands out in front of me in a surrendering gesture, I sat back on the chair. "You know I'm all for you screaming my name, but now is not the time or the place. Your shitty fucking apartment has some thin ass fucking walls."

"Your funeral was today... I saw it... on the TV... Briggs was crying... Austin... holding her... I shot you... blood... lots of it... everywhere... you... died... I... killed... you..." she stuttered, not moving an inch from her place against the headboard.

"You saw what I wanted you to see."

"What the fuck kind of an answer is that?!" she shouted. I could tell she wanted to flip the fuck out, but was trying to remain untroubled.

"The only one I have. Now stop fucking screaming and sit your ass back down on the bed. As much as I love staring at your tits. We need to talk."

She swallowed hard, slowly sliding down the headboard. Pulling her legs to her chest, hugging them close to her body in a comforting gesture. Covering her breasts that were on full display through her tight, white shirt. She cocked her head to the side, narrowing her eyes at me. Trying to figure out if I was really sitting in front of her, or if I was another illusion in her mind. She looked from me to the floor, silently telling me she was going to get off the bed. Slowly, she placed one foot on the ground then the next. Gradually stepping toward me, she reached out once she was close enough, wanting to make sure I was real. She gently touched my shoulder, her eyes wide and brazen, moving her hand along to my chest.

"But I shot you," she coaxed.

As much as I wanted to grab her hand, I didn't want to frighten her. I needed to move at her speed. "Here," I stated, placing my hand over the wound. "You barely missed my heart."

She recoiled away from me, trying to remain calm, collecting her thoughts. "How is this possible? How are you here? What is going on?"

"Let me—"

"No more lying, Alejandro."

I nodded for her to sit down. She did, resuming her position against the headboard.

I leaned forward, setting my elbows on my knees, placing my hands out in front of me in a prayer gesture. Looking deep into her eyes, I murmured, "I'm sorry, Lexi. I'm so fucking sorry."

She frowned, taking in the sincerity of my voice. I'd never apologized to her for anything I put her through in the years we were together and apart. Not once telling her I was sorry for ripping out her heart, time and time again. I regretted it every day of my fucked-up existence. I wanted to tell her. I just wasn't made that way. She knew how hard it was for me to show weakness. To anyone. Especially her. She had the power to bring me to my knees, and she never even realized it. There was still so much she needed to know. So much I needed to explain with little time to do it.

"I gave Michael, your father, four years to come clean. Four fucking years he was given to tell Amari the truth. She deserved to know how much of a piece of shit he truly was. He never loved her. I knew that since day one. Amari was blind, but love does that to you. She got pregnant with Briggs to fucking trap him, that is how desperate she was to keep him around. That is how much she loved the motherfucker. I loved my sister more than anything in this world, Lexi. There's not a day that has gone by that I haven't thought of her. Every day I find a way to beat myself up for taking her life. I see her, I feel her every goddamn second, judging me with so much disappointment in her eyes. Amari was my light, much like you are. I never had any intentions of hurting her. And if I could switch places with her, I wouldn't think twice about it. Amari got caught in the crossfire. Esteban—"

"Esteban? Briggs' bodyguard?"

"Yes, he fucked up, and it cost my sister her life. Michael was supposed to be alone. But Amari's car broke down on the side of the road, and Michael had to go rescue her and Briggs…" I closed my eyes, leaning my head into my hands. The memory of that day played out in front of me. Making me relive it again as if no time had passed. Hearing her voice on the message she left me the day she died, every goddamn day since. If I would have just answered her call, I would have been able to stop it all. She would still be alive. I wouldn't have ruined Briggs' life.

"It was pouring out. Esteban didn't see Amari and Briggs were in the car with Michael. He did what I ordered him to do. So, instead of breaking his fucking neck, I assigned him to Briggs. Making him see the broken little girl every day. Payback for taking

392

away her family. His fuck up. It was also my way of pushing her away. I couldn't handle seeing her break down, scared, and alone. I never let Briggs get close to me. I never held her while she cried. I never told her I loved her, too consumed by the shame and guilt from taking her mom away. It has been one of the biggest regrets of my entire life. I love Briggs more than anything. It's too fucking late for me to show her, the damage has been done. I've tried to make it up to her though by being the uncle I always wanted to be, with her children, Amari and Michael."

I had never shared that with anyone. No one knew the truth. I pulled my hair back away from my face. Peering up at her with glossy eyes. Not caring if she saw my raw pain, my devastation unfolding out in front of her. It was time she knew the real truth buried beneath the lies.

"I needed to get out of my penthouse. Hearing Briggs fall apart every night, knowing I was the cause of her misery, was eating me fucking alive. I would have put a bullet in my head if it weren't for her. I can't tell you how many times I stared at the loaded gun in front of me. Fighting a battle with myself not to pick it up, aim it at my head, and end it all. But I couldn't, I stayed alive for Briggs. I couldn't be selfish. My sister had made me promise to raise her if anything ever happened to her. Briggs needed me. I was the only family she had left. My punishment was to keep fucking breathing. I ended up in Rhode Island, watching you get off your school bus. You were already such a cute fucking kid. I knew Sophia was in bad shape, I knew it was only a matter of time until..." I shook the thought out of my head. "You had your arms at your sides, practicing your ballet steps. Humming a melody all the way home. Walking by yourself in a shitty fucking neighborhood like you were a grown-up. No one to watch out for you, but fuck... Lexi, that didn't stop you from fucking smiling. And it lit up your entire face."

Her eyes watered as she took in every last word that came out of my mouth.

"I couldn't help but be drawn to you. I followed you home, and you didn't even realize it, which made me hate your fucking mother a little more. Anyone could have followed you home. You walked into your house, screaming for your *momma*. I went to the side of the house and watched from the window. You found her bawling in the closet, sobbing for the lives of Michael and Amari that I took."

Tears slid down her face, knowing exactly the moment I was referring to. All I wanted to do was reach forward and wipe away all her tears.

"From that day forward, cariño. I had you watched. Not your mother, not Sophia. You. Only you."

"Why?" she whispered so low I could barely hear her.

I ignored her question. "I paid for Sophia's funeral. Feeling responsible for her death. I made it look like the money came from some trust fund of her grandparents. Your piece of shit stepdad didn't even question it. In fact, the motherfucker got a hold of some of the money I left for you, and drowned himself in whiskey. I never thought he was capable of hurting you. I'm so sorry, Lexi," I said, clearing my throat. Trying to keep it from breaking. "I tried to get to him as fast as I could. I didn't know he was touching you, hurting you until it was too late. But I made him pay. I fucking promise you, I made that son of a bitch pay for every time he went into your room."

She gasped, "You?"

"I waited until I knew you'd be gone for the day. You had your big dance recital. I paid your stepdad a little visit with my men. I made him write you a half-ass apology. Then I had one of my men show him what it felt like to be on the receiving end of what he'd been doing to you for years. He didn't last five fucking minutes before he passed out from the pain. I killed two birds with one stone that night. Briggs thought she was responsible for her parents' death. It was her fifteenth birthday, so I gave her peace of mind and I set you free. Killing the man who'd been fucking hurting you."

"Oh my God..." she wept, her lips trembling.

"I was the anonymous caller to your school. But I made sure you were placed in a decent foster home. They weren't ideal, but they were sure as shit better than what you were living with. It's why you were placed with a family so fucking fast."

Her trembling hand went up to her mouth. The truth almost too much for her to bear.

"I never expected you to show up at my strip club when you were fifteen. But fate has a funny way of fucking with you, when you least expect it. I knew who you were the second you got out of the car. I've always known who you were, Lexi. When you showed up three years later, no longer a little girl, but a fucking beautiful woman, standing in front of me. I couldn't fucking help myself. I slipped that day and called you, cariño. I had never called anyone that, except Sophia. So, you obviously know now why I kicked you the fuck out of my office. Even though I highly enjoyed the little show you put on, there was no way in hell I'd let you strip for money. It's the reason no one in the city would hire you. Lexi, I made sure of it. I just never thought you'd come to me of all people for help."

"You? It was you?"

"After I knew you got the acceptance letter to Julliard, I was going to deposit the money into your account, but you beat me to it by barging into my office uninvited. I knew ballet was all you ever had. Your happiness. I wanted you to have something to hold onto. The realtor that showed you your apartment worked for me, which is how you ended up in my building. It made it easier for my men to keep watch on you."

"So that's how you saved me from Nikolai. Did you ever take care of his men? The ones who were looking for me?"

I scoffed. "There was never anyone looking for you, cariño."

She jerked back, confused. "But you said—"

"I know what I said. It was all a lie."

"Why? I don't understand? Why did you do any of this?"

"For the same reason I pushed you away, made you hate me, treated you like shit. Kept you at arm's length, never letting you see the man you knew still lived inside of me... the man that protected you, watched over you, made sure you were fucking safe. The reason I went looking for you after you left for Europe... Watching you dance on stage, realizing I needed to let you go... The same fucking reason I went back for you, brought you home with me, took care of you, made you see what I wanted you to see..." I paused, letting my words sink in. "It's been the same reason since the first moment I laid eyes on you. I'm fucking in love with you. Te amo, I love you, Lexi. With everything left

395

inside of me, I fucking love you. I'm yours. I've been yours since I can remember."

Fresh tears rolled down her face, it was the first time I ever said those three words to her. Even though I'd been dying to say them since the second she barged into my office, when she was eighteen years old.

"Do you love me because I'm Sophia's daughter? Because I remind you of her? Because you couldn't have her, so you settled for me? Am I the rebound girl, second best, right? Is that why you love me?" she bellowed, her voice breaking.

"No," I simply stated. "I love you in spite of that."

She jolted back, surprised by my revelation. Her icy façade was dissolving layer by layer. I was getting through to her. For once, the truth may save me.

"But trust me, cariño. You couldn't be more different than Sophia if you tried. You look nothing like her. Sophia was weak, scared about everything, never fought for anything in her life. Including me. Always waiting for someone to rescue her, take care of her. She wasn't the woman for me. I thought I loved her, I thought she was the one. I couldn't have been more wrong about that. I spent years mourning the loss of a woman who never belonged with me."

Her eyes showed so many different emotions, it was almost hard to keep up.

"You're strong, you're resilient, you fight for everything you believe in, especially *me*. It didn't matter how many times I tried to push you away, knowing everything about us was wrong. You wouldn't have it. You were never scared of me, Lexi. As much as I tried to show you my Hell, you were more than willing to burn right along with me. I've never met anyone like you before. You've gone through so much and have never let it define who you were. That's one of the things I love the most about you. You were made for me, cariño. And I swear to you on my niece's life, that I've never looked at you and thought you were Sophia. I've never wanted to call out her name. It's always been just you, Lexi."

She took a deep breath, wiping away all her tears.

"You don't owe me anything. I'm fully aware of that, baby. But you need to know the truth. I owe you that and so much more." It was my turn to take a deep breath. "For the ten years you were in Europe, I was barely fucking living. I was going through the motions. Waiting for the day that someone would finally end it all. I was fucking exhausted. I am fucking exhausted. I'm too old for this shit. I was a broken compass pointing to nowhere. I missed you. I craved you. I dreamt about you. Every second of every day, I spent thinking about nothing but you. I just wanted to end it all. Living a life where no one cared if I was dead or alive finally ran its toll. I fucking needed you. For the first time in my life, I needed someone. You."

"Jesus... Alejandro," she muttered, her lips trembling.

"I know it's a lot to take in at once. If I had more time to talk to you, it would be different, but I don't. And I'm not leaving this room until you know everything. No more secrets, no more lies. No. More. Demons."

She nodded, wanting to hear the rest of what I had to say.

"The FBI had been on my ass for years. Fucking decades. Austin was so grateful for my part in Briggs and him getting back together. He gave me the heads up that his friend, Dylan was getting close to exposing me. Bringing me in. He's a narcotics detective and had been working on my case for God knows how long. That's when I realized that this was my chance to walk away. With you. To end it all. This was my demise."

She shook her head. "I don't understand."

"I wanted to come for you before you got in your car accident, but I thought I was doing the right thing staying away. When Leo told me you were badly hurt it only signified what I was doing. What I was planning. I thought I lost you. For good. When you woke up and saw me in your hospital room, everything was already set in motion."

"What?"

"My death."

She narrowed her eyes at me, still not understanding.

"I made a deal with the government. I give up the names, information on all the men they spent decades trying to get, and in return I get to walk away with a new identity. I knew it was going

397

to take time, but I never thought it would take three years. I spent those years being who I always wanted to be with you. Needing you to finally meet the man you always wanted. I let myself really be with you, for the first time. I didn't give a fuck anymore. Right or wrong. You're mine. End of story," I revealed, laying all my cards out on the table. "Cariño, I tried to give you clues the only way I possibly could. Hoping maybe you would catch on. You never did. Dylan, Austin and Leo knew from the start. They helped me with everything. Briggs knew something was going to go down, but she didn't know the specifics. It's why they let you go."

"I saw you... with the woman, she was in your bed. She was with you all the time. The newspapers—"

"You saw what I wanted you to see. The woman on my arm is a VIP. She's a fucking escort. I needed to have my enemies see me with someone else, just in case. For your safety, I needed to take the heat off of you. It was the only way I could protect you. The day you came into my house, it was planned. I needed you to hate me. I needed to reel you in. I needed to bait you to pull that fucking trigger. It was all staged. I wanted you to shoot me. That's why I was so cruel, saying things I didn't mean. I never—"

"Your mother's cross. She was wearing it. I saw—"

I pulled it out from under my collared shirt. "This one?"

Her eyes widened in disbelief.

"She was never wearing this cross. I had a duplicate made. I never wanted to hurt you again. It killed me inside to have to do this to you. The day of Michael's christening, Dylan told me I had three months to pull this off. And I was telling him and Austin that I didn't think I could go through with it anymore."

"Oh my God. Before Creed barged in. That's what you were talking about? I overheard you. And when I saw you having a deep conversation with Briggs, you were telling her?"

I nodded.

"That's why you flipped on me? You changed overnight... I thought you were having second thoughts about us. I thought—"

"The only thing that kept me going was the end result."

"Alejandro, I could have killed you."

"It was a risk I was willing to take."

"Why?"

398

I stood, walking over to her. She eyed me warily, but didn't back away. I couldn't blame her for looking at me that way. I deserved it and more. I was surprised she even let me say everything I needed to. Not that I would have given her a choice in the matter. I sat on the edge of her bed with very little distance between us.

She swallowed hard, waiting for my answer. I didn't falter, taking off my mother's cross necklace. "Because it would give me you. I could burn my past. And have a fresh future with you. I couldn't bring you into this life, Lexi, but I could have you take me away from it. I had to fake my own death. I kept your scent as my talisman," I rasped, caressing the side of her face. Trying to ease her anxiety with my touch. "I gave away my life and soul to be with you. I want you, it's only been you. I don't care where we will go, or what we will do. You are my beginning and my end."

She closed her eyes, fresh tears falling down her beautiful face. I placed the necklace around her neck. Whispering in her ear.

"It will protect you. Even when I can't."

"What happens now?" she asked with a shaky voice, taking the cross in her hand. Her eyes still shut.

"Now. I leave."

She instantly opened them. I reached into the pocket of my suit jacket, handing her an envelope. She eyed it before grabbing it out of my hand, opening it and looking at the information.

"Italy?" she stated as a question.

"It's a one-way ticket, you can use it whenever you're ready. I want you to come on your own terms. It's where I'll start my new life, praying you'll be right next to me in the place you've always dreamed to live. Everything you need to know is in this envelope. Including where to find me. My destiny is literally in your hands. It's always been in your hands. I will wait for you for the rest of my life if that's what it takes. I'm so fucking sorry, cariño. If you can give me a chance, if you can forgive me, I will spend the rest of my life making it up to you. I promise."

"Alejandro—"

She broke down, so overwhelmed with her emotions.

"I need some time to take all this information in. It's all so overwhelming. I thought I fucking killed you, I was about to turn

399

myself in. My life has been nothing but heartache with dustings of happiness. And it's not just me..." she began to sob harder. "I don't know if I can forgive you, Alejandro. You broke my heart more than once. It's just been too much. I don't think I can get past it. I don't think I can forgive you this time."

I pulled her into my arms, holding her so goddamn tight. Needing to feel her, hold her, comfort her.

Fucking love her.

"Te amo, Lexi. I love you with each breath I take. With every beat of my heart, my future belongs to you. Para siempre," I breathed out into her ear. "Please find it in your heart to forgive me. I need you. I can't live without you. I've tried..." I whispered, trying to hold it together. "Take all the time you need, but please come to me." I held her for as long as I could, but it wasn't nearly enough. "I have to go. I was only allotted an amount of time, and I've already gone way over it." I kissed her forehead, yearning to kiss her fucking lips. Holding my future in my arms.

We locked eyes.

There was so much more I wanted to say. It took everything inside of me not to throw her over my shoulder and drag her onto the plane with me. It needed to be her choice, I couldn't make decisions for her anymore. I took one last look at her.

Silently hoping...

This wasn't the end of our love story.

And I left.

Forty-three
Martinez

Three months went by and I hadn't seen or heard from Lexi. When I arrived in Italy, I made sure I had everything ready for her. Everything she could ever want or need, waiting for her like a desperate man. She never came. Old habits die hard though, and I still had Leo watching over her. In the wake of my death, I didn't know what could happen. I always kept Lexi out of the press, unknown to anyone associated with me, except Leo. Just because most of my enemies were rotting behind bars, thanks to me, didn't mean she couldn't get caught in the crossfire.

He never went into too much detail, our conversations had to remain short. He only reassured me that she was safe. Still living in that shitty fucking apartment in Manhattan, instead of in paradise with me. During the three years that the FBI were collecting information, going undercover, getting everything in order for search warrants for arrests, I made sure to get all my finances in fucking order before I had to disappear. It was why I spent so much time working.

Leo had access to all my funds, doing what he always did for me. Making sure I stayed rich as fuck. He opened up multiple untraceable bank accounts, laundering my money to the Cayman Islands and Switzerland. Where the U.S. government could never touch it. He opened up trust funds for my great niece and nephew, Amari and Michael. Their colleges, weddings, and whatever the fuck else they might need would be provided and taken care of. Briggs wasn't happy when I told her I had him open a trust for her as well, but she knew better than to argue with me about it. I still hadn't told her the truth about her father, I didn't want to ruin the illusion of the perfect dad she had in her memory. I had already created too much negativity in her life. I was waiting on Lexi, to see how she wanted to proceed with telling Briggs they were half-sisters. If she even wanted to tell her at all.

Leo opened another account for Lexi, in case she ever needed anything, it would be at her disposal. I bought a house off the Amalfi Coast, right on a cliff like Lexi wanted. I spent every night on the balcony looking up at the stars, waiting for her to come to me. I couldn't wait to show her the view, hold her in my arms and watch for shooting stars. Like the nights we spent in Colombia years ago. I thought after I left my past behind, I would finally be at peace. Possibly even be able to sleep. Neither had happened. And as more time went on, I started to think it never would. I found myself giving up on all hope that she would forgive me. God knows I didn't deserve her.

Only a few of my closest connections knew I was alive, men I knew I could trust. If they needed anything they knew to call Leo, and he would get ahold of me. No one knew where I was or how to reach me, except Leo, Briggs, and Austin. I guess Amari was already begging her parents to come see me, and I would be lying if I said I didn't miss them. There was nothing for me to do with my days anymore other than think of them.

Of her.

"Señor, you here again?" Rosa, the owner said in a thick Italian accent.

She was a little Italian woman in her mid-seventies, who stood maybe to my waist. There was something about this place that made me come back every day. It was a small restaurant on a cobblestone street in town. It reminded me of a pizzeria in Manhattan with its tables lined with red and white checkered tablecloths, and a fresh rose in a red vase.

"How come you by yourself? Every night you come. You drink. You eat. You drink more. You smoke el sigaro. You no smile. You no laugh. You no talk. But again you come. Same thing. Where is the signora?"

"No signora, Rosa," I replied, taking another puff of my cigar.

"No signora? You so handsome. I have a niece. Beautiful. Bellissima." She kissed her fingers. "I introduce."

"No, Rosa. I have a woman. One that…" I took a deep breath, "consumes me."

"Ah, señor, you in love. L'amore!" she wiggled her eyebrows, causing me to chuckle. "Where is this woman? She never here."

I took a sip of my wine. "I wish I knew, Rosa."

"You no worry. You in Italia. Paradiso di amore! She come to you. When she ready."

I nodded. "That's what I'm hoping for."

"You dinner. On me. You drink. You eat. No pay."

"Rosa, you don't—"

"Señor, I'm old enough to be your mamma. We famiglia now."

I smiled. I couldn't help it. Immediately thinking about how Lexi wanted to live here because the people were so welcoming and loving.

"There it is." She grabbed my face in between her hands. "The smile. Such a handsome man. Quanto è bello. You trust in love. She will come. I know it." She kissed my head and left.

I killed two bottles of wine and opened another one when I got home. Taking it out to the balcony with me just as the sun was about to set. Not bothering to grab a glass. I laid on the lounger, listening to the upbeat Italian music in the distance. There was always some sort of party or festival going on in the area. My thoughts drifted, picturing Lexi and I dancing around the balcony, so carefree. Wishing I had danced with her more when we were together. Nightfall took over, the music shifted into a romantic melody, and all I could imagine was laying her down on the lounger and spending hours making up for our time apart. I shook off the sentiment, taking another swig from the wine bottle. Numbing myself with alcohol, lying back to look at the stars. Wondering if she was ever looked at the same night sky thinking about me.

The breeze from the fresh air, the wine, the food, the exhaustion, finally won and I fell into a deep sleep. Dreaming of her face, hearing her voice, smelling her all around me.

"Lexi… I love you…" I groaned in my sleep.

"I love you, too."

My eyes fluttered open, blinking a few times. Thinking my mind was playing tricks on me, or the wine went straight to my goddamn head.

"I'm here, Alejandro," Lexi announced.

She was sitting in the chair next to me. Looking like a fucking goddess. Her skin was glowing. Her green eyes were shining so bright. Her soft, silky hair was down, blowing in the wind. She was wearing a yellow flowing dress.

My cock fucking twitched at the sight of her.

"Jesus Christ, you're even more breathtaking than I remember." I rolled toward her, reaching for her waist. Not wanting to waste one more second not touching her. She put her hands up, stopping me.

"Lexi, I haven't seen or felt you in so fucking long. Please at least come lay in arms." I narrowed my eyes at her.

She shyly smiled, saying, "We need to talk."

"First words every man wants to hear, cariño."

"Okay… then I need to talk to you and you need to listen. I know how hard that is for you but—"

I didn't falter, stating. "Done." And I pulled her to me.

He was relentless. When Martinez wanted something, there was no stopping the man. He was insatiable. He tugged me forward, making me straddle his waist. His hands immediately traveling up my thighs.

I stopped him again.

He grinned, devouring me with his eyes. "You said I needed to listen to you, not that I couldn't touch you."

"Alejandro…" I warned in a stern voice.

He reluctantly placed his arms behind his head, which only made him look more mouthwatering. Breaking my resolve already. He arched an eyebrow when he realized what I was thinking.

"It's okay, baby. I want you to touch me."

404

I shook my head, trying to stifle a laugh. "This is not going how I planned."

"I—"

"No talking." I placed my hand over his mouth. "Just listening. There's a lot I need to say to you before you sweet talk your way back into my life again." He kissed my palm, nipping it as he winked at me.

I pulled mine away. "First and foremost, you need to know I'm here under certain conditions. One of them being, our relationship will remain strictly platonic."

His jaw clenched.

"I have spent the last three months going back and forth with what I should do about you. About us. Weighing the pros and cons of coming here. Before I knew what I was doing, I found myself at the airport. Boarding a plane to Italy. The pros outweighing the cons in a sense."

He smiled, reaching for me again.

"Wait, let me finish," I interrupted, stopping his hands. "What I say next may hurt you, but at this point... I don't really care. I don't trust you enough not to hurt me again. You've broken my heart more times than I care to count. In fact, other women would probably tell me I'm insane for even being here. And they would probably be right."

He opened his mouth to say something, but quickly shut it when I shot him another warning glare.

"You're an asshole, Martinez. A downright fucking bastard. You treated me like shit when all I ever did was love you. I understand why you did it, now. I get that you needed to push me away. But that doesn't change the fact that you still hurt me. It doesn't take away the pain you inflicted, the memories that I'll always remember, and the nights I cried myself to sleep. Alone."

He grimaced not trying to hide it like he usually would.

"With that said, you also saved my life more times than I probably even know. You protected me, watched over me, took care of me. In a twisted way, you were like my guardian angel. I can't overlook that, and I won't. What you did for me when I was kid..." My eyes began to water. "The first time that monster came into my room, I was sleeping. I woke up to the strong scent of whiskey hovering over me. He called me Sophia over and over again as I felt his hands roam all over my body." I shuddered, a cold chill coursing through me. Shaking off the images, I continued. "I wanted him to suffer. I wanted him to die. It was the first time I experienced true evil in this world. Making me realize the entire time I was with you, Alejandro, in your world. I've never felt so safe."

The serious expression on his face captivated me in a way I had never experienced before. Which only added to the plaguing emotions that ran thick between us.

"You made sure I ended up in a decent foster home, paying for my college, giving me extra money to live off of, saving me from Nikolai, my ballet studio in your penthouse, taking care of me after my accident, spending God knows how much money on the best doctors, the best medical attention, my ballet studio, and everything else in between. Your actions spoke volumes when there were no words. You may have hurt me emotionally, but you've always taken care of me physically. No matter what, no questions asked," I expressed, needing to get it all out.

His calm, serene eyes barred into mine, igniting a fire deep within me. He wasn't looking at me. He was looking through me. Exactly the way he always had.

I peered deep into his eyes. "You were the villain in your own story, Martinez. In mine, you've always been my hero." Tears slid down my face and he wiped them all away. Skimming his calloused fingers across my cheeks. Pushing the hair away from my face. I wanted to stay lost in his eyes at that moment, savor the way he was looking at me, the way he pulled every sentiment from my body as if it belonged to him. I pulled away from his grasp, instantly missing his warmth. His touch. His love. I needed to finish what I was trying to tell him.

"All the good you've done for me, outweighed the bad. That's one of the reasons I'm here. I owe it to us to see where this could go without any demons on either of our shoulders. No pasts haunting us. Fresh start. New beginnings."

I took a deep breath, nervous for what I was going to say next. What I already divulged was the easy part. I hadn't gotten to the hard yet.

"The next and most important reason… is because I owe it to our daughter."

He was silent for the first time ever. His face was completely void of any emotion.

I let on, "She deserves to know her father. She deserves a family. The one I never had. The one I truly want to try to give her, with you of course."

More silence.

"Did you hear me, Alejandro?"

His gaze fell to my barely-there swollen belly, letting his eyes linger there for a few seconds, peering back up at my face. He rasped, "You're pregnant?"

I nodded.

"You're positive? Certain? This—"

I turned around, reaching for my purse, grabbing it off the table. Pulling out the ultrasound picture, I placed it in between us.

"I'm eighteen weeks along. She's healthy. I've had no complications, just some morning sickness during the first trimester. But I'm fine now. I started to feel her kick last week. I wish you could have been…" I didn't finish what I was about to say, not thinking about who I was saying it to.

He didn't stop looking at the picture on his chest. Like he wasn't listening to a word I was saying. "So you were pregnant the last time I saw you?"

"Yes. I found out that day. I was actually sleeping with that photo. It fell in between the bed and nightstand."

He glanced up at me. "You've been pregnant this whole fucking time? And you didn't think I had a right to know?" he questioned with so much hurt in his eyes.

"Of course you do. I was just—" I gasped, he abruptly flipped us over.

He leaned close to my face, his entire body hovering above me. Looking down with an expression I couldn't place. "You're carrying my child, a life we created, and you waited till fucking now to tell me? What's this bullshit about deserving to know her father?"

"I—"

"She should have known me from day one, Lexi. You're lucky you're pregnant, or I would put you over my goddamn knee and spank your little ass until my hand stung and your cheeks were bright fucking red."

My eyes widened. "Ale—"

He cocked his head to the side, silencing me. "I'm going to tell you how this is going to go. I'm going to forgive you for hiding the fact that you were fucking pregnant. Putting my baby girl's life in danger."

"She was never—" His finger came down on my lips, silencing me again.

"And you're going to forgive me. We're going to start over. None of this platonic bullshit of seeing where this goes…" He gestured in between us. "Because the only place it's going right now, is in the fucking bedroom so you can sit on my face and I can fuck you with my tongue. If you're a good girl, I will let you come."

My mouth parted, releasing the air I didn't realize I was holding.

"And I will win back your trust. I will never hurt you again, cariño. I promise you on our daughter's life, you've always been my world. Now she will be too." He placed his hand on my belly feeling her for the first time. "But if you ever keep something like this from me again, I won't hesitate to remind you what the palm of my hand feels like against your perky goddamn ass."

He didn't give me a chance to reply before his mouth was on mine. Crashing our lips together, kissing me gently, adoringly, fervently. Savoring every last touch, every last push and pull, every last movement of my lips working against his. It was one giant buildup of months of him wanting to feel my mouth on his. Kissing me deeper, harder, and with more determination.

The passion and the longing that radiated off of him, sent spasms down my body. Immediately making me wet. I couldn't hold back any longer. I put my arms around his neck as he pushed me further into the lounger, instantly picking me up as if I weighed nothing. Gripping my ass as I wrapped my legs around his waist, he carried me to the bedroom. Our mouths never stopped devouring one another.

He growled, slipping his tongue passed my parting lips again. Working it in ways that had me grinding my pussy against his cock. It had been so long since I felt that friction with him. He held onto the back of my neck, bringing us closer but still not nearly close enough. There was no space or distance between our ravenous bodies other than the small baby bump, as he laid me on the bed.

"I love you," he whispered in between kissing me.

"I love you, too," I murmured, not breaking our connection. "I want you."

"You have me," he groaned. "You've always fucking had me."

My dress, bra, and panties were off within seconds. He kissed his way down my body, slowly savoring the feel of my heated skin against his cool lips, stopping when he was at my stomach. I peered down at him, watching as he tenderly rubbed all along my belly, kissing every last inch.

"I'm sorry for everything I put your mama through. I promise I'll make it up to her by being the best father I can to you. I already love you so much, mi niña bonita."

My eyes watered again, hearing him speak to our unborn baby girl.

"You're going to be a Martinez because your mama is going to marry me," he murmured out of nowhere.

"Ale—" His mouth collided with mine again, taking everything I was giving to him.

He rasped, "That wasn't a question."

He spent the rest of the night making love to me. Starting the beginning of our future.

Finally, officially together.

Epilogue
Lexi

"Alejandro," I called out, walking into the living room. Only calling him by his real name in the privacy of our own home. A new name came with his new identity, but he would always be Alejandro Martinez to me.

I'd spent all morning in my ballet studio he had custom built in our home, trying to work off the baby weight. The studio was already here before I flew to Italy to be with him. He said it was one of the first things he had put in when he bought the house. Wanting to surprise me if and when I came. We had more space than we knew what to do with. The house was a massive, gorgeous Mediterranean style home situated on a cliff that overlooked the water.

Adriana Daisy Martinez was born three months ago at three A.M. in the comfort of our own home. It didn't matter what her last name was, she wasn't connected to "Alejandro Martinez" the deceased crime boss. He wouldn't have it any other way, his daughter would be a Martinez. We named her after Alejandro's mother and Briggs, two of the most important women in his life, besides Adriana and I. She weighed five pounds, six ounces when she was born, and had a full head of dark black hair and bright, tantalizing blue eyes like her daddy. I was in labor for twelve hours and Martinez never left my side for one second of it. Holding my hand through the pain, breathing right along with me. Helping the mid-wife deliver our baby girl. And just like her father, she never slept at night, but had no problem sleeping during the daytime. Austin, Briggs, and the kids flew in for Adriana's birth, and Amari couldn't have been happier to have a girl for a cousin. Seeing as the baby Briggs had a few months prior to me giving birth was just another boy, leaving Amari outnumbered.

Martinez let me decide what I wanted to do with telling Briggs the truth about our father. After giving it a lot of thought and consideration, I decided I wanted her to know I was her half-sister. Even though I knew a part of her would be heartbroken to know her father wasn't the man she remembered. Martinez and I sat her and Austin down when they came to visit a few months after I moved to Italy. She took the news harder than I imagined, but she was also happy to know she had another family member in this world other than her uncle.

I never told her the truth behind her parents' death. There was no point in shattering her heart again. It wouldn't bring her parents back and it would only take away the only family Martinez had left in the world. She would never forgive him if she knew the truth. I couldn't do that to him. It was a secret I would take to my grave.

"There you—" I stopped dead in my tracks.

He was passed out on the couch with a sleeping Adriana on his chest. She looked so tiny against him. He had his arms securely wrapped around her, holding her close to his heart. His baby girl had replaced me, and I wouldn't have it any other way. They both looked so peaceful together, I couldn't help but stand there and watch my sleeping beauties.

He stirred, opening his calm, serene eyes. Looking adoringly at me with a mischievous grin. He still loved seeing me in my ballet attire, and if he weren't holding the other girl in his life, he would have taken advantage.

"Well, hello there, Mrs. Martinez."

I smiled, leaning up against the wall. Loving that he still called me that. I preferred it to our new name.

We got married a few weeks before I gave birth. We had an intimate wedding on the beach near our home with just him and I. He was adamant that Adriana was going to be born into a marital family. Saying what kind of example would we be giving her if her parents weren't married when she was born. It's not like it mattered. He wasn't ever going to allow her to date, let alone get married. I already felt bad for the poor boy who would fall in love with her. He would have to answer to Martinez. The thought alone was scary.

Adriana had him wrapped around her little finger, and she knew it. After all these years, I woke up every morning to him lying beside me. Never alone. And once Adriana came along, he had his arms full. Most of the time I was wrapped on one side of his body and her on the other.

He finally slept.

Of course as much as a newborn would allow. Which wasn't much.

"How long has she been out?" I asked, lying next to him in the nook of his arm. He pulled me tighter.

"I just got her down a little while ago," he groggily replied, kissing the top of my head.

"Seems like she got you down too, old man," I giggled, loving that the man who never slept before no longer had that problem.

"This old man just finished working you over this morning. I'll remember that tonight when you're begging for my cock."

"Martinez," I chastised, leaning up to look him in the eye. "Is that the way you talk when you have our daughter in your arms? She's going to grow up to love a guy with your dirty mouth, just watch."

"Not if I have something to do about it. She's not dating ever. And if she does, I'll just put a hit out on him."

My mouth dropped open.

"I'm kidding. Relax. Come here."

I melted against him once again.

"I'll just have someone else do it."

I tried to look back up at him, but he chuckled, holding me down. We spent the rest of the afternoon, napping on the couch.

All together.

Martinez

My life had done a complete three-hundred-and-sixty-degree turn. I had everything I ever wanted, never in a million years, imagining I could actually deserve it. With my new identity, came my new life.

My future.

"How does something so big, come out of something so small?" I asked Adriana as I changed her diaper.

She cooed, kicking her chubby little legs. Listening to everything I was saying, like it was the most important thing in the world. Her mama still looked at me like that too. I couldn't help smiling down at the life we created together. She was so fucking perfect. With her black-as-night hair and long eyelashes.

"I wasn't always this puss…" I caught myself, "This pushover you see in front of you, mamita. Your daddy used to be feared, no one messed with him and lived to tell the tale. I walked into a room and everyone bowed down. Especially the women, but they got down in other ways. Ways you won't ever do or I'll cut off the man's balls without hesitation. You remember that, mi niña bonita, Adriana."

She smiled and it lit up her entire beautiful face.

"But none of them mattered, because they weren't your mama. She's the only woman who's ever had me by the balls, but don't tell her that. She'll let it go to her head real quick," I whispered, snapping up her onesie. "One day when you're older, I'll tell you all about how we met. How much I protected her and loved her immediately. Exactly the way I did with you." I picked her up, placing her on my chest, kissing her soft baby skin. Turning around to find Lexi standing in the doorway, wiggling the baby monitor in her hand.

"I own your balls, huh?" she grinned, laughing. "I'll have to remember that the next time you give me any shit."

"The right and the left. Since you put them in your mouth, I guess that counts for something, right?"

Her eyes widened. "Oh my God! You ruined it! You suck!"

I kissed her lips. "You swallow." She tried to slap my arm, but I caught her wrist.

"You kiss your daughter with that dirty mouth?"

"I kiss you with it." I deepened our kiss. "I love you, cariño. Te amo."

She smirked, grabbing Adriana out of my arms. She gave her a bottle, rocked her and then put her to bed. After my shower, I threw a towel around my waist and went into Adriana's room. Giving my angel one last kiss before bed. Doing the sign of the cross over her body like my mother used to do to me every night as a child. I whispered, "I love you," before quietly pulling her door closed. Anxious to go lose myself inside my wife, like I did almost every night.

I walked into our room to find Lexi lying on our bed waiting for me.

Dressed in a see-through nightie, and a bright ass fucking smile.

I grinned, leaning against the doorframe, crossing my arms over my chest. Taking in my sexy-ass, fucking wife with a predatory stare. I dropped my towel, gripping my cock in one hand and stroking it.

"I'll let you own him tonight. I know how happy he can make you."

She licked her lips, sucking her bottom one between her teeth. Eyeing my cock.

I walked over to her, each step precise and calculated. Stopping to crawl my way up her body. Kissing every last inch of her skin. Her chest rising and falling the closer I got to where she wanted me the most. Her pussy. Licking along the seams of her panties, hooking my fingers in the sides, sliding them slowly down her legs. Making my way up to devour her sweet pussy, till she was screaming name.

"Cariño—" The phone rang, cutting me off.

Lexi sat up, looking at me warily. Holding her chest, and the cross that she never took off to this day. No one called that phone, ever. She reached over grabbing it off the nightstand, handing it to me.

I answered it, not giving it a second thought. "This better be a goddamn emergency," I gritted out into the phone.

"Hey, man. Sor—"

"Leo? This better be fucking important. I'm spending some quality time with my wife," I warned, caressing Lexi's thigh.

Looking at her beautiful face, sliding my hand down to her pussy once again. She smacked it away, and I pouted at her.

"No shit. I wouldn't be calling you if it wasn't." He took a deep breath. "I don't know how to say this to you, man..."

"Quit pussyfooting around. Fucking spit it out already."

"I'm sure you're going to be getting a call from Briggs—"

"Jesus Christ, Leo. Cut the bullshit."

He took another deep breath, speaking with conviction, "Creed just called. It's Mia. She's gone fucking missing."

THE END.

For Martinez and Lexi.

It's only the beginning or is it *the end* for…
Creed and Mia
(Next in my new MC Standalone Series)

November 8ᵗʰ Pre-order:

Pre-order available now on Amazon, i-Books, Nook and Kobo

AMAZON US
AMAZON UK
AMAZON CA
AMAZON AU

64813557R00232

Made in the USA
Middletown, DE
18 February 2018